MITTO HAD NEVER CONSIDERED himself to be a greedy man—at least no greedier than any businessman. And yet he couldn't take his eyes off of the gold. With those coins, he wouldn't have to worry about hauling scratchy hay or heavy barrels of Hylan lager for miles, praying to the gods to keep the snow at bay.

Hells, with that much money, he'd not have to leave Rydah for a year!

Suddenly suspicious, he looked up at Toemis. Where had the old man gotten so much gold? Whose purse had been pilfered?

Whose throat had he slit to gain this treasure?

As though reading his thoughts, Toemis crossed his arms and said, "It's what's left of a lifetime of saving …and it can be yours for nothing more than a ride to Fort Faith."

THE RENEGADE CHRONICLES

Rebels and Fools

Heroes and Liars

Martyrs and Monsters

Heroes
and
Liars

David Michael Williams

To Kate: Beware of Goblin! DMWilliams

ONEMILLIONWORDS

ONEMILLIONWORDS

Copyright © 2016 by One Million Words, LLC
Excerpt from *Martyrs and Monsters* copyright © 2016 by One Million Words, LLC

Inquiries can be directed to onemillionwords@hotmail.com.

First published by One Million Words, LLC, Wisconsin, USA

First printing, March 2016

ISBN 978-0-9910562-2-4

Written by David Michael Williams (david-michael-williams.com)

Cover art copyright © 2016 by One Million Words, LLC

Cover design by Jake Weiss (jacobweissdesign.com)

Author photograph by Jaime Lynn Hunt (jaimelynnhunt.com)

Interior art copyright © 2016 by One Million Words, LLC

Map by David Michael Williams and Jake Weiss

Heroes and Liars is wholeheartedly dedicated to Stephanie Williams—not only because I promised when we were teenagers that I would dedicate my second novel to her, but also because without her there would be no Renegade Chronicles and, most importantly, because she taught me love can sneak up on you when you least expect it.

(Thankfully, it didn't take a goblin invasion to bring us together.)

CAPRICON
PROVINCE OF CONTINAE

North Port

Fort Honor

Tolan

Lake Tear

Port Town

Fort Milonsteron

Temple of Mystel

Pilars

Port of Balanta

Resolar

Fort Royal

EMERALD GULF

N
w — e
S

Rydah
and the Celestial Palace

WINDY
BAY

Port
Gust

Port
Valor

Crostal Wood

Fort
Faith

Port
Stone

Hylan

The Rocky Crags

Steppe

Travelers'
Stop

Isphir
Lake

The Ruins of
Bakkah

ADEN OCEAN

Part 1

Passage I

A drizzling, overcast sky had haunted him all the way from Hylan. His small team of horses plodded along uneasily as the road grew slick with mud. Meanwhile, Mitto had nothing to do but count the raindrops that pelted his hat.

With an empty wagon and two horses, the trip should have taken no more than four hours, but he had had to stop twice when sudden downpours forced him beneath the waterproof covering.

He muttered an insincere thanks to the gods when he finally pulled up to the city gates. After nearly two weeks on the road—all the way from Kraken with stops along the way—he was eager to get to an inn, order something warm to drink, and enjoy the first of several days dedicated to doing absolutely nothing at all.

Once I'm inside, it can rain for a week straight for all I care, the merchant thought as his wagon creaked to a halt.

A man stepped out of the gatehouse, a cramped, three-walled structure made of unfinished wood. Although he was covered in a long cloak and a deep cowl to protect himself from the elements, Mitto knew him for a Knight of Superius. There was no mistaking the stiff, proper march of the watchman as he approached the wagon, no mistaking the rattle of a scabbard against armored thigh.

And the city gates were always guarded by the Knights of Superius. This was the capital, after all.

"State your name and your business in Rydah," the Knight barked, resting a hand against the hilt of his sword. In the other, he carried a shuttered lantern that bathed the area in a dull yellow light.

Mitto refrained from rolling his eyes. "I am Mitto O'erlander, a traveling merchant."

A traveling merchant of some renown in these parts, he added silently.

"And what goods do you bring into the city?" the Knight asked, his eyes narrowing as he thrust the lantern near Mitto's face.

Mitto squinted. "Nothing, good sir. I dropped the last of my goods in Hylan."

The lantern loomed closer, and Mitto felt the heat of the flame against his face.

"What of Hylan's harvest? Any trader worth his wagon would have brought at least a keg or two of lager to make the trip worth his while. Yet you come to the greatest city in Capricon with nothing to sell? You are either a fool or a liar!"

Mitto was momentarily speechless. The Knight peered into the abysmally dark interior of the wagon. In spite of himself, Mitto spun around in his seat and watched the lamplight spill into cart's interior. But the lantern's glow couldn't penetrate the shadows at the far end of the wagon.

"I'd bet a month's pay you're hiding something back there," the Knight said. "Or some*one*. Might be you're a Renegade sympathizer sent to smuggle one of your rebel friends into the capital."

Cold sweat mingled with the raindrops soaking his skin. "No, sir. You have it all wrong—"

"Silence!"

The lantern was positioned once again between merchant and guard, making it impossible for Mitto to see the man's face. He knew several of the Knights stationed at Southgate. Never had he encountered one as ornery as this fellow. He was on the verge of dropping the name of an acquaintance—an old friend who surely outranked this paranoid upstart!—when the sound of deep laughter interrupted his thoughts.

"Ah, Mitto," the Knight said between chuckles, "you must forgive me for having a little fun with you. Staring into the darkness for hours on end gets so boring."

The voice the Knight used now was one Mitto knew well, so even before the light was subdued by a shutter, he knew the identity of the prankster. Old friend indeed, Mitto thought.

"I'll consider forgiving you, Baxter, if you hurry up and open the gate before winter's chill turns all of this to ice."

Baxter frowned and moved a hand back toward his weapon.

"That's *Sir Lawler* to you, Renegade!"

"Oh, shut up and open the gate!"

Baxter Lawler laughed all the way to the ironclad barrier blocking the road. After whispering the current shibboleth to a comrade on the other side of the wall, he stepped back and shook his head.

"You have to admit I got you good," he said to Mitto.

"Yeah, yeah, but he who laughs last, laughs best."

Despite the darkness, Mitto saw the Knight's smile. "Is that a threat, master merchant?"

Mitto urged his team toward the opening gates. "I would never threaten a Knight of Superius."

That earned another laugh from Baxter. As the wagon passed, he said, "I'll be sure to stop by Someplace Else after my shift so you can buy me a drink."

"I'd say it's *you* who owes *me* a drink," Mitto called over his shoulder.

Now that the Knight couldn't see him, Mitto allowed himself a slight smile. Above the splashing rain and the clip-clop of horseshoes against cobblestones, he thought he heard, "Fair enough, old friend. Fair enough," before the gates crashed closed behind him.

The rain sounds like the hiss of a sea monster. She remembers hearing stories about ferocious serpents whose long bodies could wrap around a dozen times over, dragging the doomed vessel and crew to the dark depths of the ocean.

Julian told her many stories she wasn't supposed to believe or to even think about—especially before bedtime. But she is never afraid of the snakes in the garden, and the monsters that show up in her dreams never harm her.

Anyway, she is on dry land now. She doesn't know how long they were on the ship that brought them here. She doesn't even know where *here* is, but she's confident they were at sea long enough for even the most sluggish of serpents to find them. Maybe Larissa was right about there being no monsters. Maybe Julian had been teasing her after all.

She can't ask them now, though, because they're both dead.

The street is wobbly beneath her legs. Toemis tells her she must be careful until she finds her land legs again, but she doesn't know what that means. Lately, Toemis says a lot of things she doesn't understand. But she has known him longer than she did Julian. And since Larissa and Julian are gone, only Toemis is left to take care of her.

Wherever they are, there is a lot to see, lots of buildings. This place is bigger than where they lived. She wants to see everything at once and gets dizzy trying to take it all in. Toemis looks straight ahead. He walks fast, leading her by the hand. It isn't easy to keep up with him, even though he is very old, but she does her best.

She wonders how long they will be out in the rain. Larissa never let her play in the rain.

She catches a glimpse of people seated around a table through a window when Toemis stops suddenly. She stops too and looks at what he is seeing. Someone is leading two horses and a wagon into a stable. She wants to run over and pet the horses, to look into their big eyes, but she won't leave Toemis's side. She hopes maybe he'll take her to the horses because she likes animals of all kinds—even snakes.

But instead of walking toward the horses, Toemis leads her to the door of a different building, and they go inside. It's warmer here. The people gathered around tables drink from big cups. She starts to take off her wet coat, but Toemis doesn't let her. He is strong for an old man. They sit down at a table. She wants to touch the scratched surface but doesn't want Toemis to see her do it. Toemis doesn't like it when she fidgets.

A woman comes over to them. She has blue eyes that remind her of Larissa's. The woman asks Toemis if she can get them anything, and he tells her warm milk. When she returns with two cups, Toemis digs a coin out of his pocket. With Toemis distracted, she quickly wipes her hand across the tabletop. Its roughness feels good against her skin.

Toemis tells her to be careful with the cup. It's hot. She lifts the cup with both hands and trickles some of the liquid into her mouth. She swishes it around a few times before swallowing. She hadn't had any milk since they left home, since Larissa died. The milk could've come from a cow or a goat, but she doesn't care which. She likes all animals.

After another sip, she carefully sets the cup down. Toemis does not touch his milk.

There is a lot to see inside the building, which is bigger than their room on the ship and bigger than home was. The milk-woman is sitting near a fireplace now. Toemis is looking over at the fireplace, and at first she thinks Toemis is staring at the milk-woman. But he is really watching the other person over there. He watches the man for a long time, long enough for her to make a handprint on the table. She wants to take off her wet clothes.

When the milk-woman leaves the fireplace, Toemis stands up quickly. She knows he wants her to do the same because he takes her hand again. And she knows better than to leave Toemis's side. Toemis is the only one left to protect her.

Toemis walks over to the fireplace. She walks beside him, but because her legs—land legs?—are smaller, she has a hard time keeping up with him. It wasn't always that way. He used to walk slower. These days, though, he walks fast and says things she doesn't understand. When they reach the fireplace, Toemis starts talking to the man.

She listens but doesn't say a word.

Few people walked the streets of Rydah that night. Mitto wanted to attribute the lack of passersby to the deluge that had him shivering in his seat and futilely pulling his sopping cloak tighter. But he knew it was more than that.

Situated on Capricon's northeastern peninsula, Rydah was no stranger to storms. The cityfolk never let a little rain bother them. The heaviest of downpours never kept the Rydans holed away for long.

Even when the Thief Guild was at their worst, people refused to let that secret sect dictate where and when they would walk the streets. If it meant one had to be a little more wary of cut-purses, so be it. Rydah was a big city—the largest in Capricon—so a little crime was to be expected.

Steering his team down the familiar avenues, Mitto watched a young man run from building to building, using the awnings of shops and inns to his best advantage. The fellow spared the wagon and its driver hardly a glance. Mitto wondered if the man was a member of the infamous Thief Guild, but he doubted it. Guildsmen had a reputation for being nearly invisible.

Anyway, the citizens of Rydah had something worse than thieves to worry about these days.

Mitto resisted the urge to watch the man until he disappeared from sight. He, for one, would not give into the paranoia that had people all over the island seeing rebels at every turn. He hated Renegades as much as the next guy, but they had no cause to interfere with his life. Or so he hoped.

He looked in the windows of the public houses he passed and couldn't help but notice there were far fewer patrons within compared to a year ago. But that had been before Edward Borrom and the other Kings of Continae forged the Alliance with dwarves, centaurs, midge, and even ogres.

Before the rebels started making trouble out of hate for the nonhumans, a desire to chip away at Superius hold on Capricon, and gods only knew what other reasons.

Before Capricon and Continae Proper were plunged into what some were already calling the Renegade War.

Mitto missed the days when his greatest concern was keeping an eye on his purse. One never knew what Renegades were up to or what trick they might use to strike at their enemies. It didn't matter he was an honest merchant who cared no more for politics than fashion trends in the Deathlands. At least one knew what the Thief Guild wanted—money.

Then again, there were rumors the Guild was working hand-in-hand with the Renegade movement in Rydah...

Mitto let out a long sigh as he jumped down from his perch. He hadn't even been paying attention but had instinctively known when to pull back on the reigns. He recognized the stable boy that ran out to lead the horses to their shelter, though he never could recall the lad's name.

Smiling a preoccupied smile, he flipped a copper coin into the boy's hand and said, "Clean them up, and you'll get two more just like it. And let them eat their fill of oats. Gods know they've earned it!"

Without waiting for a reply, Mitto walked toward the entrance of the inn. An old sign hung on rusty hinges from a post beside the door. Faded gray-white letters declared the name of the establishment: Someplace Else. Mitto had always thought it a terrible name for an inn, but the proprietress insisted it was perfect.

"What if two people cannot decide where they want to spend the evening?" she would propose whenever he brought up the matter. "'Let's head over to Garland's Feat,' says the first.

'Naw,' says the other, 'that place reeks. Let's try someplace else.' And sure enough, they'll end up here."

Mitto rolled his eyes—as he done the first time she explained the origin of the inn's name—and opened the door. The light in the common room was bright compared to the shadow-strewn streets outside. He saw a couple of familiar faces, but there was no mistaking that Someplace Else had seen better days.

He did his best to brush the water off his cloak and removed the saturated, three-cornered hat from off his head. He wrung the water from bedraggled hat with both of his hands. The puddle at his feet swelled into a veritable lake, and a wandering rivulet was meandering farther into the common room.

"Mitto O'erlander, quit dampening my doorstep and come to the fire before you catch your death of cold!"

The merchant's eyes were inextricably drawn to the owner of the voice. Although the woman who had spoken was roughly his age—or perhaps a bit younger than his forty-odd years—she spoke with the tone of a doting mother. Somehow, Else Fontane had a way of making him feel closer to five years old than fifty.

A wide smile stretched across her round face as she snatched up a towel from behind the bar and hurried over toward him. She was pretty—no denying that—and he had thought on more than one occasion that being more than simply friends with Else might be a grand thing.

But those thoughts tended to surface when he was more than a little drunk. She had been a dear friend for the past fifteen years. Too much time had passed for them to transcend the status of their current relationship.

And yet whenever he crossed the threshold of Someplace Else and looked into her big blue eyes, he felt as though he had come home.

Mitto caught the towel a second before it would've hit him in the face.

"Look at what the cats and dogs dragged in," she sighed, shaking her head sadly. "I've seen mermaids dance in less water than you've brought into my inn."

"If you've seen even one mermaid, then I'm the Queen of the Sea," Mitto replied, running the towel through his dark curly hair. "Tell me you have a spare room, so I don't have to go back out into the rain."

"I've always got room for you, Your Majesty," she said with

a wink. "Without the money I make playing dice with you, I'd have had to close the inn long ago."

He gave a low chuckle but then thought she might be serious. "Is business that bad?"

Now it was her turn to laugh. "Don't you worry about me, Mitto. It'll take more than a measly war to shut Someplace Else down. Come on now. Don't make me drag you to the fire. I meant what I said about winning your money, and it's no fun playing dice with someone in a sickbed."

"All right, all right," the merchant muttered, allowing himself to be led to a high-backed chair near the hearth.

"I'll be right back with a cup of tea," she promised.

He opened his mouth to correct her—he never drank tea!—but caught himself at the last moment. I must be getting old, he thought. First Baxter makes me look more gullible than a new-born midge, and then I almost believe Else would actually bring me tea.

Shaking his head at his foolishness, Mitto eased back in his seat and basked in the warm glow of the fireplace. Out of the corner of his eye, he watched the innkeeper pull out two glasses and a bottle of Dragon's Hoard, his favorite spirits, from behind the bar.

As she poured the drinks, Mitto looked around the common room and wondered how many hours he had spent there. He couldn't remember why he had chosen the inn over all of the others, but fifteen years after his first visit, Mitto now spent most of his free time at Someplace Else.

Perhaps it was the name, after all. Since he spent most of his life on the road, traveling from town to town, he did not bother with a house of his own. His whole life was about "someplace else."

Of course, he'd never admit it to Else. She was a swift-thinker and had a quick tongue to match. Someone had to keep her in check. But he wasn't so foolish as to believe he could beat her in a game of riddles. No, Else Fontane was as clever as they came.

Why, it had taken him more than a year to realize she had managed to sneak her own name into the name of her beloved inn.

Passage II

Mitto gazed contentedly into the fire, watching the flames flicker and undulate in an almost hypnotic manner. Suddenly, he was aware of someone standing behind him.

Perhaps it had been all of that thinking about thieves and rebels because he was on his feet in an instant to confront whoever it was. He didn't recognize the man who had stolen up on him as silently as a ghost. For that matter, the stranger resembled a wraith, draped, as he was, in a tattered cloak and cowl that cast most of his face in shadow. Dark, sunken eyes peered out at him from between a sharp nose.

Mitto took a step back.

The intruder pulled back his hood, revealing the wrinkled visage of a very old man. "I did not mean to startle you, boy. I only want to talk. Please sit."

His voice reminded Mitto of a creaky-hinged door in want of oiling. Because he had no reason to deny the old man's request—because there was no reason to be afraid of the ancient stranger—Mitto sat down and offered him the vacant seat.

The old man set himself down with a not-quite-stifled grunt. That was when Mitto saw the geezer wasn't alone. A second shorter form followed him to a spot on the other side of the chair. Mitto tried to discern what he could about the addition to his unexpected company, but the shorter stranger wore a long hooded coat to match the old man's.

A dwarf, maybe…or perhaps a midge? Mitto thought sourly.

He couldn't consider the bundled mystery further because the old man spoke again, drawing Mitto's gaze and full attention.

"Was that your covered wagon I saw out front?" he asked.

Mitto did not answer right away. He was lost in the intense gleam of the old man's dark eyes.

"Might be it is, might be it's not," Mitto said at last.

He had never been one to jump at bumps in the night, but there was something suspicious about the old man—something menacing.

Swallowing despite his suddenly dry throat, Mitto asked, "Who are you, and what do you want from me?"

"My name is Toemis Blisnes. I need a ride to Fort Faith…whatever is left of it."

Mitto sat back in his chair, letting the old man's croak-like voice echo in his mind. The stranger's name meant nothing to him, but the mention of Fort Faith left him bewildered.

Fort Faith was a smallish fortification out past Fort Valor, nestled up against the Rocky Crags. The place had been abandoned since the Ogre War. Nobody lived there now, except maybe the ghosts of the Knights butchered by the brutes. What could Toemis Blisnes want with a deserted fort? The man was far too old to be gallivanting halfway across Capricon…

"Will you take us there? I can pay."

Toemis withdrew a fat purse from inside his coat. The mention of "us" reminded Mitto that he and Toemis were not alone. Mitto's gaze wandered back over to the cloaked figure, but as the small stranger had taken a seat on the floor on the other side of Toemis's chair, he saw only the top of a brown hood.

"Look, Mister Blisnes—"

"Toemis."

"As you like, Toemis," Mitto said, inspecting a seam staring of the three-cornered hat on his lap. "I can't guess what interest you have in that old heap of stone, and I don't care. Fact of the matter is, I don't venture that far west…not on that road, anyway. I've been known to make deliveries to Fort Valor, but there's nothing worth my while beyond."

He glanced up at Toemis. The old man returned his stare without expression.

"My route takes me to Hylan, Steppt, and Kraken regularly. Sometimes, I'll go up to the Port of Gust if the money is right, but I've never even seen Fort Faith," Mitto said, filling the silence with facts. "There's nobody at Fort Faith to trade with."

But then Mitto remembered a rumor he had heard during his stop in Steppt while sharing a drink with Miles Tentrunks. Tentrunks, a fellow traveling merchant and notorious gossip, had heard on "good authority" that the Knights of Superius were planning to reoccupy Fort Faith due to increased Renegade activity in the region.

At the time, Mitto hadn't put much stock in his rival's words, but now...

"I can pay," Toemis repeated, holding a coin purse out to Mitto.

He resisted the urge to take the purse and look inside. The profit from his trip to Kraken and back was considerable. That sum, added to what he would make from his last run to Hylan before the first snowfall, would see him comfortably through the winter.

It's probably full of rocks...like the old man's head, he mused. *And it would take a small fortune to tear me away from Someplace Else. I've earned this little bit of respite!*

The veiny, wrinkled hand remained outstretched, the coin purse just inches away.

"I can't," Mitto protested, forcing himself to maintain eye contact with Toemis. His refusal didn't seem to dishearten Toemis Blisnes in the least. If anything, the old man looked more insistent, more determined than before.

Without a word, Toemis loosened the purse's drawstrings. The firelight made the shiny gold coins inside within sparkle and shimmer.

Mitto's eyes widened. The old man was, in fact, offering him a small fortune.

A certain fable his mother had told when he was small came unbidden to mind, and Mitto had the ridiculous notion he was face to face with the dastardly Goblin. In the stories, Goblin would give gold in exchange for a favor. But in the end, the man or woman in the tale always regretted helping Goblin with his seemingly simple request.

Beneath his supposed generosity, Goblin was as sneaky as they came.

Mitto had never considered himself to be a greedy man—at least no greedier than any businessman. And yet he couldn't take his eyes off of the gold. With those coins, he wouldn't have to worry about hauling scratchy hay or heavy barrels of Hylan lager for miles, praying to the gods to keep the snow at bay.

Hells, with that much money, he'd not have to leave Rydah for a year!

Suddenly suspicious, he looked up at Toemis. Where had the old man gotten so much gold? Whose purse had been pilfered?

Whose throat had he slit to gain this treasure?

As though reading his thoughts, Toemis crossed his arms and said, "It's what's left of a lifetime of saving…and it can be yours for nothing more than a ride to Fort Faith."

The old man could be lying. Looking down at the gold once more, Mitto was fully aware that Toemis, in spite of his age, could be a thief—could be the fabled Guildmaster, for all Mitto knew. And then there was Toemis's diminutive accomplice. Where did he fit into everything?

Mitto didn't trust the old man, and yet whatever deception Toemis and his companion might be weaving, the gold looked real enough. Of course, in the stories, the gold was always real.

"Are you two with the Guild?"

Toemis's brow furrowed in momentary confusion before he answered, "No."

"Are you Renegades?"

"No."

Even as Mitto recalled the terrible endings of those childhood tales—orchestrated, always, by Goblin—he knew he would accept the impossibly simple job. He silently cursed Toemis for the tempting offer and then cursed himself for accepting the shiny bait.

"Fine, I'll do it," he said, sounding as defeated as he felt. At least the would-be hero in the story was allowed a moment of joy before his downfall. Mitto, on the other hand, felt nothing but worry. "What do you say, half now and half when we arrive at the fort?"

Toemis closed the purse and thrust it back into his coat. "Nothing until we get there."

Mitto opened his mouth to argue but then shrugged his shoulders in surrender. He couldn't blame Toemis for being cautious. Besides, with Goblin it was always all or nothing.

"When do you want to leave?" Mitto asked.

"Now."

Mitto had that nothing Toemis could say would surprise him. He was mistaken.

"Now?" he demanded. "It's raining like mad. The city's half-flooded for gods' sakes."

Toemis's piercing black eyes didn't blink. All or nothing,

Mitto reminded himself. Well, I may be a fool for gold, but I'm not completely crazy.

"Look, Toemis, even if the gatekeepers would allow us to leave Rydah at such a suspiciously late hour and even if the Renegade War weren't lending courage to every rogue and brigand this side of the Strait, I'd still have to insist that we wait until morning on account of my horses. They need rest. It won't get you to Fort Faith any quicker if they collapse a mile outside the city."

That last bit was pure hyperbole, though the horses deserved to rest—as did he. Out of the corner of his eye, he noted a slight movement, a bobbing, as it were, of the brown hood beside Toemis's chair. The old man dropped a bony hand down atop the other's head, though Mitto couldn't decide if the gesture was intended to calm or control.

"Very well," Toemis said, rising from his chair. "We'll meet here at sunup."

Mitto nodded, and when the old man stuck out his claw-like hand, he quickly got to his feet and extended his own hand to seal their deal. Toemis's skin was warm but not as sweaty as Mitto's was. And the old man was possessed of a strength that caught Mitto off guard.

Without another word, Toemis Blisnes made his way over to the bar, where Else was trying hard to look like she hadn't been watching them the whole time. The small, silent other followed Toemis without hesitation. But the shrouded stranger did pause long enough to take a quick glance at the merchant, providing Mitto with an unobstructed, albeit brief, peek at the enigmatic creature.

Which only left him with more questions.

An hour later saw an additional chair before the fireplace. The few patrons who had shared the common room earlier were gone except for Loony Gomez, who was using one of the tables as a pillow and whose loud breathing could be heard all the way to the fireside, where the three of them sat in silence.

Mitto chewed at his thumbnail as he stared into the crackling fire. Now that Toemis had gone to one of the rooms upstairs, he had come up with a long list of reasons why he should've turned the old man down—fables aside. It might be Toemis was planning on clubbing him over the head once Rydah's alabaster walls were out of sight, taking his horses and wagon as his own…

"You can bet I'll look into this," Baxter Lawler promised for the second time.

Mitto didn't bother glancing over at the Knight. His friend was talking more to fill the stillness than anything. Mitto had told Else all that had transpired between him and the old man after the two strangers left for their room. He had repeated the story when Baxter showed up at Someplace Else not an hour ago.

It was very late, but Mitto couldn't bring himself to head upstairs yet. He needed at least one night with his friends before leaving Rydah again.

"The name doesn't sound familiar," Baxter was saying, "but that doesn't mean Mister Blisnes isn't a wanted man. Could be an alias. The Renegades are a crafty lot, and now that the Guild has thrown in with them…"

The Knight let his unpleasant thoughts trail off. Mitto just stared at the orange flames. He couldn't shake the feeling that accepting the job was akin to throwing dice with Else. But would taking Toemis to Fort Faith prove as costly as a night of gambling with the lucky innkeeper? The stakes were certainly higher. He had more to gain…and more to lose…

All or nothing.

"I'll talk to my commanding officer first thing tomorrow morning," Baxter continued, "even though it'll mean getting up at the crack of dawn on my only day off."

"How downright gallant of you, Sir Lawler," Else said from her place on the other side of Mitto. "But given the way you talk, I assumed *you* were the highest-ranking Knight in all of Capricon."

Baxter stuck his tongue out in reply, looking more like a glib youth than one of the great defenders of the realm.

Mitto turned to regard Else. After he had filled in the gaps of what she had gleaned while eavesdropping, she had said very little about her thoughts on Toemis and his offer. Years as an innkeeper had forged Else Fontane into a reliable judge of character, and Mitto respected her opinion. But aside from stating the obvious—"If something seems too good to be true…"—Else had kept her private thoughts to herself.

But Mitto had the distinct impression she didn't want him to go.

"It's just so bloody suspicious," Baxter added, "a man willing to pay that much money to go to an old fort. I suppose it's possible he has a grandson stationed there and wants to visit. Or maybe he's really a wealthy nobleman in disguise and wants a place to hide with Knights all around him...though there're Knights aplenty here in Rydah."

"So the rumor is true," Mitto said with a wry chuckle. Perhaps Miles Tentrunks wasn't the total buffoon after all.

"Which rumor?" Else asked. "And isn't Fort Faith a wreck?"

When the Knight took a long swig of Dragon's Hoard, Mitto knew he and Else were in for a lengthy explanation.

"Fort Faith *was* a wreck, but the Knights have fixed it up some from what I've heard. You see, a little while ago, a young commander and fifty or so Knights came from Continae to reoccupy the fort.

"Why, you may ask? Well, on account of all these no-good rebels roaming the countryside. At last count, there a half-dozen different factions on the island, and now there's talk of a new Renegade Leader from the Continent United."

"It's only fair," Else said sagely. "If the Renegades can call on their friends from Continae, why not the Knights?"

Baxter merely shrugged. "Maybe so, Else dear, but I'd rather they take their blasted war *away* from our idyllic island than the other way around."

"You'll hear no arguments here!" the innkeeper laughed, throwing up her hands in mock surrender. "But what about Toemis? Could he be one of the new Renegades, the Renegade Leader even?"

"I don't think Toemis is a rebel," Mitto heard himself say. He felt the others' eyes on him. "I have no proof, mind you. Just a feeling. Anyway, I've never heard of a Renegade Leader traveling in the company of a little girl before."

Neither Mitto nor Else had gotten more than a glimpse at Toemis's companion, but she was the bigger mystery in Mitto's mind.

"And you're sure she wasn't a midge?" Baxter pressed. "Many a man has mistaken one of those little scamps for a human child...until the bloody thing starts throwing spells."

"Have you ever known a midge to sit quietly for more than

two minutes?" Else countered. "No, I'd bet my inn she was an actual child."

The three of them shared the silence for another few minutes, alternatively taking swings of Dragon's Hoard. When Mitto found his way to the bottom of his mug and stood and said he wanted to get some sleep before his early start tomorrow.

"You take care now, Mitto O'erlander," Else ordered. "If anything happened to you, I'd lose my best customer."

He promised to keep his guard up—as if he were some green jaunt-about out to see the world for the first time!—and told them both he would be back in Rydah before they knew it. Then he said goodbye to both of them, though Baxter promised he would meet him at the Westgate in the morning "to get a good look at the old guy, if nothing else."

Else would also rise with the dawn, he suspected. She always seemed to get an early start on the days Mitto left the city.

Since he would likely see them both in the morning, what was the point of raising a glass to friendship or exchanging heartfelt farewells? Anyway, Mitto hated goodbyes. When one made a living by delivering goods from town to town, life was one temporary goodbye after another.

Still, as he made his way upstairs and down the dark corridor, he couldn't shake the feeling this would be the last time he shared a cup of Dragon's Hoard with the irreverent Knight and the lovely innkeeper.

Passage III

In the twilight of early dawn, Magnes Minus, the Lord of Capricon, took leave of his sleeping wife and made his way through the halls of the Celestial Palace. His pace was brisk, though not hurried. Reflex directed his feet down the appropriate corridors and stairways, inevitably leading him to the palace's library, his sanctuary from duty and distress.

There, in that shrine-like athenaeum, while combing the archives to acquaint himself with the long-dead saints and sinners who had shaped the world through their deeds, Magnes Minus paid homage to history.

He barely noticed the elaborate tapestries that graced the walls or the other ornamental embellishments of the palace's superb architecture. He passed by windows that provided the most spectacular views in all of Rydah, in all of Capricon perhaps, but paid them no heed. Even the archaic suits of armor standing on either side of one particular doorway—costly relics from the Wars of Sundering—even those souvenirs of centuries past did not earn a second glance.

The few members of the palace staff who crossed Minus's path were greeted distractedly, but surely by now those early-rising maids, attendants, and chamberlains were accustomed to the lord's faraway eyes, his furrowed brow. Some might worry for him, assuming the burden of his position and the stress of keeping Capricon safe from petty criminals, the Guild, and Renegades weighed heavily on their lord's mind.

But those who knew Magnes Minus understood that mornings were reserved not for present concerns, but for the past.

This particular morning, Minus found himself lost in a conundrum that had him both stymied and excited. While researching the life of Memndrake, Superius's third king, he had happened upon an obscure reference to one Sir Ryleigh Tristan, the grandson of Sir Tristam El'Drake, who was allegedly one of the first Knights of Superius.

Ryleigh's lineage meant very little in itself. Every great family in Superius claimed descendency from one legendary warrior or another. And yet while no knew exactly how many Knights had made up the original Order—whose virtuous exemplars who had lived before the nation of Superius itself was born—many records mentioned "Aldrake's Twelve."

Whether that number included the warrior-king Aldrake or not was up for debate. Some scholars had searched through every available resource and had managed to put a name to each of the Twelve.

Tristam El'Drake was not among them.

Yet perhaps that was not so surprising. There were so many inconsistencies in Superius's early history. Mostly people dismissed the old stories of King Aldrake and his Twelve as myth. As those stories were passed down from generation to generation, the names of the Twelve were changed, lost, and in some cases reinvented.

Normally, Lord Minus had no trouble dismissing such incongruities, history's bastard children. But there was something familiar about Sir Tristam, not to mention the obvious similarity between the Knight's surname and the given name of the first King of Superius.

Were Tristam El'Drake and his connection to King Aldrake a key to the monarch's cloudy origins?

Minus had recalled another text that referenced to a Sir Tristam, but it wasn't until last night, on the verge of falling asleep, that he had remembered a lyrical poem about Aldrake's heroic charge against the Midcanthian Emperor...

Now, as he walked ever faster toward the library, Magnes Minus prepared to take the next step in unraveling the mystery of Tristam El'Drake, the Thirteenth Knight. He felt his heart beating rapidly in his chest and smiled. So many people found the nuances of lore boring, but he reveled in it.

He took two steps through the library's threshold and stopped in his tracks. No one ever visited the archives at this time of the morning. Everyone in the Celestial Palace respected their lord's privacy during his sojourns into the past. But today, someone had gotten there first.

The intruder jumped to his feet and started scooping up papers strewn about one of the library's many desks. "Apologies, milord. I had hoped to be gone before your arrival. I am just finishing."

Minus's grin grew as he approached the man, whose face had turned a deep shade of red.

"Why, Sir Walden," he said, "this is surely the first time I have ever seen you make use of the library."

The Knight said nothing at first and busied himself with organizing the sheaths of paper and returning them to their place on a nearby shelf. Minus was dreadfully curious about what the man had been looking at, but he decided to have some fun with his old friend first. The Knight had provided him with precious little ammunition over the years.

When Sir Walden returned to the desk to retrieve his cloak, the lord cut off his retreat by interposing himself between the Knight and the only way out of the library.

"Do you mean to become a scholar, then?" he asked. "Will you exchange your sword for the quill?"

The Knight's apparent embarrassment was worth all the gold in the palace's treasury.

Bryant Walden had resided at the Celestial Palace for nearly two decades. As the High Commander of Capricon, Sir Walden was the highest-ranking Knight in Rydah and a stickler for protocol—more so than any other Knight Minus had ever met. Even after so many years of friendship, the seneschal still insisted on addressing him as "milord."

"Hardly that, milord. I am here on official business, but, by your leave, I will leave you to your work."

Resisting the urge to roll his eyes at Walden's all-pervading civility, Minus said, "First, let me ask what business you had here that could not wait until later in the day. It is not every day that you breach your routine, Sir Walden."

The Knight looked hesitant, clearly not wanting to take up more of his lord's time. Minus crossed his arms in mock impatience.

"It is probably nothing. One of my officers asked me to investigate a suspicious character." When Minus inclined an eyebrow, he quickly added, "You need not worry, milord. I came here to research the name more as a personal favor than out of any real concern.

"One of my lieutenants, Sir Baxter Lawler, has a friend who transports goods all throughout Eastern Capricon. Last night, a peculiar stranger offered him a purse full of gold in exchange for nothing more than a ride out to Fort Faith."

"Fort Faith?" Minus shouted, and the words echoed throughout the vast library. He frowned. "What is the stranger's name?"

"Toemis Blisnes, milord." Walden shared the description Sir Lawler had gotten from his merchant friend.

"And did you find any mention of Toemis Blisnes in the criminal records?" Minus asked.

"No, milord. He has never been arrested anywhere in Capricon."

Magnes Minus's fingers played at the hair of his beard. "This is suspicious indeed. Prince Eliot had left Rydah for Fort Valor just last week. Four days ago, we received word from Commander Bismarc that the Crown Prince of Superius has moved on to Fort Faith. As far as anyone knows, Eliot Borrom is still there."

Walden did not reply. As High Commander, he had known of the prince's movements. Obviously, he had not wanted to trouble his lord with Toemis Blisnes.

"It could be a coincidence," Minus said, unconvinced by his own words.

Walden shrugged. "No one has heard of this Blisnes fellow. It is best not to take chances."

"What do you have in mind?"

"I intend to send an escort of two mounted Knights. It may be better if they follow the wagon at a distance. If nothing happens before they reach Fort Faith, Sir Lawler can tell the Knights there what he knows…or, rather, what we don't know."

Magnes Minus was already nodding. As troubling as Prince Eliot's visit to the Celestial Palace had been—as much as the lord loathed the arrogant ass Eliot Borrom had grown into—he would sooner die than allow any harm to befall the Crown Prince of Superius.

Yet it was probably nothing at all…

Minus stepped aside and allowed Walden to go about his business. Whereas the athenaeum usually wrapped him in a cocoon of warm solitude, it now seemed like a lonely place. Modern concerns had pierced his shield of scholarly pursuit. The distance of centuries was no longer enough to keep present worries at bay.

With a sigh, Magnes Minus blew out the candle Walden had left on the desk and made a premature departure from the library. The Thirteenth Knight would have to wait.

Though Mitto had never been one to have a stiff drink before noon, he made an exception that morning.

He hadn't slept well, hadn't slept at all really, so when Else knocked on his door to tell him that the sun would rise within the hour, Mitto was already sitting up in bed, staring at nothing and trying to remember a childhood tale that contained Goblin, gold, and a happy ending.

Maybe Toemis isn't Goblin, he thought, but he's not a wish-granting godmother either.

Mitto was still pondering all that might go wrong on the way to Fort Faith when Toemis and the little girl descended the stairs into the common room. The old man carried a middle-sized leather bag, but they had no luggage aside from that. When Else asked them whether they wanted breakfast, Toemis declined.

Fine, let's get this over with, Mitto thought as he emptied his mug of ale.

"Wait here, and I'll bring the wagon around," he told Toemis and the girl. Placing a coin on the bar, he said to Else, "I'll be back before the week is up."

She smiled, but Mitto thought it looked forced. Her worry only increased his own and seemed to confirm last night's feeling that this was more than a simple goodbye.

Forcing his thoughts from that pernicious path, Mitto flashed a counterfeit grin of his own and strode out of Someplace Else.

Ten minutes later, he was reaching down from his perch on the wagon and taking the single, shabby travel bag Toemis held up for him. For being the only piece of luggage between his two passengers, the bag was not very heavy.

Toemis half-guided, half-pushed the girl up into the back of the wagon. Mitto tried to help, but he was at an awkward angle, so instead he took the opportunity to examine her.

The girl was wrapped in the same hooded coat she had worn yesterday. The rain had stopped at some point in the night, but the dark clouds, which smothered all but a few rays of the dawn, promised more showers to come. Mitto didn't know whether the girl was simply preparing for more foul weather or if the concealing clothes were a part of her everyday attire. Either way, Mitto's attempt to get a better look had been foiled once again.

That she had blue eyes and black hair was all he could say about the puzzling passenger.

In spite of his reservations about Toemis's character, Mitto found himself reaching out to steady the old man as he climbed up into the wagon. Not that Toemis needed any help. His movements were quick and decisive. The arm Mitto had thought to reinforce was scrawny and covered with age spots, yet holding it felt like squeezing the roots of an ancient hickory.

Once Toemis cleared the opening of the covered wagon, Mitto turned halfway around and said, "If you don't mind, Mister Blisnes, I'd like to see that gold of yours one more time."

He had to make sure the man hadn't done something tricky like bury it outside the inn so he could reclaim it later. Toemis produced the leather pouch without complaint, loosening the drawstring to reveal the coins inside. Even in the gloomy light, the gold somehow managed to shine. If Mitto had any concerns about whether the gold was genuine, he dared not take one between his fingers.

Goblin gives up his fortune freely but only when the time is right, Mitto thought.

As the old man plunged the purse back into the folds of his cloak, Mitto took a deep breath and said, "I don't suppose you want to tell me what business you have at Fort Faith."

"I thought you didn't care," Toemis replied before disappearing into the wagon's shade.

"Fair enough," Mitto muttered, though only the horses heard him.

He jerked the reigns, and the wagon lurched forward. As the wagon rolled noisily over the cobblestones, Mitto spoke reassuringly to the animals. He apologized for the brevity of their respite and promised them a long rest once they were back in Rydah again. He knew, of course, the beasts couldn't understand him, but after spending so much time together on the road, they were accustomed to hearing him speak.

Mitto's gaze wandered from one building to another. Most of the inns were still; their common rooms, empty. The smoke of breakfast fires issued forth from a few chimneys, but Mitto figured that most of the guests would sleep for at least another hour before rousing. He envied those people.

The lethargy that had evaded him throughout the night now accosted him, weighing down his eyelids and evoking powerful yawns. The morning light, although filtered through sponge-like nimbuses, stabbed at his tired eyes. Maybe I should invest in a flask of strong spirits, he considered but immediately dismissed the thought. That was probably how Miles Tentrunks started out...

If visitors to the capital were content to sleep the morning away, Rydah's citizens were already getting a start on the day. As Mitto steered the horses to the Westgate, the road began to fill with other vehicles. Coaches bearing noblemen and other officials wheeled toward to the Celestial Palace, while merchants steered their carts toward the marketplace of their choice or, like Mitto, toward the city walls.

In the twenty minutes it took Mitto to clear the distance from Someplace Else to the Westgate, Rydah had become transformed, trading the stillness of night for the bustle of business, the cacophony of crowds of people all trying to communicate at the same time.

By the time the city's wall came into view, a queue had already formed before the Westgate. The line wasn't very long, but inspections had been taking longer than usual lately. Twice as many Knights guarded the gate than the Renegade War.

Mitto waited impatiently for his turn, keeping an eye out for Baxter Lawler all the while.

By the time he finally reached the open gate, he was convinced his friend wasn't going to show. That didn't surprise him. Baxter was likely sleeping off the effects of a night spent in revelry. Despite the Knight's best intentions—and Baxter Lawler *always* had the best of intentions—he had probably stopped at one or more taverns after leaving Someplace Else.

Mitto didn't fault the man for his unreliability. It was just Baxter's nature. The Knight was too friendly for his own good. He couldn't refuse an offer stop for a drink or a throw of the dice. And if Baxter had come across any of his female admirers, then there was no guessing what time he stumbled back to the barracks.

No, Mitto couldn't fault the Knight for being popular and well-liked. Baxter was eager to please, but mostly he focused on keeping himself pleased.

For the hundredth time, Mitto wondered how Baxter had managed to become a Knight in the first place. Or perhaps the real question was how did the man keep up with the rigors of his profession while simultaneously nurturing his social life.

The officer on duty, a Knight whom Mitto didn't recognize, asked the routine questions, to which Mitto gave his memorized responses. The Knight was understandably surprised to learn Mitto was carrying not provender, but passengers. The wagon was obviously not intended to transport people. When the officer finished interrogating the driver, he moved on to the passengers, and Mitto was probably even more eager to hear Toemis Blisnes's explanation than the Knight was.

"Fort Faith, you say?" the officer asked. "What business have you there, Grandfather?"

Mitto held his breath. He half expected the old man to refuse to answer, but Toemis paused only a moment before replying. "Many, many years ago, I was a cook at Fort Faith. I have many memories from that time and want to take my granddaughter there before I die."

There was nothing in Toemis's tone that indicated he was fabricating, and at that moment, Mitto really wanted to believe the old man. Maybe it was just that simple. Toemis was certainly old enough to have been at Fort Faith before the Ogre War. And yet Mitto couldn't help but suspect there was more to Toemis's quest.

Goblin always spoke out of both sides of his mouth, mixing truth and lies in equal parts.

But the Knight was satisfied with the old man's story and gave Mitto leave to clear the gate. The wagon had covered no more than a few yards before the first raindrop struck him in the nose. Cursing his luck, Mitto retrieved his three-cornered hat from the bag at his side and planted it firmly on his head.

The dreariness of the morning suited his mood perfectly.

Passage IV

"Stand and deliver!"

The order was followed by the sudden appearance of three men on the road up ahead. Instinctively, Mitto pulled back on the reins, though later he would regret not having tried to drive over the highwaymen.

There could be no mistaking that the men were, in fact, robbers. Even if the one hadn't declared them all as thieves with three words, their attire indicated their purpose. All three were clad in dirty, ragged jerkins of brown and greenish hues that allowed them to blend in with the trees lining the highway. Two of them wore dark and dangerous expressions, but the third man's black mask hid everything but his angry eyes.

The man in the mask carried twin swords, the likes of which Mitto had never seen before. The twin blades thickened from crosspiece to tip, and while the dull edge of the blade protruded at a ninety-degree angle from the hilt, the sharp edge was slightly curved. Each of the other two brigands wore a sheathed sword at his belt, which left their hands free to carry crossbows. Both of which were currently aimed at their mark's chest.

Mitto registered all of this in the span of a second and a half. He immediately discarded the thought of reaching for the quarterstaff secreted in a niche behind his seat, and it was too late to try to pull the wagon away. A sinking feeling in his stomach, Mitto held up his palms to let the thieves know that he did not intend to make trouble. He almost smiled too, thinking how disappointed the rogues would be when they realized he carried no goods at all.

But then he remembered Toemis's gold—*his* gold.

"Jump down from the wagon," the man in the mask ordered, "or we'll kill you."

Mitto complied, never taking his eyes off of the crossbow-men. There was no telling how desperate they were, no way of knowing what they were capable of. He worried the archers would shoot his horses out of spite until he realized that they were far more likely to shoot him and take the animals for their own.

The notion that these filthy thieves could end his life at any second made Mitto's insides burn with rage. All weariness vanished instantly, granting him an almost preternatural alert-ness to everything around him. Too bad there's not a damn thing I can do about any of it! he groused.

"Zeetan, take a look in the wagon," the masked man called to someone who must have been positioned near the wagon's rear.

The bandit, presumably the leader, punctuated his command by twirling the two peculiar swords. The other men kept their crossbows trained on him. In the next few seconds, while every-body waited for Zeetan to come forward, Mitto considered the situation from a surprisingly detached perspective.

First, he pondered the nature of the rogues. Highwaymen were an extremely rare this near the capital. Even though the thick woods provided cover, the Knights of Superius regularly patrolled the area. And most traders traveled in groups or hired armed escorts, which made robbing them all the more difficult and less rewarding on the whole.

Another reason highwaymen were so scarce near Rydah was due to the Thief Guild. Robbery had become a very organized profession in the capital, and the members of the Guild preferred to make their profit within the walls of the city. Rumor had it that the Guild had a rather lavish hideout hidden somewhere in the city itself. Mitto couldn't imagine why these thieves would forsake the comfort of the city for the wilderness.

Of course, there were other rumors too, talk of changes within the Guild. According to Baxter, who felt the need to keep Mitto abreast of the more interesting rumors in the capital—the Thief Guild had signed a pact with Rydah's Renegades. But not every thief wanted to ally with the rebels, which caused a schism within the ranks of the Guild.

Some, apparently, had left Rydah altogether.

Two years ago, Mitto had been waylaid by highwaymen en route to Steppt. He had managed to fight them off with his quarterstaff. But there had been only two of the bastards then, and neither had carried bows. And he had taken a few bruises and cuts for his trouble.

His skill with a staff was modest at best. Even at the prime of his life, he would have been no match for three armed foes—four, counting Zeetan.

All thoughts of fighting his way out vanished when Zeetan walked up beside him. The young man wore a dark gray cloak decorated with myriad moons, stars, and other strange symbols. His voluminous coat was tied together by a rope belt, from which a dagger and several pouches dangled. He carried a tall staff, though he wasn't old enough to need it for a crutch. The staff looked ordinary enough, possibly crafted from the branch of a nearby elm or balsam, but Mitto suspected that the stick was far more dangerous than it looked.

Surely, Zeetan was a wizard.

Without sparing the wagon a glance, Zeetan addressed the masked man in a calm, measured voice. "The wagon is empty, Falchion, except for two passengers."

Mitto wondered if the wizard had peeked in the back of the wagon or if he had made the discovery via magic. There was little time to ponder it, however, for the swordsman, Falchion, suddenly launched into a litany of oaths and curses.

"Of all the gods-damned luck. We spend the morning squatting in the rain, and when a cart finally rolls by, it's empty! Bastard son of a filthy whore! Damn, damn, damn." Falchion was silent for a moment, before adding, "Who's that in your wagon, peddler?"

"What if they're Knights?" one of the crossbowmen asked in a whisper Mitto had no trouble hearing.

"Or Renegades?" the other added.

"Shut your mouths," Falchion said.

The swordsman stomped over to Mitto and leveled one of the heavy-bladed swords at his throat. "Tell me who your companions are, and if you try to deceive me, I'll kill you where you stand."

"It's just an old man and his granddaughter. They're no threat to anybody," Mitto answered.

"Is he a wealthy man…a nobleman?"

Mitto feigned a chuckle. "Not likely, judging by the looks of him."

Even as he bent the truth in hopes the highwaymen wouldn't

find the gold, a part of his mind screamed, "Just give them the money and be done with it!"

Falchion uttered another string of curses. Then the thief, his dark eyes boring into Mitto's from behind the mask, said, "Fetch the passengers. I want to see them for myself."

Mitto felt his stomach drop down to his boots. They would find the purse of gold, and Falchion would surely slit his throat for lying. Then again, the highwayman had probably planned on killing him from the start.

In response to Falchion's latest decree, the wizard slowly made his way up to the driver's seat. Mitto had sealed the interior of the wagon in order to keep the rain out. He watched Zeetan fumble with the knots in the leather thongs that secured the covering's flap.

After a full minute, one of the crossbowmen—a scar-faced man with a rodent-like face—yelled, "Just cut the damn thing!"

"Shut your mouth, Critter," Falchion snarled.

Mitto couldn't decide if the swordsman was upset because he had not given Critter permission to speak or because he feared the wrath of the wizard. Zeetan, for his part, followed Critter's suggestion, drawing his dagger and sawing through the leather. When the wizard was finished with the strap, he returned the blade to its sheath and pulled the flaps aside.

Now he'll find Toemis and the gold, Mitto thought glumly. At the same time, a part of him was glad to be rid of the gold. If I live through this, I'll be getting out cheap. I can be back at Someplace Else before dinnertime.

Let Goblin choke on his coins. I'm through with him and his secrets!

The sky flashed, followed immediately by a loud clap of thunder, which startled the highwaymen, Mitto, and the horses alike. At that precise moment, as Zeetan widened the slit in the wagon's covering, Toemis Blisnes sprang out of the dark recess of the wagon and plunged his dagger into the wizard's gut.

Less than an hour after Mitto passed through the Westgate, two Knights astride purebred war horses followed the road that would lead them to the heart of the island province. The two riders kept their mounts at a moderate pace in spite of the pouring rain. And although one of the Knights bore the distinct reputation of being a verbose and convivial traveling companion, the two comrades-in-arms said not a word to each another.

The higher-ranking of the two Knights, who was wont to describe himself as Rydah's finest lieutenant, lowered his visor to keep the rain out of his eyes. He trained his bloodshot eyes at the road ahead and tried to ignore the pounding inside his skull as well as the disconcerting churning of his entrails.

As the miles passed by—with nary a sign of Mitto's wagon—Sir Baxter Lawler cursed himself for getting mixed up with the fool of a merchant.

If I weren't such a good friend, he thought, I'd be squandering my free day in a soft bed, warm and dry. But look where my dedication to that lousy trader has landed me? I'm tired, drenched to the bone, and I'll be lucky if I make it halfway to Fort Valor without vomiting in my helmet. Oh, you owe me plenty for this one, Mitto…if that Toemis fellow doesn't stick a knife in your back first.

When they finally caught up to Mitto's wagon, he motioned for his companion, Sir Alban Damek, to slow down. The two Knights kept on like that for the next few hours, watching the wagon from a distance, never getting too close. Baxter had no way of knowing for sure that Mitto was still alive, but he craned in his saddle, searching for the tell-tale tricorn hat.

Baxter was alerted to trouble the instant the wagon stopped. When he saw several men emerge from the woods on either side of the highway, he urged his mount off of the road, trusting Sir Damek to do the same. Silently, he dismounted and tied the steed's reins to a low-hanging branch.

There had been talk of thieves skulking about the forest, but Baxter hadn't expected to run into any on this particular stretch of road. Few enough people found a need to travel between the capital and Fort Valor—or Fort Faith for that matter. But Baxter knew highwaymen when he saw them.

"Follow my lead," he instructed his sole companion. Then he began moving through the foliage, careful to make as little noise as possible. That wasn't easy, since both he and Sir Damek were fully armed. When they were close enough to the wagon to see and hear most of what was going on, Baxter forced himself to sit tight and learn as much as he could before acting.

As long as the crossbowmen were aiming at Mitto, the Knights would have to wait.

The chance to strike came when an old man—Toemis, presumably—jumped out of the wagon and stabbed the wizard.

"Now!" Baxter shouted, as he leaped out of the trees and charged headlong at the closer of the two crossbowmen.

He had no time to ensure Sir Damek was following him. Nor could he spare a thought for the most dangerous of the thieves, the wizard. He didn't even have a chance to acknowledge Mitto, though he very much wanted to scold the merchant for getting into such a mess.

Baxter Lawler focused on one thing only—dispatching the crossbowmen before they could fire their bolts through his coat-of-plates and the haubergeon beneath. The weapons could kill him and Sir Damek as easily as if he wore no armor at all, so ran with his sword raised heavenward and his shield held out before him, praying to Feol that he would live to drink another day.

Through the sights of his helm, Baxter locked eyes with the first crossbowman. The thief seemed to be moving in slow motion. When the shock of the Knights' sudden appearance wore off, the crossbowman swiveled his torso toward the oncoming warriors and slowly—or so it seemed to Baxter—took aim at him. Baxter was no more than five paces from the brigand when he heard the unmistakable snap of the crossbow's discharging.

He watched as the bolt flew toward him, pushed effortlessly through his wooden targe and planted itself into Baxter's upper arm.

The pain, compounded by the sheer impact of the bolt, sent Baxter stumbling back a step. Clenching his teeth against the burning ache in his arm, Baxter pushed forward. The crossbowman, who had no chance of reloading before the Knight was on him, dropped his weapon and turned to flee.

"Not so fast," Baxter taunted. "No one treats me like a pincushion and gets away with it."

With a mighty stroke of his hand-and-a-half sword, Baxter felled the crossbowman with a deep wound that stretched from shoulder to hip.

A man in the mask stood between him and the other crossbowman, blocking his path. As Baxter closed in on the leader—Falchion, he had been called—he saw the crossbowman beyond join the first in heading toward the woods. The Knight's heart skipped a beat when he noticed that thief's crossbow had also been fired.

In spite of his proximity to Falchion, Baxter glanced behind him and found Sir Damek writhing on the ground, a shaft protruding from his belly.

Baxter met Falchion's attack with an unintelligible battle cry on his lips. He parried the highwayman's slashes with his blade and damaged shield. Each time his enemy's heavy-bladed sword—which looked more like a barnyard tool than an accouterment of war—made contact with the targe, the impact sent waves of pain up his injured arm.

But Baxter had no choice. He must either defend with both sword and shield, or he was done for.

Falchion waged a brutal offensive, favoring fast and powerful strokes over measured and accurate ones. The brigand clearly wasn't the most skillful of swordsmen, but what he lacked in form he made up for with intensity. It was all Baxter could do to keep the over-sized kitchen cleavers from biting into him. Finally, he was forced to take a blow in order to gain some offensive momentum of his own.

Rather than raise his hand-and-a-half sword to deflect the oncoming weapon, Baxter allowed the thrust to connect with the steel covering his chest. Predictably, the blunted tip of his opponent's sword did little but dent his coat-of-plates. Before Falchion could pull back, Baxter wrenched his own sword upward. The movement was awkward, and he wasn't able to put much force into it.

Nonetheless, the blade's edge met Falchion's poorly protected forearm. The masked man let out a cry as he dropped one of his weapons.

It will be over in a matter of seconds, Baxter thought, for he knew Falchion was no match for him now. In truth, the highwayman had never been a fair rival, even with a crossbow bolt jutting out just below his shoulder. As a Knight of Superius, Baxter had been trained by the best, and his equipment was superior too.

Even as Falchion desperately swung his remaining blade at Baxter's well-protected head, Baxter calculated the rogue's defeat in three moves.

He was on the verge of impaling the swordsman, already thinking of how he would run over to poor Sir Damek afterward, when came the sound of several people rushing through the very overgrowth he and Sir Damek had used for cover.

The bastards have reinforcements! Baxter thought. Instead of dispatching Falchion, he half-turned to get a look at how many highwaymen he would have to kill before the day was done.

But they weren't highwaymen at all.

Like the thieves around him, Mitto was temporarily stunned by Toemis's attack on the wizard. For the split second that followed, he debated whether to stand by and watch the highwaymen slaughter Toemis Blisnes or join in the hopeless fight and get dying over with more quickly.

When two Knights appeared out of nowhere, Mitto's mind was made up for him. With Falchion and the two crossbowmen distracted by the new threat, he turned back to the wagon.

Toemis was still grappling with the wizard, who, in turn, was doing his best to keep the old man's knife from stabbing him again. Somehow, the two combatants managed to remain balanced on the driver's seat, and Mitto did his best to avoid flailing arms and legs as he withdrew the quarterstaff from its hiding place behind the seat.

Because the old man was lying atop Zeetan, there was no opening for Mitto. He hesitated before abandoning the wagon, however, because he worried that Toemis would not be able to finish him off. If the wizard were allowed to speak even one spell, the Knights' rescue would be in vain.

But Mitto's help was needed elsewhere. Already, one of the Knights was curled up on the road. The remaining Knight—whose coat of arms identified him as none other than Baxter Lawler—had cut down one of the crossbowmen and was preparing to engage Falchion. That left the other crossbowman for Mitto.

He had taken no more than two steps toward Critter when the sound of boots against gravel alerted him to someone coming up from behind. He swung around in time to find a fifth brigand stealing up on the action. Probably the newcomer had been keeping watch near the rear of the wagon, Mitto reasoned.

Hoping the thief was, in fact, the final member of the band—and praying he himself hadn't gotten too rusty from lack of practice—Mitto held the quarterstaff out across his body and waited for his opponent to come. The highwayman slowed a bit when he saw the merchant standing between him and his cohorts but then rushed forward, a series of deep furrows wrinkling his protruding brow.

The man carried only a long-handled axe, the type a wood-cutter might wield against a tree. He ran with his weapon held high above his head, as though he intended to hew Mitto in half like a log of firewood. Mitto waited until the last second to bring up his staff, careful to catch the descending axe well below the sharpened head. Wood met wood with a loud crack. For a moment, the two weapons locked tight together.

The axeman pushed with all of his might, hoping to over-power the older merchant. But having hefted heavy barrels and crates for the majority of his life, Mitto was more than the thief's equal in strength. Slowly, the single-edged axe began to inch back toward its owner.

With a grunt, the axeman relented and hauled back for anoth-er swing. Mitto saw that the next attack would take the form of a horizontal slice. He adjusted his hold on his staff and bent his knees to keep his center of gravity as low as possible.

The axeman's second assault was less powerful than the first had been, but Mitto grunted at the impact nevertheless. Once more, he positioned the quarterstaff so that it would catch the axe's long handle, but this time, he was not grasping the staff near its middle.

As soon as the two weapons crashed together, Mitto sent the longer end of the quarterstaff straight at the axeman's ribs. His opponent had no chance to avoid the blow, which sent him staggering back a few steps. Mitto didn't give the man time to recover. As soon as the axe head was a safe distance away, he slammed the blunt tip of the staff into his opponent's stomach.

The axeman doubled over with a groan, grasping at his mid-section with his left hand.

His right hand, however, had maintained its grip on the axe. As Mitto came forward, the thief made a clumsy swing, a hope-less attempt to keep the merchant at bay. This time, the quarter-staff caught the head of the axe and from underneath and, using the superior strength of his two arms against the axeman's one, Mitto wrenched the weapon right out of the man's hands.

The axe sailed harmlessly into the woods, and before the brigand could react one way or another, Mitto swung low with the opposite end of the quarterstaff. The staff hit a little too low, missing the man's knee by a couple of inches, but the blow had been solid enough to send the man pitching sideways, completely off-balanced.

Mitto struck his opponent in the kidney on his way down for good measure. When the highwayman hit the road, practically face-first, he made no move to get back up. Breathing heavily, from exhilaration and exhaustion alike, Mitto left the unarmed thief and turned back to see how Baxter was faring.

There was no Critter, there was no sign, and Falchion was down to one sword. Glancing over at the wagon, he was alarmed to find that both Toemis and Zeetan had disappeared. He might have suspected magic as the cause, except then he noticed how the wagon was rocking. Apparently, the old man and the wizard had relocated their skirmish to the inside of the wagon.

Since there was no doubt in his mind Baxter could finish off the lone swordsman, Mitto hopped up onto the driver's seat and lifted a corner of the covering's flap to peer inside. There was no time, however, to make out much of anything in the dark, for suddenly five more Knights of Superius, all on foot, burst out of woods from almost exactly the same spot Baxter and his comrade had.

Why had Baxter's allies held back instead of overwhelming the highwaymen from the start? he wondered.

But Mitto realized all too soon that the newcomers were not there to rescue him and that the Knights themselves were in need of rescuing.

Passage V

Of the five Knights, Baxter Lawler recognized only one, the tallest of the lot, upon whose surcoat was emblazoned the image of a red stallion surrounded by a yellow sunburst. It was Vearghal Ahern, a fellow lieutenant and Baxter's archrival.

Ahern was an impossibly rigid man who hadn't a humorous bone in his body. But he did have a sharp wit, which he often honed—Baxter's flaws being his favorite whetstone. Ahern's unit, comprised of twenty Knights, had been sent out a week ago to comb the forest east of Rydah for clues concerning the disappearance of some local woodsmen.

Ahern had thought himself above the dull mission, believing that the woodcutters had likely drunk too much, wandered off, and gotten lost. He had pointed out to the High Commander that dealing with drunkards was more up Baxter's alley than his own.

Upon being reunited with the pompous Vearghal Ahern, two questions came to Baxter's mind: where were the rest of the lieutenant's men, and what was that tar-like substance splattered all over the Knights' tabards?

"Did you guide your men into a bog, Sir Ahern?" Baxter asked, keeping half an eye on Falchion.

But the tall Knight—whom Else Fontane had dubbed the Immovable Tower—did not reply. He said something to his men behind him, and, immediately, the four Knights began to run as fast as their cumbersome armor allowed them in the direction of the capital. At the same time, Ahern hurried over to Baxter, raising his visor as he neared.

"What in the hell is going on? Aren't you supposed to be on the other side of Rydah?" Baxter asked.

"Silence that infernal tongue of yours, Lawler," Vearghal Ahern growled, "and for once in your gods-forsaken life just *listen.* You have to get these people out of here. We are all in grave—"

The lieutenant's words were cut off by a most dreadful racket. Baxter had never heard anything like it before. It sounded like mourners wailing, only the cries were too brazen, too fierce. A shiver ran down Baxter's spine, and without thinking, he took a few steps toward the woods, trying to see past Mitto's wagon to where the unnerving clamor originated.

Ahern's Knights kept on running up the road, seemingly oblivious to the horrifying din around them. Suddenly, a mass of dark shapes emerged from the woods to their left, swarming the Knights like a cloud of overgrown mosquitoes. Baxter watched helplessly as the unidentifiable fiends hacked away at the Knights, throwing themselves bodily at the men to impede their retreat—which was surely what Ahern had ordered them to do and what Ahern himself had been doing until he stumbled upon Baxter and the wagon.

Up the road, the Knights tried to organize themselves into a defensive position, but their strange enemies would not give ground or time to get organized. The Knights were greatly outnumbered and were taking quite a beating.

"What enemy is this?" Baxter wondered aloud. He was on the verge of dashing over to help the Knights when he felt a heavy hand on his shoulder.

Baxter spun around, suddenly remembering the swordsman, but Falchion stood perfectly still, his gaze locked on the battle between the Knights and...whomever. It was the Immovable Tower who had grabbed him by the pauldron.

"Listen to me, man," Ahern said. "We don't know *what* they are. I've never seen the like. They ambushed us in the forest and killed fifteen of my men. I don't know how many there are, but there are too many for us to handle alone."

Baxter Lawler was speechless. Looking uncomprehendingly from the lieutenant to the pitched battle up the road, he finally asked, "They're not human?"

Ahern ignored the question. "Get on the wagon and get out here. Your only chance is to outrun them. Take word to Fort Valor—"

The lieutenant didn't have a chance to say more for the enemy was upon them, tearing through the undergrowth and leaping out of the forest like monstrous jack-in-the-boxes. Baxter stared wide-eyed at the creatures, which were definitely not human. They stood as tall as men, he thought, but it was hard to tell because they were somewhat hunched.

They wore only the lightest of armor, a motley collection of mail that covered some areas while leaving other parts entirely unprotected. One wore a chain-linked coif, but the others wore nothing at all on their bald heads, leaving their hideous faces exposed.

It was like coming face to face with a nightmare. Grayish yellow skin stretched taught over bony visages. Pointed ears and sharp noses jutted out at sharp angles. Sickly, sickle-shaped eyes regarded him hungrily. And the teeth—all incisors, knifelike, carnivorous. As if their teeth and claw-like fingers weren't enough, each of the creatures carried one or more weapons, including spears, knives, axes, and in one instance, the pilfered broadsword of a fallen Knight.

Anger quickly overpowered his terror, and Baxter raised his sword, eager to destroy the monsters. But then Ahern stepped between him and the fiends and gave him a push back.

"Get out of here!" he shouted. "That's an order!"

Baxter wanted to argue that Ahern was in no position to be giving him orders, since they were both the same rank. But his real desire to disobey the lieutenant had more to do with not wanting to abandon him than anything else.

You brave, stupid bastard, he silently seethed as he turned his back on Vearghal Ahern and ran over to the wagon.

Mitto, half-kneeling and half-standing on the driver's seat, stared in disbelief at the monsters.

"Snap out of it," Baxter yelled. "We have to get out of here."

Leaping up beside his friend, Baxter grabbed the reigns and looked further down the road in time to see Falchion vanish into the woods. Ahern was swinging his broadsword in wide arcs before him, slashing at any creature that attempted to get past him. When the first spearhead penetrated the lieutenant's defenses, smashing into the Knight's breastplate, Baxter looked away, unwilling to witness the toppling of the Immovable Tower.

He gave the reins a wild shake and shouted "Yah!"

The horses needed no further insistence. Between the monsters' strange scent and the smell of blood, it was a miracle that the animals hadn't bolted earlier. At the sudden lurching of the wagon, Mitto nearly lost his balance and might have tumbled over the side if Baxter hadn't caught him by an arm.

"Thanks," Mitto muttered.

"Don't mention it," Baxter replied, interrupting the medley of commands and curses he was directing at the two stallions.

When a third group of the ghastly creatures began pouring out onto the road far ahead, Baxter's swearing reached a whole new level of intensity and creativity. He pushed Mitto back into the covered section of the cart and positioned his damaged targe to cover as much of his crouching body as possible.

He feared the horses would buck and rear—they were draft animals, after all, not chargers—but the beasts didn't falter, and the wagon careened ever faster down the gravely highway. *If we don't break an axle or lose a wheel, we might get out of this yet,* he thought.

The foes up ahead were getting ready for the only chance they would have to prevent the wagon's escape. A few of the creatures were hastily firing arrows from shortbows, aiming, Baxter noted in dismay, at the horses. He saw a row of the fiends with spears held aloft, ready to throw their deadly missiles at the equine flanks.

Baxter swallowed another curse, tossed his shield aside, and threw himself bodily forward. He landed on the horse's broad back with a bone-jarring thud that sent a wave of agony lancing through his injured arm

Marveling that he hadn't crippled himself or the poor beast, he wrapped his free hand around the bridle and used the hand-and-a-half sword to free the animal from the harness connecting it to the other horse and the wagon altogether. Kicking at the horse's ribs with his heavy boot, he drove the terrified animal forward.

Liberated from the heavy weight of the cart, Baxter's mount quickly outpaced the other horse and the wagon. He was upon the monsters almost instantly, swinging his sword at the spear-wielders and pushing his mount into their ranks like a living battering ram.

The creatures scattered, but Baxter's wild charge could not hope to frighten away the entire horde. But he had known all along the limitations of a cavalry of one. His mount reared suddenly, an arrow piercing its rump. It was all Baxter could do to maintain his hold on the bridle.

The flailing front hooves connected with one of the creatures, sending it flying into one of its allies, but Baxter took little comfort in that unexpected help. The impetus of his charge spent, he had no way of putting any distance between him and the monsters.

Spears and axes ripped into the terrified animal, and Baxter was pulled down by claw-like hands.

The wagon quaking all around him, Mitto rolled heels-over-head backward before coming to a painful halt at the back of the wagon. He just sat there in the darkness for a moment, disoriented and confused.

But not even a bump on the head could make him forget the frightening...*things*...that had flooded out onto the road like a tainted black river.

His brain searched for some sort of an explanation. What could they have been? There had to be a logical explanation. They were something out of one of his mother's fables. The hungry monster that lives under the bridge...the sinister ghoul that snatches brats who sneak out after dark...

"What's going on?"

Mitto jumped at the sound of the voice. He peered into the darkness shadow, fearing that one of the monsters had followed him inside.

Someone—something?—started moving toward the front of the cart and opened the flap to peer out at the world, which was flying past them. The daylight that poured through the narrow opening revealed the silhouette of Toemis Blisnes.

"Get down!" the old man shouted.

Then the wagon was bathed in blackness once more. Mitto threw himself face-first to the planks that made up the wagon bed. Pinpoints of light appeared around him as arrows cut through the flimsy material of the wagon's covering. A larger missile landed a hand's breadth from Mitto's head.

The wagon shuddered beneath the onslaught, but no arrows or spears managed to pierce the low wooden wall behind which Mitto, Toemis, and his granddaughter had taken cover. After a few seconds, the arrows ceased. Before Mitto could expel a sigh of relief, something solid and heavy collided with the back of the wagon.

He rolled over onto his back and propped himself up on his elbows. The unfastened flaps at the rear of the cart billowed out behind the vehicle like pennants, but he couldn't see anything out of the ordinary. Whatever the monsters had thrown at the retreating wagon—for, he realized with a surge of joy, they were surely past the mob of creatures by now—had not even dented the guardrail.

His elation evaporated, however, when he saw a most terrible countenance rise up over the edge to peer at him over the wooden rail.

As the monster pulled itself up into the back of the wagon, Mitto denied his instinct to scurry away and instead dove forward to where his quarterstaff had rolled snug up against the guardrail. The fiend let out a fearsome cry and, with only its upper-body propped up over the railing, took a swipe at the merchant with one hand.

Sharp fingernails raked across Mitto's upper back and neck. Stifling a cry, he scooped up the quarterstaff and drove one end of it up at the creature's chest. He pushed with all his might in an attempt to dislodge the monster, but the lanky-armed, narrow-chested monster was stronger than its body otherwise indicated.

With both hands shoving off against the top of the guardrail, it tried to heave itself into the wagon in spite of the quarterstaff planted in its chest.

Mitto had little leverage in the maladroit position he had been forced to take, and he felt the strength in his arms ebbing. He dared not move his quarterstaff, though, for at the moment, it was all that was keeping the creature from entering the wagon.

Unable to come up with a better idea, Mitto shifted his weight and used the staff like a lever, using the monster's own power to propel it up and over the wagon's threshold, where it landed unceremoniously on its head in the wagon bed.

The fiend quickly recovered from his short flight, and before Mitto could bring the quarterstaff into a suitable position, the thing sprang at him. It kept one hand wrapped tightly around the staff, forcing the weapon down and out of the way, pressing it uncomfortably against Mitto's abdomen. Its other hand went for his neck. Mitto managed to catch the creature's wrist at the last second, the long, filthy fingernails a mere inch from his flesh.

Now that they were on equal footing, Mitto realized the full extent of his peril. Not only was the creature stronger than it looked, it was clearly stronger than him. Mitto fought back with every ounce of his might, but slowly the claws made their way to his throat.

He continued to struggle, staring fearfully into his adversary's bestial eyes. Even when he began to accept his inevitable death, he didn't stop clawing at the squeezing fingers, though he did close his eyes shut out his killer's grotesque face.

Then, inexplicably, the talons were gone. Mitto gasped for air and opened his eyes to find the monster doing a strange dance, its gangly limbs flapping like a bird about to take flight. When the creature pitched to one side, Mitto saw Toemis Blisnes's knife buried in the small of its back.

The old man flung himself at the fiend, first removing the blade and then driving it home repeatedly. All the while, the monster grabbed at him and tried everything it could to shake him loose. Finally, the creature's bony elbow connected with Toemis's forehead, and the old man went sprawling into a corner of the wagon.

By this time, however, Mitto had recovered from his initial encounter with the monster. When it turned to finish off Toemis, it found Mitto waiting. The powerful, deadly hands started to rise to fend off the blow, but there was no chance of that. Mitto swung with every fiber of his being and heard a satisfying crunch when the quarterstaff connected with the monster's skull.

The force sent the thing staggering into the side of the wagon, where it collided with the tarp and promptly fell to the floor, unmoving. To be sure that the thing wasn't merely stunned, the merchant knelt beside it and investigated. A stream of black gore was oozing from its caved-in temple.

Mitto slumped back against the canvas, his mind reeling. Toemis's granddaughter was curled up into a ball in the far corner of the wagon, completely concealed in the material of her hooded cloak. In another corner lay Zeetan, his arms and legs bound together, a gag in his mouth. He stared at Mitto with wide eyes.

Wizard or not, Zeetan looked scared out of his wits.

Ignoring Zeetan and the girl, Mitto crawled over to Toemis. He was relieved to find the old man alive, and this surprised him, considering how much he had loathed him earlier. Toemis had nearly gotten them all killed when he instigated the fight with the brigands. And yet, after their clash with the monsters, everything else was ancient history.

"Are you all right?" he asked Toemis, trying to help the old man up into a sitting position.

Toemis let out a loud cough, cleared his throat, and nodded. Even in the poor light of the wagon, Mitto could see an ugly bruise on the old man's forehead that stared back at him like a third eye. "I'll be fine, but you'd better get those horses of yours under control before they overturn the wagon."

That said, the old man pushed past him and made his way over to the girl. Still clutching the quarterstaff as though it were an extension of his arm, Mitto poked his head out between the front flaps, expecting to find Baxter Lawler at the reigns.

But the Knight was gone, and he had apparently taken one of the horses with him.

Mitto crawled out onto the driver's seat and looked around. On either side of the wagon, the forest was a green blur. Not far up ahead, the road crested the top of a small hill. If they maintained their current speed, the cart would likely lose all four wheels on the way down.

"Whoa!" he yelled at the remaining horse. "Whoa!"

Eventually, the beast complied, slowing to a safer pace. Although the animal's hide was sleek with sweat, the stallion showed no sign of stopping, which was fine with Mitto. He had no wish to give the monsters a chance to catch up.

He tried to steal a backward glance but couldn't see past the bulk of the wagon. There was no sign of Baxter or the missing horse anywhere.

"What foolhardy thing did you do this time?" Mitto asked, blinking back tears.

He felt the blows raining down on him, though his coat-of-plates turned aside the spearheads. The heavier impacts of axe and sword left dents in the armor, but none of the weapons punctured through the layers of metal. Swinging his hand-and-a-half sword in an effort to force the monsters back, Baxter fought his way to his feet and almost tripped over the dying stallion.

When he saw the wagon careen past him on the road with only handful of the monsters in a position to fire their arrows at vehicle, Baxter let out a loud laugh. His audacity had worked. None of the missiles had found their way to the remaining horse.

Never mind that he himself was doomed…

Baxter pushed the thought from his mind. Gripping his sword with both hands, he waged an assault that sent pieces of the creatures flying in every direction. Geysers of hot black blood soaked his surcoat.

He howled when a war-hammer crushed his upper arm, crumpling his pauldron and shattering the bone beneath. He let the useless limb fall to his side and went into a great spin. Holding the hand-and-a-half sword in one hand now, he severed the head of the creature that had so grievously wounded him.

His victory was short-lived, however, for another monster was already beating the spiked head of its mace into his helm. A second assailant had managed to pierce both his coat-of-plates and the haubergeon beneath with a barbed spear.

Baxter managed to slay three more of the fiends before the weakness of his injuries drove him to the ground. Clawed fingers tore at his armor, tearing off his coat-of-plates, tugging off his battered helm. Within a matter of seconds, they had removed his haubergeon as well, and it appeared as though a few of the creatures were fighting over who would inherit the piece of armor. One of the demons was already painfully poking him with the tip of his own hand-and-a-half sword.

"Well, go ahead and get it over with." He had to shout to be heard over the creatures, which were shrieking and yelling at one another in a language Baxter couldn't understand. "I accept defeat, knowing you'll never have the others."

He laughed again and recognized the hysteria for what it was. The monsters didn't seem to share in his mirth. They regarded him with sinister expressions, and more than a few spearheads prodded his exposed flesh.

"Come on and finish the job, you bloody cowards!" he roared, but none of the monsters appeared to be in much of a hurry to comply.

Have it your way, he thought, and made a play for the knife tucked in his boot.

That spurred the creatures into action. A cacophony of discordant cries erupted from all around him. The spearheads and sword tips bit deeper into his body, but that was not enough to stop the Knight. Finally, one of the monsters kicked him in the side of the head hard enough to flop him over on his stomach. As he blacked out for what he knew would be the last time, he let out a final chuckle.

Looks like I'll be seeing the Immovable Tower sooner than I wanted…

Passage VI

They stopped only when Mitto realized he was on the verge of killing his horse. While he certainly didn't want the animal keeling over from exhaustion, he allowed only ten minutes of rest each break. Whenever he was tempted to take more time, all he had to do was look at the corpse in the wagon, and that was enough to make him forget about his cramped legs and stiff joints.

When dusk enveloped them, Mitto knew he should find a place to wait out the night. As much as he wanted to get to the safety of Fort Valor, traveling at night was out of the question. Too many dangers lurked in the darkness, including concealed rocks that could cripple a horse and wild animals.

As he steered the wagon off the main road, he tried to calm his nerves, reminding himself they had put quite a few miles between themselves and the monsters. Hopefully, the monsters had given up the chase long ago.

But as night descended, logic became an ineffectual weapon against his fears, and he started seeing the monsters concealed in every shadow.

"Why have we turned off the road?"

The query made Mitto's entire body tense. Scolding himself for being so jumpy, he loosened his grip on the quarterstaff and glanced back at Toemis. The old man, his skull-like head and scarecrow neck protruding from between the flaps of cloth, wore a decidedly disapproving look.

"I know of a place where we can rest for the night," Mitto told him. When a soft, low sound escaped the old man's lips, Mitto turned his attention back to the road ahead. He wore a frown to match Toemis's. "You didn't think we'd ride day and night without rest until we reached our destination, did you?"

Mitto took Toemis's silence as a testament to the affirmative.

"Look, I'd like nothing more than to go nonstop to Fort Valor—"

"Fort Faith," Toemis corrected.

Mitto swallowed a harsh retort. Did the old man really think he was just going to bypass Fort Valor? He took a deep breath before continuing. "It's too dangerous to be wandering around at night. All it would take was one exposed root or an unseen stone, and we'd lose another horse faster than you can say…" His mind blanked, but he pressed on. "Besides, there are other hazards."

He left it at that, waiting for the old man to argue with him, to thrust the bag of gold under his nose once more. Well, just try it, Mitto thought scornfully. I'll throw each and every coin back at you. Look what your tainted treasure has cost me so far.

The missing horse was a constant reminder of what he had lost, though he could always buy another one. Baxter Lawler, one the other hand, was one of a kind…

Toemis didn't press his point, and when Mitto glanced back over his shoulder, he saw the old man had already withdrawn back inside the wagon. After a few more minutes, Mitto slowed the wagon and then stopped entirely, his eyes locked on a boxy building made of wood and the empty posts before it.

There were no horses secured to the posts, which meant no other travelers were using the lodge tonight. Never in his life could Mitto recall wanting so much to find company for the night—if only because there was safety in numbers.

Swearing under his breath, Mitto jumped down from the driver's seat. He spoke neither to himself nor to the horse as he disengaged the animal from its harness. He wasn't in any mood for conversation.

He heard something hit the ground and found Toemis standing beside the wagon, looking at the lodge.

"Where are we?" he asked.

Where do you think we are? he wanted to shout. We're in the middle of nowhere with gods-only-know how many of those wretched creatures lurking in the woods!

Mitto took a slow breath and tied the horse's reins to a post. "It's a lodge. Travelers caught on the road at nightfall use it. The Knights are in charge of its upkeep, which means it passes for adequate shelter. If nothing else, it'll keep us dry."

And keep a wall between us and the monsters, he added silently.

Toemis just nodded, still staring at the simple structure. His eyes held a faraway look, giving Mitto the distinct impression he wasn't really seeing the lodge at all. Unexpectedly, the old man spoke.

"Not one of the Knights ran from battle today, even though they were hopelessly outnumbered."

"The Knights of Superius are a brave lot," Mitto replied, not knowing what else to say. "They'll do anything in the name of chivalry."

That last part had held more than a hint of sarcasm, and Mitto felt guilty for it. But he couldn't help being angry with Baxter for throwing his life away to save them. Yes, it was part of the Knight's job, his sworn duty even, but that wasn't enough consolation for Mitto. He'd gladly have traded a dozen Toemis Blisneses for one Baxter Lawler.

As if breaking free of whatever strange whim had possessed him, Toemis turned around to face the driver's seat and said, "Zusha."

Only when the little girl's face pushed through the flaps did Mitto realize Toemis had spoken his granddaughter's name for the first time. Zusha stepped out onto the driver's seat. Then Toemis, placing his outstretched hands under her armpits, lowered her down to the earth. Somewhere in the process, the girl's ever-present hood fell back, and Mitto made a startling discovery.

Earlier, he had been struck by the girl's blue eyes, for they had reminded him a little of Else Fontane's. Mitto had always thought that Else's eyes were a fraction too large for her face, and their prominence tended to draw one's attention—and admiration even.

Yes, he distinctly recalled seeing Zusha's blue eyes back in Rydah, but now, as he unabashedly stared at her profile, he saw her eyes were as dark as Toemis's.

He took a step forward, trying to get a better look, thinking perhaps it was a trick of the fading light, but as soon as the girl's foot hit the ground, Toemis pulled up her hood and began leading her toward the lodge.

In all the bedlam of that afternoon, Mitto had almost forgotten how much he distrusted Toemis Blisnes. Never mind that the old man had probably saved his life. Toemis's skill with his knife, not to mention his eagerness to use it, was another piece of the puzzle.

Why are you really going to Fort Faith, old man? Mitto wondered. *Why do you hide your granddaughter's face beneath a hood? Is she even your granddaughter?*

But Mitto did not voice any of his many questions. He was about to join his enigmatic passengers at the lodge when he suddenly realized he had a third companion to contend with. Spitting out a stream of curses that would have rivaled even Falchion's most colorful oaths, Mitto leaped back up onto the driver's seat, pulled open the flaps, and stared down at the hog-tied spell-caster, wondering just what in the hells he should do with Zeetan.

It was a night like many others at Someplace Else, which was not necessarily a good thing in the mind of the inn's proprietress. Lately, she could count her customers on one hand, and once they were finished with supper, the majority of them would either go up to their rooms or back to their homes.

Only Loony Gomez was wont to stay until she locked up, and he'd be too drunk to make it to the door on his own. She had become an innkeeper because she was a social animal by nature, but lately she had had fewer and fewer patrons, which meant less companionship—and less money.

Else was staring at the fire across the room, pretending to listen to one of Gomez's favorite stories—a bawdy tale about a lonely carpenter's daughter who carved an imaginary lover out of wood—when a brassy jingle from the bell above the door announced the arrival of a new customer.

Snapping out of her daydreaming—which had been about Mitto O'erlander, she realized self-consciously—Else abandoned the bar and walked over to the newcomer.

Normally, her customers didn't receive a personal greeting at the door, but it wasn't as though she had anything else to do. Truth be told, she was grateful for the arrival of anyone who might break up the monotony of another predictable evening with Loony Gomez. And from all appearances, this was no ordinary customer.

The man's stiff gait, broad shoulders, and most importantly, the scabbard that protruded from underneath his overcoat declared him a Knight of Superius.

Rydah's Knights seldom visited Someplace Else. Her establishment was too far away from the gatehouses, barracks, and the Celestial Palace to attract the city's defenders. She couldn't even remember the last time a Knight walked through the door, with the exception of Baxter Lawler, of course, and Baxter only showed up only when Mitto was in town.

"May I take your coat, good sir?"

The Knight's cloudy gray eyes blinked twice, and the corners of his mouth twitched into a polite smile. "No thank you, madam. But might I have a word with whoever was on duty last night?"

The Knight made no move to remove his coat, which was pockmarked with the dark splotches of raindrops. Shrugging inwardly, Else replied, "I run the show here every night, and if I had ever needed an assistant, I couldn't afford to keep them on now."

Else, who had never been too proud to discuss her problems with complete strangers, suddenly felt a twinge of embarrassment well up from some unexpected reservoir. She had no way of knowing whether the man was well-to-do, but judging from his fine overcoat—and the fact that the Knights of Superius were reputed to reap wages that befitted the nobility of lesser realms—the man was far from impoverished.

"Might we have a talk over by the fire, madam?"

It dawned on her that she had been lost in her own thoughts again, and she desperately hoped she hadn't been standing there too long, staring stupidly at him. If her cheeks had flushed earlier, they surely traded their rosy hue for a much darker shade now.

"Of course," she said, quickly turned her back on the Knight.

On her way over to the fireplace, she mentally reprimanded herself for acting like some heartsick filly. When was the last time a man made me blush? she demanded of herself. She answered that question with another: When was the last time a man called me "madam"?

Else had never paired the Knighthood and romance in the same thought. Oh, the Knights of Superius were a chivalrous lot—courageous and gallant and all that—but they were also, by the same token, impossibly rigid creatures, strict with themselves as well as those around them.

"Dull, dull, dull," she had told Baxter one night when she, Baxter, and Mitto had polished off a bottle of Dragon's Hoard among the three of them. "Let the young maidens sigh and make eyes at those walking cans of tin. I'd sooner court the Guild-master than the High Commander. At least with a thief, you'll only lose your money. A Knight can go riding off with your heart without even realizing it.

"Anyway, what happens at night, when the Knight is no longer a Knight? I'd bet my inn that the gauntlets...er...gloves come off then, and underneath it all, there's nothing courtly about any one of them. Present company excluded, of course."

But Baxter hadn't argued at all. Sir Lawler was, perhaps, a good deal better than his comrades in that he didn't put on airs. True, Baxter was more or less infamous for his gambling, drinking, and wenching, but while the Knighthood frowned upon such behavior, Else was grateful to find abundant weaknesses in a Knight of Superius. Even with his armor on, Baxter was just a man—no more, no less.

"To what do I owe this pleasure, Sir Knight?" Else asked once the unfamiliar Knight was seated beside her by the fire.

His eyebrows arched in surprise. "Why do you suppose I am a Knight?"

"Well, if you're *not* a Knight, then I must ask you to leave your sword at the bar."

That brought a full-fledged smile to the man's handsome face. And it was handsome, Else had to admit. The Knight looked to be in his early fifties—maybe over a decade older than she—judging by the silvery hair at his temples and the age-worn grooves by his mouth and eyes.

Maybe I ought to consider changing my policy on courting Knights, she thought, returning his smile.

Immediately, she felt guilty. Hadn't she been hunched miserably over the bar a moment ago, practically sick with worry for her dear friend Mitto? Yes, *friend*, an inner voice argued, and nothing more than that. There was no reason she couldn't be charmed by a new face. That imperceptive merchant had no claims on her, and she had no claims on him.

"I confess I am indeed a Knight...Sir Bryant Walden, High Commander."

He paused, clearly waiting for Else to give her name in fair exchange, but suddenly her tongue lost the ability to move. Here she was, face to face with the highest-ranking Knight in Rydah—nay, in all of Capricon!—and she had spent the last few minutes ogling him as though he were the prize bull at a beef auction.

"My name is Else Fontane," she managed at last. "It is a pleasure to make your acquaintance."

"The pleasure is all mine," Sir Walden said, but then his features straightened to a grim expression, and he sat a bit taller in his chair. "I have come to discuss an important matter with you, Madam Fontane."

"What is it?"

"I understand that a man by the name of Toemis Blisnes stayed at your inn last night."

An icy fist clutched her heart, and she found herself worrying about Mitto all over again.

At the onset of the showers, the night had grown terribly cold, so cold that Mitto had finally started a fire despite the smoke that would escape through the lodge's chimney. But it was necessary, if not for his sake, then for Zusha's—not that Toemis had seemed concerned for his shivering granddaughter.

The old man hadn't said a word since entering the lodge, and he now sat, unmoving, on the floor with his back up against the wall. He gazed sightlessly at the worn planks at his feet. Zusha sat beside him, more like an obedient pet than a cherished loved-one.

Like Toemis, Zusha sat on the floor, hardly moving, except for turning her head every now and again, careful to keep her hood in place.

Mitto, resting his feet up on the edge of the hearth, sneaked another glance over at the two of them. Zusha herself was stealing longing looks over at the fire. Not for the first time, Mitto thought Toemis was a wholly unsuitable guardian for the girl. Finally, after adding another couple of logs to the blaze, the merchant could stand it no longer.

"Maybe you ought to move closer to the fireplace," he suggested, shattering the oppressive silence between them. "You don't want your granddaughter to get sick, do you?"

Toemis's reaction was immediate. Jerking his head up as fast

51

as a striking serpent, the old man glared at Mitto.

"It is none of your concern," he spat.

"Well, at least take some of this food," he offered, gesturing toward the box of dried fruit and salted meat he had lugged in from the wagon. "I don't care if you starve, old man, but at least take some for the girl."

Toemis winced, and Mitto braced himself, half-expecting the old man to rush at him with that knife of his. But Toemis didn't move. "It is none of your concern," he repeated more slowly.

Wary though he was of Toemis's knife, Mitto had heard enough. "Look, you might not care about her welfare—"

Then both men were on their feet, with Mitto following Toemis's lead. He reached for his quarterstaff, but the old man showed no sign of coming any closer to him.

"You ought not talk about things you know nothing about!" Mitto could see the fire's reflection in Toemis's coal-black eyes. The intensity in those dark spheres flared to new dimensions as he continued his rant. "No one cares for Zusha more than I do. No one! You know nothing about her…about us. If you did, you would not concern yourself with her comfort. Oh, you would drag her over to the fire, perhaps, but…"

Toemis let his words trail off. He was trembling, his scrawny shoulders rising and falling with each hurried breath. He let one of his hands fall down to pat the girl's covered head. Keeping his eyes fixed on Mitto, he slowly sat back down and said, "We have our own provisions."

Shaking his head in surrender, Mitto slumped back down in the chair he had dragged over by the fireplace. He was trying to puzzle out everything the old man had said—and had left unsaid—when he heard a sound down at his feet.

Lying on the floor a few paces away from the fire was Zeetan. Mitto had been loath to haul the wizard into the lodge, but he didn't have the heart to let him freeze to death out in the wagon—even if he was a crook and a spell-caster to boot. The makeshift bonds Toemis had wrapped around Zeetan's wrists and ankles remained firmly in place.

And the gag was still crammed in the man's mouth, which was why Zeetan's words were coming out all muffled and garbled.

"What's the matter…cat got your tongue?" Mitto snapped.

Zeetan shook his head from left to right to left urgently.

"I'm not taking the gag off," Mitto told him.

Zeetan's head slumped back down to the floor, though he continued to repeat the same three sounds over and over again.

"'I earn nothing'?" Mitto translated.

Zeetan rolled his eyes and uttered a piteous moan.

"Fine." Mitto knelt beside Zeetan. "I'll take off the gag, but if I hear one unfamiliar sound...just one strange syllable...I'll crush your windpipe. Got it?"

The wizard nodded, looking wide-eyed at the quarterstaff.

"Now," Mitto began, keeping the staff pressed up against the wizard's throat as he pulled the soggy ball of cloth out of his mouth, "what do you want?"

"I *heard* something," Zeetan whispered.

"What—"

But Mitto was unable to say more because, just then the front door swung wide open.

Passage VII

Sweat dripped down Ruben Zeetan's face. His body was stiff and cramped from lying in the same position for the past few hours, and, thanks to the bonds that bound his wrists to his ankles, he hadn't been at all comfortable since the old man had taken him prisoner. On top of all that, he was pretty sure he was bleeding to death.

Because he had been busy grappling with the old man—trying to prevent him from scoring a second hit with the knife—Ruben had missed the arrival of the gray-skinned fiends. He had no idea where they had come from or when they had interrupted the robbery. Furthermore, he knew nothing of his fellow thieves' fates, though he suspected Falchion and the others had turned tail and run at the first sign of danger.

If he had doubted his eyes when one of the creatures pushed its head over the guardrail—had wanted to dismiss the grim sight as a hallucination—he had had plenty of time to convince himself of the truth while sharing the wagon with the damn thing's body.

He had no idea what the old man and the merchant planned to do with him, but he instantly forgot about these problems when his suspicions were confirmed and the lodge's only door opened.

"Oh, gods," he squeaked, trying to bring his immobilized hands up to cover his face.

The old man and the merchant jumped to their feet at the same time, but since Ruben closed his eyes, he didn't see what happened next. If he hadn't been so terrified of the extermination that was sure to come, he might have thought back to the single decision that had brought his life to this path—or, rather, its inglorious dead end.

Eyes clamped shut, Ruben Zeetan heard these words:

"I am Commander Stannel Bismarc of Fort Valor. I had hoped my men and I might share this lodge with you for the night, but first, I must insist that you explain what exactly is going on here."

The words did not belong in the mouth of a fiend. Bewildered, Ruben opened one eye ever so slightly. Sure enough, the lodge was not crawling with a horde of screaming demons. In place of the monsters stood six humans.

Ruben wanted to cry out in joy, but not wanting to risk a return of the gag, he kept quiet. He did his best to ignore the fact that Knights of Superius were probably the last people in the world who would want help him. For the moment, it was enough to be alive.

So as not to draw undue attention to himself, Ruben remained absolutely silent as the merchant told his story to the commander. From Mitto's hurried account of recent events, he learned that the merchant and his two passengers had been headed for Fort Faith when the highwaymen appeared.

When the story referenced him personally—as "Zeetan" or "the wizard"—Ruben fixed his gaze on the floor and tried to look invisible. Yes, it's all over now, he thought. The Knights will imprison me for sure. Or worse.

As for the Knights, they said not a word as Mitto O'erlander told his tale. And since the old man, Toemis, seemed content to let the merchant do all the talking, it was Mitto alone who spoke. When the topic turned to monsters, Ruben dared another peek at their interrogator.

The commander— his name already forgotten—stood at the front of the group while the other Knights held back. He carried a helm in the crook of his arm, and the firelight revealed a face with well-defined and somewhat angular bone structure. His beard and mustache were impeccably neat, and the short-cropped hair atop his head shared the same hue as the fire that illuminated it—aside from the patches of white frost among the red.

When Mitto was finished, the lodge was consumed by silence for several long seconds.

"Had your elucidation been any less farfetched, I might have doubted you," the commander in a soft and steady voice. "But no one would compose a lie of such fantastic magnitude when a simpler one would suffice."

"The proof is in my wagon," Mitto said. "I'll show you the monster's carcass right now if you want."

The commander paused as though considering the merchant's offer, but before he could reply one way or another, someone pushed past the Knights and came to stand beside the commander.

"What's going on in here?" asked a woman clad from head to toe in a long, white robe.

Even before she tossed back her hood to reveal a face that was fair in both senses of the word, Ruben's eyes had been drawn to the places where the gown hugged undeniably feminine curves.

After she revealed her comely countenance, however, Ruben could not wrench his gaze away from her perfect face, which was framed by long, beautiful locks, the color of ripe strawberries. When she made eye contact with him, he nearly swallowed his tongue.

"Why is that man tied up like a beast bound for slaughter?" Her tone carried with it a sense of astonishment and indignation.

She looked to the commander for an answer, but it was Mitto who replied, "Begging your pardon, ma'am, but he's a wizard. There's no telling what spells he would throw at us if he could."

She glared back at the merchant, and at that moment, Ruben fell in love.

"I myself have skills that one might define as magical," she retorted coolly. "Do you plan to treat me likewise?"

Although Ruben couldn't see Mitto's face, he was sure the man was blushing. What mortal man could look into the eyes of such a beauty and not feel ashamed for provoking her anger?

As it was, Mitto sputtered an unintelligible rebuttal, looking from Toemis to the commander for some help. It was the Knight who came to Mitto's aid.

The commander set a hand on the woman's shoulder, not to restrain her, Ruben realized, but to pacify her. Giving her shoulder a gentle squeeze, he said, "Please excuse Sister Aric's zeal. She simply cannot abide the sight of a man suffering, no matter his crimes."

Upon hearing that final clause, the woman's shoulders slumped slightly, and a hint of a flush blossomed across her cheeks. If the woman—Aric—had looked lovely while upset, she appeared ten times prettier in her embarrassment. Ruben wanted to thank her for her concern and added a lengthy, heart-felt confession of all his sins as well, except he still couldn't find his voice.

"Yes, please excuse me," Sister Aric said, though in Ruben's mind she was Lady Aric. Princess Aric. The Goddess Aric. Her name sounded too base to belong to such an enchantress, but, at the same time, she was all the more attractive for her modest appellation.

Mitto mumbled something that resembled an acquittal.

"Sister Aric is a priestess of Mystel, and Fort Valor is honored to have her as its chief healer." With a wry grin, the commander added, "I trust you will not find it necessary to hog-tie the poor girl."

Aric playfully smacked the Knight on the shoulder. The two of them reminded Ruben of siblings, and the fact that both of them had red hair seemed to confirm it. He could only pray to whichever god pitied unlucky wretches like himself that the two of them weren't lovers.

"Enough, Stannel," Aric said. Then turning to Mitto, she added, "Might I inquire what this wizard has done to warrant such treatment?"

The commander held up a hand to stay the merchant's reply. "That will have to wait for now. There is a certain matter concerning monsters that must be straightened out first."

"Monsters?" Aric asked.

As if on cue, there came a series of sounds from outside the lodge. First, a familiar cry filled the otherwise silent night, followed by the clang of steel against steel.

Ruben's skin prickled with gooseflesh. It has to be the monsters. Who else could it be? Surely not Falchion and the others, who'd sooner wrestle a family of wolverines than face Knights in battle.

Despite his decision to face death with dignity in the presence of Lady Aric, Ruben couldn't quite stifle the terrified squeal that welled up from deep inside him as the fiends flooded into the lodge.

Else couldn't tell High Commander Walden much about Toemis Blisnes. She had never seen the old man before last night, and he had stayed only one night, visiting the common room a quarter-hour at most. But she related everything Mitto had told her, including the abundant supply of gold in the old man's possession.

The Knight digested the information impassively, as though none of it were news to him.

"He spoke with no one other than your friend, the merchant?" Sir Walden asked.

Else shrugged. "Not that I saw, unless he knew one of the other guests already in a room upstairs."

She fetched the ledger from behind the bar and showed him the names of the few patrons from last night. Bryant Walden's steely eyes scanned the page.

"Are any of them staying here again tonight?" he asked, not taking his eyes from the ledger.

She shook her head. "Most of Someplace Else's guests are traders. They stay in Rydah a night or two before returning to the road."

"What about those who do not stay the night?" Sir Walden handed the ledger back to her, as his eyes scanned the common room.

"Sad to say," she began, but then cut herself short, deciding she would reveal no more of her financial woes to the Knight. "Someplace Else hasn't many regulars these days."

She turned in her chair to get a look at the inn's drinking society. She didn't recognize any of the four men who sat at a nearby table. The rest of the furniture was unoccupied. None of the customers were paying her and the Knight the least bit of attention. They said little to one another as they nursed a bottle of Bylentine rum.

Glancing over at the bar, she added, "Only Loony Gomez comes here…"

Else trailed off when her eyes met the empty seat. "Well, where in the hells did he get off to?" she wondered aloud, half-expecting to see him pop up from behind the counter with a fresh mug of ale. "Gomez never leaves this early."

Bryant Walden was silent for a moment, digesting all of the information he had been given. "Maybe he's had some trouble with the law and got spooked by my presence," he offered.

"I can't believe Loony Gomez is capable of serious wrong-doing…unless he had an accident while drunk," she told the Knight.

Sir Walden grunted noncommittally. "Nevertheless, I would appreciate it if you kept an eye on this 'Loony Gomez' fellow. Probably, he has no connection to Toemis Blisnes, but he might represent a different kind of trouble."

Else gave a slight nod, took a deep breath, and made up her mind to ask a question of her own. "As I've told you, Mitto is dear friend of mine. With someone as important as yourself inquiring about a man in his company, I fear his life is in jeopardy. Can you tell me why the Knighthood is so concerned with Toemis Blisnes?"

When Bryant Walden frowned, she feared she had over-stepped her bounds. Who was she to question the High Com-mander of Capricon?

But then the Knight leaned forward and looked her in the eye. As he spoke, he kept his voice soft but firm. "I probably should not tell you any more than you already know, Madam Fontane, but I can see you genuinely care for the merchant. I will tell you what I know. You have no doubt heard the rumor that the Crown Prince of Superius was recently in Rydah?"

The query took Else by surprise for it seemed far off topic. She had indeed caught ear of the gossip regarding Prince Eliot Borrom's surprise visit to the island. There were many versions of the rumor because no one could guess why the prince had made an unexpected voyage across the Strait of Liliae.

Some claimed Eliot had secret business elsewhere in Capri-con, while others alleged that the prince had taken up residence at the Celestial Palace. Else had dismissed the chatter as drivel, stories fabricated out of sheer boredom, but now…

Sir Walden continued, his voice barely above a whisper. "I personally presented the prince to Lord Minus. What words were exchanged between the two men is not of importance here, but suffice it to say, Prince Eliot decided not to linger in Rydah. He left the next day, his departure as clandestine as his arrival. He took the highway to Fort Valor."

Else considered the Knight's words, overwhelmed by the news that Prince Eliot had actually been in Rydah no more than a week before and confused about how it tied in with Mitto and Toemis.

"We have received word from the Commander of Fort Valor that the prince has already quit Fort Valor for Fort Faith."

Now Else was even more baffled. What interest did the

Crown Prince of Superius, son of the greatest among the Kings of Continae, have in some old ruins? But then she recalled what Baxter had said about the Knights' reoccupation of Fort Faith. As her thoughts sped down this new path, she quickly made the connection: Prince Eliot had taken up residence at Fort Faith, which was also Toemis Blisnes's destination.

Before she could ask another question, Bryant Walden said, "We have no evidence that the old man is out to harm Prince Eliot, but neither can we be sure that he is not a Renegade assassin. And this is why I have sent two of my finest men to follow them. You can rest assured your merchant friend is in the best of hands."

Although she was sure she knew the answer, Else asked, "Sir Baxter Lawler wouldn't happen to be one of them, would he?"

The Knight arched his eyebrow in surprise. "Why, yes, how did you know?"

Feeling dumfounded by everything she had learned, Else fell back in her chair and shook her head. She couldn't decide whether to be grateful or further worried that Mitto's life was in Baxter's unpredictable hands.

The battle within the wintry lodge lasted less than ten minutes in reality, but to Ruben Zeetan it might have lasted days. Throughout the harrowing ordeal, he waited for one of the fiends to impale him with a serrated blade. Since his hands and feet were bound securely—and painfully—behind his back, he could only do his best to squirm over to a far corner of the room.

He nearly fainted when he felt someone touch his arm and probably would have screamed like a maiden in distress had he not lost his voice completely. When the razor-sharp edge of a sword failed to pierce his flesh, he opened his eyes. He was greatly rewarded; kneeling over him was Sister Aric.

She said something to him, but he couldn't hear her over the din of the melee. She looked like nothing less than a goddess just then. While Mitto, Toemis, and the Knights had forgotten him entirely—leaving him for dead by the fireplace—Aric had overlooked his crimes and come to offer him whatever succor she could. He hoped his eyes did not betray the terror that clutched at his entrails.

His self-consciousness quickly abated when the decapitated

head of one of the Knights rolled over to him, settling against his chest.

Tears streamed down Aric's cheeks, but the sight of the disembodied head didn't cause her to swoon. Slowly, almost reverently, she pushed the bloody head away from them. Watching Aric, Ruben was suddenly aware that the two of them were not alone in the corner. The bundled-up body of Toemis's granddaughter sat on the other side of the priestess. Aric had the child pressed up against her, cradling the girl and whispering comforting words into her ear.

Ruben had never been so jealous of anyone in his life.

When his attention was drawn back to the battle, he was suddenly aware of a strange light emanating from the warriors' midst. As he searched for the source of the brilliance, which cast a metallic light over the combatants, Ruben saw Mitto O'erlander swinging his quarterstaff with deadly accuracy. He spotted Toemis just as one of the fiends scored a vicious slash across the old man's flank.

Toemis hit the floor hard and didn't get up. When his attacker reared back to make the killing stroke, one of the Knights threw himself at the fiend, impaling it with his bloodstained sword.

Ruben watched in mute horror as two more of the fiends detached themselves from the fray and came at the heroic Knight from both sides. The man managed to block the first creature's sword but could do nothing as the other plunged a barbed spearhead through his chain-link vest. The Knight fell under the serious blow only to be stabbed twice more by each of the monsters until he lay still.

Mitto and the remaining Knights were greatly outnumbered. Of the Knights, only four remained on their feet. The others, like Toemis Blisnes, had either passed out or died. Ruben would have guessed the fiends' number at somewhere near twenty. The one-room lodge was literally crawling with murderous vermin. Nothing short of a miracle would turn the tide of the battle, and once the fiends finished with the warriors, he and his ladylove would be next.

It took a moment for him to realize all four of his limbs were free. He stared at Aric blankly when she shouted into his ear.

"I've cut you free! Use your magic to help them!"

Ruben gasped. He would rather have died while tied up than

demonstrate his true helplessness before Sister Aric. Gawking stupidly at his hands, which were discolored from hours of bad circulation, Ruben nearly perished from humiliation right then and there.

She was depending on him to save them all. How could he admit to her he was incapable of casting even the feeblest of spells?

As he struggled with his shameful confession—the words that would likely be his last—the uncanny light grew brighter until Ruben thought that the sun had abandoned its place in the heavens. Both he and Aric turned to peer into the impossible sunrise, forgetting everything but the inexplicable golden splendor.

He followed the sunburst to its source and found the Commander of Fort Valor, whose name he still couldn't remember, swinging an enormous sword in one hand and a smaller weapon in the other. The bronze glow originated from that second, rod-like weapon.

Ruben had never seen anything like it. He was on the verge of asking Aric if her eyes were playing ticks too when the commander threw his sword like a javelin and took the gleaming club with both hands.

The Knight reared back, and as he swung the extraordinary weapon in a wide arc, the brassy light engulfed the lodge, fully blinding Ruben.

Passage VIII

He had awoken to countless hangovers in the past. They were often the consequence of celebration, the inescapable result of revelry, and he had long ago come to accept that. He would not give up drinking and merrymaking into the wee hours of the morning—never that!—and so there was no use complaining about the aftereffects.

"It's as pointless cursing the mosquito whose unseen feeding leaves you scratching your arm all day...as futile as reasoning with a midge," Else Fontane had once said of hangovers.

Now he silently cursed the innkeeper, thinking surely she had something to do with his present condition. Only at Someplace Else, it seemed, did he sometimes forget his limits and over-indulge. It was that damn Dragon's Hoard, he decided. Else and Mitto drank the stuff like water, but spirits always hit him harder.

His skull throbbed in time with the beating of his heart, and his insides roiled and churned like the angry sea. He lay on something hard and moist, which was a disheartening discovery to be sure. He could only hope that he was wet with sweat and not something worse. The others in the barracks would never let him live it down if he had soiled himself like some snot-nosed tot!

As he tried to recall when his next shift began, Baxter resolved to open his eyes in spite of the painful sunlight that would surely assail his sensitive eyes.

One opened, but the other lid wouldn't budge.

Very curious, he thought and brought a hand up to touch the uncooperative eye. Or rather, he would have done this if he had had any control over his arms. As it was, when he tried to move either one of them, a searing pain raced up from his wrists.

Baxter blinked away the film covering his good eye and saw he was not, in fact, anywhere near the Knights' barracks. He was lying on the ground in a forest, bereft of all clothing, and suffering the effects of something far worse than alcohol. Managing to raise his head slightly, he looked down at his hands, which were bound tightly with a barbed wire.

His memory of the clash with the monsters returned to him with the force of a war-hammer.

I should be dead, he thought. A second survey of his condition found that his body was riddled with many cuts and wounds, and a layer of blood and filth coated his flesh like a second skin.

I should be dead, along with Sir Damek and Ahern and his men, he reasoned. But he had been spared. The realization did nothing to improve his spirits.

His next thought was that of escape, but there was little chance of that. At the moment, the blinding rays of the rising sun were blocked out by shade provided by three distinct bodies looming over him. Their faces were cast in shadow, but by their shape, he knew them to be the same inhuman foes as yesterday.

One of the monsters uttered a series of sharp syllables, only to be interrupted by the middle creature when it interjected with a single sound that resembled a snarl. The same creature then burst into a short dialogue that was all harsh consonants and guttural vowels. Baxter had never heard anything like it, and he had been privy to more than a few foreign tongues throughout his tenure as a Rydah gatekeeper.

After the monster in the middle finished speaking, it made a sudden gesture with the long pole it was carrying, and the other creatures backed away out of sight. The remaining monster strolled over and looked down at him. Baxter stared up at the abomination, wondering what heartless deity was responsible for breathing life into such twisted creatures.

Everything about the creature's face promised cruelty and violence. The feral eyes were a dull orange and held no more emotion than a prowling cat on the verge of pouncing. Fang-like teeth peeked out as the monster opened its mouth to speak.

Baxter's ears heard the creature's nonsensical sentence, but then, impossibly, he understood what it had said.

"They want to kill you, you know."

The words echoed through his head like his own thoughts,

but he knew beyond a doubt that it was the creature that had put them there. It was a dizzying sensation, and for a moment he feared he was losing his mind.

The creature resumed its discordant chatter, and again, the translation found a way into Baxter's brain.

"That is why you are here, outside of the camp, where my soldiers will not be tempted to put a spear through your bowels."

Baxter didn't reply. The creature's words were sinking in. They had set up a camp in the forest, and there was no telling how many of them there were. The monster before him had spoken of its kind as soldiers, had said "my soldiers." Hence, he was in the presence of one of their leaders. The idea that these creatures were organized to that extent made Baxter's despair only greater.

"But I saved you from their enthusiasm. I will not let them undo all the work I did to keep you alive because I spared you for a reason, human. You will tell me everything I need to know."

"Like hells, I will," Baxter said, not caring whether the monster understood him or not. Torture wouldn't loosen his tongue. He'd use the barbed fetters to saw through his veins before he betrayed anyone to the walking nightmares.

The monster laughed. "Your cooperation is not necessary."

The creature pointed the long pole it was carrying at Baxter's head. He had dismissed the thing as a spear, but now he could see, with the tip of it mere inches from his face, it was a staff of some sort. Inky black feathers sprouted from the base of a leering skull, and the pole itself resembled wood except for its dark, gray color.

When the hollow sockets of the skull lit up with a reddish flame, Baxter felt a vice clamp over his heart and fought the panic welling up inside of him.

The Knight knew magic when he saw it, and he had no intention of falling under the monster's spell. He plunged his thorny bonds into his thigh for leverage and began pressing the tiny barbs into the flesh of his leg and his wrists, eager to get on with his noble suicide.

But no sooner had he made the first cut into his thigh than he found his body completely paralyzed. He couldn't even turn his head away from the fire-eyed skull and its silent scream.

"Let us start with something easy," the creature said. "Tell me where the men in the wagon are headed."

"No!" Baxter shouted, or at least he thought he tried to.

Despite his greatest efforts, his mouth opened, and he heard himself say, "Fort Faith."

Anger, fear, self-pity, and, above all, hate for his captor swelled inside of him until he thought he would burst. He wanted to wrench the staff out of his tormentor's hand and crack it over the creature's head, shattering both skulls simultaneously. He wanted to kill every last one of them and water the forest with their dark blood. But Baxter Lawler couldn't even weep as the creature asked him more questions.

And he answered every one of them, betraying himself, the Knighthood, and all of Capricon.

When Ruben awoke, he was in the arms of an angel. Aric wasn't looking at him, at least not at his face. She had unbuttoned his robe and was examining what lay beneath.

Ruben jerked away, pulling his robe shut. The pain that shot up through his abdomen almost sent him back into a swoon.

"You've been injured," Aric explained patiently. "I need to tend to it, or it will fester."

His cheeks afire, he gave a quick nod and settled back to the floor. Careful to avoid the woman's eyes, he stared up at the ceiling, and that was when he saw that the lodge no longer had a ceiling.

Further inspection revealed that almost half of the lodge was missing. The logs that had made up the walls and ceiling had splintered into a million pieces. He remembered the commander's mighty stroke with the glowing rod and how the lodge had lit up like a falling star.

"I didn't even see you get wounded," Aric was saying. "It must have happened at the beginning of the fight."

Ruben didn't answer her. He didn't have the heart to tell her that he had gotten stabbed by the old man while trying to rob him. Instead, he gasped and produced an agonized expression, though he actually felt little pain. Aric's hands were as soft as satin, as gentle as a lover's caress.

"With the goddess's blessing, I have mended you," she told him, "but you should wear this poultice for a day or so to guard against infection."

"Thank you," he muttered, though the words seemed woefully inadequate.

Aric smiled prettily. "Thank the *goddess*. I am but Mystel's lowly servant."

Ruben didn't think Sister Aric was a lowly anything, but he found himself incapable of telling her so—or to communicate anything to the beautiful woman. He had never been able speak to the fairer sex, and Aric was the fairest female he had ever met. He knew he should forget about her and surrender to the truth that Aric would never return his love.

Neither tall nor handsome, Ruben Zeetan had come to terms with his slight build and gangly arms and legs long ago. His nose was too long, and the acne from adolescence had left scars on his cheeks. He was no maiden's dream.

Realizing that he had been gaping at Aric, he gathered the front of his robe and began buttoning furiously. The healer had done an outstanding job at patching him up. While Toemis's knife had missed any vital organs, the wound had hurt him plenty. His dark gray robe bore a considerable bloodstain as a testament to the trauma.

When Aric made no move to leave his side, Ruben thought to say something witty, something charming, but nothing came to mind.

Probably for the better, he reasoned. I should keep my mouth shut and forget all about her. If she knew me for what I was—a captured highwayman who dresses like a wizard to instill a false fear in his victims—she would not have wasted her or her goddess's time on me.

Aric's attention was drawn away from him when Mitto and Commander What's-his-name approached.

"Why did you untie him?" Mitto demanded.

He came forward, but then Aric was on her feet, barring the merchant's way.

"Be civil, good sir," she told Mitto, her voice firm though not unkind. "If the wizard wanted you dead, you can rest assured that you would be already."

Arms akimbo, Mitto glared past the woman and down at Ruben. With a sigh, he dropped his hands to his side and said, "I am in your debt for your ministrations, Sister Aric, and I do not wish to insult you, but I fear you underestimate this man. Zeetan is a despicable thief."

If the merchant's words stung him, the look Aric gave him was a deathblow. He saw disappointment in her pale blue eyes, a sadness that made him want to curl up and die. He mourned the loss his defender, but more importantly, he lamented the loss of her respect. Maybe it was better to surrender completely and tell her—tell them all—he was no more a wizard than he was the King of Superius.

"Wait a minute," Mitto said. "Was *he* responsible for the explosion that killed all those things...and destroyed half the lodge with them?"

The merchant was looking at him now with a grudging approval, and Ruben decided that now was definitely not the time to unburden his conscience.

The Commander of Fort Valor cleared his throat. "I do not think this is the appropriate time for such a discussion. We should not linger on the past. Moreover, we should not linger *here*. There is no telling how many more enemies are about."

"Agreed," Aric said quickly. "We should set out immediately. If we hurry, we should be able to make it to Rydah before the next sunset."

In all of the excitement, Ruben hadn't noticed that night had passed and morning arrived. How long did I sleep? he wondered.

"We're not going to Rydah."

Mitto and the commander turned to face the owner of that mild voice. Toemis's granddaughter stood before them all, her hood up and small hands folded before her. It was the first time Ruben had ever heard the girl speak—and the first time he had seen her without the old man beside her.

"Toemis said we are going to Fort Faith," the girl added, her softly spoken words drifting out from under the capacious hood.

Aric strode over to the girl and knelt down beside her. "Your grandfather is sick and needs more help than I alone can give. He can get the treatment he requires in Rydah."

Then the Commander of Fort Valor surprised everyone by saying, "The girl is right. We aren't going to Rydah."

Amazingly, Mitto's remaining horse as well as one of the Knights' had survived the butchering at the lodge. The monsters had killed the other mounts in order to prevent a retreat.

Either that, or they just like to kill things, Mitto thought gloomily.

He supposed he shouldn't complain. In addition to his horse and wagon, he still had his life. He wondered how long that was likely to last. Gods only knew know how many more of the creatures stood between them and their destination...

No one said much of anything as they prepared to set out. Only two of the commander's men had survived the night. One of them mounted the solitary war horse and took point, and the other watched their rear from the back of Mitto's wagon. Aric, Zusha, Toemis, and the wizard also climbed into the wagon bed, where the healer continued to attend to Toemis, who looked more dead than alive.

Commander Stannel Bismarc, on the other hand, joined Mitto on the driver's seat. The two men shared a heavy silence.

Mitto wanted to pepper him with questions, but the older man's stony expression was not a welcoming one. Stannel Bismarc had much on his mind, and judging from body language alone, he was in no mood to open up to a stranger.

Not that Mitto could blame the man for his reticence. Stannel had lost six of his eight men to the monsters. He pitied the man for his loss, but at the same time, there was something a bit odd about the Knight.

Mitto suddenly had the impression the commander wasn't mourning his men at all. Those bright blue eyes had shed no tears. The Knight is looking forward, not backward, Mitto thought. He's not grieving. He's thinking...calculating... scheming...

Shaking his head, Mitto silently scolded himself. He didn't know the commander at all. Anyway, who was he to condemn a Knight of Superius? It's those damned creatures, he decided. They've got me seeing monsters all around me.

Even Toemis Blisnes, old Goblin himself, seemed harmless when compared to those things.

"Do you have any idea what they are?" Mitto asked the commander.

Without looking at him, Stannel replied, "I cannot be sure, but I have my suspicions."

Mitto waited for the commander to elaborate. When it was clear he didn't intend to, Mitto pressed the matter. "Do you mind sharing your suspicions? I, for one, have never heard of any animal remotely like them."

"They are not animals. They are goblins, I think."

Mitto might have tumbled off the driver's seat if the commander hadn't been there to steady him. "That...that's impossible," he stammered when he regained his balance and his voice. "Goblins aren't real. They're the stuff of fables... monsters meant to frighten children on long, winter nights."

In spite of his best efforts, he was having great difficulty keeping his voice steady. Surely it was coincidence that the creatures shared the name he had secretly given Toemis.

"That is all the goblins have become to humans," Stannel said. "Or at least, to most humans. But there are records of a war nearly four hundred years ago. It took place on this very island, only back then, it wasn't called Capricon. Before the formation of the Confederacy of Continae, Glenning alone held claim to this land, and the Glenningers called it Novislond."

Mitto, who cared very little about history, couldn't guess what that had to do with goblins, but he let the Knight speak on. If nothing else, Stannel's story would keep his mind off the present.

"Novislond..." Stannel chuckled. "It means New Land, and according to legend, the Glenningers had taken the island from a clan of dwarves. But that's neither here nor there...or perhaps it is at that. You see, all of that happened shortly after the Wars of Sundering destroyed the three great empires of Western Arabond."

Now Mitto was lost. The Knight was talking about ancient history. If Mitto wasn't terribly mistaken, the Wars of Sundering had taken place more than seven hundred years ago!

"Bear with me," Stannel said. "I'm getting to the goblins. Much of human knowledge was lost during the Wars of Sundering, so if any of the Three Kingdoms were aware of this island's past before Canth, Yelhorm, and Nebronem were divided into countless territories and city-states, it didn't survive the years of chaos that followed.

"But getting back to Novislond...or forward to it, as the case may be...the Glenningers moved in after pushing the dwarves out. They likely thought they were safe when the dwarves didn't try to take back the island. And Novislond did enjoy many years of peace and prosperity...until an unknown enemy appeared, sailing across the Aden Ocean in a fleet that spanned from one end of the horizon to the other.

"They were a new race...or new to the Glenningers at least, and they fought with a brutality the Knights of Eaglehand had never before encountered. As a matter of fact, Glenning had to appeal to Superius for help, lest Novislond be overwhelmed by the foreign armies. Knights of Eaglehand and Knights of Superius fought side by side for the first time, and after three years of bitter war, the goblins were repelled. They left the island as suddenly and mysteriously as they had come."

Mitto scoffed. "You can't seriously believe all that. Why hasn't anyone in Capricon ever heard of these...*goblins* before?"

"Time," Stannel replied, as though the single word explained everything. After a long pause, he added, "You have never heard of the Goblin War, but rest assured, it happened. The goblins were pushed back almost four hundred years ago. It is believed that they came from the other side of the world. And since none returned in all that time, it is understandable that their existence has been largely forgotten."

"And now they're back?" Mitto asked, his voice rich with incredulity. "After four hundred years, they show up again, just like that?"

"Just as they had the first time," Stannel said.

It was too much for Mitto to take in. He couldn't believe it, *wouldn't* believe it.

But what else could they be?

"If we *are* facing a goblin invasion, why go west?" Mitto asked. "Shouldn't we warn Lord Minus and the rest of the capital?"

"No," the commander replied without hesitation.

"Why not?"

"That," Stannel said, "is a secret."

Passage IX

She sits beside Toemis in the back of the wagon. Toemis is breathing, and every once in a while, he says something in his sleep. She can't understand him, though, because he isn't using real words. She is worried because Toemis is very, very old, and if he dies, there won't be anyone left to take care of her.

She runs a hand through Toemis's thin, coarse hair. It reminds her of a horse's mane, but the thought of horses makes her feel sad. When they left the log-house that broke in half, she saw some dead horses, which made her want to cry.

Horses are big, strong, pretty animals. They like to run very fast, and when they whinny to each other, they are talking. But those horses didn't move. They would never run or talk again. Just thinking about it makes her want to cry all over again.

Toemis's forehead is warm and sticky. The woman in white says he has a fever. She doesn't know what she will do if Toemis dies. She knows he really wants to go to a place called Fort Faith. She doesn't know why.

There is a big bruise on Toemis's forehead, and his shirt is red where he was stabbed. She wants to look at the hole in his side, but the woman in white has covered it up with bandages. The woman told her that her grandfather will be fine, that he just needs to rest. She doesn't know if she believes the woman in white because Toemis looks like he might die soon. The woman in white might just be lying to make her feel better.

She likes the woman in white. The woman has long, wavy red hair and smiles a lot. She wonders whether the woman in white will take care of her like Larissa used to, if Toemis dies. She thinks the woman in white would make a good mother.

Toemis brought her to this new place. He told people that he is going to Fort Faith because he worked there once, but she doesn't believe Toemis used to be a cook. She has eaten Toemis's cooking, and it always tastes bad.

There is not much to do in the wagon. Even though Toemis is not awake, she will not leave his side. After Larissa died, she promised she would obey Toemis, and he told her she must stay by him at all times. She wants to take off the heavy coat or at least remove the hood because it's beginning to smell funny. But Toemis said the coat was for her protection, and she won't disobey Toemis.

Nobody in the wagon is talking. Besides Toemis, herself, and the woman in white, there are two others in the wagon with her. The man in the gray dress is the same one Toemis fought with yesterday. The other man, the man in metal, must be a knight.

Julian used to tell her stories about knights. Knights like to fight, and they are good at it. Knights kill monsters, and Julian once told her a story about how a knight killed a dragon. Larissa said dragons aren't real, just like sea serpents aren't real. Larissa told her not to believe Julian's stories.

But she isn't afraid of monsters anyway. Dragons are just big lizards with wings. She once saw a lizard by the river, and she wasn't scared of it at all. When she dreams about dragons, they are always nice to her. They don't burn her with fire or anything.

She thinks the thing that hurt Toemis might have been a monster. These knights killed the monsters, just like in the stories Julian told her. Maybe Larissa was wrong. Maybe Julian was telling the truth. Before she was even born, Julian had left Larissa to travel around the world. Larissa never saw knights and dragons and sea monsters, but Julian said he had.

The monsters that killed the horses look like people, but they look like animals, too. They have sharp teeth like wolves and eyes like the old tomcat that used to come by the house looking for scraps. Are monsters animals? Or are they people?

She won't ask the woman in white about the monsters because Toemis doesn't like her talking to strangers. She likes animals, and she knows that some animals eat other animals. Some animals even attack people, but she knows that it isn't because they are mean. It's just what they are made to do. So she shouldn't hate the monsters for killing the horses and those knights or for hurting Toemis. It's just their nature.

She likes all animals, even slimy snakes and creepy, crawly spiders. Therefore, she should like the monsters too... *if* they are animals. She wants to ask the woman in white for the name of the monsters, but she won't. But if Toemis dies, she will ask the woman in white to be her new mother.

Mitto spent a long time thinking over what Stannel had told him about the goblins and decided he believed him. He didn't know what to make of the man's secretiveness regarding their destination, but who was he to question a Superian commander?

Anyway, Stannel Bismarc wasn't opposed to making conversation. He simply wouldn't let the subject be steered down certain avenues. The man obviously put a lot of thought into everything he said. If that made him seem guarded or circumspect, well, there was no crime in that.

All else aside, the Knight certainly knew a lot about history. He sounded more like a scholar than a warrior, and when Mitto had told him so, Stannel smiled and said, "I am not a true scholar, though you may be surprised to learn that every Knight must study history to some extent.

"Anyway, what little I know about human history is confined to Superius's and Glenning's past."

Neither man had spoken for a while after that. There was nary a sound from the interior of the cart, so as the miles passed beneath them, Mitto had little else to do but let his mind wander. It was an old trick he had picked up long ago. When one spent so much time alone on the road, one had to do something to pass the time.

Today, however, no matter how hard he tried to let his mind roam free, his thoughts invariably homed in on the same few topics, and of those limited mysteries, the goblins always won out.

It still disturbed him that the monsters shared the name with Goblin, the character from his mother's fables. But what bothered him more was they hadn't a clue as to how many more goblins were out there.

As daylight began to fade, Mitto's imagination grew more and more active. He saw goblins peeking up over hills and creeping within copses. If he had been a little anxious throughout the long ride that day, he was downright tense at twilight. When the sight of a hare bounding across the road made him jump, he knew that he had to get his mind off of the monsters.

"There is something I ought to tell you," Mitto said to Stannel, who hadn't left his side all day. "The old man, Toemis ...I don't trust him."

Stannel gave him a thoughtful look. "Does your suspicion have anything to do with this?"

Mitto's breath caught in his throat when Stannel produced Toemis's coin purse. His surprise immediately gave way to anger. What right did the commander have to search the old man?

That's my gold, not yours! he silently screamed. Not trusting himself to speak, Mitto simply stared at the familiar pouch.

"Aric found it while tending to him," Stannel explained. "Do you know what is inside?"

Mitto was about to disavow all knowledge of the old man's treasure when it dawned on him how foolish he was behaving. Stannel would not have produced the purse if he planned to keep it for himself. He had been on the verge of sharing his suspicions about Toemis to the Knight, so why did he feel the need to conceal the truth?

Mitto told Stannel everything about his meeting with Toemis and his granddaughter, careful to keep his voice low. He confessed he hadn't fully believed the story the old man had fed the Knights at Rydah's Westgate, though he had absolutely no idea what the man really wanted with the remote fortress.

Stannel listened in silence, his face betraying nothing of his thoughts. When Mitto finished, he said, "The matter is undeniably curious."

When he said nothing more, Mitto added, "I have...*had*...a friend among the Knights in Rydah. He was there when the goblins first attacked us. I had told him about Toemis and his strange offer the night before. Then during the brush with the highwayman, Baxter...Sir Lawler, that is...and another Knight came to our aid. I think maybe they were sent to keep an eye on the old man."

"Or," Stannel said, "Sir Lawler was simply worried about his friend, and his commanding officer allowed him to do you this personal favor."

Stannel's statement was logical, but somehow Mitto got the impression the commander was again holding something back.

Mitto sighed. "I suppose you're right. After all, there's nothing particularly important about Fort Faith. What harm could one old man do there?"

That hit the mark. Stannel turned sideways in his seat and appraised him with a searching stare. When he turned away, bringing his eyes looking forward once more, the Knight said, "You suspect Toemis's reason for going to Fort Faith and my decision to go west rather than to Rydah are somehow connected."

"Are they?"

"I cannot say."

"You can't say, or you *won't* say?" Mitto pressed.

"A little of both," Stannel replied, "for how am I to understand the old man's intentions any clearer than you?"

Mitto smiled in spite of himself. "Point taken."

Thinking the conversation was over, he settled back and stared up into the western sky, where the setting sun painted the horizon in oranges and yellows. Rather like the color of gold, Mitto thought wryly. The commander's next words caught him by surprise.

"What about the little girl? What is her name?"

"Zusha," Mitto muttered. "I think she warrants watching to."

"The girl is also more than she seems?"

"Maybe. If nothing else, she's tied to Toemis."

"Culpable through association," the Knight provided.

Mitto scoffed. "Something like that. I can't say she's anything more than a simple child, but there is something about her that's not quite right. For one thing, she's always covered by that big cloak of hers. I've not gotten more than a quick glance at her face."

He recalled the mystery of the girl's eyes, how one day they had been blue and then brown the next, but he didn't mention it to Stannel because he might have simply been wrong the first time. But then he remembered something about Zusha that did warrant mentioning, something he had almost forgotten in all of the confusion following the battle at the lodge.

"I saw her during our fight with the goblins," Mitto began, lowering his voice even more. "That healer of yours, Sister Aric, had taken her out of harm's way. In the midst of it all, I glanced over at her. Now, wouldn't you think a child would be crying with all that bloodshed and those horrifying monsters all about? Wouldn't you think she'd be bawling her eyes out on the account of her grandfather's injuries?"

"Perhaps," Stannel replied. "Unless she was in shock."

Mitto grunted. "Shock. Yeah, well, that might be it. But I don't think so. When I looked over at her, she wasn't crying or trembling or hiding her face. No, she was just watching it all as calm as can be…like it meant nothing to her. You can say it was shock, and maybe it was, but my blood runs cold when I think of it."

Stannel didn't respond. He seemed to be digesting the information, perhaps storing it away for later use. By now, Mitto took the Commander of Fort Valor to be an intelligent man, a good deal wiser than the average Knight. Certainly, he was smarter than Baxter…that damned, brave fool…

"Let me see if I have this straight," Stannel said. "When our paths crossed, you were traveling in the company of three people whom you did not trust."

Mitto chuckled in spite of himself. "That's right."

Their conversation soon turned to a more practical subject—specifically, where they would make camp for the night. Because of their late start and their horse shortage, they wouldn't make Fort Valor before darkness fell.

"The goblins have the advantage at night," Stannel told him. "They can see better in the dark than we can, if the old stories are true. Better we find a place where we can defend ourselves if we must than risk a confrontation on the open road."

Stannel seemed to take it for granted that they'd be able to fend off another attack, even though there were only three Knights left, including the commander. Mitto had survived the first two encounters with the goblins by sheer chance. He doubted that he would be so lucky a third time, but he did take some comfort in Stannel's confidence.

Mitto trusted the commander—secrets or no secrets. He trusted him with his very life, which, he reminded himself, was more valuable than gold.

Ruben didn't like the idea of stopping for the night. There had been no sign of the fiends that day, but he suspected they were out there somewhere. They had tracked them all the way to the lodge, after all. Why stop there?

He didn't know what the demons wanted, and he didn't care—so long as he never had to face them again. And if the fiends were still tracking them, it made no sense to stop and give them a chance to catch up again.

The Commander of Fort Valor—he had heard Aric call him "Stannel" at one point during the long ride—was in charge, and no one else questioned him. So Ruben held his tongue. He had done his best to fade into the background all day, fearing the Knights would follow Mitto's advice and bind and gag him again.

Stannel seemed far too preoccupied to worry about a highwayman, however, and the Knight who kept watch from the rear of the wagon had his attention fixed on the road, glancing at Ruben only every now and then. If Aric thought he was a threat, she didn't voice her concerns in his presence.

Only Mitto seemed to remember that he was a captive, and not just another passenger.

When they pulled off the road and they stopped at a dried-up riverbed, everyone climbed down from the wagon. Mitto suggested once more that they tie up "the wizard." Stannel flatly refused.

"He'll kill us in our sleep," the merchant argued. "The minute our backs are turned, it'll start raining fire, and Zeetan will escape."

"Escape," Stannel repeated, looking past Mitto at Ruben. "Escape to where? Wizards aren't known for being fools, and he knows as well as the rest of us that a single man…spell-caster or not…is no match for an army of goblins."

Ruben quickly shifted his eyes, pretending he hadn't heard the exchange.

Mitto started to dispute the point but stopped mid-sentence. "Wait…what's that you said about an *army* of goblins?"

The Commander of Fort Valor then launched into his theory about the fiends—the goblins, as he named them—but Ruben didn't want to hear any more about them. He was beginning to think spending a few years in Fort Valor's dungeon might do him some good. If nothing else, it would give him time to reevaluate his life as well as protection from the goblins.

Anyway, Stannel seemed like a decent enough fellow. If he was in charge of the fort, how bad could things be?

Stannel forbade the lighting of a fire. They sat together in a small circle, sharing what rations they had salvaged from the dead Knights' saddlebags. Eating the food of the fallen, they spoke nothing of their fears.

The two Knights who were to take the first watch took to their task stolidly, as though keeping an eye out for monsters was just part of the job. He envied the Knights their courage, that virtue they had earned through years of training and experience. Ruben, for one, was scared out of his wits.

After the frugal supper, Stannel told them to get some rest. The ground was rocky and hard, and while the Knights had extra bedrolls, Ruben couldn't get comfortable. The chill of late autumn seeped through the thin material, biting into his bones. Every time the wind howled through the trees, he jerked upright, earning him alarmed glances from the Knights on watch.

Mitto and Stannel were to take the second and final watch of the night. Ruben felt ashamed yet grateful he was exempt from the responsibility. If a goblin jumped out at him from the quiet woods, he'd likely faint or run away.

But he didn't want Aric to know what a coward he was, so he volunteered to help, only to be told by Stannel that prisoners were not expected to post watch.

So there was nothing to do but rest his head against the cold earth, close his eyes, and will himself to fall to sleep. His attempts were as fruitless as yesterday's robbery had been, however. As he waited for sleep, he sneaked an occasional look at Aric, who lay beside the little girl. Meanwhile, Zusha snuggled up against the old man in effort to keep them both warm.

Ruben thought that he'd like to keep Aric warm in that way.

As he stared up at the overcast sky, which was further obscured by the balding branches of the winter-ready trees, Stannel's words came back to him: "Wizards aren't known for being fools."

He couldn't shake the feeling Stannel saw through his disguise. The commander's eyes seemed to hold a secret knowledge. It was almost as if the Knight had looked into his soul.

If Stannel *did* know that Ruben was not a wizard—and the lack of ropes and a gag seemed proof of that—then he was surely playing with him. Stannel might have said, "If you want to keep up the pretense you are a wizard, then you must play the part to the end."

He couldn't guess why the commander didn't expose him for what he truly was—an ordinary human being with no more magic in his blood than fat on his frame. Maybe Stannel hadn't guessed the truth, after all.

And why haven't I confessed yet? he wondered. That would get Mitto off my back if nothing else. They might even let me go. But where would I go?

Yes, he thought, better to play my part to the end. At least if they think I am useful, they won't throw me from the wagon like a leaky barrel.

Yet there was another reason why he didn't come clean. He had seen a measure of respect in Aric's eyes when she had asked him to use his magic to stop the goblins at the lodge. A cleric herself, Aric saw him as a kindred spirit.

In the end, he knew he would continue to live the lie if for no other reason than to maintain his Aric's respect—no matter how fleeting her feelings toward him were. She might never love him like he loved her, but he didn't think he could endure her disgust.

When Ruben finally drifted off to sleep, he was assailed by terrible nightmares of two distinct varieties. The first kind, which had been common enough in his youth, were dreams of monsters chasing him around a dark forest, jumping out at him, snapping their teeth in attempt to tear him limb from limb. He couldn't run fast enough to get away, but they never really caught up to him either.

The second type of nightmare was all the more terrifying for its novelty. Just as Ruben had given up fantasizing about women during his waking hours, so had he banished them from his nocturnal reveries.

But one female managed to invade his unconsciousness that night, and whenever she denounced him as a fraud, he died as surely as if a spearhead tore his heart in twain. Unlike the imagined goblins, Ruben could never outrun his guilt and self-loathing.

Passage X

For the first time in weeks, Loony Gomez didn't spend the evening at Someplace Else. A few guests idled in the common room, sipping drinks and keeping to themselves, but there was no sign of the crazy old man. Though Gomez's drunkenness sometimes got out of hand, Else missed his company. She even missed those lewd stories he told again and again.

Between welcoming new guests and refilling mugs, she kept an eye on the door, expecting Gomez to wander in at any moment. As the hours passed in a most tedious fashion—none of her customers were in the mood for chitchat—she found herself looking for Gomez more and more.

When she finally locked up, a sick feeling settled the pit of her stomach.

She couldn't help but feel Loony Gomez's absence was a bad omen. Maybe the old drunk was just sick. Or maybe he had chosen a different inn for once. That in itself wasn't the happiest of possibilities for Loony Gomez was her most reliable patron.

But she knew there had to be more to it. She recalled his impromptu departure the night Sir Walden visited. That too had been suspicious. Now Else seriously considered the old sot might be in trouble with the law. Gomez must have recognized Bryant Walden for a Knight of Superius and was avoiding Someplace Else.

Her sleep was troubled that night, though she couldn't remember her dreams when she woke the next morning. She rose at the same time she always did. After years of following the same routine, she didn't need the rooster's crow to tell her it was time to get up. The few guests who had spent the night at Someplace Else would not likely rise for another hour, giving her plenty of time to go to the local market and buy the food she would need for breakfast, lunch, and dinner.

She reached for her coat and headed down the stairs, her mind was already planning the menu. Her thoughts were far from the worries that had plagued her last night, and so she was considerably startled to find Loony Gomez standing in the midst of the common room.

"What is the meaning of this?" she demanded. Her suspicions from the night before assailed her. She had never thought of Loony Gomez as a threat, but the fact that he had apparently broken into the inn made her all the more wary.

Before Gomez answered, he glanced behind himself at a roadside window, reinforcing Else's fear that the old drunk really was a wanted man. Meanwhile, Else edged closer to the bar, where a number of bottles rested within easy reach. If Loony Gomez tried anything funny, she resolved to club the scoundrel over the head and then run for the nearest constable.

She shrank back when Gomez spun away from the window and took three great steps toward her. "You 'ave friends among the Knights."

It was a statement, not a question, so Else didn't answer him.

"I saw Commander Walden in 'ere two nights past," he whispered. "Do ya deny it?"

The fact that Gomez was trying to keep their conversation quiet made Else even more nervous. When she finally answered him, she spoke more forcefully—and more loudly—than she might have otherwise, burying her apprehension beneath a façade of anger.

"I will not deny or confirm anything until you tell me what you are about, Gomez."

The man winced at her vehemence—or perhaps it was the volume of her voice. He took a step back and brought up his hands, as though to pacify a hysterical woman.

"I'm not tryin' t' scare ya, girl," Gomez said, keeping his tone calm. "I'm here t' save yer life an' with any luck, many more lives too."

"What are you talking about? Are you drunk?"

Gomez blinked twice, and a crooked smile splayed his chapped lips. "No, m'dear. I'm dreadfully sober at the moment. There're some things I must tell ya, things you must promise t' pass on t' yer Knight friends…t' Bryant Walden hisself if ya can manage it."

Else could scarcely believe what she was hearing. "You want me to be your messenger?"

"You'll want to be yer own messenger once ya 'ear what I got t' say," Gomez replied.

She had her reservations, but there was something in the man's eyes that conveyed a seriousness—and a sentience—she had never witnessed in him before. If the man really was crazy, his madness had taken a new turn.

"Go on then," she said with a sigh.

"What I'm about t' tell ya may seem unbelievable, but bear with me, girl. The fate of Rydah may well rest on yer pretty li'l shoulders."

Having survived the night with no sign of goblins, the motely company shared a cheerless breakfast of cold leftovers before setting out on the road again.

Mitto's back ached from sleeping on the ground, and even though he and Stannel had been up for many hours—they had stood watch from early dawn—the merchant couldn't stifle the great yawns that sporadically wracked his body. Few words were exchanged as everyone resumed their places from the day before.

From the driver's seat, Stannel Bismarc beside him once more, Mitto let his thoughts drift to all matter of topics. Of course, the goblins weighed heavily on his mind, and he uttered a silent prayer to Pintor, god of protection, to keep them safe on their journey.

He thought about Baxter Lawler, his old friend. His anger at Baxter's suicidal—albeit heroic—act against the goblins had dissipated only to be replaced by a hollow feeling. The world seemed a far more dismal place without the mischievous Knight in it.

Baxter hadn't been the only Knight to fall to the goblins, and Mitto feared many more would perish before the goblins were chased from Capricon—*if* they could be chased from the island.

The past couple of days had brought Mitto face to face with his own mortality. The goblin encounters left him wondering if he would even be missed should one of their spearheads hit home. His work took him all throughout the eastern half of the island.

He had more acquaintances scattered throughout Capricon than he knew what to do with, but none of them would mourn his death, not really. Baxter might have raised a glass to his memory, but nothing—short of the Knight's own death—would have kept Baxter down for long.

It was depressing thought, but he knew there was someone who would be truly saddened by his death. He had seen her face flash before his eyes during the battle at the lodge. And he had fought hard so that he might see that face in the flesh one more time.

Today, Mitto feared Else might be in just as much danger as he was.

He knew now he cared for Else Fontane more than he had let himself believe. Maybe it was love, and maybe it wasn't. All Mitto knew was that he would have given all the gold in Toemis's purse and then some to be with her at Someplace Else.

"Stop," Stannel ordered.

Mitto obeyed, glancing left and right for hints of danger but seeing none. He knew where he was. Fort Valor stood about an hour down the road. Up ahead, a narrow, overgrown path forked off from the highway curving left. Mitto had heard tell the trail was a route to Fort Faith, a route that bypassed Fort Valor altogether.

"Why did we stop?" Sister Aric had poked her head through opening of the wagon and now looked from Stannel to Mitto for an answer. "Is there trouble?"

"No trouble," Stannel assured her.

The commander eased himself over the side of the wagon and walked up to the mounted Knight, who had turned his horse around. The Knight lifted the visor of his helm, Stannel spent the next few minutes conversing with the man. Although they were too far away for Mitto to hear anything of what was said, it was apparent Stannel was doing all of the talking.

Mitto leaned back and crossed his arms. "I think he likes keeping people in the dark."

"It's true that he keeps many things to himself," Sister Aric said, "but you can rest assured he'll tell you what you need to know."

Mitto flinched. He hadn't meant for the healer to hear him.

The rider saluted, lowered his visor, and urged his horse into a gallop. Predictably, the Knight followed the main road, heading for Fort Valor. He'll herald our arrival, Mitto predicted.

When Stannel ascended the wagon, Aric said, "You must think we have left the goblins far behind if you send our scout away before the fort is in sight."

Mitto watched Stannel's reaction out of the corner of his eye. The man was, after all, the Commander of Fort Valor. He probably wasn't accustomed to having to explain himself to anyone. But if Stannel was surprised by the healer's audacity, he did not show it.

"We are not going to Fort Valor," Stannel said. "I have sent Sir Ostler there in our stead to spread the word about what has befallen us on the road."

"Where *are* we going?" Mitto asked.

They were no more than an hour away from Fort Valor. He could already taste the wine, feel hearth's warmth. And now Stannel was going to take that away from him?

"That way," Stannel replied, pointing down the road less traveled.

Mitto gaped at the offshoot, which looked even more forsaken than it had before. Dead leaves rustled through the dying grass. Bare branches reached down over the path, as though waiting to snatch up unsuspecting travelers. Even if he hadn't had goblins on the brain, Mitto would have been wary about turning off the main road at this juncture.

"You mean for us to go on to Fort Faith," Mitto stated flatly.

Stannel gave a sharp nod. He too had been staring down the wild path, but now he turned to regard Sister Aric. "I would have offered you the chance to join Sir Ostler, but I knew you would have refused to leave your patient."

The healer smiled. "Well, you're right about that, Stannel. Let us pray you are right in taking this further risk."

Stannel said nothing. His face was impassive, unreadable.

"I know it's not my place to question your decisions, Commander," Mitto began, "but wouldn't it make more sense for us all to go to Fort Valor first? We could pick up provisions and acquire reinforcements for the trip to Fort Faith."

The Knight shook his head. "We must make for Fort Faith with all haste."

Having said that, Stannel took the liberty of instructing the horses to start up again. The Knight steered the wagon onto the overgrown path. Not trusting himself to address the man in a remotely civil tone—Mitto was not accustomed to taking orders from anyone, and he certainly was not used to anyone else guiding his wagon—he turned to face Aric.

"Do *you* know why we're going to Fort Faith?"

The woman nodded.

"We aren't going there so that Toemis can see the place one last time before he croaks, are we?"

Aric narrowed her eyes and looked annoyed at his heartless reference to Toemis's suffering. Then the healer's face eased back into her typical expression—a paradox of power and passivity. "No, I don't suppose that is the only reason."

Feeling more frustrated by the second, Mitto straightened himself in the seat and scowled out at the encroaching trees. He couldn't decide which was more irritating—Toemis's statements, which could be all lies, or Stannel and Aric's honesty when withholding information from him.

Either way you look at it, I'm in the dark, he decided. Whatever it is that's got everyone rushing to Fort Faith had better be damn worth it!

Else didn't make it to the market that day. When her guests finally dragged themselves down into the common room, she apologized profusely and told them they would have to find their meal someplace other than Someplace Else.

Fortunately, not a one of them had any interest in staying a second night, so following closely on the heels of the last guest, she wrapped a shawl around her and left the inn.

She couldn't remember the last time she had closed down so early in the day. When she turned the key and heard the bolt slide home, she felt a shudder run through her. I'll be back, she told herself. This isn't goodbye.

Thrusting the key into the pocket of her jacket, she cast a look back at Someplace Else and started to run down the street toward the center of town, where the ivory spires of the Celestial Palace glinted in the morning light.

As she hurried down one avenue after another, the words of Loony Gomez bounced around in her brain. "The fate of Rydah may rest on yer pretty li'l shoulders," he had said, and she had almost laughed in his face, certain that Gomez was inebriated. She had humored him by listening to his outrageous tale, smiling politely.

But slowly, her smile had faded...

"The first thing ya got t' know is I was once part of the Guild."

There had been no reason to ask Gomez which guild he meant. Whenever someone spoke of the Guild in Rydah, he or she was most certainly referring to the Thief Guild. The thought of Loony Gomez stumbling through the streets, trying to cut purse strings with his unsteady hands almost had her laughing out loud.

"I was with the Guild for many a year...most of m'life, in fact. When the Renegades started poppin' up in Rydah, we were content to leave 'em alone, ignorin' them so long as they ignored us. Their business was none of our concern, an' for nearly a year, the two organizations stayed outta each other's way.

"But after a while, not long ago, the Renegade Leader of Rydah requested a meetin' with the Guildmaster. The Renegades wanted t' join forces with the Guild in order t' boost their numbers...and t' fund their war, I'd wager.

"The Guildmaster wanted nothin' to do with the rebels, though. The Guild had always been 'bout one thing and one thing only. Profit. An' the Guild was always at its best in times of peace and prosperity. A'ready there were more Knights in Rydah, thanks t' the Renegades.

"So the Guildmaster refused the Renegade Leader, an' that shoulda been that since the Guildmaster speaks for all the Guild. But there was a guildsman who'd been waitin' for his chance t' take over. He saw this as the perfect opportunity to do, an' when he declared his allegiance t' the Renegades, a bunch of the others with him.

"Now the punishment for leavin' the Guild had always been a swift death so as t' maintain secrecy, ya understand. But the Guild couldn't manage so many quitters at one time. An' besides, they had the Renegades on their side. The Guild was forced t' disband for the first time in over two hundred years."

At this point in his story, Else had still thought Gomez was making it all, piecing together various rumors that had been circulating throughout the capital quicker than counterfeit coin.

"What's so bad about that?" she had demanded. "The death of the Guild sounds like good news to me. Anyway, you have no proof anything you've said is true. I see you as a retired shoemaker or maybe a washed-up bard, but I can't picture you as a thief, Gomez."

"That's the best kind of thief," Gomez had replied with a wink.

She had rolled her eyes. "I think it's time for you to leave. Thanks for the story, but—"

"Six years ago your inn was robbed. There were no signs of a break in, but the chest you keep hidden under the floorboard behind the bar was emptied of its contents...a sum of nineteen pieces of silver and thirty-eight coppers. But your personal savings, which you keep secreted inside your mattress, was not touched."

Else had been so shaken, she hadn't even notice how much his style of speech had changed.

"How...how do you know that?"

Gomez had smiled sadly. "Everything I told you is true, Else. And the worst has yet to be said."

She had had so many questions. Had Gomez personally burgled her inn those many years ago? Where was the fabled Hall of Thieves located? What was the name of Rydah's mysterious Renegade Leader? How many rebels were there?

But then Gomez had continued, more hurried than before.

"I have reason to believe the Renegades are preparing for a coup d'état." He had pressed on despite her gasp. "I don't know the specifics, but I do know when. This evening, when the sun dips below the western wall, the rebels will start the attack from within.

"Some of them will make for the Celestial Palace. Others will concentrate on the city's gates, making sure they remain open...and securing a route for forces waiting *outside* of the city."

"Forces? What kind of forces?"

"I cannot say," Gomez had replied with a shrug of his shoulders. "It took some trouble to learn as much as I have. Maybe there is a Renegade battalion hidden in the forests outside Rydah. There has been talk of a Renegade Leader newly arrived from Continae. Maybe he brought an army with him. I honestly don't know, and I don't intend to stick around and find out.

"If you have any brains in that pretty head of yours, you'll do the same...after you alert the Knights, of course. I'd do it myself, but I simply can't risk it."

Else had already made up her mind to take up the mission—crazy though it sounded—but she had had to ask at least one question before Loony Gomez disappeared from her life forever.

"Why tell me any this? If you were once a member of the Guild, why do you care if the Knights, your sworn enemies, are prepared for a coup?"

Gomez had taken a few steps toward the door before answering. "Even if I didn't have a reason to hate the Renegades, I'd never sit idly by as Rydah was sacked. I may be a thief, but Rydah is my home too."

Then Gomez exited the inn without looking back, leaving the proprietress of Someplace Else to consider his warnings and begin preparing for her first—and perhaps last—trip to the Celestial Palace.

Passage XI

Her thoughts aflutter, Else ran as fast as legs would carry her toward the Celestial Palace. If she could get word to the Knights, maybe the Renegades could be stopped before the capital was besieged.

The burden of such a great and unwelcome responsibility weighed heavily on her. She was a simple innkeeper, for gods' sakes!

Else pushed past people in her way, plunging through the crowds and dashing dangerously in front of oncoming vehicles. When she was nearly run over by a wagon, she forced herself to take a deep breath and continue at a safer pace. It wouldn't do the city any good if she were trampled on her way to the palace—except for the Renegades.

Now that she was paying more attention to her surroundings, she thought she saw rebels everywhere. Neighbors and strangers alike seemed to harbor sinister intentions. You've never been one to let your imagination run wild, Else Fontane, so don't start now, she silently scolded.

Even if some of the rebels were walking the street just then, none of them knew what she knew.

Or did they? Might someone have seen Loony Gomez leave Someplace Else that morning? Perhaps she was being followed at that very moment...

She glanced over her shoulder several times, but no one appeared to be stalking her. Refusing to give into her paranoia, she kept her eyes fixed on the towering Celestial Palace at the city's center. Anyway, she doubted the Renegades would make a move against her in broad daylight.

But with an army hiding outside the city, who could say how bold they had become?

Her legs were starting to ache, but she ignored the pain. If only Mitto were here, she thought. Then I wouldn't have to deal with this alone. And I'd be much more comfortable in that old wagon. We'd probably already be at the Celestial Palace.

She had worried about Mitto ever since he left Rydah with Toemis Blisnes, but now a part of her was grateful the man was far from the city, far from danger.

Unless, of course, Baxter was right, and Toemis Blisnes really was the new Renegade Leader in Capricon. For all she knew, Mitto was being held prisoner in some Renegade army camp.

By the time she reached that broad stairway that climbed from the street up to the tall arches of the palace's main entrance, Else thought she might collapse. Her legs were shaky, and her heart pounded in her breast. Staring up at the steps, she wondered if she had ever gotten so much exercise in one day.

She had made it halfway up the stairway before she noticed the sentries flanking each of the three arches. When she reached the top, the two guards at the central arch broke away from their posts and approached her.

"Good day, madam," one said. "What business have you at the Celestial Palace today?"

The sentry's voice was polite, but Else noticed how the two of them had casually blocked her path. Aside from their open-faced helms, whatever other armor the men wore was hidden beneath resplendent surcoats of red and gold, which distinguished them as palace guards. Both guards carried halberds, with swords hanging at their sides.

Else couldn't decide if these men were actual Knights of Superius or if they had come from the pool of lesser soldiers that supplemented the Knights' regiments. Not that it made much of difference.

"I have an urgent message for Lord Minus," she said with as much confidence as she could muster.

The sentries shared a glance. The man who had spoken earlier smiled amiably and said, "The Lord of Capricon is a very busy man, but we would be happy to pass along your message."

Else felt her cheeks burn. Maybe they would pass on her warning to their commanding officer, but then again, maybe they wouldn't. That wasn't good enough, not today when so much—including the lives of these two idiots—was riding on her.

If Baxter hadn't followed after Mitto, she might have gone to him, but as it was, she was left with one option.

"I am a personal friend of High Commander Bryant Walden," she announced. "Please tell me where I can find him."

The two sentries shared another glance.

"High Commander Walden is *also* a busy man," said the same guard as before. "If you would please give us your message, I give my word that we will deliver—"

"I will not! I have sensitive information that is for more important ears than yours. So if you will not take me to Lord Minus or Sir Walden, I will wait here until one of them passes by."

Without preamble, she lowered herself to ground. Her back erect and legs folded, she sat in the middle of the marble walkway and regarded the sentries smugly.

She had no idea if Magnes Minus or Bryant Walden ever used this egress, but she had a feeling she wouldn't be waiting there long.

Ignoring the flustered guards' glares, she said, "If you wish, I can sing while we wait. Some say I have the most beautiful voice in all of Rydah."

She was bluffing—she couldn't carry a tune to save her life—but her words had the desired effect. One of the men swore softly and called back to the other sentries.

"Get the sergeant!" he barked and then turned back to Else. "We'll let him decide what to do with you."

Else shrugged unconcernedly. She wasn't cowed by them. She'd tell the sergeant exactly what she told the sentries. Sooner or later they would bring her to the High Commander just to get rid of her.

She just hoped that by the time she finished jumping through bureaucratic hoops, her information wouldn't be old news.

Ruben shared Mitto's disappointment when he learned they weren't stopping at Fort Valor. For one thing, he was sick of getting jostled around in the back of the wagon, and for another, he was worried that the goblins would make another attempt at exterminating them.

He had been looking forward to reaching Fort Valor, if only

to surround himself by more warriors and to place walls of stone between him and the goblins. He knew nothing of the Commander of Fort Faith, his future jailer.

Ruben couldn't guess why they had forsaken Stannel's stronghold for Fort Faith, but unlike Mitto, he didn't put the question into words. In fact, he hadn't said more than two words all day. The Knight who kept watch out the back paid him no mind whatsoever. Ruben might as well have been a barrel of flour or a sack of potatoes.

It was almost as though he had become invisible without the benefit of magic.

Aric spent most of her time looking out the front of the wagon and chatting with Stannel. Ruben wished he were as comfortable talking with the woman as Stannel was. He wondered what, exactly, the nature of their relationship was. Were the commander and healer merely colleagues, or was there more to it than that?

When she wasn't keeping the commander company, Sister Aric looked after her patient. Toemis still hadn't awoken by the time they stopped for lunch, which had consisted of nothing more than hardtack. Aric had poured trickles of water down Toemis's throat, whispering words Ruben couldn't quite hear.

The healer took good care of her patient, and in spite of Toemis's age and his injuries, Ruben actually envied the old man. What he wouldn't have given to receive that much attention from Aric. As it was, he dared not engage her in even the most trivial of banter, lest he inadvertently reveal his lie.

At one point, Toemis began to toss his head from side to side. He moaned and even muttered in his restless sleep. Most of what the old man said was nonsense, as far as Ruben could tell, but there were some actual words mixed in with the gibberish. More than once, Toemis uttered the name Julian, or maybe it was Julia. Ruben couldn't be certain, but there was no mistaking the old man's words when he suddenly sat straight up, opened his eyes to reveal just the whites, and looked straight through Ruben.

"It'll all be over soon. I have come to make amends."

Then Toemis fell back down to the bedroll.

Ruben nearly fainted himself. The episode had been haunting, surreal, and even though the old man had been in the grip of a fever dream—or so Aric said—he thought there was something frighteningly prophetic about Toemis's declaration.

The healer mopped Toemis's brow and whispered reassuringly into his ear. Aric's touch seemed to calm the old man, who settled back into a deep sleep, but not before saying "Julia"—or was it "Julian"?—twice more.

After making sure Toemis was resting comfortably, Aric crept over to sit beside the little girl, who hadn't removed her heavy cloak even when the noonday sun had heated up the wagon like an oven. Aric told the child her grandfather would be all right and wrapped her in a hug.

While the girl didn't pull away, she didn't exactly return the embrace either. Ruben wasn't able to see her face, mostly because of the hood, but nothing he had witnessed in the little girl indicated she was upset about her grandfather. Come to think of it, she hadn't even flinched when Toemis sat up and spoke.

The more Ruben thought about her, the more he was certain there was something a bit off about the girl. He was still staring at the child, enveloped in Aric's arms, when the girl quickly— and none too gently—extracted herself from the healer and scooted to the rear of the wagon to sit beside the Knight.

Ruben had just enough time to exchange a baffled look with Aric before the Knight let out a startled cry. He and Aric turned their heads as one in the direction of the soldier and the little girl, who kneeled unnoticed at the Knight's side.

"Goblins!" cried the Knight. "Coming fast!"

Else had had to speak to not only a sergeant, but also a captain before she was allowed to enter the Celestial Palace. She had told both men the same thing—she had important news for Lord Minus and High Commander Bryant that could not wait for an appointment and she would not leave until she was granted an audience with one of them.

The captain had gone so far as to threaten to throw her in a cell for disturbing the peace, but Else had only repeated she was a personal friend of Sir Bryant—an exaggeration, to be sure— and that any harsh treatment of her would result in the most dire of demotions.

The captain had not been impressed by her threat, but clearly the man had had his fill of Else Fontane.

"If she's such a good friend of the Knights, let *them* deal with her," the captain muttered. "Take her to Lieutenant Ahern."

She recognized the name. Baxter had often griped about Vearghal Ahern, his archrival and antithesis. According to Baxter, Ahern was the most rigid and impossibly proper Knight in all of the Order. Now it seemed she was going to meet the Immovable Tower in person, though she wasn't sure whether she should be satisfied with herself for getting past the threshold or disappointed in reaching what might end up being the equivalent of a stone wall.

If Ahern was as impossible as Baxter made him out to be, her threats would prove useless against him.

Even as she plotted a strategy for getting around Lieutenant Ahern, Else couldn't help but be impressed by her surroundings. Bold tapestries bearing coats-of-arms and exquisite paintings of historical personages lined the corridors. Far above her, the vaulted ceilings were covered with murals and friezes depicting scenes in exquisite detail.

After traversing richly embellished flights of stairs up to the third story of the palace, the captain led her to a small foyer. The man stepped up to an unremarkable door and knocked. When there was no reply, he rapped louder, but again there was no answer. The captain tried the doorknob, only to find it locked.

Cursing to himself, but loud enough for Else to catch each and every word, the man stopped as though he were considering his options. Finally, he gestured toward one of several chairs pressed up against the wall of the antechamber.

"Looks like Sir Ahern has stepped out," he told her. "You can wait for him here. It's bound to be more comfortable than sitting outside on the steps."

Else muttered an oath of her own once she was certain that she was alone. She supposed the guards had a right to be distrustful of her. Nevertheless, she found herself wishing something bad would befall the captain and his underlings—until she remembered how bad things were about to get for Rydah's defenders.

She was aware of every minute passing in that small, silent room. What if Lieutenant Ahern had already left the palace for the day and had no intention of returning? Every second brought the Renegades closer to their attack, and here she was, hunkered down outside an absent Knight's office.

Impatient—and more than a little flustered—Else stood up, stormed out of the lobby, and collided with someone. For a moment, she feared she had run into the Immovable Tower. But although the fellow wore armor, he was no taller than Baxter. Relieved and disappointed at the same time, Else apologized for her carelessness.

"No harm done," the Knight replied cordially, but then a puzzled expression creased his features. "Might I inquire who you are and why you are skulking about outside Sir Ahern's office?"

She gave her name and added, "I came to the Celestial Palace to deliver an urgent message to High Commander Walden but was brought here instead."

The Knight snorted. "You would have been waiting for quite some time. Lieutenant Ahern is away on a mission, and no one knows when he will return."

Else scowled. "Now listen to me carefully. I need to see Bryant Walden. Now. He knows me, and the news I have cannot wait another second. Do you understand?"

The Knight blinked twice, probably surprised by the woman's brazenness. "I will be happy to take you to the high commander's office. I do not know for certain that he is in, but it is a good place to start."

Else nodded wearily. There was a window behind the Knight, and she noted with alarm that the sun had already passed its zenith. Time was running out.

The Knight walked quickly, and she was grateful for his haste, even if her legs ached from hiking across the city and through the labyrinthine halls of the Celestial Palace. As she followed her newest guide, she lost track of how many staircases she had ascended since entering the palace. Judging from the view out one of the windows, she had climbed more than half-way to the top of the towering palace.

From her vantage, she caught glimpses of the city that stretched for miles in every direction. Seeing so much of Rydah all at once made Else worry all the more for the capital. Who could guess how much damage the Renegades might inflict before they were subjugated?

When she was certain her legs couldn't survive another flight of stairs, the Knight stopped before another antechamber that was almost identical to the one she had just left. In lieu of a doorway, however, the room lacked a front wall altogether. But as with Ahern's lobby, this room also led up to a second room, presumably the high commander's office.

The door was shut.

Please be inside! Please, please, please! she silently begged. She couldn't remember wishing for anything so desperately. She nearly pushed past the Knight and pounded on the door herself, but at the last moment she held herself back and impatiently waited for her guide to knock.

There was no response, and only silence answered the Knight's second and third attempt. Else was almost giddy with disbelief. Why do these people even have offices if they never use them? she wondered.

She might have kicked the door down in frustration, but she felt too defeated to do much of anything. The thought of exploring more of the palace to locate Bryant Walden—or Lord Magnes Minus, for that matter—nearly sent her collapsing into the closest chair.

"Miss Fontane," a familiar voice said, "I did not expect to have the pleasure of seeing you again so soon."

Else spun around, and there was Bryant Walden, standing in the expansive entryway of the lobby. She wanted to run up to the man and give him a hug but immediately dismissed the ridiculous urge. Still, the sense of relief that washed over her was overwhelming.

She opened her mouth in order to say hello, but suddenly her mind was assailed by Gomez's warning, and she ended up choking on her words.

Perhaps it was a combination of physical exhaustion and the stressful nature of her visit to the palace for her lightheadedness became full-fledged dizziness. She felt herself falling but didn't understand at first that she was fainting. No! her mind screamed. I can't fail now, not when I've finally found Walden!

Nevertheless, her legs gave out beneath her, and the last thing she saw was Bryant Walden running forward to catch her.

Passage XII

Only minutes after the overgrown path rejoined the main high-way again, Mitto saw Fort Faith in the distance. By his estimation, they would reach the fort in half of an hour.

He had never seen Fort Faith before—until recently he imag-ined it was nothing but a pile of rubble—and even though he knew the castle to be inferior to Fort Valor in size and splendor, he breathed a sigh of relief at the sight of the place nonetheless.

Then he heard the Knight's cry of alarm, and his speculations about Fort Faith's accommodations burst like a balloon. Mitto let out a roar of frustration and pushed the horse harder. Not again, he pleaded. Not when we're so close.

He wanted to grab one of the goblins by their necks, give them a good shake, and ask them why in the hells it couldn't leave them alone.

He prodded the horse into a grueling pace. As the wagon sped up, Mitto tried to catch a glimpse of their pursuers, but he could see nothing of the goblins from his vantage. Beside him, Stannel maneuvered himself into a more-or-less standing position and attempted to peer over the covered section of the wagon.

"What do you see?" Mitto asked.

Stannel carefully lowered himself back down to the driver's seat before answering. "There are quite a few of them. No mounts of any sort, but they are moving very quickly."

Mitto swore. "Can we outrun them? We're almost to Fort Faith for gods' sakes!"

"Maybe," Stannel allowed, and he said no more. Mitto glanced over at the commander, but Stannel Bismarc, his eyes closed, seemed lost in his own thoughts.

He swore again. "Hold on, everyone!" he shouted over his

shoulder and gave the reigns another jolt. "Come on, you lousy excuse for shoe leather! Move! Move! Move!"

Running was their only hope. Luck had seen him through two encounters with the goblins, and he didn't trust that fickle mistress to intervene a third time. Even a small party of the monsters would easily tear them apart—and Stannel had said there were "quite a few." Fighting was out of the question, even if they did have a wizard among them.

"Hey, wizard, now might be a good time to throw some fire-balls or something!" he yelled into the back of the wagon.

When they had covered half the distance to Fort Faith, Mitto let out a little laugh. "We're going to make it! Feol's fools, we're actually going to—"

Mitto hadn't seen the stone in their path—or whatever it had been—but suddenly the wagon was running on only two wheels. The front two were airborne for a fraction of a second before they came crashing back down to the road. The whole wagon shuddered on impact, and then it shook even more violently as the front, left wheel fractured and broke apart completely.

A second later, the other front wheel shattered.

The wagon pitched, and Mitto nearly fell off. He held fast to the driver's seat with one hand and to the reins with the other. As the vehicle slowed to a bumpy halt—for the horse had given up on the pulling the ruined wagon—a thick cloud of dust rose up from where the bottom of the wagon had scraped against the road, making seeing and breathing difficult.

It had all happened in the span of seconds, but now that the wagon had stopped completely, Mitto took a moment to get his bearings. Stannel, on the other hand, wasted no time in leaping from his perch and drawing his sword.

"Wake up, man!" he said to Mitto. "The goblins will be on us in no time."

Mitto didn't want to wake up. On the contrary, he wanted very much to close his eyes and hope when he opened them again, the nightmare would be over. He certainly didn't want to ready himself for another clash with the gruesome creatures that had murdered Baxter Lawler. I'm a merchant, not a warrior, he almost shouted at Stannel, at the goblins, and at the gods them-selves.

Instead, he muttered, "Let's get this over with" and jumped down from the driver's seat, quarterstaff in hand.

He followed Stannel to the rear of the wagon. There was no sign of the Knight who had been keeping watch from the back. Mitto figured the poor bastard must have gotten tossed over the guardrail. The dust made it impossible to make out anything from farther down the highway.

Someone inside the wagon handed the little girl, Zusha, to Stannel, who helped her down to the road. In spite of the gravity of the situation, Mitto found himself enthralled by the little bundle of brown cloth. The child neither cried nor complained. She was as silent as the grave, and her calmness seemed to Mitto an unnatural thing. As Ruben crawled out of the wrecked wagon, Mitto continued to watch the girl.

Zusha was looking down the road, where the dust was slowly settling and the unmistakable shape of the goblins could be seen. But she didn't scream or run over to one of the adults. She just watched them. When she finally pulled off her hood—possibly to get a better look at the monsters—Mitto snapped out of his trance and ran over to her.

Kneeling down in front of the girl, Mitto said, "I want you to run that way as fast as you can. Run to the castle!"

He pointed up to the road to where Fort Faith's blocky frame broke up the monotony of the flatlands around it. They were close enough for the guards to have spotted them, but Mitto knew that the Knights would never reach them before the goblins did.

As he spoke to the girl, Mitto noticed two things. First, she was older than he had estimated—a lot older. Before, he would have guessed her age at seven or maybe eight. But looking at her so closely, he saw that in spite of her size, she was at most a year or two away from adolescence.

The other thing he saw was that he had not been mistaken about the girl's eyes. Mitto found himself staring into two eyes of different hues. One was as blue as the Aden Ocean, while the other resembled the dark brown of blackbean tea.

"I can't leave Toemis," she told him calmly. "He's all I have."

Mitto broke away from her mismatched stare. "If you stay here, you'll die." He forcefully turned the girl around and gave her a shove in the direction of Fort Faith. "Get going!"

He watched her take a few tentative steps toward the horse, glancing back at the wagon, where Stannel and Aric were arguing about what to do with the old man. He saw Zusha approach the stallion and pet the beast's flank. He was about to yell at her again—a threat this time—but he became aware of a great clamor behind him.

Slowly, tragically, he turned around.

The goblins—there had to be thirty of the bastards—spread out, forming a circle of blades. Some of them goblins spoke to one another in a harsh tongue. Others were clearly laughing at their prey. They shook their weapons, which ran the gamut in size and shape, at the ensnared company. Slowly, ever so slowly, they stepped forward, closing in on the humans.

Only Stannel and Mitto were armed. The Commander of Fort Valor held his sword in two hands and stood protectively in front of Aric. As for the healer, she had no weapon and when Stannel offered her a dagger, she declined.

Then Mitto remembered Zeetan. He found the highwayman pressed up against the back of the wagon, gawking wide-eyed at the ever-encroaching ring of goblins.

"What are you waiting for? Cast a spell, or we're all dead!"

The wizard shook his head frantically, "I...I c-can't."

Mitto cursed the pathetic excuse of a spell-caster. Hadn't Zeetan nearly brought the lodge down on top of them during the last fight? Where was that spectacular power now?

As if in answer to his unspoken query, the roar of crackling flame whooshed past him and engulfed three of the fiends in a blanket of orange fire. The goblins shrieked in agony, flapping their arms impotently against the hungry inferno. Those nearest the ones burning alive backed away from their doomed companions.

A goblin to his right screamed and clutched its abdomen, where the small shaft of an arrow protruded.

Mitto spun around, trying to figure out what in the hells was going on. A large chunk of the goblin's circle had broken away, as many of the monsters were now rolling on the ground in an attempt to extinguish the flames that greedily ate at their gray and mottled flesh. He was even more surprised to find three new faces.

One of the newcomers, a short man in blue robes who looked more like a wizard than Zeetan ever had, carried a wooden staff that appeared to be the source of the fireballs. There was also a red-haired woman who was in the process of reloading a crossbow.

The third stranger was only slightly taller than the spell-caster. He wore a dark suit of armor that was unlike anything Mitto had ever seen. Along with a horned helm that hid his face entirely, the armor covered the man's entire body. No, the fellow's hands were bare, and his skin was as black as coal.

Despite his diminutive stature, he spoke with a deep voice that might have belonged to a giant. "What're you waiting for? Fight for your life!"

The short, thick-bodied man—if it was a man!—then raised a battle-axe that was nearly as tall as he was and threw himself at the goblins nearest the terrified stallion. Stannel was already hacking away at the monsters surging toward him and Aric.

Although nothing seemed to be making sense anymore, Mitto had enough sense to raise his weapon as a goblin charged at him. Thrusting and bashing with his quarterstaff, he managed to drop two of the creatures in a series of desperate moves.

Breathing heavily, he waited for the next fiend to come at him, only to realize the battle was over. All but a few of the goblins were dead or dying. Some resembled little more than charred piles of meat, though many others were riddled with deep wounds wrought by sword, axe, and crossbow. The bodies near the stranger in the horned helm were missing arms, legs, and in some cases, heads.

Of the motely band, only Zeetan appeared injured. He had slumped to the road and was clutching an arrow that had pierced his belly.

The remaining three goblins were making a swift retreat, but the blue-robed wizard—who was surely a midge—had given chase. A final blast from his staff sent a particularly big conflagration at them. The fireball sent the monsters thrashing to the ground, but no matter how much they rolled around, the flames would not abate.

Mitto watched the midge saunter back over to the wagon. With a sweep of his conical hat, he bowed and said, "On behalf of Commander Colt, welcome to Fort Faith!"

Else opened her eyes and looked up at a ceiling she didn't recognize. Fighting through the cobwebs in her mind, she sat up.

She was alone in a sparsely decorated room with stone walls.

Swinging her feet over the side of the small couch, she examined the small room, desperately seeking something familiar. Why aren't I at Someplace Else? she wondered. What has happened?

When she saw Bryant Walden's face, everything returned to her in a sudden jolt of clarity—the warning from Loony Gomez, her struggle to reach the Celestial Palace's upper echelon, and the impending attack on the city.

The high commander took a couple of steps into his office and came to halt when he saw she was awake. "Well, Madam Fontane, I am glad to see you are awake. You gave us quite a scare. I had just called for one of the palace's healers."

"My apologies, High Commander," Else replied. Her cheeks burn, and she wondered what it was about the Knight that made her feel like a bashful maiden. "I have come here to give you some dire news."

"About Toemis Blisnes?" Walden took a seat behind his desk, which was littered with papers, quills, and what looked to be part of a gauntlet.

Else shook her head and got to her feet. "This is far more serious than one old man."

Walden leaned forward in his seat. "I have already summoned Lord Minus. I sent for him when I was under the impression you had learned something about Toemis. But if this is not about your merchant friend and his curious passengers, then what?"

Else took a deep breath. She knew she should tell the Knight everything and not leave a single detail out, though she was hesitant about mentioning Loony Gomez. It wasn't that she was worried about betraying the old thief—Gomez had said he was leaving Rydah anyway—but she was concerned Bryant Walden wouldn't believe her after learning the source of her knowledge.

And she didn't have time for lengthy explanations. Time...

"Dear gods in heaven, what time is it?" she asked, and the volume of her voice made the Knight start. "How far is the sun from the western walls?"

Walden regarded her uncertainly before leaning back to look out the window behind him. "The sun will not touch the wall for two hours or more. Else, what is going on?"

Before she could answer, a man of sixty-or-so years wearing the finery of a nobleman entered the room. Else had lived in Rydah her whole life, and the closest she had ever gotten to the

Capricon's lord was when she had caught a glimpse of him at a parade years ago.

Yet there was no doubt in her mind she now stood face to face with Lord Magnes Minus.

The first thing that struck her about Lord Minus was that he had a kind face, and aside from his fancy garments, the man didn't dress the part of an opulent aristocrat. She had always thought that lords and ladies wore no fewer than a dozen golden necklaces at any given time and that their wrists and fingers were also always covered with sparkling jewelry. Minus wore only a gold pendent declaring his lordly position and a single silver band on his left hand.

As he entered the office, Lord Minus smiled and nodded politely to her. Forgetting herself—she had never been in the presence of nobility before—Else performed a hasty curtsey, though she was wearing trousers, not a dress. She felt very ordinary, very simple before these two important men.

"You must be Miss Fontane," Lord Minus said. "It is a pleasure to make your acquaintance. Am I to understand you have news regarding Toemis Blisnes?"

Else could sense an eagerness beneath the lord's calm exterior. At that moment, she wanted nothing more than to unravel the mystery of Toemis Blisnes to the Lord of Capricon, but of course, she couldn't.

"I'm afraid she has come here for a different purpose entirely," Sir Walden said when Else didn't immediately reply.

"Ah, yes," she stammered. "Milord. High Commander. I am here to warn you of an invasion that is to occur this very evening."

Neither man said anything for what seemed like a long time.

"I know it sounds ludicrous," she continued, "but I am absolutely certain the Renegades are planning to attack the Celestial Palace when the setting sun touches the western wall. In an hour or so, the Renegades of Rydah, along with the members of the Thief Guild who have thrown in with them, will try to take this palace. At the same time, others will make sure the city gates are open for the army that is to attack from without."

After another long pause, Lord Minus turned to Bryant Walden and said, "Is this not the innkeeper you spoke of yesterday? Or she one of our spies?"

"I am an innkeeper, milord. But I have learned this information from a very reliable source—"

"From whom?" Sir Walden asked.

Else let out a loud sigh. "There's not time to explain. It's true that I have no proof to back my claims, but it couldn't hurt to increase the city's defenses for just one night. If I am wrong, you lose nothing. But if I am right, hundreds...maybe even thousands of lives will be saved."

Lord Minus looked to Bryant Walden, who slowly rose to his feet.

"I trust her," he said to Lord Minus, but then to her, he added, "We have found signs of an impending Renegade offensive, but we had no idea it would come so soon. Yet there has been nothing to suggest an attack from outside..."

"You mentioned an army, my dear," Lord Minus said. "What kind of an army?"

"I haven't a clue," Else confessed. "It may be more Renegades, or maybe the rebels have assembled more allies like the Guild. I don't know anything else. I wish I did, but I don't."

"Perhaps that will be enough." The high commander's voice was soft and reassuring. When he turned back to Lord Minus, however, he adopted the tone of a true officer. "I will ready the men for the attack. As always, our defenses are strong, and the men are wary, but I will supplement the sentries along the wall with our reserve units.

As he spoke, Bryant Walden walked around his desk and headed for the door. "I must beg your pardon, madam, but duty calls."

She did not want to see the high commander go. Just being around him made her feel safer, but of course, he had to ready his men for battle. Now she was alone with Lord Magnes Minus, the ruler of all Capricon. Tearing her eyes away from the empty doorway, she glanced over at the lord and found him staring vacantly out a window.

He turned toward her and gave another warm smile. "You need not worry, Miss Fontane. The city is in Commander Walden's capable hands. However, if the Celestial Palace may soon be visited by violence, I must insist you accompany my wife, Lady Corrine, and myself to the castle's keep, where we will safely wait out the attack."

"Milord, I wouldn't dare impose—"

Minus waved away her argument. "I insist, and I will not

take no for an answer. Come, let me show you the way."

He took her arm gently and led her out of the office. But before they had even cleared the threshold, several loud booms shook the palace, rattling the glass in its pane. Lord Minus dropped her arm and ran back over to the window. Else was right behind him.

The blasts had sounded like thunder, but there wasn't a cloud in the sky. The window provided a vast view of just a fraction of the city, and although they were quite a way up, Else had no trouble making out the shapes of people running—panicking—in the streets below.

"What in Pintor's name…?"

The lord wasn't looking at the streets, she noticed, but out at the Aden. She saw nothing amiss at first, but when she shifted her gaze from the coastal roads to the water itself, her breath caught in her throat.

Dozens, perhaps even one hundred, dark shapes moved atop the waves, coming ever nearer to the capital. It was a fleet of some kind, but Else had never heard of any vessel resembling the tower-like ships sailing toward Rydah.

Another boom shook the palace, and this seemed to rouse Lord Minus.

"We must make haste for the keep," he said, pulling her away from the window.

Else allowed herself to be led out of the office and through a series of corridors. She was oblivious to her surroundings. Her mind was stuck on those foreign ships and what they portended for the capital.

And with every impossible thunderclap that shook the palace's alabaster walls, Else Fontane could only conclude that the Renegades—and their mysterious army—were running ahead of schedule.

Part 2

Passage I

At the first cry of alarm, Colt headed for the eastern wing.

The vantage of Fort Faith's tallest tower afforded him a panoramic view of the entire area. Movement on the highway drew his attention. The travelers were still too far away to identify, but he made out a solitary wagon speeding toward the fort at a break-neck pace.

There was no mistaking the creatures giving chase.

"Goblins."

He spat out the word like a bad taste in his mouth. It hadn't even been a part of his vocabulary until a week ago. But now he knew the monsters for what they were, and a score or more of them chased the wagon in the distance.

He watched the battle as it began, unable to make out many details. When he saw the streams of fire streaking all around the goblins, however, a smile tugged at the corners of his mouth. Knights, as a rule, disdained magic, but he was beginning to see the usefulness of having a spell-caster around.

Colt's smile didn't linger. Between the distance and the smoke billowing up from the scattered fires, he couldn't discern who had the upper hand. He worried about his friends—and gods above, how he wished he could be with them!

But he wasn't allowed to leave the fort whenever he fancied. Vanguard aside, he wouldn't have been welcome among the party of Knights riding hard to join his three friends in their rescue mission. As the Commander of Fort Faith, he couldn't risk his life needlessly. And so he was forced to watch the action from afar, praying to the gods to watch over his men and dear friends.

It wasn't the first time he wished he weren't in charge, and he doubted it would be the last.

If his lieutenant had anything to say about it, he'd never see another battle as long as he lived. From the tower, he could see Gaelor Petton and a handful of other Knights racing toward the battle, but he knew they wouldn't arrive before it was over—one way or another.

He couldn't blame Petton for protecting him, but at the same time, he longed to share in his comrades' danger. And he wanted a chance to strike back at the goblins.

By the time Petton and his men reached the wagon, the battle had indeed ended. He saw no sign of any living goblins, and knowing Cholk, Opal, and Noel, there weren't any survivors. They left the wagon where it was, but not before unbridling the horses. Then combined company started down the road back to Fort Faith.

Eventually, Colt abandoned the tower and hurried down four flights of stairs to join with Sir Silvercrown and a few other Knights awaiting the newcomers. No one spoke as the assembly drew near—and what a strange assembly it was!

The mounted Knights formed a circle around the unyoked carthorse and those who were traveling on foot, which included a midge, a dwarf, and a human girl. That, on its own, was an odd combination, but as all three of them currently resided at Fort Faith, he had gotten used to them.

As for the newcomers, there appeared to be four of them. He assumed the man bedecked in armor was a Knight, and the woman in white was either a priestess or a wizardess. There was also a man in a three-cornered hat and a girl who was only slightly taller than the midge and wore a big brown coat.

When Petton and Knights came to a full stop before him, he was able to make out two more people in the group. An ancient-looking man lay draped across the back of a black stallion. The second man, atop the same horse, sat doubled-over, his face pressed against the beast's mane. The old one appeared to be unconscious, but the other fellow was awake despite the fact that his eyes were tightly closed. His moaning could be heard above the clopping of the horses' hooves.

Lieutenant Petton dismounted and led the unknown Knight up to where he, Sir Silvercrown, and the others waited. With a crisp salute, Petton said, "Commander Crystalus, I present Sir Stannel Bismarc, Commander of Fort Valor."

Colt didn't bother to hide his surprise, but he quickly recovered his composure. After clearing his throat, he said,

"Welcome to Fort Faith, Commander Bismarc."

He returned Stannel Bismarc's salute and was on the verge of asking him a dozen questions at once, but the visiting commander said, "The pleasure is all mine, Commander Crystalus...or is it 'Commander Colt'?"

He felt his face flush at the use of the nickname his older brothers had given him long ago. He had never cared much for his real name, and so he encouraged his friends to call him Colt. Even some of his men affectionately referred to him as Commander Colt, but hearing that name from the lips of this stranger—a fellow commander, no less—made him feel all of five years old again.

"You may call me either," he told the Commander of Fort Valor.

"And you may call me Stannel," he said with a grim smile. "There are important matters we must discuss immediately. In private."

Colt nodded. There were plenty of things he needed to say to the other man too.

"Come, I will take you to a place where we can talk." When Stannel cast a preoccupied glance back at the others who had been in the wagon, Colt added, "My lieutenant will escort them to our infirmary."

"You have my gratitude." Stannel pointed to the woman in white, and now that she was closer, Colt saw the light blue sash that crossed her chest and encircled her slim waist as well as a silver medallion around her neck. "Sister Aric is a priestess of Mystel. She will help treat the wounded."

"Very good," Colt replied, thinking her assistance would be a true blessing. Fort Faith was currently without a surgeon. At the moment, a certain woodsman was taking care of the Fort Faith's wounded.

But the story behind the forester's presence—and the presence of several others at the fort—was far too long to get into just then.

Colt led Stannel inside. As they ascended the first great staircase in the entry hall, he asked the other commander whether he needed any medical attention of his own or if he required any refreshment. Stannel curtly refused food and drink, insisting that there were higher priorities.

"You have come in response to my letter?" Colt asked by

way of broaching the subject. They were not yet to the commander's makeshift office in the eastern wing, but he didn't worry about anyone eavesdropping. Anyway, everyone at the fort was already well aware of the current predicament.

Stannel stopped suddenly, and Colt took two more steps before realizing his guest was no longer beside him. "I have received no letter from you, Commander," he said. "I have been away from Fort Valor these three days past."

"Then why—?"

Stannel forestalled him with a raised hand. Fort Valor's commander made a cursory glance up and down the hallway before saying, "I was on my way to Rydah when my party was ambushed by those same creatures that waylaid us near your fort. I believe they are goblins. I do not know how many of them currently reside in Capricon, but unless I am greatly mistaken, there are very many...an entire army perhaps.

"But what I must know, what I cannot wait any longer to ask, is whether Eliot Borrom made it safely to Fort Faith. Is our prince alive and well?"

Colt drew in a deep breath and let it out slowly. He had sent a lengthy missive with one of his Knights, instructing the man to present the letter to Stannel before taking it further to Lord Minus in Rydah. He had worried the goblins might slay the messenger before he reached his destinations, and Stannel's con-fession seemed to confirm that possibility for the rider had left for Fort Valor a week ago.

Now Colt hardly knew where to begin.

"Prince Eliot did *not* make it safely to Fort Faith," he said at last. "It's a long story, Commander, and you have had a long journey. Let's have a seat in my office, and I'll tell you everything."

Colt started to lead the way once more, but Stannel stood rooted in place. "I insist you tell me the prince's whereabouts immediately."

Looking at an unremarkable stone in the wall, Colt said, "As far as I can tell, the goblins have Prince Eliot in their custody ...and they've had him for some time."

Stannel's face paled. "Then it is as I feared."

"It's *worse* than you have feared," Colt said bitterly. "The man you, I, and even Lord Magnes Minus took for Prince Eliot was no man at all, but a goblin shaman in disguise."

*   *   *

Klye held the book close to his face. Even though his eyes
scanned the words on the pages, he wasn't really reading them.
Colt had found the manuscript, along with a few other books,
stashed away in a small, dusty room that might have served as
Fort Faith's library before the Thanatan Conflict.

The book had escaped the ogres' notice during the pillaging
that had surely followed the sacking of the fort. Not that that was
surprising. Ogres weren't known for their interest in literary
works.

From what Klye had gathered from the first few paragraphs,
the book was a diary of some low-ranking Knight who had been
stationed at Fort Faith more than three hundred years ago, back
when the fort was newly erected. The Knight wrote at length
about the dullest topics, and Klye would have discarded the
journal altogether except that the long-dead Knight's tedious
record was far more engaging than the words of the man in the
sickbed beside him.

"It's not like the pirates did anything worse than the rest of
us," Plake was saying—despite Klye's obvious show of ignoring
him. "It ain't right that they're down there in the dungeon by
themselves while everyone else is free to walk around the fort."

Unable to restrain himself any longer, Klye dropped the book
on his lap and said, "I can arrange for you to join them, though
your company would make it a worse punishment."

Plake scowled. "Very funny. But if you have so much sway
with Colt, why don't you just ask him to let them out of there?
They're *your* responsibility."

Klye retrieved the diary. Let the rancher rant the afternoon
away. He didn't have to justify himself to the likes of Plake
Nelway. Like everyone else in the infirmary, Klye would tune
him out.

"Some leader you are," Plake grumbled. "If anyone should
be down in that dungeon, it's you. You're the Renegade Leader.
You brought us all here!"

Klye gritted his teeth, resisting the urge to throw the diary at
him. If I were quick enough, I might even hit his broken nose, he
thought.

When Lieutenant Petton entered the infirmary, Klye forgot
all about Plake. He watched the Knight warily. If the lieutenant

had had his way, he, Plake, and the rest of the Renegades would be sharing the dungeon with the pirates. Gaelor Petton had made no secret of his distrust and dislike for Klye and his band.

And the feeling was mutual.

Klye had not seen Petton the past couple of days, and he had never come to the infirmary without Colt before. He wondered if he had come to add to the threats he had already issued—promises both spoken and unspoken. But the lieutenant didn't even glance his way as he passed by his bed.

Petton was not alone. Following him was an unusual entourage, including a white-robed woman and a man dressed like a wizard. The latter clutched at his stomach and looked to be on the verge of passing out. Two Knights carried another man into the room, though Klye couldn't get a good look at him. The wounded were laid to rest on the vacant beds on the other side of Sir Matthew Fisk.

Upon seeing Fisk, the woman asked, "Is this man alive?"

"He lives," Petton answered, "though just barely. This man has kept him from the clutches of death for the past few days."

When the lieutenant indicated the tall man standing silently in one corner of the infirmary, he didn't even bother to look at him.

"I know you will have your hands full, Sister Aric, but if you have a moment, please say a prayer for Sir Fisk," Petton said.

Still staring at the unconscious Knight's ashen face, the woman nodded solemnly.

Petton turned and headed for the door. "I am sorry to leave you so hastily, but I have other duties to attend to. These men will provide you with anything you need."

The two guards standing near the doorway saluted sharply. Then Petton and the other Knights departed. The woman's brow crinkled in uncertainty as she took in the armed sentries. When her gaze fell upon him and Plake, Klye smiled inwardly. She has no idea who we are, he thought.

Even Plake was silent as Sister Aric—who, Klye presumed, was a cleric of Mystel—attended the man in the blood-smeared gray robe. The patient lay still, not making a sound. Many questions swirled around Klye's mind, but he contented himself with studying the healer and her two patients, trying to learn everything he could about them.

The priestess found bandages in a cabinet. Klye noted she

didn't use a needle and thread to treat the wounded man. Either the injury was not too severe, or the woman possessed healing magic. Klye had seen similar skills demonstrated at the Temple of Mystel in Western Capricon, and while he didn't believe in gods, he couldn't argue against the existence of magic.

Throughout his adventures, he had seen both the curative and the catastrophic aspects of the arcane arts. So what if the woman thought her magic came from a benevolent deity? he thought.

Sister Aric spent the next few minutes standing over the injured man, her eyes closed and her hands placed atop his wound. Her mouth moved, but she made no sound. No one in the infirmary stirred, and as he watched the healer, Klye was reminded again of his time at the Temple of Mystel. The healers there had helped them despite the fact that they were being chased by Knights.

It all seemed so long ago...

When Sister Aric finished with the man in the gray robe, she moved to her next patient. But rather than attend to the other new arrival, she ran a hand along Fisk's neck, checking his pulse. She then placed her ear to his chest. When she removed the Knight's bandage, she gasped and took a step back.

Sister Aric looked away from the Knight and found both Klye and Plake staring at her. "Did the *goblins* do this?"

For once, Plake kept his mouth shut.

"No," Klye told her evenly, "a Renegade did."

"Renegades?" she asked. "I didn't think there were any rebels in this area...unless...there really is a new Renegade Leader in Capricon?"

At that, Klye laughed out loud. "There is, and you're looking at him."

To the woman's credit, she didn't shriek or faint. She merely blinked twice and then returned her attention to Matthew Fisk, praying over the dying man's body. Next, she concocted a salve with the ingredients on hand and made a new poultice. When she was finished treating Fisk, she walked back over to the door, pointedly avoiding Klye's eyes.

"Who has been treating that Knight?" she asked the guards.

They both pointed toward the corner of the room. Sister Aric walked up to Othello, who had watched Sister Aric's activities without a word.

"I am Sister Aric Narrestif, Fort Valor's healer. Tell me,

friend, are you also one of Mystel's gifted?"

"No."

If the woman was disconcerted by the man's curt reply, she didn't let that stop her from pressing onward.

"I must say I am impressed by your work. It is a testament to your skill that the Knight yet lives." She paused, giving the man a chance to say something, but when he didn't reply, she added, "I have been treating Knights for the past few years, and I have never come across a wound that so cleanly dealt. Tell me, what manner of weapon was responsible?"

Othello glanced at Klye.

"It was an enchanted weapon," Klye said. "A vorpal sword."

"Is that true?" Sister Aric asked Othello.

"Yes."

Klye watched as the healer looked Othello up and down, perhaps noticing his strange attire for the first time. He wore pants and a shirt made of buckskin and shoes that were more suitable for mucking around the woods than making rounds in an infirmary. Instead of carrying a delicate surgeon's blade, the man wore a large hunting knife at his hip.

"Are you the healer here at Fort Faith?" she asked him.

"No."

"But you've been tending to that man, the Knight?"

"Yes."

"Then who *are* you?" She didn't shout the words, but there was no mistaking the exasperation in her voice. Klye couldn't quite stifle a grin.

"Othello."

"He's one of my Renegades," Klye added.

Sister Aric cast the Renegade Leader a skeptical glance. "Is this true?" she asked the sentries.

They nodded.

The woman shook her head. "There's a Renegade Leader in the infirmary and another rebel serving as the fort's healer. There's talk of a magical sword. Just what in the world is going on?"

Passage II

Mitto watched the Commander of Fort Faith lead Stannel up a great flight of stairs. Lieutenant Petton and Sister Aric followed at a distance, along with the Knights who had been charged with delivering the wounded to the fort's infirmary. But Mitto, who had miraculously all but the most superficial of wounds, was left behind in the entry hall, forgotten by everyone except for the strange trio who had appeared out of nowhere and rescued them from the goblins.

The horn-helmeted warrior and the midge were arguing about something, while the red-haired woman looked on with a bemused expression. They were like something out of a bard's tale—or a bad joke.

When the warrior took a swing at the midge with his mailed fist, the archer stepped between the shorter figures and said something Mitto couldn't hear to the man in the black armor. The warrior then folded his arms, but rather than make a retort, he withdrew from the group in a huff, stomping his way up the wide staircase.

The woman looked as though she was on the verge of saying something to the midge, but the little spell-caster had noticed Mitto by this time and was walking over toward him.

The irrational urge to flee struck Mitto like a bucket of cold water. Or maybe it wasn't so irrational, after all. Most sane people did their best to avoid midge. Popular opinion held that interacting with a midge was not conducive to a long, happy life.

And yet this midge had saved his life. Were it not for the small wizard's magic, the goblins would have likely slaughtered them to a man. Mitto owed him a debt of gratitude. Anyway, the doors had been locked fast behind him, so there wasn't anywhere to run.

The midge came to stop at an uncomfortable two and a half feet away from Mitto.

"Hi. My name is Noel. What's yours?"

During his time in Rydah, Mitto had seen dwarves, half-elves, and even a centaur on one occasion. And there had been an occasional midge too. While none of the other races harbored any great love for the midge, the local authorities couldn't legally keep them from visiting the capital.

Like most sensible people, Mitto had always tried to keep his distance. It wasn't that midge were intentionally malevolent—not like goblins. They were, however, the most powerful spell-casters in Altaerra. Rumor had it every midge was capable of wielding great magic. That fact alone would make them intimidating, but there was more to it than that.

In their infinite wisdom, the gods had also granted the midge an immature and naïve nature. They were in essence a race of childish wizards. Midge were incredibly capricious, and they had the power to realize just about any of their whims.

Noel might have looked like an ordinary, bright-eyed human youth, except for his outfit, which was comprised of an over-sized blue robe; a wide-brimmed, conical hat made of straw; and a thick belt—with an even thicker brass buckle—from which hung an assortment of vials and purses. Add the red-wooded staff with its blue bauble tip, and Noel looked like a child playing dress-up.

"Uh, hello. I'm Mitto O'erlander."

The midge laughed out loud, which caused Mitto to flinch. "That's a funny name. Mitto. It sounds like something a gnome would come up with!"

Not knowing how to respond to that, Mitto just smiled while his mind scrambled to find an excuse to extricate himself from the midge's company.

"The gods sent me here to protect my friends," Noel continued. "Well, they weren't really my friends until *after* I came. Except for Klye, of course, but I didn't even know he was going to be here. The last time I saw him was in a different world altogether, but I think maybe the gods wanted us to meet again here at Fort Faith."

After a quick breath, the midge added, "Why are you here?"

"You needn't be frightened of Noel," said the woman, coming to stand beside them. "He may sound crazy, but he's relatively civilized for a midge."

Noel beamed and puffed out his chest, as though he had been awarded a great compliment. "This is my friend Opal," he said. "She lives here too. She's friends with Colt, like me, but she doesn't like Klye so much. Opal, this is Mitto. Isn't that a silly name? Mitto!"

"Hello," Mitto said, blushing in spite of himself. "It's a pleasure to make your acquaintance."

Even as he uttered the formality, Mitto realized it wasn't an overstatement. Now that he was face to face with her, he realized Opal was a truly beautiful woman. She had glittery green eyes and flawless skin. Her smooth, ovular face was framed by long, shiny hair the color of a perfect sunrise. She was slender but not without curves.

"Well met, Mitto," she said. Even her voice was lovely.

Despite her feminine stature, however, Opal didn't dress the part of a lady. The well-worn trousers and loose-fitting shirt seemed better suited for a man than a woman. The quiver strapped to her back and the crossbow she carried also seemed in contrast with her feminine features.

Mitto had seen her shoot. She was as much a warrior as her companions. And the plain outfit and the weapons did nothing to dilute her natural beauty. The stark contrast of hard and soft made Opal all the more attractive.

Suddenly aware he was ogling the girl, Mitto forced his eyes to meet hers, but Opal was no longer looking at him. She was staring past him and off to one side.

"Is that your daughter over there?" she asked.

"What? Where?" Mitto spun around and found Zusha Blisnes peeking out from behind one of the pillars that lined the hall. "Oh, her. No, actually she was one of my passengers. I'm a traveling merchant. Her grandfather wanted to bring them to Fort Faith because, apparently, the old man was once a cook here. It's a long story."

Opal nodded as though it all made perfect sense. The midge was already bounding over to Zusha. At first, Mitto feared the sight of the eccentrically dressed midge would frighten the little girl, but then he recalled how Zusha hadn't balked during the goblins' attacks.

And he had to remind himself she wasn't exactly a *little* girl.

Noel introduce himself. Zusha didn't give her name, but that didn't seem to bother the midge, who launched into a lengthy speech about his duty as Fort Faith's protector.

"The Knights say they don't like my magic, but where would they be without it? Hmm? Colt always seems to come around, though he likes to wait until the last possible second. Hey, did you know that your eyes are two different colors?"

When Mitto turned back Opal, she was smiling at him. "The Knights here are always so busy, especially now that the goblins have made themselves known. I don't think Colt would mind if I showed you some hospitality. Are you hungry?"

She didn't wait for an answer, and with his stomach all but empty, Mitto dared not refuse her. He followed close behind her, glancing behind to make sure Zusha was coming too. With Toemis incapacitated, he felt responsible for the girl.

Noel continued to carry on his one-sided conversation with Zusha while leading her by the hand. They all followed Opal through a doorway and into a narrower corridor. Once again, Mitto found his eyes straying, taking in Opal's comely form, but as soon as he realized what he was doing, a wave of guilt washed over him. A voice that resembled Else Fontane's reminded him she was likely more than a decade his junior.

At the thought of Else, Mitto's mood darkened. Even though he was safe inside a fortress with Knights of Superius, he was eager to be gone. No matter how hospitable Fort Faith might prove to be, it could never match Someplace Else.

Silently, he vowed to return to Rydah as soon as possible.

The two commanders stared at each other across an ancient writing desk. Colt leaned back in his stiff-backed chair, waiting to hear Stannel's reaction to his extraordinary tale. Stannel, for his part, had not moved at all during the younger Knight's speech and continued to stare at his counterpart in silence for several seconds.

Finally, the Commander of Fort Valor cleared his throat and said, "Let me make sure I understand. The supposed Crown Prince of Superius left my fortress and came here to Fort Faith as planned. But his arrival was witnessed by a Renegade Leader named Klye Tristan. That very night, the rebels invaded Fort Faith with the use of magic…that midge's magic…in an attempt to kidnap Prince Eliot.

"Some of the Renegades made it all the way to the western wing, where you and your men had secured the prince. Klye Tristan was among that group, but ultimately, he and his accomplices failed. When Prince Eliot ordered you to kill the Renegade Leader, you hesitated, and that was when your sword…"

Stannel trailed off, prompting Colt to repeat the next part.

"That was when Klye told me to look at my sword…to look at the prince through the blade," Colt said.

During the course of his story, Colt had unsheathed his sword and laid it on the desk. Now both commanders' gazes landed upon the weapon. There was nothing spectacular about the hilt, except for the intricate engravings that revealed the masterful workmanship of a bygone era. Many Knights possessed ancient swords, the arms of their ancestors. This was true for Colt as well, though his blade was a rarity among rarities.

Colt watched Stannel run a finger along the flat of the long, transparent blade. Whereas the hilt and crosspiece looked ordinary enough, the blade was a truly remarkable sight. No one—not even Colt's grandfather—knew what the blade was made of. It was as clear as glass yet harder than steel.

Colt's father had given him *Chrysaal-rûn* before he left Superius for Capricon. Since coming to Fort Faith, the young commander had found two occasions to brandish the unusual weapon, and in both situations, he had learned that the crystal sword possessed powers beyond his—or any of the other Knights'—understanding. He had seen the gemlike blade shed a pale, blue light when he needed illumination, and during the heat of battle, it had cleaved through metal as though it were old parchment.

"And when you looked at Prince Eliot through the blade, you saw not a man, but a goblin?" Stannel prompted.

"Yes," Colt said, trying his best to gauge Stannel's reaction. "*Chrysaal-rûn* revealed the shaman's true face, at which point, the false prince brandished strong magic against the Knights and Renegades alike.

"The goblin might have killed us all if it weren't for the efforts of a certain Renegade…a rogue Knight of Superius…and Opal, the archer who came to your aid against the goblins on the highway. They defeated the goblin shaman, but he escaped in the end."

Colt knew it sounded fantastic. He might not have believed it himself if he hadn't been there when T'slect nearly destroyed him and his friends to keep his plans a secret.

"What of the Renegades?" Stannel asked.

The question caught Colt off guard.

"We have detained the entire band," Colt said. "I have measured each of the rebels individually and am managing them according to their crimes and likelihood of repeat offenses. Obviously, the goblins are the greater threat, but since I cannot let them free without an official pardon from Superius, I see no reason to treat them poorly. As far as I am concerned, they have redeemed themselves by their actions against the shaman.

"Two of them, including the Renegade Leader, are currently in the infirmary, while two others are locked up in the dungeon. The rest are allowed to walk freely about the fort as long as they don't get in the way."

"And the midge fights for the Knights now?" Stannel asked.

"Yes...well...Noel is a tricky case. He's loyal to both the Knights and the Renegades."

Stannel folded his hands on the table. "Let us speak of the present...and the future. The goblins have compromised Continae's government, though the extent of their subterfuge remains unknown. Neither do we know how many goblins are hiding in Capricon, whether we face a small battalion or a great army. On top of everything, the real Prince Eliot is either in the goblins' possession or dead."

"Yes," Colt said softly, his voice faltering.

Stannel cradled his chin in his hands, and stared at a spot on the desk for a few seconds before he spoke again.

"Prince Eliot...or, rather, the goblin posing as our prince...had stayed at Fort Valor for a very short time, but he raised a few questions during his visit," Stannel began. "His visit left me feeling uneasy, for he had hinted that King Edward was displeased with the Knights in Capricon because we had not yet snuffed out the rebellion. His words were demoralizing to say the least.

"Of course, now I know that it was all lies, but at the time, I wanted to discuss the prince's unannounced visit to the island with Lord Minus. Sister Aric, who has friends in the capital, elected to come along. En route to Rydah, we were to spend the night at a certain lodge. That is where I crossed paths with the company you found me with. That is also where I first encountered the goblins."

Colt listened patiently as the Commander of Fort Valor recounted the battle at the lodge and their hurried flight to Fort Faith.

"Were it not for your friends, we would have been slaughtered," Stannel said. "I would like to give them my thanks personally."

Colt found himself smiling for the first time since he sat down behind the desk. "I will be sure to introduce you to them. I think you are one of very few Knights who would thank a midge for anything."

Stannel shrugged. "I would thank anyone who has earned my gratitude, regardless of his race. Anyway, you are one of very few Knights brave enough to count a midge among his troops."

"Yes, I allow him to stay, but it's mostly because I can't think of a way to get him to leave," Colt confessed.

Now Stannel smiled. "I recognized the midge for what he on the battlefield, and the woman with the crossbow was obviously a human, but what about the warrior in the dark armor?"

"A dwarf," Colt said, "but he's not from Afren-Ckile. Cholk is from the Deathlands. He saved my life before I left Continae, and we've been friends ever since."

"A midge, a woman, a dwarf, and a slew of rebels...Fort Faith truly is a unique castle."

"I suppose I'm not a traditional commander," Colt replied. "If it were up to my lieutenant, there would be no one here but Knights, and the Renegades would all be locked up in the dungeon." He paused before asking, "What do you think, Commander?"

Stannel raised an eyebrow and then said, "I think, Commander, that it is none of my business how you run your fort."

Realizing that he had been holding his breath, Colt let it all out at once. A part of him had expected Stannel to start scolding him just as the false Prince of Superius had. As the youngest commander in Capricon—at twenty-four years, he was younger than most of his men—Colt found himself constantly doubting his abilities and his worthiness to command.

It had even occurred to him that T'slect or some other imposter had sent him to Fort Faith to undermine the Knights' leadership on the island.

But with Stannel sitting across from him, he felt more confident than he had in a long time.

"I would like to hear all about your adventures, Colt, but I shall not be able to impose upon your hospitality for long," Stannel said, rising suddenly. "I must return to Fort Valor and from there send word of the goblins to Rydah."

Colt stood too. "If my messenger didn't make it to Fort Valor, we must conclude that the goblins are watching the highway."

"Nevertheless, I shall leave for my fort at first light tomorrow. If you could provide me with a worthy steed, I would be in your debt."

"It would be my honor," Colt said. "And I insist you allow some of my men to escort you—"

Stannel held up a hand. "That will not be necessary."

Colt gave Stannel a quizzical look, but the only explanation he provided was, "I will travel all the faster if I have only myself to worry about. Besides, you are terribly undermanned here as it is. I will not take your men from their posts. There is, however, one more favor I must ask you."

"Yes, of course. Anything I have is at your disposal."

"Because I will travel light, I must ask that you allow Sister Aric to remain at Fort Faith."

"Certainly, though adding a healer to our ranks is a blessing, not a burden." Colt paused. "What about the other people you were traveling with?"

Now Stannel's bright blue eyes seemed to twinkle. "I got them here safely, Colt. They're your problem now."

Passage III

Baxter was only vaguely aware of the passing of time. Inside the tent, it was most always dark, affording him only a limited view of his surroundings. And because he couldn't turn his head in any direction, whatever light the sun provided revealed little more than the top of the canopy.

The monster's foul magic had robbed him of any control over his body. Aside from involuntary activities, such as breathing and passing water, his body was lifeless.

In spite of his paralysis, Baxter was still very aware of his senses. He could see, smell, and hear. Most of all, however, he could feel. He could feel the stream of drool running down his cheek, the hunger gnawing at his belly, and the chill of late autumn biting his exposed flesh. Also, his captors had done nothing to care for his wounds, so his injuries were a source of great preoccupation.

But after a while, even the throbbing in his head faded into the background, swallowed up by the tedium of his twilight existence.

Lying prone and helpless for countless consecutive hours, Baxter had had a lot of time to think. At first he had dwelled upon his misery, cursing his captors, himself, the gods. When his impotent rage had fizzled away, the Knight examined his situation from a detached perspective—and tried to formulate a strategy for reversing his fate.

The creature who had initially asked him about Mitto and the others had come to Baxter twice more since then. During these terrible conversations with the monster, he had learned a few things about his captors. First, he had learned a name for them: goblins. He wasn't sure if that was what they called themselves, but when his inquisitor—who was always the same—referred to his soldiers, he had used that word.

Or at least Baxter's mind had translated "goblins" from the creature's twisted language.

When the goblin had pried the secrets of Rydah's defenses from his mind, he concluded the invaders were planning an attack on the capital. Unwillingly, he dispensed all of the information he knew of the Knights' battle tactics for defending the city—and as a lieutenant, Baxter Lawler had known quite a lot.

On another occasion, the goblin had forced him detail all of the island's military forces, from the Knights' fortresses down to local militias. Surely, the goblin army intended to conquer all of Capricon.

Baxter had also learned a little about the interrogator himself. While the goblin never referred to himself by name, he had revealed his rank. His interrogator was the general of the army. And it was by the general's word alone that Baxter still lived. And live he would until he had no more useful information to give.

But the goblin general had made no secret of Baxter's eventual death. Even if he didn't slit Baxter's throat, the Knight would eventually starve.

The general was straightforward with the human about most things, but Baxter had inferred a few things on his own. The general's staff, for instance—the goblin always carried the skull-tipped rod. Baxter believed the staff was responsible for not only overcoming the language barrier, but also his paralysis.

The staff was undeniably a potent talisman, but Baxter had noted a curious thing about the staff and its owner. Whenever the general used the staff's magic, he grimaced. For all the staff's power, the general seemed reluctant to use the tool. Baxter didn't know what to make of it, but he filed the information away, hoping it might prove useful.

Baxter couldn't guess how much time had passed between the dreadful visits, but at some point, the goblin general returned to stand over him again. He saw the hideous visage of the monster for an instant before the leering skull replaced it as the only thing in his limited field of vision. The memory of past interrogations welled up inside of him, and the Knight surely would have broken down and sobbed were he able to.

"Tell me everything you know about Fort Valor," said the familiar voice in his head.

He felt his heart pounding in his chest, felt beads of cold sweat tickling his naked body. The helplessness was maddening. At that moment, Baxter Lawler hated the goblin more than he had ever hated anyone. And he hated himself for what he knew he would do.

Thanks to the goblin general and his staff with the scarlet-eyed skull, Sir Baxter Lawler had become the Great Betrayer of Capricon.

Silently, he slipped out of bed. He moved slowly, but the grace he had previously possessed was compromised by a weakness that threatened to take him to the ground. First using the sickbed as a crutch and then leaning on the foot of an adjacent bed, he gradually made his way toward the door of the infirmary.

It seemed to Klye that he could feel his energy draining with every step, but he kept going anyway. Night had plunged the infirmary into a heavy darkness, but his eyes had adjusted enough to see the Knights who had stood guard on either side of the doors were gone. Now, with nothing but open space between him and the door, he steadied his breathing, released his hold on the bed, and took the first step toward freedom.

Fighting to maintain his balance with each movement he made, he eventually reached the door. When his hand found the doorknob, he grasped it tightly. For a moment, he enjoyed the luxury of leaning against the unyielding wood of the door. When his breathing had returned to normal, he cautiously turned the knob, wary of any noise the act made.

He was not in the least surprised to fine the door locked. The Knights weren't fools and, therefore, weren't likely to leave the door to a room full of criminals unsecured as an invitation.

No, he was not surprised. In fact, he was relieved. If the door had been unlocked, it would have meant there were guards on the other side. While he was in no condition to contend even a single sentry, a locked door was no obstacle whatsoever.

Klye reached beneath the overlarge shirt the Knights had given him and down into the waistband of his trousers, where he felt cool metal pressing snugly against his hip. He carefully retrieved the scalpel and worked the thin-tipped blade into the keyhole. He chewed at his lower lip as he used the tool to explore the inner-workings of the lock.

A few seconds later, he heard a satisfying click, and the door opened a fraction of an inch.

Smiling, he tucked the scalpel away and opened the door with a sudden burst of movement. Normally, he would have pushed the door open little by little, but Fort Faith was an old fortress, and he had noted how the infirmary door squeaked whenever the Knights came in and out. Had he drawn out the act of opening the portal, anyone in the near vicinity would have been privy to a grating sound that resembled the cry of a dying cat.

As it was, the door made only the briefest of noises as he thrust it open. When he was certain that the contained creak had roused no one with or without the infirmary, he slinked through the narrow passage and hastily closed the door behind him.

He stood with his back pressed up against the door, staring down the black corridor. Then he began his slow and steady trudge away from the infirmary, using the walls for guidance and support.

At a snail's pace, he followed the crisscrossing corridors. His path was an aimless one because he knew almost nothing about the fort's interior. One path was as good as another, so he wasted no time pondering his course. He concentrated solely on his movements, sluggish though they were, all the while committing every twist and turn to memory.

When a light appeared behind him, he tensed, and his free hand—the one that wasn't pressed against the cold wall— reached for the scalpel secreted at his side. His first thought was to press himself flat up against the wall and hope that whoever was out there didn't bother to look his way.

The person with the lantern was approaching from a perpendicular hallway. Perhaps he or she would keep on going straight…

Or perhaps not.

Klye watched as the light-barer unhesitatingly turned down his corridor. He had the sudden urge to run and nearly laughed out loud at the notion. He wouldn't get more than three steps before he fell flat on his face, and he'd sooner die than let anyone—friend or foe—see him in just a condition.

Conjuring an unconcerned smile, he leaned against the wall and waited.

"What the…? Klye Tristan, is that you?"

He recognized the voice before he could make out the commander of Fort Faith's face.

"At your service," Klye replied.

He watched as the baffled Knight tried to puzzle out the mystery of his presence in the hall. Colt eyed him warily, as though he expected him to make a desperate move. After a moment, however, the other man's face eased into a smile of his own.

"You must tell me how you managed it," Colt said.

Klye shrugged. "I wouldn't be much of a Renegade Leader if I let something as small as a near-death experience and a rickety, old door stand between me and freedom."

"So you intend to escape?" Colt asked.

"Yes," Klye said, quickly adding, "from the infirmary, at any rate. I'm not used to staying cooped up for days at a time. I thought a walk about your fine fortress would do me some good."

"You look like you can barely stand," Colt pointed out. "Why don't you have a seat?"

His legs felt like they were made of pudding. "I'll stand, thank you."

Colt let out an exasperated laugh. "At least tell me how you picked the lock."

Klye withdrew the scalpel from his waistband and held it up for the commander to see. He then altered his grip, pressing the blade between his thumb and index finger, and offered the handle to Colt. The Knight hesitated briefly before accepting the scalpel.

"I procured it last night," Klye said, "but I wanted to save my strength for tonight's walk."

Colt laughed again. "You are a cunning man, Klye."

"Like I said, I wouldn't be much of a Renegade Leader if I weren't."

Colt's friendly expression didn't alter as he said, "But you aren't a Renegade Leader anymore. The rebellion is over...at least for you and your band."

Klye scoffed. "True, but I still have the loyalty of warriors who everyone refers to as 'the Renegades'...including you. It's a matter of semantics, Colt."

Colt shrugged. "Very well, but what now? You know I cannot allow you to prowl the fort on your own."

"You let Othello 'prowl' alone," Klye said.

Colt looked taken aback by statement. "Yes, I suppose I do, but Othello has shown me he can be trusted. If it weren't for him, Sir Fisk would have passed away days ago. He has been treating Knights and...Renegade alike since the battle against T'slect."

"The bottom line is that you don't trust me," Klye said.

"If I didn't trust you at all," said the commander, "you would be in the dungeon right now, and even with all of your impressive abilities, you'd not find a way out of there."

"Perhaps," Klye allowed. "But speaking of the dungeon, I must ask you again to let Crooker and Pistol out. I know they're rough around the edges, but I give you my word they won't cause any trouble."

Colt let out a long sigh. "We've been over this before. My men are uncomfortable enough as it is with so many former rebels roaming the fort. The pirates are...well, worse. Who can number the violent crimes they are guilty of? Pistol admits that he was the leader, the pirate king, of a particularly vicious lot of buccaneers. I simply cannot allow them walk around freely."

Klye did not blink. "Will I be joining them once I recover?"

"It seems you are already well on your way to recovery," Colt said. "When you are stronger, I promise I will take you to them so you can see for yourself that they are not being mistreated. But I won't make you stay there, Klye. There is little enough to burgle from Fort Faith, after all."

Klye said nothing. Plake's accusations rang loudly in his ears, and he felt more than a little guilty that Pistol and Crooker were being treated differently from him and the others. It was beyond his control, however, and Klye reminded himself that things might have ended a whole lot worse. In truth, Klye counted Colt as an ally, and in time, he supposed the two of them might even become friends.

But there were those at the fort who were not as understanding as the young commander.

When Colt had alluded to his men being uncomfortable with the rebels living among them, Klye pictured two people who would actively try to poison the commander's mind against him. Gaelor Petton was second-in-command at Fort Faith, and Colt valued the veteran Knight's opinion.

The other naysayer wasn't a Knight, wasn't even a man. And

Klye had seen how Colt looked at Opal. He could guess how deep the commander's feelings ran for the red-haired archer. Thus, Opal was the more formidable foe by a long shot.

He didn't know if Opal cared for Colt as deeply as he cared for her, but Klye did know Opal openly scorned the Renegades. Between Petton and Opal, it was a wonder Colt hadn't tossed the lot of them in the dungeon.

"You shouldn't make promises you can't keep," Klye said after a moment. "With so many unexpected guests dropping by, the dungeon might be the only space vacant by the time I'm healed."

"Is that your way of asking me how many newcomers arrived today?"

Klye scoffed again. "Sister Aric wasn't very talkative once she found out she was surrounded by rebels...I mean *former* rebels."

"There are six of them, including the healer," Colt said. "They've come from the east. The goblins made several attempts on their lives, including an attack on the highway near our fort."

Klye wanted more details. Who were the other newcomers? How had they managed to escape the goblins? How many monsters had there been? But now was not the time for lengthy explanations. As it was, he feared he would collapse at any moment.

"They're growing bolder," Klye said.

Colt nodded. "It seems like the goblins are ready to come out of hiding."

"Well, that's a good thing, isn't it?" Klye asked. "Now that the Knights know about the goblins, they can organize a defensive strategy to force them off the island."

"Perhaps," Colt said, though the trailing sigh revealed his true opinion. "The messenger I sent to Fort Valor and Rydah never made it to his destinations. The Knights' first encounter with the goblins could well be their last, depending on how many of the damned creatures are skulking around the island."

Klye knew very little about Capricon's defenses. He was new to the island and had never been farther east than Fort Faith. He had no idea how many soldiers were stationed at Fort Valor and Rydah. But if Colt was worried, then Klye feared the worst.

One thing seemed certain—unless the Knights could repel the invaders quickly, the defenders of Fort Faith would see action before long.

Most of the Knights were eager for an opportunity to prove themselves against the foreign warriors. Not only were the goblins a threat to Capricon, but also there was a score to be settled. T'slect, the goblin shaman who had posed as Prince Eliot Borrom, had duped them all. The Renegade War was, by and large, the result of the goblins' political machinations.

Knights and Renegades alike thirsted for revenge.

Klye could only hope he would recover quickly so that he could fight alongside the fort's defenders when the time came.

As though to mock him, Klye's leg chose that moment to buckle. He shifted his weight and grabbed for the wall. The movement was awkward and uncoordinated, but he managed to catch himself. Colt came forward, but Klye warded him off with a sharp look. Accepting help from others was still something new for him.

"Come," Colt said, offering his arm. "I'll escort you back to the infirmary. I'll be sure to come by more often. Perhaps we can take another walk soon. I like being able to talk to you without so many ears nearby."

Taking a deep breath, Klye allowed the commander to take his arm. Recently, he had come to terms with his own limitations. Without the support of his Renegades, he would have perished long ago. And so he ignored his bruised pride as Colt helped him back to the infirmary.

Commander and Renegade Leader walked in silence, each lost in his own thoughts. Somewhere between that random hallway and the infirmary, it occurred to Klye that Colt had never mentioned why *he* had been walking the corridors in the middle of the night.

Colt hadn't seemed to be in any great hurry. It was as if the man's path had been as aimless as Klye's.

The two men parted ways at the infirmary's door. Klye made his way back to bed, already replaying the encounter with Colt over in his mind. In the end, he was forced to conclude that he wasn't the only man in Fort Faith with many things on his mind.

Passage IV

True to his word, Stannel was up before sunrise, and Colt was there to see him off. He again insisted that Fort Valor's commander take a small entourage with him, but the older man would hear none of it.

Colt hardly knew what else to say to Stannel. He was loath to see the other commander leave, for even though they had just met, Stannel Bismarc struck him as a good man and a capable ally. He had no real reason to detain him, however.

I'll see him again, Colt told himself. We're neighbors, after all.

Colt might have tried further to persuade Stannel into accepting help, but Stannel's voice brooked no argument. The serenity, the absolute fearlessness in Stannel's expression bespoke of incredible confidence—and maybe something more. The man seemed not at all concerned about the hoard of goblins prowling the countryside. For all the anxiety he exhibited that morning, Stannel might have been on his way to visit an old friend.

But Stannel wasn't dressed the part of a lay traveler. He was bedecked in his full suit of armor and wore a great sword strapped to his back. Although Colt had not seen the blade drawn, he recognized the weapon by its crosspiece, which was ringed on each end. It was a claymore, a combination longsword and broadsword traditionally associated with Glenning.

The claymore in itself was not such an unusual sight. Though claymores had originated in Glenning, many Knights preferred it to the lighter blades forged in Superius. In addition to the sword, Stannel kept a sheathed dagger at his belt. On the other hip, however, rested an object that Colt had not noticed before. It was this final weapon—a tool designed not for cutting, but for bashing—that held Colt's attention.

The mace's length was about the span of man's elbow to fingertips with the approximate girth of his forearm. Fashioned completely out of what appeared to be bronze, the mace looked solid and heavy. The head of the weapon was covered with rounded studs but lacked the spikes of deadlier versions. Colt thought he saw engraved sigils running along the shaft, but he never got a close enough look.

It wasn't uncommon for a Knight to carry more than one means of offense. In the heat of battle, weapons tended to break. But there was something about the mace that seemed out of place to Colt. He might have asked Stannel about it, but by the time he had noticed it, Stannel was already walking his mount out of the stable.

"Even though your path is fraught with peril, somehow I know you will succeed," Colt told Stannel as they made their way to the road. "Your confidence inspires me."

Stannel glanced down from the horse and smiled cryptically. "My confidence is borne of faith. My safety lies in the hands of Pintor, the Great Protector, and what better insurance is there?"

Stannel saluted and gave the palfrey a sudden kick, which sent the animal launching into a gallop. Colt watched the commander's retreating form for several minutes, considering his words. Pintor was the patron god of the Knights of Superius, though most Knights referred to Pintor as "the Warriorlord."

Colt thought he shouldn't be surprised Stannel Bismarc honored Pintor with a different appellation. He was beginning to think Stannel was very different from other Knights. Many Knights claimed to serve the Warriorlord, but when Stannel mentioned his faith in the Great Protector, Colt couldn't dismiss it as cliché.

When the veteran commander was little more than a speck on the horizon, Colt headed back for the stable. He was not at all surprised to find Opal there. Predictably, the woman was inside the farthest stall, tending to her horse.

She didn't seem to notice him, so Colt tiptoed past the rows of war horses and came to a stop outside the stall where Opal worked. With her back to him, she tenderly swept a brush across the coat of a white mare. All the while she spoke to the animal in a gentle voice.

Colt felt his affection for Opal swell as he watched her interact with Nisson. Opal had no memory of her childhood, had no memory of her life prior to a handful of years ago. Consequently, she had few friends. Nisson was one of Opal's oldest and dearest friends.

Colt was pleased to count himself among her friends too, even if he wished their relationship could evolve further.

While Opal was almost as tight-lipped about her inner-thoughts as she was about her past, Colt suspected she told Nisson quite a bit more about her feelings than she did any man or woman. Suddenly, he felt guilty, as though he were intruding upon an intimate moment.

"It's rather brisk this morning, wouldn't you say?" he asked her, hoping it sounded like something one would say upon just arriving.

Opal jumped to her feet and was already reaching for her crossbow when she recognized Colt.

"If you ever sneak up on me like that again, you might just find a bolt lodged in your chest, Saerylton Crystalus!"

Although the woman was glowering at him—and despite the fact that she had employed the use of his full name—Colt knew Opal was more startled than angry. A hint of a smile tugged at the corner of her lips.

If only he could tell her that she already had pierced his heart...

"You have my sincerest apologies."

"Anyway, what are you doing down here at this time of the morning?" she asked. "Shouldn't you be sloughing off behind a desk or something?"

Colt rolled his eyes. "Very funny. I came to see Commander Bismarc off. He left for Fort Valor a few minutes ago."

"That was a short visit. Did he go alone?"

"He did."

She had been stroking behind Nisson's ears but stopped suddenly. "Really? Maybe he should have taken Mitto...that merchant...along with him. I got the impression yesterday he was in a hurry to get back to Rydah. He's worried about what the goblins are planning."

"Aren't we all?" Colt muttered sourly. "Wait, you aren't planning on going for a ride this morning, are you?"

Opal shrugged. "What if I am?"

He sighed. Despite how much he had come to care for Opal, he could have done with a little less stubbornness. "You saw how bold those goblins were yesterday. They were practically in our backyard when they accosted Stannel and his companions."

"And you saw how their audacity was rewarded," Opal countered. She flashed a mischievous grin and patted the butt of her crossbow.

Colt sighed again. He had eighty men under his command at Fort Faith, and every one of them would obey his order—any order—without question. But Opal was a civilian. He couldn't make her stay inside the fort, even if he knew it was in her best interest.

Well, technically he could, but he didn't want to think about what would happen if he tried.

"I know you can take care of yourself," he began, choosing his words carefully, "but sometimes it's your enemy's lucky day. You understand my meaning? Take your run-in with the Renegades, for instance—"

Opal's glare stopped Colt short. "Klye Tristan caught me unawares because I was careless. I didn't expect to find a bunch of Renegades in the middle of nowhere. But I *know* the goblins are out there. Let them come after me if they dare!"

Colt decided not to press the point. He should have known better than to bring up the incident. During one of her many rides across the plains, Opal had happened upon the Renegade Leader and some of his men—or, rather, they had happened upon her. When one of them recognized her as a resident of Fort Faith, they took her captive in hopes of using her as a bargaining chip against the Knights. In the end, Colt and a handful of his men had had to rescue her.

That she had needed rescuing was still a sore spot with Opal, and she despised Klye for having put her in that position.

"But for your information, I'll not be riding this morning." Opal didn't look at him as she spoke, busy, as she was, with grooming the mare. "Like you said, it's a bit chilly out there. I only came to the stables so Nisson won't think I've forgotten about her."

"When you do decide to ride"—he would not use the word "if"—"please let me know."

"Why, so you can send a Knight or two to babysit me?"

When Colt didn't answer, she set the brush down, gave Nisson a loving pat on the rump, and approached the wooden door of the stall. "I don't mean to snap at you, Colt. I just hate feeling trapped here. Don't get me wrong, this is a great fort and everything...you can't beat the rent...but I'm used to being able to come and go as I please. If we let the goblins dictate the events of our daily lives...well...it's like they've already won."

"I don't like it any more than you do, but you have to be reasonable. You can't ignore a danger just because it's inconvenient."

"I know that. And I'll begrudgingly accept company on my morning rides if I must...at least until you send the goblins back to T'Ruel."

"It's for your protection. I care about you." He hastily added, "You're my friend...one of the few people at Fort Faith who don't call me 'sir.'"

Opal chuckled as she closed the stall door behind her. "The day I call you 'sir' is the day I marry a midge."

"Best not to get Noel's hopes up. Speaking of our resident spell-caster, I promised him I'd have breakfast with him. He says he has a list of suggestions on how magic can improve our lives at the fort. Care to join us?"

"Oh, I wouldn't want to get in the way," Opal declared in mock-seriousness.

"You'd be doing me a personal favor," Colt said. "You know how Noel can get. It's hard to keep him focused for long. I swear, sometimes I understand only one sentence in ten. Anyway, he'll be more likely to behave himself if you're there."

Opal smiled. "Maybe it's because I'm one of the few people around here who isn't afraid to tell him what's what. Midge or not, Noel needs to understand there are rules everyone must follow. Gods, don't I sound like a mother? Still, I have to admit the little guy's growing on me."

"Does that mean you'll have breakfast with us?"

Opal made a grandiose bow. "It would be my honor."

She put out her arm, and Colt took it with all the airs of a proper nobleman—never mind that Colt *was* a nobleman. The smile he wore as they made their way to the dining room was genuine. The mantle of command sometimes made him feel decades older, but Opal always treated him like a peer.

Traversing the corridors of Fort Faith, heading unerringly toward the spacious dining hall, Colt basked in the moment. With Opal beside him—though, sadly, they were no longer arm-in-arm—Colt willed himself to forget about the Renegades inside his fort, the goblins lurking without, and a certain midge who never tired of getting into trouble.

In that moment, he also shut out the voice of reason and dared to hope that someday Opal might return his feelings. Perhaps one day, she would hold his hand and mean it.

Despite an exhaustion borne of fighting for his life, Mitto did not sleep well the first night at Fort Faith. After having a night-mare—wherein his dear friend Baxter Lawler was being tor-mented by pitchfork-wielding goblins—he was afraid to fall back asleep, lest he have to witness the horrible scene all over again.

He told himself it was foolish to worry about Baxter. After all, the Knight was surely dead, and Mitto had always believed once you were dead, you were free from the pain and suffering of life.

But the nightmare had seemed so real that he now found himself fretting about Baxter's immortal soul. For the first time in many, many years, Mitto O'erlander uttered a serious prayer to the Gods of Good, imploring them to watch over his deceased friend.

Baxter was not the only person he worried about that night. His thoughts drifted back to Rydah, to Someplace Else. No matter how many times he told himself the inn and its namesake were safe, he couldn't shake the feeling Else was in danger. He regretted having left her, hated himself for following Toemis Blisnes on his fool's errand.

Nothing but trouble had found him since Toemis came into his life, and Mitto cursed the old man and his gold.

There were things about Fort Faith that Mitto found troubling too—the midge, for instance. In all his life, he had never slept under the same roof as a midge. Noel seemed harmless enough, but could one ever really trust someone so unpredictable and dangerous? And yet Noel wasn't even Mitto's biggest concern when it came to Fort Faith's inhabitants.

According to Opal, there was an entire band of Renegades currently residing at the fort, including a Renegade Leader. During their dinner together, Opal had told him how Klye Tris-tan and his Renegades had boldly stormed Fort Faith when they thought it housed the Crown Prince of Superius. Mitto nearly choked on his venison when he learned that a goblin spell-caster had been parading as Prince Eliot for gods only knew how long.

He had sat with his fork poised halfway between mouth and plate as the woman recounted the catastrophic battle that ended with the goblin trickster using its magic to escape.

Instead of throwing all of the Renegades into the dungeon, Fort Faith's commander—whose name, strangely enough, was Colt—took the wounded rebels to the fort's infirmary. Those who were not gravely injured were allowed to remain under house arrest if they promised not cause trouble. Only two of the Renegades, former pirates, were taken to the dungeon.

From the way Opal relayed the information, Mitto got the distinct impression she didn't agree with how Colt dealt with the Renegades.

In spite of the midge and rebels, he somehow managed to fall back asleep. He might have slept well into the afternoon but for a knock on the door. More than a little confused by his un-familiar surroundings, Mitto dragged himself out of bed. He expected to find a Knight—perhaps Commander Colt himself— or maybe Opal on the other side. Instead, he found a different red-haired woman standing there.

Sister Aric wore the same white gown with its cerulean cord of a belt. She looked well-rested.

"What time is it?" he asked, scratching his head through a mop of hair that was probably sticking up in every possible direction.

Standing there, shirtless and shoeless and with only trousers interrupting his nakedness, Mitto felt a wave of self-consciousness wash over him. Averting his eyes from hers, he mumbled an incoherent apology and walked over to where his shirt was draped over the back of a chair.

"It's nearly noon," the healer said as he pulled the tunic over his head.

"Damn, I hadn't meant to sleep this late." Mitto plopped down on the chair and reached for a sock. He didn't know what else to say to the woman, who had been a perfect stranger up until a few days ago. Chance—or misfortune—had thrown them together, but now that things had quieted down some, he realized he knew virtually nothing about her.

And now didn't really seem like the appropriate time to ask for her story.

"How are the…uh…patients?" he asked, glancing up at her.

Aric hadn't been smiling before, but now her face truly fell. "Toemis still has not awoken. I have done what I can for his body, but I fear he suffers from an ailment of the mind. He has fallen into a coma. All we can do now is pray."

Mitto nodded understandingly, as though prayer were part of his everyday routine.

"Ruben, on the other hand, is well on his way to recovery," she added, her countenance brightening.

Mitto paused in lacing his boot. "Who?"

"Ruben," she repeated. "Ruben Zeetan."

"Oh, the wizard," Mitto sneered. "I'm sure he'll fit in splendidly at this fort. Did you know there's a band of Renegades living here?"

Aric smiled thoughtfully. "Yes, I did. Several of the rebels are staying in the infirmary."

"And doesn't that bother you?" The merchant was now down on his hands and knees, searching for his boot's missing mate.

"It did at first," she admitted. "But they seem like nice enough people. The Renegade Leader is a bit too sarcastic for my liking, and Plake has a vulgar tongue, but for rebels, they are decent enough. And Othello has been doing a fine job as a healer, considering he has had no formal training."

Mitto seized the wayward boot, which had somehow managed to wander all the way under the bed, and sat down on the old mattress. "Well, it sounds like you've gotten cozy here rather quickly."

He didn't know what he had meant by that or why he felt annoyed with the woman for accepting the Renegades so easily. All he knew was he didn't intend to stick around and make friends with anyone, let alone rebels. When he glanced up from tying his bootlace, he found Sister Aric regarding him carefully.

"You forget, Master O'erlander. I have spent the past few years of my life working for the Knights at a fortress similar to this one."

He was half-tempted to ask her why she had chosen to waste the best years of her life at a fort but decided not to press the point. It wasn't any of his business. He stood up and walked over to her.

"Speaking of Fort Valor," he began, "do you know where I might find its commander? I thought maybe we could travel back east together whenever he plans on returning home."

Aric's face told an unhappy story.

"What?" he asked.

"I don't know how to tell you this, but Stannel has already gone."

"What!"

"He departed early this morning. Alone."

Mitto bit his tongue to stay the slew of curses that threatened to spill out of his mouth. Breathing heavily, he pushed past the healer and stormed out of the guestroom. He didn't know where he was going, and he didn't care.

How could Stannel have left without telling me? he fumed. Granted, we've only known each other for a couple of days, but after working together for our very survival…well…doesn't that mean *something*?

"Where are you going?" Aric called from the doorway of his room.

Mitto stopped suddenly. He had all but forgotten about the woman. "Where will I find Commander Colt? *He* didn't fly the coop, did he?"

"Of course not," the healer replied. "I've only just arrived here myself, Mitto. I don't know east from west at the moment, but I'm sure if you just took a deep breath and looked for someone who lives here…"

Mitto was already moving. The walls of Fort Faith were pressing in on him. He had to leave, had to get back to Rydah. "Forget Colt," he said, "I just want to find the way out. If Stannel can make it to Fort Valor alone, then so can I!"

The bravado of his words sounded hollow even to him, but he didn't care. What choice did he have? Sit and rot in this old castle like everyone else at Fort Faith? Hide away from the goblins and hope they disappear on their own? No, he couldn't wait around and hope for the best. He had to go.

"You're rather impulsive, you know that?" Aric said from several paces behind him. "I came to your room for a reason…to give you this."

As a businessman, Mitto was about as far from impulsive as a person could get—or at least he had been until he met Toemis Blisnes. Ever since that fateful moment, it had been one desperate decision after another.

But wasn't that always the way in the stories? The bag of

gold—which Aric was now presenting him—always brings nothing but trouble for the doomed fellow.

Well, unlike the character in the fables, Mitto wasn't going to play by Goblin's rules any more.

"You can keep the gold," he told her.

Maybe he was being impulsive, but at that moment, he cared only about getting back to Else.

Passage V

The first rays of morning light bathed the eastern horizon in a golden hue as Stannel, hunkered low on the back of his mount, raced with all speed away from Fort Faith. As far as he knew, there were but two viable routes to Fort Valor, and while the lesser-used path had seen them all safely to Fort Faith, Stannel kept to the main road.

It was the quickest route, and he figured the goblins had learned of the other path by now.

From what Mitto had told him about his encounters with the goblins and from what Stannel himself had observed of them, he would not have been surprised to encounter a barricade blocking his way. Despite the fact that most stories painted goblins as brutish, bestial killers, Stannel suspected they were far cleverer than most predators.

The goblins were not only intelligent, but also organized.

The notion of coming head to head with a brigade of goblins was not a pleasant one, but neither was Stannel overly concerned with the prospect of such an encounter.

Though the morning was but freshly begun, Stannel had been up for several hours. He had refused Colt's offers to join him for some wine the night before and had instead retreated to the privacy of his room.

Stannel Bismarc valued solitude above a good many things. It wasn't that he shunned the company of others Rather, he appreciated the opportunity to deliberate and meditate. Had anyone walked in on him last night, he would have found Stannel sitting with eyes closed and legs folded beneath him. Not many Knights meditated, as far as he knew, but he had come to terms with the fact that he was unlike most Knights in quite a few ways.

He had tried to tell some of his comrades at Fort Valor about the benefits of meditation, but no one had been interested in the idea of sitting idle for an hour or more. Then again, some Knights would not trade even an hour of sleep for all the gold in Superius.

Stannel never pressured his men. If they were to embrace a new path of living, they would have to make the decision on their own. Sometimes, however, it was difficult not to preach, particularly when he could see the weight of so many worries burdening a Knight. Perhaps at one time, he too had thought of meditation as a chore, something he *had* to do, but now he regarded the practice as a privilege and a pleasure.

He might have taken advantage of the ride to Fort Valor to engage in more meditation, but he knew better than to trade common sense for potential enlightenment. The goblins were a very real problem. He would keep all of his focus on watching for foes.

As he and the palfrey sped ever eastward into the warm light of the dawn, Stannel reflected back on his meeting with the young commander of Fort Faith. He saw a lot of potential in Saerylton Crystalus, but he also saw a fair measure of self-doubt and shortsightedness. Still, Colt had come off as a well-meaning and caring individual. In many ways, Stannel respected good intentions more than strict adherence to rules.

But that was always a source of tension within Stannel's own soul: the knightly way wasn't always the best way in his mind.

With a slight smile, Stannel recalled the look of shocked alarm on Colt's face when he had told him that he intended to travel to Fort Valor alone. Of course, Stannel had never used the word "alone." And at that moment, he did not feel alone. Ever since he had finished meditating that morning, he had been in near-constant commune with the Great Protector. The god's presence was as invigorating as the sunshine, and his company was as welcome as—no, *more* welcome than—a squadron of Knights riding at his side.

Stannel saw no sign of the goblins throughout the morn. At noontime, he was forced to rein the horse in for a rest a few yards off to one side of the road. The palfrey breathed hard, and her coat was slick with sweat, but the horse was otherwise comfortable as she chewed on the tall, withered stalks of vegetation. Stannel stretched his legs and munched distractedly on some hardtack, though he was not especially hungry.

He was alerted to the presence of goblins a split second before the palfrey flicked her ears and uttered an uneasy whinny. Between one bite of biscuit and the next, an eerie sensation had washed over him, filling him with feeling that something was wrong.

Dropping the half-eaten chunk of hardtack, Stannel reached not for the claymore strapped across his back, but for the mace that hung from his belt. He briefly considered a quick return to the saddle and an even quicker retreat from the vicinity, but somehow he knew it was too late to run. As he turned around in a circle in search of enemies, he studied the layout of his surroundings. With trees all around him, it would prove to be a confined battlefield, but then again, he was just one man. The obstacles were to his advantage.

Next, he ordered the horse to run away, punctuating his command with a swift slap to the palfrey's hindquarters. The horse obeyed, all too eager to flee. Almost immediately, he heard the snapping of twigs and the sound of mail scraping against the trunks of trees all around him. The enemy had wisely chosen to surround him in order to cut off his retreat.

As he lowered the visor of his helm, Stannel forced the stiffness from his frame, willed his heartbeat to slow to a normal pace, and cleared his mind of all distractions.

The feeling of wrongness intensified as, one by one, the goblins tore through the forest to form a circle around him. The soldiers glared and shouted foreign words at him. They waved their myriad weapons out before them and seemed to be waiting. Maybe, he thought, they expect me to drop my weapon and cower.

If that had been the goblins' expectations, they were to be sorely disappointed. Stannel placed his mace out before him, reached out to the Great Protector, and swung the blunt weapon in a three hundred and sixty-degree arc. The rounded head of the mace emitted a bronze light.

The goblins had only enough time to avert their eyes or scream out an obscenity before the ever-widening ring engulfed them. The circle of light struck with the force of a tempest, flinging the long-limbed creatures into trees, into one another, and to the ground. Some of the trees nearby were toppled as well.

When Stannel opened his eyes and took in the scene of

devastation he had wrought, he was filled with mixed emotions. He murmured his thanks to Pintor for granting him such power. At the same time, however, he mourned for the fallen trees. He even felt remorse for the goblins strewn across the forest floor.

He despised killing, and goblins, in spite of their repulsive appearance and wicked intentions, were still living beings. But all too frequently, a Knight had no choice but to kill in order to protect the innocent.

Judging by how few of the goblins were attempting to rise, he had killed all but five of the thirty-some creatures. Those who had hung back a bit had been spared the brunt of the bright barrage. Two of the five took to the forest without looking back. However, the remaining three flung themselves at him, probably hoping to bury their blades into him before he had the chance to release a second squall from the mace.

But Stannel didn't need the mace to dispatch three opponents in hand-to-hand combat.

Tossing the mace from his right hand to the left, he drew the claymore from its scabbard. In a flurry of movement, he relieved the first goblin of his spear weapon and then his head. All the while, a second goblin tried to press in on the Knight's flank, but Stannel used the mace to block the initial blow and forced the creature back with a swing of his own.

As the first goblin fell, the third one jumped over the still-warm body of his comrade and came at the Knight with a pair of mismatched swords.

The goblin to his left wielded a small axe and a dagger. Rather than attempt to parry the newcomer's swords, Stannel shifted to the right suddenly. As he did so, he swung his claymore, catching the third goblin in the arm and nearly tearing that limb from its socket. Meanwhile, the second goblin lunged forward and mistakenly impaled his ally with the dagger.

Out of an instinctual reaction—or perhaps the move was deliberate—the stabbed goblin howled and swung a rusty, curved blade at the one who had accidentally wounded him. Caught by surprise, the other goblin was in no position to do anything but scream as the saber ripped through his unprotected face.

The goblin dropped axe and dagger and fell to the ground, grasping at his ruined visage.

But Stannel had not been idle. When the goblin with the pair of swords turned on his fellow goblin, the commander quickly regained his balance and jabbed his claymore forward. His attention split between ally and enemy, the goblin could only make a desperate, futile attempt to knock the claymore aside with his remaining blade.

The move did nothing to impede Stannel's attack, and the claymore pierced the goblin's ragtag coat of chain mail and his chest. Goblin number three quickly followed goblin number two to the ground. Stannel cut the throat of the warrior clutching his mutilated face.

Other goblins were suffering a slow route to death, but Stannel left them where they lay-- not out of cruelty, but because he had no idea whether there were more enemies in the area. He hastily wiped the black blood from his blade and returned the claymore to its scabbard.

The mace remained in his hand, however, as he hunted for his missing steed.

The palfrey had escaped the notice of the goblins as well as the power of his mace. Stannel found the beast a few yards from the battlefield, grazing contentedly, as though it had never caught scent of the goblins. After sending silent thanks up to Pintor, Stannel mounted the horse and urged it back toward the road.

Fallen timber and goblin carcasses littered a forest floor stained with the goblins' dark blood. The sight made Stannel sick. Pintor's power was a multifaceted gift, but he never took pleasure in the destructive aspects of it. But Knight knew war was sometimes an unfortunate step in maintaining peace.

Saying another prayer of thanks to the Great Protector, he urged the horse to a full gallop. Without any further interruptions, he would reach Fort Valor, his home, before sunset.

Mitto never did find the Commander of Fort Faith that morning, and when he eventually ended up back at the entry hall, there was no sign of anyone. Aric had returned to the infirmary but not before reminding him how impetuous he was behaving.

Alone in the hall, Mitto stared at the thick doors standing between him and the freedom of the road—a road milling with goblins.

A part of him was tempted to throw open the doors, retrieve

his stallion from the stable, and take off after Stannel. But even if he was competent with a quarterstaff, he was a merchant, not a soldier. He likely wouldn't make it a mile before a black-headed arrow found its way to his throat. It was a disheartening thought, and his powerlessness only made him angrier.

Someone behind him cleared his throat.

Mitto, who had thought himself alone in the cavernous hall, started and spun around. He didn't recognize the man standing there. The fellow looked to be at least two decades younger than Mitto, probably in his mid-twenties. He was about the same height but he lacked the merchant's solid build.

Donned in a striped shirt and dull brown trousers, the man might have looked like nothing out of the ordinary except for the black hood that covered his entire head but left his face visible. He was smiling, but between the hood and the man's somewhat impish features, Mitto didn't know what to make of the gesture.

"Hi," the hooded fellow said, coming forward and holding out his hand. "I'm Scout. You're new here, right?"

Mitto shook his hand. "You could say that, but I'm not planning on staying long."

Scout laughed. "I wish I could say the same. I was following you for a while back there, and you didn't seem to know your way around. That's how I knew you were new...well, that and the fact that I had never seen you before. What do you say I give you a tour?"

Mitto regarded the man warily. He wanted nothing more than to be alone with his misery. "Thanks anyway."

"Come on. It's not like there's anything else to do, and the Knight's aren't going to let you wander outside."

"I'm not a prisoner here," Mitto snapped, and as he said it, it occurred to him that Scout could be.

"True enough," Scout said, "but with goblins prowling the countryside, the Knights'll make you stay for your own safety. At least, that's my guess. You know, you look kind of familiar. What's your name?"

"What?"

"You never told me your name."

"Oh. Sorry. I'm Mitto." As he spoke, he looked past Scout, searching for a tactful way out of the conversation.

Scout scratched his head, and as he did so, the hood pulled back far enough to reveal a few strands of brownish blond hair.

"Mitto...Mitto...hmmm... Well, it doesn't sound familiar. Maybe I've seen you during my travels. I get around...or at least I used to. Where are you from, Mitto?"

"Rydah," Mitto replied. "I'm a traveling merchant. I've been just about everywhere this side of the Crags."

"Really?" Scout asked. "I've been to Rydah a couple of times, mostly to deliver messages for Leslie. She's the Renegade Leader in Port Town. Did I mention I'm a Renegade?"

"No," Mitto said flatly.

"It was my job to deliver Leslie's messages to the other Renegade Leaders across the island," the rebel said, seemingly oblivious to Mitto's discomfort. "I never met the Renegade Leader in Rydah, though. I always had to talk with one of his lackeys. But I did meet Domacles Herronin. Have you ever heard of him?"

The name sounded familiar, but Mitto responded with a firm, "No. If you'll excuse me..."

He maneuvered around the Renegade and started walking back into the far reaches of the fortress. Undaunted, Scout followed right beside him.

"Well, like I said, I mainly worked with Leslie Beryl. In Port Town. But then Klye came through, and he needed someone to show him how to get to Fort Faith, so I volunteered. I guess technically I'm a member of his band now."

"Uh-huh."

"This hall will take you to the dining room," Scout told him as they proceeded down the path Mitto had randomly chosen. "Are you hungry?"

"No."

Scout smirked. "You sound like Othello. He's another Renegade in Klye's band. He doesn't talk much, but he's a good guy. Do you want to know why Klye and the rest of us came here in the first place?"

Mitto said nothing and kept on walking.

"Well, back in Continae...Superius, if I'm not mistaken ...Klye learned from someone that the Knights were going to reoccupy Fort Faith, so he and his friends...back then it was just him, Horcalus, Othello, and Plake...oh, and Ragellan. But Ragellan was killed be an assassin along the way." Scout confided that last part in a low tone.

"But, anyway, they came to Capricon...to Port Town...and

that's where they met me. Klye told Leslie he wanted to get here before the Knights did so the Renegades could claim the fort. Neither Les nor I could figure out just how he intended to hold out against Colt and his men…"

After a few more minutes of storytelling, Scout took a big breath. "Well, that brings us to Fort Faith. I was captured while spying, and then the rest of the band got caught while trying to capture the Prince of Superius—"

"Hold on!" Mitto stopped and glared at the man in the hood. "Now I know you're lying. You expect me to believe Eliot Borrom was here?"

"Yes…well, actually, no," Scout said. "We all thought it was Prince Eliot, but it was really a goblin shaman in disguise. He used dark magic…or *vuudu*, as Noel calls it…to make himself look like the prince. But we foiled the his plan…well, not me personally. I was locked in the dungeon the whole time."

Mitto stared in stupefied wonder at the Renegade. He didn't know what to make of Scout. A part of him was certain that the man was addled or at the very least, a pathological liar. And yet what he said contained enough elements of the truth to keep him guessing.

"Come on," Scout urged. "You might as well let me show you around. Unless I'm mistaken, you're going to be spending some time here."

Surrendering to the Renegade's discouraging logic, Mitto sighed and nodded.

Passage VI

When he heard the knock, Colt had half a mind to ignore it, fearing Noel had followed him to his office.

After listening to the midge's long list of advice on how magic could enrich the lives of the fort's inhabitants—suggestions that ranged from the impractical to the impossible—Colt needed a break. No one would blame him for ditching Noel, not that an old wooden door was going to stop the spell-caster.

And Noel wasn't known for knocking before entering...

The idea that it was someone else rapping on his door did nothing to lift Colt's spirits. And he couldn't quite stifle a groan at the thought of engaging in another meeting so soon. Each day seemed to bring new problems, and no one ever delivered good news. The temptation to disregard the knock was strong, but an inner voice demanded, "What kind of commander would I be if I hid from my responsibilities?"

"Enter," Colt called.

The door opened to reveal a man nearly twice as tall as any midge. Although Colt had never asked the man's age, he had always imagined his lieutenant to be in his late thirties, roughly the same age as his eldest brother. Gaelor Petton reminded Colt of his brother in other ways too. Both men were officers of high rank, and both of them had a penchant for gravity.

In truth, Colt knew very little about his second-in-command. They had met in Port Errnot only a couple of months ago. The long voyage across the Strait of Liliae had afforded Colt the opportunity to get to know many of his Knights, and he had spent much of the time in conversation with Gaelor Petton.

Mostly, though, they had discussed affairs of the Knighthood, including the myriad problems and concerns they would face while making Fort Faith habitable again. No "nonessential personnel" had been sent along with Colt's garrison—which was small enough as it was—which meant the Knights alone were expected to see to every task themselves. Divvying up the civilian duties, which ranged from carpentry to cooking, had been no small chore in itself.

But Petton had been up to the challenge. Colt's first impression of his lieutenant was that the man was incredibly dedicated. The Knights of Superius had a reputation for being a rigid and sometimes stuffy lot.

Gaelor Petton took that reputation to a whole new level.

It was as though Petton's devotion to duty had smothered all other aspects of his personality. Petton eat, drank, and breathed the Knighthood. Colt could count the number of times he had seen his lieutenant smile on one hand.

Since Petton almost never talked about himself or his past, most of what Colt knew about him came from the men. Word had it Petton had been stationed at a number of stations throughout his career. He had spent most of his time at Fort Majesty, where he had attained the rank of lieutenant.

But when Fort Majesty's commander retired, a lieutenant of lesser years had been promoted in Petton's stead. The men claimed Petton's disinterest in the human element was why he had been passed by. In other words, Gaelor Petton was not a "people person."

Colt had dismissed the rumor at the time, but now he thought the scenario was credible. Other tales claimed the lieutenant's stubbornness was the barricade that blocked his advancement. One Knight even claimed Petton had been found guilty of insubordination.

Colt thought Petton was far too concerned with promoting the chain of command to have ever broken it himself, but he did recall a conversation where Petton had hinted that his transfer from Fort Majesty to Fort Faith was a punishment for his outspokenness.

In many ways—in most ways, in fact—Gaelor Petton was more qualified to serve as the Commander of Fort Faith than Colt was. Thankfully, Petton had never acted resentful, and Colt valued Petton's opinions and suggestions.

Lately, however, the two of them seemed to be having the same disagreements over and over again.

Today, Colt would not be adding another smile to Petton's

meager tally. Upon entering the office, the lieutenant saluted stiffly, walked over to a vacant seat, and lowered himself into it. Although Petton did not slouch in the slightest, the man looked tired.

Every Knight at Fort Faith was accustomed to working hard, but ever since the goblin threat had been revealed, they had all been working longer hours in preparation for war. Petton had likely stayed up long after nightfall, only to wake before sunrise.

As routine dictated, Petton started the meeting with logistical assessments. How is the castle's larder? Stocked well enough for a typical winter but unsuitable for a drawn-out siege. How go the repairs to the western wing? The damage is isolated and not likely to escalate, but proper repairs cannot be made until true craftsmen can be brought in.

What else can be done to prepare for a goblin assault?

How are the men responding to the increased workload?

How is morale?

Colt was loath to ask that last question, even though he needed the answer. To his credit, Petton didn't launch into his familiar speech—at least not immediately.

"The men appear to be holding up well considering the circumstances," Petton said. "Most of them are eager to confront the goblins, but they understand the need for caution. I suppose it is natural to feel a little on edge while treading on the brink of war. Sir Silvercrown and I are confident in the men's preparedness for an attack.

"Of course, we'd be able to focus *all* of our energy on repelling the threat from without if we didn't have to worry about danger from within…"

For some reason, Colt decided to take the bait. "The men have been complaining?"

"In so many words," Petton replied. "One gets wary of constantly looking over his shoulder."

Careful to keep his voice even, Colt asked, "Why haven't any of them spoken to me about it?"

"You are their commander. They trust your decisions even if they are not what they themselves would choose in your place."

"Am I the only one who sees that the Renegades are not our enemy anymore?" When Petton didn't answer, Colt added, "Well, at least one of my men isn't afraid of expressing his opinion to me."

He had tried to keep the sarcasm out of his tone, but truthfully, he was getting tired of defending the rebels—or, more accurately, his trust in Klye and his band. Couldn't anyone else see that the Renegades were as enthusiastic about fighting the goblins as the Knights were? Couldn't they understand that any additional warriors would be an asset to the fort's defenses?

If Colt's comment had offended him, Petton hid it well. "The Renegades aren't the men's only worry."

Colt knew that Petton was referring to Noel. If the lieutenant despised anyone more than Klye Tristan, it was the midge.

"Noel has already proven his worth as far as I'm concerned," Colt argued. "Stannel and his entourage would have perished on the road...long before you and your men reached them."

Petton frowned, and Colt regretted his phrasing. The lieutenant wasn't bound to like Noel any better after being reminded of his own inadequacies. Of course, it was Noel's extraordinary qualities—namely, his magic—that made him a source of scorn for Petton in the first place.

Colt cleared his throat. "What I meant was—"

"I know what you meant, Commander. The midge's magic is an admittedly potent weapon, but may I remind you that fire burns human flesh as easily as goblins'."

Colt didn't respond. No words of his would change the lieutenant's opinion of Noel. He could only hope that Petton and the other Knights would come to see Noel's—and the Renegades'—virtues in time.

Since there was nothing else to say on the matter, Colt changed the subject back to the goblins. The two officers debated the idea of sending another messenger eastward, but in the end, they both agreed that waiting to hear from Stannel was the wiser move.

Stannel Bismarc had made a valid point about conserving Fort Faith's troops. Colt didn't know how many troops were stationed at the neighboring fortress, but Fort Faith would need all of its defenders, especially if T'slect's armies had already reached Capricon.

When it was obvious neither man had anything more to say, Petton rose, saluted, and headed for the door without saying goodbye. Colt tried not to take it personally, though he couldn't help but wonder if the lieutenant behaved so aloofly with all of his associates.

Colt blew out a breath he had been unconsciously holding when Petton shut the door behind him. There were times when he found Petton more frustrating than Noel. At least Noel had an excuse—he was a midge. Colt was beginning to suspect Petton would never give up trying to convince him of Noel's and the Renegades' evils.

And yet he couldn't blame Petton for trying to keep Fort Faith safe. And Colt couldn't deny his own leadership style was unconventional at best.

But even if my impressions of Klye and his band prove tragically amiss, I can't ignore the dictates of my conscience, Colt thought. Maybe Petton should have been named commander in my place, but since he wasn't, he'll just have to respect my decisions.

His thoughts adrift in a sea of melancholy, Colt couldn't quite stifle the yawn that overcame him. Although it wasn't yet noon, he felt ready to call it a day. It was at times like this that Colt wondered how any foot soldier could aspire for a command of his own.

Diplomacy was far more exhausting than swinging a sword!

The woman in white told her Toemis isn't dead but that he is still very sick. Sitting quietly beside Toemis's bed, she thinks he sure looks dead. He looks small too.

When Toemis is up and walking around, she always feels much smaller than him. Toemis is a grownup, but lying there in the bed, he looks more like a rag-doll than a person. His chest rises and falls. He breathes, but he doesn't wake up.

The woman in white says he is not dead, but what's the difference between dying and sleeping forever?

She has seen dead people before. She was there when Julian died. She was also there when Larissa died. Both times there was a lot of blood, but Toemis is not bleeding at all. He has an ugly scab on his forehead. Maybe if Toemis bleeds, he will die. Maybe you can't die unless you bleed, she thinks.

When Julian died, Larissa was still around to take care of her, and when Larissa died, she still had Toemis. The woman in white is very kind to her. She has pretty red hair, and she is young. At night, she sleeps in the same room with the woman in white, even though she would rather stay with Toemis. She thinks that if Toemis wakes up in the middle of the night, he might get confused and leave without her.

But she doesn't fuss when the woman in white talks her into going with her. Toemis always told her not to talk to strangers, but the woman in white has done nothing but help her since Toemis got sick. And she's helping Toemis, so she can't be a wicked woman.

Julian used to tell stories about witches and harpies who used spells to make themselves look young and beautiful, even though they are really old crones. Sometimes, it looks like the woman in white is making spells.

The woman in white told her she is a healer, but if she is a healer, why can't she make Toemis wake up? But when the woman gives her food to eat and tucks her into bed at night, she thinks the woman is nice—even if she is a witch. Maybe there are good witches.

Julian told her many stories about monsters, witches, and men with swords. Larissa told her not to believe Julian, but since leaving home, she has seen monsters, magic, and men with swords. So Julian was right after all.

She doesn't know where she is, but she knows she is where Toemis wanted them to be. Toemis never told her why they were coming to this place or even what a Fort Faith is, and she never asked him. She didn't want to make Toemis mad by bothering him with questions because Toemis doesn't like to talk much.

But if Toemis never wakes up, she will never know why she came to a place full of men with swords.

She is watching Toemis now, waiting for him to wake up. She decides the first thing she must ask him is why they *really* are here. He told a lot of other people that he used to have a job here, but she doesn't think that is true. Before Julian and Larissa lost their blood and died, Toemis never lied even once, but Toemis has changed a lot since then.

Sometimes he seems like someone else.

Julian or Larissa never talked about Toemis being a cook. And Toemis's food always tastes like burnt.

When the woman in white asks her about her grandfather, she doesn't tell her anything. Sometimes she is so silent that the other people in the room forget she is there. She listens to what they say and has heard many interesting stories. They remind her of Julian's stories.

*   *   *

As day eased into evening, the air became heavy with a damp chill. Stannel wore a thick cloak over his armor, but it did little to temper the bite of the cold autumn night. The sunless sky shone almost white, and although it had not snowed yet, he could smell hints of winter in every breeze.

Little more than a month ago, he had sweated in the bright summer sun. But summer had ended abruptly, and now it seemed that autumn too was preparing to depart.

Capricon's weather was irregular at best. Having lived on the island for the past twenty-five years, Stannel was accustomed to the unpredictability of the seasons, yet it was almost as though winter were eager to conquer the land with its bitter cold and heavy snows

Better winter than the goblins, he thought.

Winter was the bane of war. Even light snowfall delayed troop movements, and heavy blizzards could defeat a battalion as effectively as any mortal foe. Unless the goblins knew of methods he himself was unfamiliar with, Stannel thought that the invaders would have a difficult time so late in the year. The defender almost always had the advantage during long winters, especially if the castle was well stocked. Waging a winter siege was tantamount to suicide.

But the Commander of Fort Valor knew nothing of goblin tactics. Maybe the goblins would withdraw from the island at the first freeze. More likely, they had their own ways to counter winter's complications. If the goblin army employed magic-users—like T'slect, the shaman Colt had told him about—then that would bring an entirely new dynamic to the Knights' offensive and defensive strategies.

Slowing his tired steed to a brisk walk, Stannel tried to recall everything he had ever read about the goblin war that had been fought on the island centuries ago. Like his good friend Magnes Minus, he had an interest in studying the past, but unlike the Lord of Capricon, who combed ancient texts and newer resources alike, Stannel preferred the history of Glenning and Superius exclusively.

In fact, it was the goblins' invasion of Novislond that prompted the first alliance between the two kingdoms.

Stannel prayed to Pintor to unlock his memory and reveal the details he had long ago gleaned about specific battles and skirmishes. He had tried this exercise earlier, during the trek from the lodge to Fort Faith, but the same bits of information surfaced repeatedly in his mind. The goblins had overwhelmed both knightly factions with sheer numbers. In most clashes, the disciplined human warriors had been no match for the ferocious and frenzied tactics of the goblins. He also remembered reading about barbaric traps and snares.

The greatest advantage the goblins had held, however, was the element of surprise—an advantage they maintained three hundred years later.

Unless the population of Capricon could be warned and prepared, Stannel thought.

Despite the low temperature, Stannel urged his mount into a run. Truth be told, Stannel didn't mind the cold. At first, the crisp, frigid air had sharpened his senses, and he was ever watchful for goblins. But as the hours passed, the cold seeped into his bones.

Focusing his thoughts and directing them inward, the Knight willed the blood flowing through his veins and arteries to quicken. After that, Stannel hardly noticed the cold.

The trek from Fort Faith to Fort Valor was not so long, considering that many of Capricon's cities and towns were a full day's travel apart. Normally, Stannel would have enjoyed such a jaunt. He had often traversed the highway from his fortress to Rydah while on official business for the Knighthood. He had also visited the capital for personal reasons.

No matter his purpose, Stannel always enjoyed the sights, sounds, and smells of the forest that covered most all of the island's northeastern region. He enjoyed the opportunity to bask in the natural beauty of Capricon, his adopted home.

But today, riding with on such an urgent errand and with the threat of goblins hanging as heavily as the moisture in the air, Stannel hardly noticed the grand trees, which were almost completely bare. The only smell that filled his nostrils was the tang of rotting vegetation.

No, there was something else too, a new odor, though Stannel couldn't immediately identify it. The scent reminded him of a campfire, but at the same time, there was a sickening taint to the otherwise agreeable aroma.

His skin prickling, Stannel urged the palfrey ever faster. His heart pounded in his ears, but he did nothing to slow his pulse. Once he crested the hill before him, he would have an unencumbered view of Fort Valor.

But what to make of the gloomy haze darkening the sky?

Then he understood.

A metal-clad fist seemed to take hold of his insides and squeeze mercilessly when he reached the top of the hill. He doubled over in his saddle and closed his eyes to block out the terrible sight, tears streaming down his beard.

Passage VII

Thanks to Scout, Mitto had seen most of Fort Faith on his first full day there. All throughout the tour, the rebel spoke of people Mitto had never heard of, including the Mayor of Port Town and his daughter, Leslie, who had become a Renegade Leader somewhere along the line. Scout also talked about the men—and woman—who made of Klye Tristan's band, regaling Mitto with a most incredible story.

Scout had even offered to introduce him to Klye, who was recovering in the infirmary, but Mitto flat out refused him. It wasn't that he was intimidated by the prospect of meeting a Renegade Leader—well, that wasn't the entire reason.

It was the sickroom's other occupants he was really avoiding. He guessed Zusha, the girl who looked and acted like a young child but wasn't, spent most of her time there, and he wanted nothing to do with her or her grandfather.

Let Sister Aric take care of the girl. She wasn't his responsibility. And as for the healer, Mitto held an admittedly irrational grudge against her. Since Stannel wasn't there to bear the brunt of his anger, Aric would have to pick up the tab.

However, by his second morning at the fort—really, his third day at Fort Faith—Mitto was tempted to call a truce in his one-sided grudge with the healer. Opal had proven good company that first evening, but he had not seen much of her since then. And since the Knights seemed to have neither the time nor inclination to converse with him, his companionship was limited to the very man whom, yesterday, he had done all he could to ditch.

Most of that second morning was spent in conversation at the breakfast table, where Scout retold just about all of same stories as yesterday. By this time, Mitto was beginning to see how all of the tales fit together. And since the major details remained the same from one telling to the next, he was forced to concede that Scout could be telling the truth.

He listened closely as the Renegade spoke of his encounters with goblins, beginning with an ambush in the sewers of Port Town.

"I'd been down there before," Scout said between mouthfuls of porridge. "In the sewers, I mean. It's not the most pleasant of places, but when you're on the wrong side of the law, you have to make do with what you have…and it's not like anyone in the Three Guards was likely to follow you down there."

Scout, who apparently didn't even remove his black hood during meals, took a big bite of bread before continuing. "Of course, now that I know there are goblins living down there, I'll steer clear of the underground passages for a while."

Mitto surprised himself by asking, "But the goblins attacked you, right?"

"Yeah," Scout said, his mouth full of food. After swallowing, he added, "I was taking Leslie and Klye to an inn called Oars and Omens. Klye's men were staying there, and so were a clan of pirates who were considering an alliance with Les's Renegades."

Mitto remembered Scout telling him how Leslie Beryl had sought out some pirates, hoping to supplement her own forces with the battle-ready buccaneers. The two pirates who were locked in a cell beneath Fort Faith had been from that clan, though Mitto couldn't recall why Pistol and Crooker had joined Klye's band.

There was simply too much to keep straight, and Mitto was interested only in how the goblins fit into everything.

Still, after learning of Leslie's plan to hire mercenary pirates to fight beside her Renegades, Mitto couldn't help but wonder at how far the rebellion might have gone if the goblins hadn't been revealed as the true threat. The Knights and Renegades at Fort Faith had put aside their differences in the face of foreign invasion, but would others follow suit before it was too late?

Scout was also worried about those he had left behind in Port Town.

"None of us knew what the monsters were at first," the rebel was saying. "We thought maybe they were new creatures that no one had ever happened upon before…that maybe they had lived down there since the days when dwarves ruled the island. We had no way of knowing the goblins were planning an invasion."

Scout's expression soured as he spoke. "For all I know, Les still doesn't know what the goblins have planned. She's probably still under the impression that her father, the mayor, is the enemy. I'd bet all the beer in Hylan that the goblins are somehow using their *vuudu* to control him. I've known Crofton Beryl since I was no taller than this table. He used to be a hero to the people, but now he's a menace. If I could only convince the Knights to let me go so I can go back and warn everyone…"

The man lapsed into an uncharacteristic, brooding silence. For the rest of the meal, he said nothing, and Mitto likewise remained silent. Hearing Scout's account of the goblins in Port Town's sewers sent chills down his spine. If the goblins had settled beneath that city, who could say what kind of a hold they might have in Rydah?

Most of all, Mitto wondered how many of the damned monsters already called Capricon home.

It was a depressing subject to ponder, so when Scout offered—as he had offered the day before—to introduce him to some of the other Renegades, Mitto thought twice before turning him down. On one hand, he had little else to do, since he hadn't yet thought of a plan to get him safely from Fort Faith to Rydah.

On the other hand, the other Renegades might provide more information about the goblins. Scout hadn't been there for the actual fight that had taken place in Fort Faith's war room, the battle that had pitched Knight and Renegade alike against a powerful goblin wizard.

Deciding that he ought to learn everything he could about the enemy before returning to Rydah, Mitto said, "All right."

From what Scout had told him yesterday the Renegades were allowed to roam Fort Faith freely. Their weapons had been confiscated, though Scout still wore a small, empty sheath at his belt. Aside from the two rebels recovering in the infirmary and the one who was assisting Sister Aric, the others spent most of their time together in an empty storeroom.

Mitto had passed by the room with barely a look yesterday, but today he followed Scout through the wide entryway, feeling both nervous and excited.

Ultimately, he was disappointed to find nothing more than an old table, some chairs, and a lot of open space inside. He had envisioned a room full of rough-looking, battle-scarred men huddled together, plotting their escape from confinement. Instead of a small mob, he found no more than three people occupying the room.

One of them sat beside the table, staring out a window. He looked to be no more than sixteen years old, which was far too young to be a Renegade, as far as Mitto was concerned. The other two rebels, a man and a woman, were engaged in combat.

While the rebels had been forced to forfeit their weapons, the wooden practice swords that the warriors wielded apparently posed no threat to the Knights. As he followed Scout over to the young man by the window, Mitto didn't take his eyes off the duelists.

The man, who stood a half a foot taller than the woman, had an almost mechanical style, his body and weapon acting and reacting in carefully measured movements. The woman, who wore her blond hair in a short ponytail, attacked and counter-attacked in a similar style, but Mitto thought she had to work a little harder than her opponent. Her face was slick with sweat, and unlike the man, she was breathing hard.

"Mitto, I'd like you to meet Arthur," Scout said. "Arthur, this is Mitto."

The boy merely glanced at the two of them for a moment before returning his gaze to something out the window.

"Pleased to make your acquaintance," Mitto muttered.

Scout made a face at the boy's turned head before leading Mitto away from the table.

"You have to forgive him," Scout whispered. "He's been like this ever since we got here. No one knows why. Even Horcalus, who is a bit claustrophobic, has taken to captivity better than Arthur. But he's young…he'll bounce back…I think."

Mitto nodded absently. He had already dismissed the dismal youth from his thoughts and was once more watching the man and woman swing at each other with the blunt swords. It wasn't the merchant's first time seeing a woman warrior, though many cities refused to employ female soldier—and the Knights of Superius had yet to admit a single woman in their ranks.

Women warriors typically found employment in mercenary bands, where skill, not gender, decided one's pay. After hearing so much about Leslie Beryl and now seeing this blond swords-woman engaged in mock battle, Mitto realized the sex was overlooked within the rebellion too.

And he was impressed with the Renegade woman, who fought as passionately and skillfully as any Knight Mitto had witnessed. As he watched the woman gracefully avoid her rival's weapon, he noticed for the first time something inherently intimate in the struggle of life and death, even when it was merely an imitation.

When the couple's swords locked, the man proved stronger of the two, though the woman pushed back with all of her might. Then, she suddenly darted to one side. At the sudden loss of support, the man pitched forward a step. The woman tried to take the advantage, spinning around with her wooden sword extended in hope of catching the man in the back.

Unfortunately—because Mitto found himself rooting for the woman—the man nimbly dodged the blow and countered with a strike of his own, aimed at the hilt of his opponent's weapon.

The dull sword hit the woman's hand with a loud thwack. Crying out in surprise and probably pain, she dropped her weapon and grasped her offended hand with the other. Smoothly, almost routinely, the man followed through with his move, returning his mock blade to the ready before bringing his elbow back and thrusting the sword forward into his rival's belly.

"You are dead," the man announced and then drew back his sword, which had stopped an inch from her abdomen.

The woman flapped her wounded hand like she was trying to dislodge the pain. Then she brought her knuckles up to her mouth. Mitto expected her to be angry in defeat, that the passion of the fight would overflow into the aftermath of the struggle, but to his surprise, the woman laughed.

"I thought I had you there at the end," she said.

The man shrugged. "You weren't far from it."

Mitto watched their body language, hoping to find some hint about the nature of their relationship. But if the two were anything more than practice partners, he couldn't discern it. Truth be told, he was having some difficulty believing the two of them were Renegades. They seemed too...civil.

Beside him, Scout burst into applause. "Well done, Horcalus." To the woman he said, "You'll get him next time."

Both combatants regarded Scout and Mitto blankly.

Mitto cleared his throat.

"Oh, yeah, right," Scout began. "This is Mitto O'erlander.

He's a traveling merchant who got stranded here because first highwaymen and then goblins attacked his wagon. Mitto, this is Dominic Horcalus and Lilac Zephyr."

Horcalus made a slight bow. "Well met, Master O'erlander."

"Please, call me Mitto."

The swordsman nodded, but said nothing more. Lilac took his hand gingerly and gave it a slight shake. Her knuckles were still red from where Horcalus's blade had smacked them.

"It's nice to meet you," she said.

Now that he was standing face-to-face with her, he saw she was rather plain, and yet her smile had a charm all of its own.

Before any of them could say anything more—not that Mitto really knew what to say—the boy beside the window jumped to his feet so suddenly his chair clattered noisily against the table.

"What is it, Arthur?" Horcalus was already moving toward the boy.

Arthur didn't reply, and when Lilac and Scout followed Horcalus over to the window, Mitto joined them.

"Look! Someone is coming...riding hard," Scout said, pointing at a shape on the horizon.

The four of them watched in silence as the solitary rider drew nearer. Mitto squinted against the brightness of the sun, for the window faced east, and the day was still young.

A second later, Mitto recognized the man who racing toward the Fort.

Colt nearly had to run to keep up with the older commander. Stannel said not a word as the two of them retraced the steps they had taken just two days prior. Colt stole sidelong glances at his fellow commander, trying to find whatever clues he could, but Stannel's stolid stare, which focused unwaveringly before him, revealed nothing about why he had returned to Fort Faith so soon.

Colt didn't even know whether Stannel had made it to Fort Valor before turning back to Fort Faith. It didn't seem likely, judging at how short a time Stannel had been gone. Why, he would have had to turn around immediately upon reaching his fortress to make it back so soon, Colt reasoned. And even then he would've had to travel day and night alike.

When they finally reached Colt's office, the younger commander gestured for Stannel to take a seat, which he did without comment. Colt took his own place across the desk and waited for the Knight to explain himself.

Staring into Stannel's green-blue eyes, Colt might have thought he was looking at a different man altogether. Stannel looked older somehow, as though all of his years—and then some—had caught up with him all at once. The image of the depleted Knight lingered for but a moment. Then the Commander of Fort Valor took a deep breath and began his tale.

Colt sat engrossed as he listened to Stannel recount his encounter with the goblins while taking a rest off the road. Stannel glossed over much of the details of the battle, sufficing it to say that the Great Protector had seen him through the struggle. He explained how little else of consequence had occurred during his trek to Fort Valor, but when Stannel spoke of the peculiar feeling that came over him and the strange smell in the air that grew stronger as he neared his destination, Colt felt something heavy in the pit of his stomach.

"There is nothing but rubble left of Fort Valor."

The words nearly knocked Colt off his chair. Surely, he had misheard the man. "What?"

Keeping his gaze level, Stannel said, "Fort Valor is no more."

"But...but how?" Colt stammered. While he had never seen the place with his own eyes, he suddenly found it impossible to believe the fort was gone.

"I do not know how. The battle was over before I arrived." Stannel said these last words with just a hint of bitterness. "All I know is that my fortress has been utterly destroyed. The towers were felled like trees, and the walls resemble those of a sandcastle that cannot hope to withstand the tide. Everywhere is the stain and stench of fire, as though something had burned through solid stone."

Colt could only shake his head. He had seen many marvels since his arrival, had witnessed magic in its many forms—from the powers of his own crystal sword to T'slect's *vuudu* spells that had destroyed much of Fort Faith's western wing—but he simply couldn't imagine any spell powerful enough to burn a stone fortress to the ground.

What chance did the Knights have against a foe that could decimate a castle just by uttering a few words?

He didn't know what to say to Stannel, could not conjure up any words of comfort. Nothing could ever make up for what the man had lost. Colt had yet to forgive himself for the men who had been killed by T'slect. The loss of everything—and everyone at the fort—would have surely crippled him.

"I found no sign of survivors," Stannel said, answering Colt's unasked question. "There were bodies of men and goblins alike strewn about the area. The Knights were picked clean of weapons and armor. The goblins cared as little for their own dead as they did the bodies of their enemies, leaving them to rot where they fell. Then again, I am no better for I did not linger long enough to dig graves."

"Stannel, I am so dearly sorry—"

The elder Knight cut him off. "There is no time for that now, Colt. I left the corpses for the vultures because I know they are beyond my help...beyond the help of any man now. Their souls reside in Paradise beside Pintor and the other Gods of Good. Now is not the time to lose ourselves in sadness or regret. Now is the time to act."

Stannel's calm exterior made the ardor of words all the more powerful. The Knight was hurting inside, Colt was sure, but Stannel appeared to be using his pain as an impetus rather than another obstacle.

Pushing his own pain aside, Colt swallowed hard and asked, "What do you propose we do?"

"We now know for certain there is at least one goblin army in Capricon. We must spread word as far as we can, from one coast to another, if possible. But our priority still lies with warning Lord Minus and the capital."

Thinking Stannel was perhaps planning to take on that mission alone, Colt said, "I agree, but such an important task cannot be trusted to one man alone."

"Yes," Stannel said, "but the group must be small so they can travel with all speed while avoiding detection."

Colt was already nodding. "My own forces are small, but I can spare Knights for this mission."

"No."

Colt blinked in confusion.

Stannel added, "We do not know where the goblins will turn next. If they set their sights on your fortress, you will need each and every one of your men ready to defend it."

It was a logical argument, but...

"If we don't send Knights to Rydah, who will go?"

Immediately after uttering the question, Colt realized he already knew the answer.

"You have come to trust the Renegades because they want to defeat the goblins as badly as you do," Stannel said. "Well, now is the time to put your faith to the test."

Colt couldn't find the words to speak.

Stannel got to his feet. "The fate of Capricon may well rest in the hands of our former enemies."

Passage VIII

Klye hid his surprise when Lieutenant Petton and two other Knights arrived to escort him from the infirmary. Petton led the way, not bothering to see if his prisoner was keeping up. The Knights who flanked him took hold of his arms, a position that simultaneously supported and confined him.

Perhaps Colt has decided to toss me in the dungeon after all, Klye thought.

He allowed the Knights to guide him down one passage after another and was relieved when Petton went up a flight of stairs rather than down. While he knew little about fort's layout, he was certain that the dungeon was somewhere below.

But he refused to give Petton the satisfaction of asking where they were going.

The lieutenant, for his part, seemed distracted. He hadn't even taken the time to glare at him. Petton led him into a room where Colt was sitting behind an unremarkable desk. Aside from Petton, who had initially questioned him and threw the occasional derogatory comment his way, Colt was the only Knight at the fort who ever spoke with him.

He wondered why Colt hadn't come for him himself but was prepared to wait for an answer.

A second man sat off to the side, not beside Colt, but not quite facing him either. The man regarded Klye impassively as the two Knights lowered him into an empty chair. Colt then dismissed the men, though, to Klye's disappointment, Petton was allowed to remain.

The three of them—Colt, Petton, and the mystery man—stared at him in silence for a moment. Klye was accustomed to the lieutenant's hard stares, and he thought he knew where he stood with Colt, so he concentrated on the third man, returning the man's gaze with a scrutinizing stare of his own.

The man was dressed like a Knight, bedecked in plate armor with a hefty sword strapped to his back. Judging by the white in his hair and the few wrinkles near his eyes and mouth, Klye guessed he was quite a few years older than Colt.

"Commander," Colt said to the man, "this is Klye Tristan, the Renegade Leader of which I have told you. Klye, this Sir Stannel Bismarc, Commander of Fort Valor."

Before Klye could reply, the older man said, "I am the *former* Commander of Fort Valor. Fort Valor has been destroyed by the goblins."

Klye listened in mute wonder as Stannel recounted his hasty ride to Fort Valor yesterday and the macabre sight that met him when he finally reached his destination. While T'slect had told them the goblins were planning to invade Capricon, Klye never expected the invasion to come so swiftly—or so devastatingly.

"We have no way of knowing whether the goblins have attacked the capital yet," Stannel was saying, "or even if Lord Minus is aware of the invaders. But if Capricon is to prevail, we must get word to Rydah and coordinate our efforts."

All right, Klye thought, that makes sense. But what does any of this have to do with me?

"I'm no military strategist," Klye said, "but I've had a few clashes with the goblins. I'll tell you whatever I can if it'll help."

"Your help is indeed essential," Stannel said, "but story telling is not what we had in mind."

Klye mulled over the cryptic words, looking at Colt for some help. The young commander had said nothing since introducing him to Stannel, and even now he seemed reluctant to speak. Klye found Colt's silent stare unnerving. What? Klye wondered. Do I have something hanging from my nose?

Finally, Colt let out a long breath and spoke. "With Fort Valor…gone, Fort Faith is the only strictly martial fortification left in this region. Rydah may have many more Knights in its garrison, but those soldiers are burdened with defending a large civilian population. Even if Rydah has escaped the goblins' attention thus far, the capital alone cannot hope to protect the other towns of eastern Capricon."

"All right…" Klye drawled, prodding Colt to get to the point.

"Because Fort Faith has become…quite unexpectedly, a key factor in the island's security, we cannot reduce our already insufficient numbers by sending Knights away from their post, even though we must get word to Rydah of what has occurred at Fort Valor."

Then it became perfectly clear.

"You need expendable soldiers to take on this all-important-yet-incredibly-dangerous mission," Klye deduced. "And you have my Renegades in mind for the job."

Colt said nothing, but Petton's scowl told Klye he had hit the mark. He glanced at Stannel, wondering where the former commander's opinion lay, but Stannel's features had not altered one way or another. He continued to stare at Klye, perhaps waiting for him to say more.

Colt also looked expectant and perhaps unsure whether he was doing the right thing—not that Klye could blame him.

"You know I want to do my part," Klye said. "I have a score to settle with T'slect and all goblins, for that matter. We all do. But as you can see, I'm in no position to go traipsing around the war-torn countryside on a suicide mission."

"I thought suicide missions were right up your alley," Petton muttered.

Colt raised a hand to silence the lieutenant and, likely, to stay Klye's sarcastic reply. When the young commander spoke again, his voice was softer. "I know you are still too weak to take on such an arduous task, Klye, though both of us wish you weren't. There's no way you can go to Rydah, but there are members of your band who are in better condition, warriors who might help us if you gave them your blessing."

My blessing? Klye scoffed inwardly. I'm their leader, not their god. Still, he knew his Renegades were a loyal lot, and some of them wouldn't comply with the Knights' requests unless they knew he had sanctioned it.

But Klye also knew Colt was asking for more than his permission.

He decided to press his luck.

"I'll do whatever I can," he replied. "As you well know, my men tire of wasting away in this old fort. Most of them are itching for another chance to fight the goblins. My men are few, but they are capable...the fact that we're all still alive is proof of that. But we work best as a team. Granted, I won't be able to join them all on this quest, but—"

"They are not *all* going," Petton said flatly.

Klye glared at the lieutenant but bit back a sharp retort. He wouldn't let the antagonistic Gaelor Petton bait him into an argument. He was finally in a position to help his Renegades, the men—and woman—who had risked their very lives under his command. It was his fault they were stuck at Fort Faith, and even though the Knights were treating them well, it was his responsibility to fight on their behalf.

"So who *is* going?" Klye asked Colt.

"That has not been decided yet." Colt fixed his gaze on his fingers, which were folded and resting on the desk. "That is why we have asked you here."

I don't remember being asked, Klye thought wryly. "Well, who do you have in mind?"

Colt took a deep breath. "The party bound for Rydah must take a circumspect route, avoiding the main road at all costs. We need someone with a wary eye…someone who is accustomed to traversing stretches of untamed land."

"Othello," Klye concluded.

Colt nodded. "From everything you have told me of him, Othello would be the perfect guide for the party."

"What about Scout?" Klye asked. "He's been all over Capricon, including Rydah. Othello makes a great lookout, but like me, he's new to the island. With both Othello and Scout in the party, you'll increase the likelihood of success."

Colt met and held Klye's gaze. "Scout will not be leaving the fort."

Klye waited for the commander to explain himself.

"I don't doubt his abilities. But Scout has been quite vocal about his desire to return to Port Town so that he can warn the Renegade Leader there about the goblins, which, as you know, is not the most important objective at this point."

"You doubt his loyalty," Klye stated.

Colt sighed again. "I don't believe Scout would actively jeopardize the mission, but he might take advantage of his freedom to further his own agenda."

"And you aren't going to change your mind?"

"I'm afraid not."

Scout's eagerness and honesty had done him in. Klye was forced to conclude that there was nothing he could do for the man. "Othello it is then," Klye concluded helplessly. "He's a talented archer, but that skill is severely undermined in a melee.

You will need warriors trained for close combat…men who will fight as viciously and fearlessly as the goblins themselves."

"You are referring to the pirates," Colt said with a faint smile.

Klye nodded.

"That isn't possible," Colt said. "They are too unpredictable, and they stand to gain the most from deserting." Klye opened his mouth to argue, but Colt quickly added, "And, no, I am not going to change my mind."

Klye folded his arms. "Why did you bother to 'ask' me here if you've already made up your mind?"

"We have not made up our minds about everyone," Colt said. "Lilac, for instance…she joined the Renegades after she learned the false Prince Eliot had her brother, a Knight, killed. She sought out your band because she had also learned the imposter sent assassins to hunt down Chester Ragellan and Dominic Horcalus."

Klye said nothing. He and Colt had been over it all before. He had told the commander all about the misadventures that had brought him to Fort Faith, including everything he himself had learned about the Renegades in his band.

Colt went on. "Out of all of your men, she is perhaps the least guilty of wrongdoing. And then there is the matter of her sword."

Klye could hold back his sarcasm no longer. "So you intend to let them carry weapons? What if they decide to throw in with the goblins? Lilac's vorpal sword can cut through a Knight's mail as easily as a goblin's."

"He makes a valuable point," Petton said smugly.

"Klye, this is a delicate issue. Up until a week ago, the Renegades were our enemy. We are investing an awful lot of faith, so please have some patience here."

Klye had never seen Colt so exasperated. "Fine, fine. I'm sorry. Yes, I'll vouch for Lilac. Even without her enchanted blade, she's an effective warrior."

"What about Plake?" Colt asked.

"He's lousy in a fight that requires more than bare fists. He's obnoxious, pugnacious, and doesn't like to follow orders. As much as I'd love to get him out of the infirmary and far away from the fort, I wouldn't recommend adding him to the party."

"Very well. What about Arthur?"

Klye nearly laughed out loud. Arthur had not so much joined his band as gotten swept away with it. Out of everyone in the band, he knew the least about Arthur.

"Arthur is even more useless in combat than Plake. He's young and inexperienced."

Klye didn't bother mentioning that Arthur's disposition had taken a turn for the peculiar since the Renegades had gotten caught. Horcalus was very worried about the boy, but neither he nor Klye knew what to do to buoy Arthur's spirits. Lately, the boy kept to himself.

"That leaves Horcalus," Klye said after a moment. "As a former Knight, he's the most qualified to lead the party."

Colt exchanged a glance with Petton before saying, "We remain undecided about whether to allow Horcalus to join the party. I am convinced of his loyalty to Superius, but Lieutenant Petton has his reservations."

I'll just bet he does, Klye thought.

"You'll find no better swordsman in my band," Klye argued. "He is honorable and fair, not to mention an experienced warrior. Unless you plan on sending Othello and Lilac alone, I suggest you include him."

Petton opened his mouth—likely to object—but then there came the sounds of a scuffle from on the other side of the door. The sound of a man's voice could be heard, followed by the harsh replies of the sentries. Something knocked against the door, and all three Knights—Stannel, Colt, and Petton—rose to their feet.

Klye, thinking it best to conserve his strength, remained seated, though he craned his neck to look back at the door.

With one hand on the hilt of his sheathed broadsword, Petton wrenched open the door, revealing a single man who was in the process of struggling against the sentries. To Klye's relief, it was not one of his Renegades.

"I demand you let me in!" the stranger shouted. "I must speak with Stannel before he sneaks off again!"

While Klye had never seen the middle-aged, three-cornered-hat-wearing man before, he did recognize faces in the crowd behind him. Lilac, Horcalus, and Scout looked equally surprised to find the stranger grappling with the Knights. And when Opal and Noel came to a stop behind the Renegades, Klye thought Colt's office was far too small for so large an audience.

*   *   *

Since it was obvious that the private meeting had come to an abrupt end, Colt decided that the best thing to do—indeed, the *only* thing to do—was to bring the matter before the assembled company. They relocated the conference to the dining hall, which was empty at this time of the day.

Colt took his place at the head of one of the long tables, with Stannel seated on one side and Lieutenant Petton on the other. Klye chose the spot next to Stannel, and the other Renegades—Horcalus, Lilac, and Scout—joined him on the same side. Opposite the Renegades sat Opal, Noel, and Cholk, the dwarf having joined the procession en route to the dining hall.

He waited for a few minutes before starting, saying not a word until the final two invitees entered the room. When Othello and Sister Aric took their place beside the merchant at the foot of the table, Colt rose and told everyone the ill tidings of Fort Valor's demise.

Predictably, everyone was taken aback by the report, though no one was struck harder than Sister Aric, who bowed her head and silently wept. There were angry mutters from rebels and civilians alike. Colt didn't know why the merchant, Mitto, had barged into his office to begin with, but now the man traded his indignant expression for one of silent shock.

The buzz of curses and threats against the goblins ceased when Colt resumed his speech. He explained the dire importance of sending a small company to Rydah in order to inform them of the tragedy and to appraise the situation at the capital. When he told them of Stannel's plan to send a few of the Renegades to accomplish this vital task, the room was plunged into a stunned silence.

The stillness did not last long, however.

"With all due respect, Colt, do you really think you can trust the Renegades?" Opal asked. "What's to stop them from running off?"

"Klye would never do that!" Noel insisted from beside her.

"The Renegade Leader isn't going anywhere," Petton told the midge, "though *you* are welcome to leave anytime you wish."

The three rebels seated to Klye's right regarded him curiously, waiting for a further explanation from their leader. Klye merely shrugged and said, "It's up to Colt to say who will be allowed to go, but nobody has to go."

"We're eager to help," Scout insisted. "The goblins are responsible for killing Ragellan…and Lilac's brother. Just tell us when, and we'll be ready."

"They won't let you go, Scout," Klye said. "Or the pirates. And I'm not even sure if they'll let you go, Horcalus."

Colt's eyes were drawn to Mitto, who had risen to his feet. "I don't care if the company is made up of rebels, pirates, and half-dozen midge, I'm coming along!"

Sister Aric sat silently. For a moment, Colt thought that she was staring into space, her mind wandering, but then he realized that she was looking at Stannel. The former Commander of Fort Valor had met her gaze, and Colt forced himself to look away, not wanting to intrude upon their private grief.

"Can I come along too?" The insistent, almost whiny voice of the midge caught Colt's attention next, and when he glanced over at that side of the table, he saw that Noel was pulling at Opal's sleeve. "I'll be a big help!"

Opal, ignoring Noel, was exchanging words with Cholk, though Colt could not hear them due to the clamor of all the voices. Above it all, Gaelor Petton was yelling across the table at Scout, who was himself complaining at the injustice of allowing Lilac and Horcalus to go but not him.

"The rogue knight won't be going anywhere if I have anything to say about it!" Petton promised.

Realizing that he had lost all control over the assembly, Colt shouted, "Silence!"

Everyone hushed, except for Noel, who demanded, "Why can't everybody just be friends?" before slouching down in his chair.

Eleven pairs of eyes watched him, waiting for him to judiciously settle all disputes. But Colt was through with playing mediator. Enough was enough. He was the commander.

"No one is going anywhere without my say-so," Colt told them all. "I don't care if you are a civilian or the King of Superius. Capricon is at war, and I must assume responsibility for everyone currently residing within my fort. If you have a problem with this, I will be happy to personally escort you to a cell where you will remain until the goblins are defeated."

No one said a word, and more than a few of them regarded him with astonished expressions. Colt was surprised to find he enjoyed their reactions. For the first time since he had assumed command of Fort Faith—for perhaps the first time in his life—he refused to second-guess himself.

The freedom from doubt was almost intoxicating.

"We must all be united in our purpose," he continued, "but if you cannot rise above your petty squabbles and look at the situation objectively, then it is up to me to take the appropriate steps without your counsel.

"Of the Renegades, Lilac and Othello will be joining the party bound for Rydah."

"What about Horcalus?" Lilac dared to ask.

Colt didn't back down. "I do not doubt your honor, Sir Horcalus," he said, stressing the former Knight's title. "On the contrary, I hope I can count on you to supplement the forces here at Fort Faith should the goblins turn their sights our way."

"I am yours to command," the rogue knight swore, but not before a quick look to Klye.

"Who is going to lead the party?" The query came from the merchant, Mitto. "I'll follow regardless, but I'd like to know who's to be in charge."

Colt saw Stannel shift in his seat, but before he could say a word, Colt said, "I will lead the party."

The shocked expressions regarding him now rivaled the earlier looks.

Opal rose then, her hands planted on her hips. "Well, I don't care what you say, Saerylton Crystalus. I'm coming with you, and if you try to lock me in a cell, I'll blacken both of your eyes."

"And that goes double for me!" Cholk announced, pounding his fist on the table.

Colt looked upon the unlikely pair with mixed emotions. At first he was angry they were challenging his authority, but his ire quickly faded, replaced by an intense fondness for them. Here were his two dearest friends, willing to risk their lives and fight beside him.

Part of him did want to lock Opal away, to keep her safe from all dangers, but another part of him—a greater part—wouldn't have traded her company for anything.

The room had once more plunged into a sea of voices, but Colt ignored them for now, reveling in the notion he was finally going to get a chance to take action against the goblins.

Passage IX

Baxter yearned for death more than he had ever wanted anything in life.

In many ways, he already *felt* dead. When he managed to sleep—a shallow slumber somewhere between consciousness and unconsciousness—his dreams were rife with torment. During these nightmares, he feared death had overtaken him at last. And instead of releasing him from his misery, the supposed Afterlife increased it tenfold.

But then he would wake to his suspended reality.

The dreams were one of the few things that interrupted the limbo his life had become. In some sick way, he appreciated the nightmares, for at least in those twisted dreams, he could run or fight back against his assailants. Horrible though they were, the dreams also provided him with some diversion to break up the bleak emptiness of existence.

When the goblin general entered the tent, a perverse joy overcame him. The general was his only companion—the only other being in the world, as far as he was concerned.

Baxter had lost track of the rising and setting of the sun. And though it felt as though he had been imprisoned for months, he knew it couldn't be so. The general had not seen it fit to feed him, so it couldn't have been more than a few days.

His desperate hunger brought a madness all its own.

At that moment, he would have gladly traded his immortal soul for the chance—just the *chance*—to kill the general. He imagined roasting the creature's sinewy limbs and drinking the thick black blood. So ludicrous was the idea that he might have laughed out loud if he could.

The general had interrogated him about Rydah and its defenses. The next time he had come, he ordered Baxter to him to tell him everything he knew about Fort Valor. No matter how much he had tried to resist the fire-eyed skull-staff, his tongue would inevitably—nay, eagerly—reveal every modicum of information he had ever gleaned, starting with when it was constructed, the number of times he had been there, and even the names of the Knights he knew who were stationed there.

The worse part of his unwilling treachery was that he didn't know what the general was doing with the information. For all Baxter knew, both Rydah and Fort Valor were under siege. Worst-case scenarios played out in his mind, and in every one of his dark musings, he saw himself as the sword with which the goblins struck Capricon. Families were butchered; his comrades, slaughtered. Both Fort Valor and the Celestial Palace lay in rubble.

There was no one left to save him because he had doomed everyone.

The goblin general now stood directly over him. This was the only way he could see his interrogator, since Baxter could not turn his head even a fraction of an inch. He stared up at the grotesque visage that plagued his unending dreams. The goblin's eyes were a yellowish-orange hue that reminded him of a festering wound. The creature's thin purple lips stretched back in a rictus grin that held no mirth.

The general spoke no word of greeting. He never gloated or taunted his captive. Baxter was merely a tool. He studied his prisoner's face as though appraising the integrity of a blade, searching it for signs of weakness and deciding if it could stand the rigors of another battle.

Baxter wondered if the skull-staff's powers would continue to work on a deranged man. Could a crazed mind surrender sensible information? He wondered if wanting to embrace madness was a sign of madness or, given the circumstances, sanity.

Apparently deciding his living weapon could endure at least one more round, the goblin general positioned the skull above Baxter's unblinking eyes. Not for the first time, he wondered what the death's-head might have looked like in life. Was it the head of a goblin or a human or something else entirely?

In his nightmares the decapitated member taunted him with the general's voice. In Baxter's less lucid moments, the decapitated head and the goblin general's head were one and the same.

Predictably, the eye-sockets began to glow an unearthly red, and Baxter felt the spell reach deep into his own head, invading the private recesses of his very being. This time, he didn't bother to struggle.

"Tell me about Fort Faith," the general said.

I already told you everything I know about all of the island's redoubts, Baxter wanted to scream, but instead, he began reciting statistics.

"Fort Faith was recently repopulated with eighty-three Knights, led by Commander Saerylton Crystalus of Superius. The fortress itself spans—"

"Enough," the goblin interrupted, and instantly Baxter's speech ceased. "I know all of that. I want to know about Fort Faith's unofficial residents. Tell me about the spell-caster that lives there. Tell me about the midge."

Baxter's mouth opened to comply, but no words came out. He couldn't tell the goblin anything about a midge because he didn't *know* anything about a midge at Fort Faith. His unexpected—and unintentional—opposition filled him with smug satisfaction, though it was a small victory.

"Tell me about the midge!" the general repeated in a louder voice.

The power of the spell swelled inside his mind, as though the tendrils of magic were squeezing his brain like a sponge. It was like suffering from a sudden, stabbing headache, but what was worse than the pain was the humiliation of his helplessness.

His lips trembled as he replied. "I...can't...tell you...what I don't...know!"

The ferocity of the attack subsided somewhat.

"Tell me about the dwarf that lives at Fort Faith, and the woman with the crossbow," the general said.

Baxter's mouth tried to form words, but, again, there were no words to expel. He knew very little about Fort Faith's new occupants, and he had heard absolutely nothing about a midge, a dwarf, or a woman. As far as he knew, there were eighty-three Knights stationed at the fort, and that was all.

While it was an unpleasant realization that the goblins already knew more about the goings-on around Capricon than the he, a Knight of Superius, did, Baxter was nevertheless filled with satisfaction by the fact he could in no way help the invaders this time.

"Tell me about the Renegade Leader Klye Tristan and his band."

"I know nothing about a Renegade Leader by that name," Baxter replied, overjoyed by the fact that his words would have been exactly the same had he consciously chosen them.

Now the skull-tipped staff wavered unsteadily just inches above his face, as though the goblin was contemplating striking him with it. Baxter reveled in the moment. So, he thought, the blade has dulled beyond use. Mayhap it's time to discard the tool...

If he had had any control over his mouth, Baxter would have uttered a few choice insults to further goad the general. But there was no way he could prod the goblin into killing him. He could only ask the Warriorlord to have mercy on him and end the cruel charade his life had become.

But mercy would have to wait, for without another word, the general stormed out of the tent, leaving Baxter to stare up at the dreary canopy of his private tent, a thin cloth which couldn't keep out the cold but which trapped him as veritably as a wall of steel.

He grieved at the postponement of his final rest, but at the same time, he felt a new optimism grow inside of him. The goblins hadn't won yet, and as long as there were those resisting the conquerors—like the defenders of Fort Faith—there was still hope for the island.

Baxter knew almost nothing about the Commander of Fort Faith and his men, but at that moment he prayed with all of his heart to the Warriorlord to give them strength. The goblin general was obviously preoccupied with the "unofficial" residents of the fort, which meant they posed a threat.

And if it took a midge, a dwarf, a lady with a crossbow, and a Renegade Leader to push the goblins back to wherever they came from, so be it!

"You can't be serious about this."

No sooner had Colt closed the door to his private workroom than his lieutenant spoke the incredulous words. Gaelor Petton, his arms folded in front of him, wore a mighty frown that was made more ferocious by the Knight's dark, bushy eyebrows, which were so narrowed as to almost be touching.

Colt had seen such disapproving expressions on the face of his father and older brothers when scolding him for one mistake or another. Once upon a time, Colt might have shrunk under Petton's blatant disapproval, but not today. Today, Colt felt like a new man.

No, he felt like a man for the first time in his life.

"I have never been more serious in my life," he told Petton, whose face did not at all soften at the news.

"It is highly irregular for a commander of a fort to abandon his keep in times of war. You are needed here. Sir Silvercrown or I can take charge of the band destined for Rydah."

Colt turned a shrewd eye on the lieutenant. "You would sooner stick your sword in any one of the Renegades than work beside them."

Petton jerked as though physically struck by the verbal jab. For an instant, Colt regretted his strong words, but at the same time, he wanted Petton to know he was not going to be challenged on this issue. He had made up his mind, and no one was going to dissuade him.

Petton cleared his throat. "While it is true that I am far less…trusting when it comes to the rebels, it is unfair to assume I cannot set aside my prejudices to accomplish what needs to be done. I beg you to reconsider."

Colt shook his head. "Internal strife can vanquish a regiment as assuredly as an external threat. For good or for ill, I have done my best to act justly toward the Renegades. I can only pray that they will repay me with their loyalty."

"If not me, then send Sir Silvercrown or Sir Vesparis."

"No," Colt replied, a bit too emphatically perhaps. "We already know that the goblins are capable on taking on the guise of humans, and *Chrysaal-rûn* might be the only thing we have to thwart their enchantments.

"This is something I must do, Petton. You saw how the sword burned Klye when he tried to wield it. For all we know, I am the only one who can hold it without suffering ill effects. It's a matter of practically. It doesn't matter whether I am a commander or a novice foot soldier. I wield the crystal sword, so I am the most logical choice for leading the company to Rydah."

Petton opened his mouth as if to object, but then scowled fiercely at the floor.

"And where might I fit into your plans, Commander?"

The mild question caught Colt off-guard. He had all but for-gotten Stannel had followed the two of them back to his office. Now Colt turned his attention to the other commander, who sat, unperturbed, in a chair beside him.

"Well," Colt began slowly.

In truth, he hadn't thought about Stannel one way or another. The decision to lead the mission had come to him so suddenly and so strongly he hadn't considered how Stannel might feel about the situation.

If anyone had more of a right to take charge of the party, it was Stannel Bismarc…

"I cannot presume to give you orders, Stannel," Colt contin-ued. Then, all at once, the perfect solution came to him. "But I would be honored if you would take command of Fort Faith in my absence."

The room fell into a heavy silence. After a moment, Stannel replied. "While I am honored by the offer, Commander, I fear it is not as simple as that. There is a matter of protocol."

"What do you mean?" Colt asked. A veteran officer like Stannel—or Petton, for that matter—would be well-versed in the subtleties of knightly decorum, but Colt was still new to the job.

"My station is Fort Valor," Stannel explained. "I cannot transfer my service from one fort to another without approval from the Knights' Council in Superius…just as you cannot forfeit your post without the Council's permission."

Colt clenched his fists in impotent rage, but his anger quickly faded, only to be replaced by despair. He was bound by the laws of the Knighthood. How foolish he had been to think he could abandon his command.

"Sir Bismarc would be a worthy substitute as the party commander," Petton pointed out.

The wind stolen from his sails, Colt nearly collapsed into one of the vacant chairs. I am doomed to serve my king and my country from behind this desk, he concluded gloomily.

Stannel cleared his throat. "It is true I had pictured myself in that very position, but upon further reflection, I do not think I am the best candidate for the job. The goblins have wronged the Knighthood and everyone in Capricon, but I feel the effects of their despicable crimes more acutely than most. The thirst for personal vengeance may cloud my judgement. With your permission, Commander, I would like to remain at Fort Faith until I can regain my objectivity."

Colt nodded absently. He had expected Stannel to jump at the chance to lead the party, to fight back against the goblins in any way he could. That was what Colt had wanted to do ever since the battle against the goblin shaman.

The goblins had killed three of his men, and he craved vengeance. Stannel, on the other hand, saw such desires as a weakness.

"Well, *someone* has to do it," Petton said. "Shall we go over the list of candidates again?"

Then something inside Colt awoke—or perhaps it re-awoke. No, he thought, I'm not giving up so easily. His convictions were fueled by passion, but he didn't care.

Can't a person do something because he wants it so badly *and* because it's the right thing to do? he wondered.

"There has to be a way," he muttered.

"Pardon?" Stannel asked.

"You said you can't take command of Fort Faith without permission from the Knights' Council," Colt said.

"Correct."

"And even the goblins weren't running amok on the island, it could take months before the Council's decision would reach us."

"Correct."

"Aren't there any exceptions to the rule?" Colt asked. "What about emergencies?"

Stannel thought for a moment. "If you were dead or in some way unfit to lead, then your lieutenant could step up to fill your place."

"But if I'm unfit to serve as Commander of Fort Faith, then I'd be likewise unfit to serve as the leader of the party."

"I am afraid so," Stannel said.

Damn it! he fumed. There must be a way. There must...

"Is there any law against changing a fort's name?" Colt offered in jest.

Stannel considered the question seriously. "Actually, I do not think I have ever heard of a rule that states that explicitly. Why do you ask?"

Colt did his best to contain his mounting excitement. "Well, theoretically, couldn't I change the name of Fort Faith to Fort Valor? Wouldn't that automatically make you the commander of this fortress?"

"Well, I suppose—"

"Now wait a minute," Petton said. "If this becomes Fort Valor instead of Fort Faith, then all of the men stationed at Fort Faith will be displaced."

Colt looked to Stannel for help.

"That is not necessarily true," Stannel said. "In times of war, when there is no time to seek the Council's approval, two commanders may exchange troops as they see fit. In theory, Colt could relinquish each and every one of his men to serve under me."

Petton threw up his hands. "This is crazy!"

"But is it possible?" Colt asked.

Stannel thought for a moment before replying, "It is an admittedly sly maneuver, but as far as I know, it is legal."

Petton opened and closed his mouth several times, his face turning a deep red. Colt had not wanted to offend the man, but he wasn't about to back off simply because Petton felt slighted. Maybe it was the lieutenant's right to lead in Colt's absence, but since that wasn't possible, Petton would have to find a way to deal with it.

Besides, Colt thought, Stannel will treat the Renegades with more patience than Petton would have.

"Will you do it?" Colt asked Stannel with more than a little trepidation. All Stannel had to do was refuse, and the scheme would be over before it began.

"I should like to meditate on such a heady decision for at least a day," he began, "but since time of the essence, I will give you my answer now. I agree to your terms, Colt. I failed in my duty to protect the original Fort Valor from the goblins. Perhaps the gods are giving me a second chance with new Fort Valor."

Colt was almost dizzy with the realization that he had actually pulled it off. Stannel's face revealed nothing of his feelings. Petton's expression, however, betrayed deep reservations. Colt vowed to have a private word with the lieutenant before he departed in an attempt to smooth things over, but at the moment, he felt like nothing in the world mattered except that he was getting his chance to make a difference in the war.

And while the party bound for Rydah would avoid battle at all costs, Colt couldn't help but hope that they would run into T'slect along the way.

Passage X

Mitto received word they would be leaving for Rydah immediately after sunset and that everyone who was going was to meet in the entry hall at that time.

He was a little surprised to be included in the group—not that he would have stood for being left out. Recalling the great confusion that had erupted during the meeting in the dining room, he wondered who else had made the cut. But not wanting to press his luck, he didn't ask the messenger, a Knight whose name he didn't know.

Mitto tried to sleep that afternoon, but his mind was awhirl at the magnitude of what he was about to do. Excitement and anxiety gripped him, causing his stomach to roil. He was eager to leave for Rydah, but a part of him feared what he would find when he arrived

And then there were the goblins on the road...

He dozed on and off for the next few hours, and when twilight washed the sky a pale gray, he dressed, gathered the few possessions he would need for the journey, tucked his quarterstaff under one arm, and proceeded to the entry hall.

The vestibule was packed with an odd assortment of folks. The Renegades, including Klye Tristan, made up one small group, and a second crowd had formed around the young Commander of Fort Faith. Stannel was there too, but the Knight did not look as though he were leaving.

Opal, Noel, and the dwarf—or so Scout had called him—stood off to one side, and true to their word, both the woman and the black-clad warrior were dressed for travel. They wore thick, hooded cloaks and were openly armed. Noel wore the same blue robe as before, so Mitto couldn't be sure if the midge was coming along or not. He recalled the damage the wizard's fireballs had wrought during the scrimmage near Fort Faith, and a part of him thought having Noel along might not be such a bad idea.

He almost laughed out loud. The situation must indeed be desperate if I'm in favor of a having a midge for a traveling companion! he thought.

Mitto made his way over to Opal's group and uttered a perfunctory greeting. The dwarf—Mitto couldn't remember having ever heard his name—grunted indifferently, never taking his eyes off of the throng of Knights. The dwarf's eyes were so dark as to appear black, matching his ebony skin.

Not that Mitto could see much of the dwarf's skin now for he was clad the same peculiar armor that he had been wearing on that first day when he, Opal, and Noel had rushed into the fray to save him. In that dark, lusterless suit of armor—topped with the horned helm—the dwarf cut a truly fearsome picture. The double-bladed battle-axe strapped to his back made him look all the fiercer.

Opal wore a quiver on her back, but she kept her crossbow at easy reach on her belt. She also eyed the assembly of Knights, but Mitto couldn't guess what she might be feeling. From what the two of them had said during the meeting in the dining hall, Mitto knew Opal and the dwarf were close friends of Fort Faith's commander. Maybe they were worried about the man, who was knowingly placing himself in great danger, or maybe they were jealous of all of the attention he was receiving.

None of the other Knights looked very eager to say goodbye to them.

"That's a nice stick."

The strange comment snapped Mitto out of his reverie. Glancing over—or, rather, down—at the speaker, Mitto found Noel staring appreciatively at his quarterstaff.

"It's important to find the right stick when you're making a staff. Take mine, for instance." The midge held out his reddish rod with the blue-gem tip. "It's made from the finest wood in Pickelo. Oh, and it's enchanted too. Do you want me to cast a spell on your staff?"

"Ah…no thank you," Mitto replied, clutching his quarterstaff protectively.

"It takes a long time to make an enchantment…well…stick," Noel said. "It took me almost a year to make my staff as powerful as it is, and sometimes when I have nothing better to do, I add more magic to it. It's kind of hard to explain, but I could put a single weak enchantment on yours."

"I'm good," Mitto insisted. "This staff has seen me through more than a few scuffles. I like it the way it is."

Noel shrugged. "It's longer and thicker than mine, but we midge are taught from an early age that magic can more than make up for physical disadvantages. Mine may be smaller, but it's capable of a lot more than your ordinary stick."

Mitto studied Noel, trying to discern whether he was speaking in innuendo, but Noel's smile was devoid of all guile. Not knowing what else to say, Mitto asked, "So, ah, Noel, will you be joining us on the road?"

The midge seemed to shrink before his very eyes. "No," he uttered miserably. "Colt wants me to stay here to protect the fort while he's gone. I'd really like to come along, but maybe it's better if I stay. Klye is still very sick. Did you know he and I are good friends? Well, we are. We were friends before I met Colt. Anyway, Opal and Cholk promised they would watch over Colt, so I guess I'll stay here and make sure Klye gets better."

Mitto nodded as though he understood every word. Well, at least I know the dwarf's name, he thought.

Cholk smiled. "It'll be a far shot easier to keep an eye on Colt without having to keep an eye on *you* at the same time," he told the midge.

Noel stuck out his tongue.

"Play nice, you two," was Opal's reflexive reply. "What about you, Mitto? I know you're from Rydah, but why are so eager to get back? Why not just wait out the war at Fort Faith?"

Mitto blinked twice and tried to put his thoughts in order. "I have friends in Rydah. I wasn't born there, but it's my home. I lost one of my dearest friends on the way here, and I want to make sure that nothing has happened to the other...*others*."

Opal's scrutiny made Mitto more than a little uncomfortable. There was something in her eyes that suggested she suspected there was more to it than what he told her. What is it about beautiful women that makes them seem like they know more than the rest of the world? he wondered.

Mitto's attention was drawn to the Commander of Fort Faith, who was separating himself from the other Knights. He climbed halfway up the grand stairway, stopped, and turned to regard everyone below. An expectant hush fell over those gathered.

Mitto waited for the young Knight to launch into a lengthy oration, but to his surprise, he unsheathed his sword and said no more than six words:

"To Fort Faith! To Fort Valor!"

The other Knights in the room raised their blades and let out a great cheer. But Mitto was still staring up at the commander's weapon. The blade appeared transparent, as though wrought from glass. Mitto might have dismissed it as a ceremonial implement, except the commander then returned the sword to the scabbard on his hip and drew his traveling coat over the weapon.

Mitto was still pondering the mystery of the clear-bladed sword when the commander descended the stairs and was once more enveloped by his men.

Meanwhile, two Renegades left their party and came over to where he, Opal, and the others were waiting. Mitto recognized Lilac, the woman warrior whom he had watched duel that morning. Recalling the ease with which she wielded the wooden practice sword, he was glad to have her in the group, though he might have hoped to have Horcalus along too.

Lilac no longer carried a practice sword. A well-crafted, silver-colored hilt protruded from the scabbard at her hip. Her companion had come late to the gathering in the dining room. The tall man had entered alongside Sister Aric, and further questioning had revealed the rebel had been serving as the fort's healer before the priestess arrived.

Aside from that knowledge and the man's name—Othello—Mitto knew nothing about him.

Standing more than a head taller than anyone else in the party, Othello wore an outfit made of buckskin. Even his boots looked to be made of deer leather. A large hunting knife hung to his belt, and he had draped a longbow over one shoulder. The quiver on his back was filled with green-feathered arrows.

Othello certainly dressed the part of a forester, and the beginnings of a yellowish beard that covered his face made him look all the wilder.

The two Renegades said nothing to Opal, Cholk, and Noel, who in turn made no move to speak to the rebels. The midge had, in fact, detached himself from the group and was hurrying over to where the other Renegades stood. Mitto watched as the little wizard approach Klye Tristan and started talking.

All too aware of the palpable discomfort, Mitto decided to

breech the silence by introducing himself to Othello.

Othello accepted his hand in a wordless greeting but made no attempt to nurture the dialogue. The expression on his face was not unfriendly, per se. There was no contempt in those bright green eyes, but neither was there anything to suggest amiability. Deciding not to press the rebel, Mitto took a step back, ready to resume the awkward silence.

To Mitto's surprise—and relief—Lilac dispelled the silence. "I think it would be best for us all if we put the past behind us. We're on the same side now, with the same goal in mind."

"Let's just make sure it stays that way," Opal snapped, and Mitto thought that Lilac looked physically stricken by the other woman's comment.

The unbearable stillness might have resumed but for the arrival of the sixth and final member of the party. The young commander wore a vest of leather armor beneath his unbuttoned coat. He carried no shield, wore no helmet. At the moment, he looked less like a commander—less like a *Knight*—than the armor-covered dwarf.

"Is everybody ready?" he asked.

Everyone nodded.

"All right," the Knight said. "Then let's go."

They left under the cover of darkness, though Colt wondered how much they gained from that. According to Cholk, goblins could see in the dark nearly as well as dwarves could—not to mention the goblins' magic was surely powerful enough to overcome an overcast night.

Still, Colt knew they would have to make use of every possible advantage, no matter how small. Slipping away at night was better than departing in broad daylight.

Innate abilities aside, the goblins had another edge over the island's defenders. The Knights knew next to nothing about the goblins' troop placements—or even an estimate of their numbers.

In the face of such formidable unknowns, Colt had opted for stealth over speed, hoping to avoid the invaders altogether. Since the goblins were almost certainly watching the road, the party would traverse the game trails—or cut a path of their own— through the dense forest that stretched all the way to Rydah. Not only would the trees provide additional cover, but also the confined setting would work against the goblins' greater numbers if it came to battle.

Cholk led the way, using his inherently keen vision to pierce the veil of night. Although Colt had initially thought to appoint Othello as the group's guide, he assigned the archer to rearguard for now. Othello carried his bow at the ready, an arrow already nocked. Having witnessed the archer's deadly accuracy with the longbow, Colt was surprised how comfortable he was walking with his back to the tall, silent Renegade.

But for good or for ill, he trusted Othello.

Up ahead, Lilac followed closely behind Cholk. Colt wondered if she wasn't more dangerous than Othello. When she had fought against the Knights, Colt had seen her impossibly sharp blade cut through armor as effortlessly as a scythe through wheat. From his interview with her after the battle with T'slect, he had learned that, like *Chrysaal-rûn*, Lilac's vorpal sword was a family heirloom.

Both rebels could escape at any time, but Colt's thoughts didn't linger on the possibility. Neither had joined the rebellion out of discontent with the government or out of hatred for the Knights. By all accounts, Othello had gotten caught up with Klye's band after killing several men in self-defense.

Lilac, on the other hand, was the daughter of a respectable Superian lord. She had joined Klye's band to protect Chester Ragellan and Dominic Horcalus from assassins hired by T'slect—a honorable cause to be sure.

If either chose to betray the mission, it would be for their Renegade Leader's sake, Colt knew. But he and Klye had come to an understanding. Even if Klye might have more tricks up his sleeve, there was no doubt in Colt's mind that Klye hated the goblins as much as he did. Besides, Klye wouldn't be foolish enough to think Lilac and Othello were capable of carrying out a rescue mission at Fort Faith on their own.

Fort *Valor*, Colt reminded himself with a smile.

Colt realized he wasn't the only one watching Lilac. Whenever he glanced over at Opal—under the pretext of watching their left flank—he saw the woman's gaze was glued to the swordswoman.

He had wanted to have a frank discussion with Opal before they left the fort, but with all of the planning for the mission, he hadn't had time. Or maybe that was just an excuse to avoid confronting the woman about her enmity for the Renegades.

Perhaps the tension would fade with time. Opal hadn't done or said anything to provoke the former rebels. Anyway, she didn't have to like her teammates; she only had to do her job without adding more problems to their already precarious situation. For her swift temper, Opal wouldn't jeopardize the mission over petty differences and past grudges.

At least Colt prayed she wouldn't.

They walked into the early morning, stopping for only the briefest of breaks. Throughout the hike, Colt took occasional glances back at the sixth member of the party, the man he knew the least about. He had had some reservations about allowing the merchant to tag along, but from Stannel's testimony, Mitto was an honest man—and he was handy with a quarterstaff.

From all appearances, the man was holding up well. He looked tired and a bit careworn, but there was determination in his eyes. Here is a man who is no stranger to hardship, Colt thought.

He watched as Mitto used his quarterstaff to brush vines and other clinging plants out of his path, seemingly undaunted by the threat of goblins. The merchant went about his work without complaint and with a single-minded dedication of a true soldier.

The party walked in silence. Colt had forbidden talking altogether, and even whispers were to be kept to a minimum. In all of the stillness, with only birdsong to fill the void, he couldn't help but dwell on the desperate decision he had made.

The long hours of introspection since departing had revived his doubts, which began weaving holes through his resolve as a whole. He tried to shake away the uncertainties, but soon he found himself analyzing his motivations. Had he done the right thing in quitting his post? Was he really the best choice to lead the dangerous mission?

Wasn't he really just running away from responsibilities at the fort?

He tried to imagine what his father would say when he learned of his son's actions. Would he praise Colt's voluntary demotion as an act of valor or condemn it as cowardice? Wasn't it, truthfully, a little of both?

Stannel was quite capable of running the fort in his stead. Stannel became a Knight of Superius before Colt was even born, and he had served as Commander of Fort Valor for more than a decade. His prowess in battle was dwarfed only by his wisdom. He was fair-minded and even-handed.

Really, the fortress was better off without "Commander Colt."

The thought might have been depressing, except he had recognized his inadequacies long ago. Someday, perhaps, he would be a great leader, but presently he was ignorant of many aspects of protocol and, more importantly, he lacked experience.

In spite of his shortcomings, Colt couldn't deny a part of him regretted yielding his authority to Stannel. There was nothing to ensure that the older Knight would reinvest power back into him...if Colt even wanted it.

That line of thought soon had Colt examining the very reasons he had become a Knight. Yes, there had been some pressure to follow in his father's and brothers' footsteps, but he could have become anything he wanted—an artisan, a scholar, or even a priest.

Had he chosen the path of the warrior simply to prove that he was as good as his brothers? Hadn't he been overjoyed at his unexpected promotion to Commander of Fort Faith because it had proven his legitimacy as the progeny of Laenghot Crystalus and suggested he could be a hero like his father before him?

And when his father had bestowed to him the crystal sword, hadn't that been the best day of his life?

Stealing across the silent countryside, the hilt of *Chrysaalrûn* inches from his hand, Colt knew there was more to it than that. For better or for worse, he had been raised on stories of honor and valor, had drunk the milk of adventure since infancy.

If he could go back and do it all again, he knew he would choose the Knighthood again. What excitement was there in the life of a sage or craftsman? What could be more noble than being a Knight? Let the priests worry about the souls of their countrymen. I am content to protect their lives, he thought.

Maybe he had made mistakes along the way, but he had always tried his best. What more could the gods ask of him?

His spirits bolstered and sense of purpose restored, he was suddenly struck by the importance of what he and his troupe had set out to do. The men and women around him had risen to the call of duty despite the overwhelming odds against them.

He wished he could share his epiphany with the others in the group, but even if he hadn't prohibited nonessential conversation, Colt knew he wouldn't have been able to put his feelings into words. Not even mundane activities—such as making and breaking camp, followed by more hiking—could sap the paradoxical excitement and calm that possessed him.

And yet his contentment and confidence proved to be short-lived.

Passage XI

Mitto couldn't remember the last time he crept through a forest in the middle of the night, but he did recall one occasion from his childhood, when he and a few of the local boys had decided to go on an adventure.

They had carried sticks, slings, and pocketknives, seeing monsters lurking in every shadow. He remembered being thrilled and afraid at the same time. The quest had come to an immediate halt, however, when a sinister rustling in the brush sent them all dashing back to their beds.

Now he felt as though he were reliving that experience. Except this time there really were monsters, and if the goblins found them, running home to hide under his blanket wasn't an option. He tried to take comfort in the fact he was surrounded by people who knew about adventures and were no stranger to fighting their way out of a scrap.

As the hours of walking passed without incident, Mitto relaxed somewhat. By the end of the first night, he was more tired than anything else. Not even the threat of a goblin attack could keep him from falling into a deep sleep when they finally made camp.

They renewed their hike the following evening, but by this time, Mitto was more preoccupied with the stiffness in his joints and a plethora of cramps than he was worried about the goblins.

As the sun dipped beneath the horizon behind him, he concluded two things about the nature of adventures. First, being on one wasn't nearly as exciting as the fables made them out to be. It was more walking than anything. And second, he wasn't built for it, at least not anymore.

While his arms were strong from hefting and hauling heavy freight, he had grown soft around the middle, the result of spending so many hours sitting on his arse while the horses pulled him and the wagon along. He also blamed Dragon's Hoard for the roundness of his midsection.

It's no wonder why the heroes in the tales are always young and in shape, he thought. An older guy like me would only slow the story down!

Of course, he never mentioned his fatigue and aches to his companions, not even when his began to fear he would collapse. It was all he could do to keep from dropping to the ground the moment Colt called for a break. As the second night of their trek began to wane, Mitto worried he would keel over long before they reached Rydah.

If not for his determination to see Else Fontane again, he might have already quit.

Mitto was searching for a hidden reserve of strength—though he feared he had spent that on the first night—when a strange cry erupted from somewhere off in the distance.

The sound, which caused the hairs on the back of his neck to rise, was surely the call of some woodland animal. But what that beast might be, Mitto couldn't hazard a guess. He had never heard the likes of that haunting, wail-like noise before in his life.

Colt called the party to a halt, whispering the command sharply. The six of them spent the next few seconds peering into the gloom around them, trying to locate the source of the sound. A light fog had blanketed the forest floor on the previous morning, and today, the mist had accumulated, bathing the vicinity in an impenetrable murky whiteness. Mitto felt something clamp around his heart and his bowels turn to ice water when a second howl, coming from the opposite direction, echoed the first.

The panic welling up inside threatened to rob him of reason. He wanted to run but instead clenched the quarterstaff so tightly that his knuckles hurt and waited for Colt's next order. Mitto had never fought under the orders of a trained professional, and he found himself hoping that the ordeal would be less terrifying for it.

"Cholk, can you see anything?" Colt asked.

The dwarf let out a deep rumbling sound Mitto took for a no.

Colt turned next to the forester. "Othello?"

To Mitto's surprise, the archer's eyes were closed. "There are many, and they're spreading out."

"They'll try to surround us," Colt concluded, stared into the fog.

More ghastly cries were drifting among the trees, growing louder, closer.

Then Colt gave the only reasonable command: "Retreat!"

The small company burst into flight. Their retreat lacked grace, but at least they all went the same direction—east.

Mitto instantly forgot about his weariness and ran with renewed vigor. His body seemed to have a mind of its own as his arms and legs pumped furiously. Curiously, his own thoughts were of Goblin, that fictional antagonist whose resemblance he had seen in Toemis Blisnes.

This shouldn't be happening to me, he reasoned. I gave up the gold. I've turned from the path of greed and have embarked on a selfless quest, putting myself in danger for the greater good.

Gods damn it, didn't Goblin's dupes ever get a happy ending?

The fog was so thick Mitto almost ran headlong into a tree. He managed to keep one of his companions in view, though even at a few paces behind, he couldn't identify the person he was following. Nevertheless, he kept his eyes fixed on the shape before him, watching it cleave a swath through the thick, damp air.

He and his phantom-like guide ran for perhaps three full minutes before Mitto saw other shapes in the coalescing fog. He didn't bother to glance behind him, not wishing to confirm what he feared he would find there.

In the best of circumstances, Mitto might have been able to fend off two or even three of the monsters at once. Judging from the weird calls that reverberated throughout the murky forest, however, he estimated there were more foes out there than there had been in all of his previous goblin encounters combined.

As the fiends closed in on him, he understood his luck had finally run out.

He felt somewhat detached from everything, as though he were watching someone else run for his life. His thoughts returned to the childhood stories. Like the fools from the fables, he had found himself in increasingly worse situations. The tragic character always sought a way out, but the price for Goblin's gold was always a life.

Well, Mitto thought as he skidded to a halt and brandished

his quarterstaff, I'll not die without a fight.

He slammed the butt of his staff into the first goblin's chest, and although the monster wore an oversized shirt of chainmail, the blow sent it staggering back. He then brought his staff up just in time deflect the downward slash of a curved blade, but this new opponent wielded two weapons, and he could only throw himself to the side as the second blade—a serrated knife—homed in on his gut.

Mitto couldn't evade the attack completely. The blade ripped open the flesh between his belly and hip. He fell back, but as he did so, he swung the quarterstaff out hard. He heard the satisfying crack of wood against bone when it connected with the goblin's unprotected head.

The monster collapsed lifelessly, but it was replaced by two more.

His back up against the thick trunk of a tree, Mitto made desperate swings with the quarterstaff, forcing the fiends to keep their distance. Pain lanced through his side, threatening to rob him of his senses. The two goblins separated, clearly planning to rush him from opposite sides.

Then, unexpectedly, the goblin to his right let out a strangled cry and pitched face-first to the ground. The second monster, seemingly undaunted by the loss of his companion, lunged at Mitto with a barbed spear.

Mitto knocked the weapon aside, but even as he sparred with the remaining opponent, he saw a sea of dark shapes tearing through the fog. It was only a matter of seconds before he would face a foe on every side.

He was on the verge of countering his opponent's second swing when the monster suddenly dropped and joined its comrade in writhing on the ground. The goblin groped at its chest, and it took a moment for Mitto to realize it was reaching for an arrow protruding from its sternum. Mitto glanced up and found his savior coming toward him.

"Can you run?" Not waiting for an answer, Othello grabbed Mitto's arm and began to sprint.

Mitto didn't protest, though every step sent a plume of red-hot pain through his side. He gripped the Renegade's buckskin shirt as tightly as if he were holding onto life itself. As they ran, he saw further evidence of the archer's handiwork. Here and there, arrow-pierced goblins lay in various states of dying.

He didn't know where Othello was taking him, and he didn't care. All he could think about was his own agony, but he dared not stop. Suffering was better than death.

They might have run for two days straight. He was only dimly aware of times when the archer would stop in order to dispatch a goblin on the verge of overtaking them. Perhaps it was the white haze that bathed the forest that made it all seem like a dream.

For his part, Mitto could do nothing to help their cause, and after a short time, his feet give out from underneath him. Surrendering to pain and hopelessness, Mitto closed his eyes and sank into the depths of unconsciousness.

Colt almost immediately lost his sense of direction—along with his allies.

He tried to stay beside Opal, but at one point, he had swerved right while she went left. Now he saw no sign of the woman. He thought Othello and the merchant were somewhere behind him, but he dared not stop to confirm his suspicions.

Chrysaal-rûn in hand, Colt pushed himself hard and prayed that he was still heading east. If there had been any chance of prevailing against the goblins, he would have dug in and tried to fight them off, but his gut told him victory was not possible.

The only thing that mattered now was to get to Rydah. If just one of them could make it to the capital and inform the Lord of Capricon of all that was transpiring, then the deaths of the others would not be in vain.

Meanwhile, the goblins giving chase behind him were drawing ever nearer. He head the clatter of their armor, the pounding of their boots. He thought that he could even smell them—a sickening blend of spoiled meat and metallic blood.

Then a cluster of dark shapes appeared in the mist before him. Colt offered up a prayer to Pintor the Warriorlord, asking the benevolent god to guide his sword arm.

The goblins that had been tailing him quickly joined the newcomers and surrounded him. They charged in, but Colt was ready for them. He swung *Chrysaal-rûn* viciously, strewing the ground with pieces of weapons and warriors. Startled by the devastation that the Knight's blade was wreaking, members of the vanguard faltered and fell back.

Those that didn't were summarily slain.

An occasional arrow whizzed through the thick air, but none of them struck Colt, who had cut a path through the invaders and was running once more. The goblins gave chase. In spite of the thick fog, Colt could make out signs of more enemies coming at him from what he assumed was northeast and southeast. In the haze, he might have believed there were thousands of them.

He saw only one hope of escaping the ever-tightening circle of goblins. If he kept going straight at full speed, he might be able to slip through the proverbial fingers as they tried to close in around him.

As he ran, Colt said a prayer to Feol, the god of luck.

Either the fog was fading or Colt's eyes had adjusted to the gloom for he soon found that he was able to see further than before. The goblins up ahead appeared to be adjusting their paths to intercept him, but he knew he would easily avoid them if he maintained his course and speed. If his fortune held out, he might eventually lose his pursuers once he passed them.

He knew something was amiss, however, when the northern branch of the ambush came to a sudden halt. When the sounds of battle assailed his ears, he realized the goblins there were surely preoccupied with one or more of his companions.

Further inspection revealed the identity of the goblins' bane—a solitary warrior of short stature, swinging a massive battle-axe.

Cholk was hopelessly outnumbered, though at the moment, he appeared to be keeping his enemies at bay. Between the dwarf's prowess in battle and his savage hatred for all goblinkind, Cholk would probably kill a dozen of the monsters or more before all was said and done.

But in the end, even the dwarf's ferocity could not save him from whichever spear or sword would inevitably slip through the plates of his armor. Unless Colt came to his aid, Cholk was doomed.

Colt had mere seconds to make a decision, but in that time, he came up with several reasons why he should abandon the dwarf. For one thing, their objective was far more important than any member of the company. Also, Cholk had volunteered for the mission knowing full well the danger ahead and that death was a very real possibility, if not a probability.

And Colt knew that even if he joined the dwarf in combat,

there was no guarantee he could save him.

A good commander knew when to make sacrifices.

But Colt had never claimed to be a worthy leader.

Back in Continae, Cholk had betrayed a Renegade Leader—had risked his own life—to save Colt's life. Now, as he charged into the fray in hopes of returning the favor, Colt wondered whether this would prove to be the last mistake he ever made.

"About time you got here," Cholk shouted, his deep voice hewing through the din of the melee. "I thought you were going to miss all the fun."

Colt came at the first row of attackers with a wordless war cry on his lips. *Chrysaal-rûn* whirred through the air, not at all slowed by the weapons, shields, and bodies that got in its way. Cholk wasted no time in pressing his attack, hacking at the suddenly uncertain foes and sending many of the monsters to the ground.

Shouting with every swing of the enchanted blade, Colt scattered the goblins before him. Seconds later, the enemy fell back to regroup, and Knight and dwarf were provided a moment's reprieve.

"I thought I was done for," the dwarf confessed. A thin trail of red mixed with the black goblin blood spattered across his breastplate, but otherwise Cholk looked none the worse for the skirmish.

"It's not over yet," Colt said between shallow breaths.

Indeed, the woods were full of whooping, snarling goblins. The fiends Colt had worked so hard to outpace had caught up, and they wasted no time in encircling their prey. Even if Colt had had the stamina to renew his retreat, he wouldn't have gotten far before having to stop and defend himself again.

Escape was now impossible; it was time to make a stand.

He counted more than fifty goblins around them, and distant shouts foretold of more to come. The monsters' advance was tentative though, and Colt could only presume word of the crystal sword's keen blade had already circulated among them.

"Do you fear death?"

Cholk's question took Colt by surprise, but what was more startling was the fact Colt *didn't* feel afraid. He was far too preoccupied with the situation to fret about its probable outcome.

"My people don't mourn the loss of kith and kin," Cholk

continued. "Death comes for all, and it is up to the gods to decide when each dwarf...or man...will leave this world. To die bravely in battle is the best way for a dwarf to die. We call it The Last Great Deed."

Throughout their brief but cherished friendship, Cholk had remained tightlipped about his homeland and its customs. To this day, Colt didn't know what had caused the dwarf to wander so far from Thanatan or how he had ended up with a band of Renegades.

To hear Cholk speak so frankly about his beliefs was as welcomed as it was unexpected.

"Each Knight is trained to accept death as a possible consequence of battle." Despite the tightening circle of fiends surrounding them, Colt's voice wasn't the least bit shaky. "Knights fight so that others might live. Dying in service to others is the greatest honor we can achieve."

Though Colt would have given almost anything for the two of them to live, he meant what he had said. His only regret was that he didn't know whether Opal or any of the others had broken through the enemy's line.

So long as *someone* makes it to Rydah, our deaths won't be in vain, he thought.

As the goblins snarled and taunted them, Opal's face flashed in his mind's eye. His only regret just then was that he had never told her how he felt about her—such a small feat in comparison to what he faced now. If he could find courage in death, why had it eluded him in life?

Goblins carrying shortbows and crossbows shouldered their way to the front of the ring. The monsters were obviously planning to attack from afar to avoid putting themselves at further risk of the crystal sword's sting.

Colt had other plans.

"For Superius, Continae, and the Alliance!" he shouted, hurling himself at the line of archers.

Cholk roared something in his native tongue and followed. The two of them met the enemy with the crashing of metal against metal and blade against bone. The goblin battalion surged forward to meet them, and they were cast in a sea of sneering faces and wicked blades.

Colt lost sight of Cholk almost instantly, and soon after, everything else.

Passage XII

The first thing he was aware of was the smell of damp earth. The scent was so strong he could almost taste it.

Mitto opened his eyes, only to find himself enveloped by darkness. For one terrifying moment, he feared he had awoken in his own grave. He jerked, flinging his arms out, and was relieved to find open space around him. The jolt of pain that shot through his abdomen proved he was still alive.

But how had he escaped the monsters?

He sat up slowly, mindful of his injury, but something big and hard hovered over him. As his eyes adjusted to the darkness, he realized that he was under a narrow structure of some sort, possibly a bridge. He also saw he was not alone. When he recognized the tall Renegade archer, he nearly swooned with relief.

"But...*how*?" Mitto asked when Othello crouched down next to him.

"Hush. You are hurt, and the goblins are still out there."

Othello, balancing on the balls of his feet, reached for the bottom of Mitto's blood-soaked shirt. Remembering how Othello had served as the healer at Fort Faith until Sister Aric's arrival, Mitto sighed and braced himself for the sight of what was sure to be a gruesome wound.

To his surprise, a bandage of sorts was already wrapped around his waist, though that too was saturated with blood. As Othello treated the wound—again—Mitto tried to distract himself from the pain by studying his surroundings. He confirmed they were, in fact, under a small bridge, which stretched across a brook that must have been wider in years past. Judging by its simple architecture and the rotting beams, the bridge had been built long ago.

He was sure he had never seen it before, which meant that he had never been here.

Before he could ask Othello where they were, a cold, wet sensation seeped into his torn skin. Biting his lip, Mitto tried to think of something else beside the pain. Looking out beyond the narrow bridge, he tried to gauge the time of day, but there were few enough clues from his vantage. It might have been twilight or just an overcast afternoon.

There was no sign of anyone else. Despairingly, he imagined the other members of the company getting cut down by the goblins. He thought of the valiant woman warrior and the beautiful, red-haired archer. Surely, they and the Knight and the dwarf, had been overtaken.

Or was there a chance they had escaped like Mitto and the forester?

"I have nothing to dull the pain," Othello said in a low voice, "and nothing to mend the wound."

"It's that deep?"

Othello didn't reply, but Mitto heard the sound of cloth tearing. Then he felt the Renegade's strong, callused hands reach around his waist. As the new makeshift bandage was drawn tightly, Mitto watched Othello make a complex knot to secure the strip of cloth.

"Thank you," Mitto said quietly. He owed Othello far more than gratitude. The man had risked his own life to carry him, a complete stranger, to safety. "Do you know what happened to the others?"

He shook his head.

"Where—"

Othello held up a hand to silence him. "When the sun sets, we'll set out again. For now, rest."

The forester's words left no room for argument, and Mitto wasn't inclined to disagree. A few more hours of sleep would do him good. Anyway, he was too tired to balk at the idea of renewing their hike to Rydah. For the moment, he was content to close his eyes and forget everything.

The next thing Mitto knew, Othello was shaking him awake. He recalled the Renegade's promise that they would leave the sanctuary of the old bridge at nightfall. Now that the time had come, he was less than eager to get on with the mission.

But he knew they couldn't stay there forever. He allowed Othello to help him out of the damp recess, grunting when his wound protested against the movement. Although he had slept through much of the day, he still felt lightheaded and weak. The thought of walking around the treacherous forest all night was nearly enough to send him crawling back down into the muck.

Certainly, Othello would have a better chance of reaching Rydah without him.

But in spite of his physical discomfort and the perils beyond the bridge, Mitto had not lost his resolve to reach the capital. The thought of Someplace Else—and Else Fontane's—warm embrace was all that was keeping him on his feet.

The stories I'll have for her! he thought. She won't believe everything I've been through this past week. Hells, *I* hardly believe it.

Othello quickly outpaced Mitto, who, using his quarterstaff as a cane, could manage no better than a slow gait. When the Renegade disappeared from sight, Mitto feared he had decided to set off on his own after all. Moments later, however, Othello reappeared off to one side. He was apparently scouting the area, making sure no goblins were nearby.

Mitto plodded along, grimacing against the pain.

They went on like this for more than an hour. Finally, Mitto had to stop. Leaning up against a knotty oak, the merchant waited for his breathing to return to normal. The pain in his side was gradually subsiding into a dull, throbbing ache, but that would change as soon as he started moving again.

Othello reemerged from the trees a few seconds later. Without asking for an explanation or offering any word of reassurance, he shouldered his longbow and took up position at an adjacent tree.

"How far are we from Rydah?" Mitto asked.

Othello shrugged. "I've never been there."

That was nearly enough to send Mitto slumping to the ground. "What? Then how do you intend to lead us there?"

Othello took an abrupt step forward, unslung his bow, and reached for an arrow.

"Look, I didn't mean—"

Othello cut him off with a look as sharp as any arrowhead. He then turned away, looking off to the north. Using the tree as a brace, Mitto adjusted his stance and peered into the all-encompassing darkness. In the frail light of the crescent moon, he saw nothing but still, sleeping woods.

"Somebody's out there."

Although Othello had spoken in a slow, calm manner—like he always seemed to—Mitto's heart began racing. A hundred questions assailed him, but he was too frightened to put any of them into words. He had the sudden and ridiculous urge to shimmy up the tree and press his face against the bark, something he hadn't done since he was a little boy.

Goblins, however, were far more likely to climb up after him than his short-tempered father had been.

Or they'd just fell the damned tree.

The thought of facing even one goblin was enough to make his knees go weak. He had never thought of himself as a coward, but this recent string of near-death experiences had frayed the fiber of his courage.

After a minute or two, Mitto heard the sound of someone—or more than one someone—scuttling through the forest. He knew without a doubt they were drawing nearer. He altered his grip on the quarterstaff.

Come and get me, Goblin, and let's be done with it, he silently taunted.

Othello drew back his bowstring but then let the string go slack again and pointed the tip of the arrow at the ground. Mitto gave the Renegade a perplexed look, but Othello was paying him no attention whatsoever.

By this time, Mitto could make out two distinct shapes in the night, and he nearly laughed out loud when he recognized them.

Opal stopped dead in her path. She must not have immediately identified them because she hefted her crossbow up. Likewise, Lilac raised her sword and look up a defensive stance. Then both women seemed to recognize their allies at the same time for they lowered their weapons.

"Thank the gods," Lilac said quietly. "We feared you both were dead."

The female Renegade was all smiles as she came forward and wrapped Othello in a tight hug. The man stiffened at Lilac's embrace but didn't push her away. Tentatively, awkwardly, he patted her on the back.

"Where are the others?" Opal asked with a hand on her hip.

When Othello didn't answer, Mitto stammered, "Um, well, we haven't seen them since we got separated."

Opal's shoulders slumped, but then her expression grew even more determined. "We have to search for them."

"What?" Lilac demanded. "That wasn't what we decided!"

"I changed my mind." Opal replied, her voice growing louder with every word. "If these two escaped the goblins, Colt and Cholk might have too. We have to find them."

"We still have a mission to complete," Lilac protested.

"And we will," Opal assured her, "but first, we will learn what happened to our...to *my* friends."

Lilac shook her head helplessly, and Mitto understood this wasn't the first time they had debated the topic. He thought it was a small miracle the two women had come to any sort of agreement, given their prickly relationship.

Perhaps the bigger miracle was they hadn't killed each other before now.

"Colt would have wanted us to complete the mission," Lilac said. "For all we know, he and Cholk are still en route to Rydah. We may well find him waiting for us there."

Opal might not have even heard her. "With Colt and Cholk missing, I am the next logical choice for leader, and I say locating the missing members of our band is our highest priority."

Throughout the exchange, Othello hadn't said a word. Whatever was decided, he seemed content to go along with it. So when Opal's bold declaration provoked a lull in the conversation, Mitto found both women looking at him, as though expecting him to cast the deciding vote.

He looked helplessly from Lilac to Opal. Both women had made viable points, and Mitto didn't want to anger either of them. He thought Lilac was right about Colt wanting them to continue without him, but he also saw the fear beneath Opal's mask of obstinacy.

How could he ask her to leave her friends behind? Othello had risked everything to save him. Shouldn't they all do the same for Colt and Cholk?

"Um...well...I...I just don't know," he said at length.

Disappointment darkened both women's expressions.

"You are not my leader," Lilac told Opal. "If you want to waste your time wandering blindly through these woods, be my guest, but it's only a matter of time before the goblins find you…and kill you. I, for one, am going to Rydah."

Without waiting for Opal's reply, Lilac stormed away in the direction she and Opal had been headed before. Othello gave Opal an unreadable look before following after Lilac. When he overtook Lilac, he said something that caused the woman to pause briefly. When Lilac resumed her brisk pace, she had adjusted her course so that she was going the way Othello had been leading.

Othello followed close behind her. Neither Renegade bothered to look back.

"Coward!" Opal shouted after them. She looked tempted to fire a bolt into Lilac's back.

But she didn't. Cursing furiously, Opal stormed after the Renegades. Mitto was left to hustle clumsily after them.

"If you think I'm going to let you escape, you're crazy," Opal said. "You're still prisoners of the Knights of Superius."

Lilac didn't respond. The two women walked side by side, looking at everything but each other. Othello took the lead once more, guiding the party through the dense forest and looking back every now and then to make sure they were following.

Mitto brought up the rear. It was not a strategic or even an intentional move. At one point, Opal glanced back to find him straggling. He expected her to scold him, but she must have noticed his limp or how he was leaning on his quarterstaff for support because she muttered something to Lilac. After that, the party's pace slowed noticeably.

They walked all night, taking only brief rests. No one spoke during these short respites.

When the first rays of morning began poking down through the forest canopy, they were forced to find a place to sleep. They chose a spot that didn't seem much different from anywhere else, though a cluster of birch trees provided some cover from the west.

Othello took first watch, followed by Opal and, finally, Lilac. When it came to Mitto's turn, more than half of the day had already expired, and everyone was ready to press on despite the remaining hours of sunlight. Silently, the company of four pressed on. After a while, the monotonous activity began to play with Mitto's mind. He imagined he was trapped in a fever dream where he couldn't deviate from the repetition.

Little did he know the true nightmare was yet to come.

*   *   *

The following day proved as uneventful as the prior one. Mitto was beginning to fear they had gotten turned around. Surely, they should have reached Rydah by now!

Midway through the next day, however, they came upon a road that intersected their own path perpendicularly. Having traversed the road more times than he could recall, Mitto knew it for the highway that connected Rydah to the rural community Hylan.

Practically dizzy with delight, he told the others they were, at most, a handful of miles from the capital. Following his advice, they turned north. The company held fast to the edge of the forest, ready to return to the cover of the trees at the first sign of danger. They met no one—friend or foe—during that last leg of their journey.

True to Mitto's prediction, they reached the Rydah before nightfall.

But Mitto's joy at finally arriving home was dispelled at the first sight of the city. A dark cloud stretched over the city, a thunderhead made of smoke wafting up from the capital. The next thing Mitto noticed was the Celestial Palace—or, rather, the lack thereof.

Even at a great distance, a traveler could see the palace's spires, which stretched heavenward like the fingers of the faithful reaching up to the heavens. Not only was the Celestial Palace gone, but Rydah's alabaster walls, too, had all but vanished.

Mitto quickened his pace, heedless of the discomfort of his wound. His mind had gone numb, and the closer he got to the ruined capital, the less real it all seemed.

Southgate and the walls around it had been reduced to a mass of jagged masonry, allowing Mitto a view of the city itself. Most all of the buildings—homes and shops alike—had been burned to the ground. The corpses of Rydah's citizens were strewn about the blood-stained streets. Men, women, and children alike lay in various horrible poses.

Goblin corpses also littered the ground. Some of the monsters still clutched the weapons they had used to butcher the defenseless townsfolk.

As Mitto stepped over what remained of the southern wall, his shock wore off, and he stumbled. Down on his hands and knees, he purged the contents of his all-but-empty stomach onto the soiled street. After a time, someone came over and helped him to his feet.

Only partially aware of Opal, who continued to support him, Mitto once more took in the absolute ruin that Rydah had become in his absence.

Lilac knelt beside the headless body of a child who couldn't have been older than three. "This can't be happening," she whispered, though the last word was choked off.

"It's so much worse than we feared," Opal said a faraway voice.

"Don't move!"

In the ghoulish silence, the sudden shout caused all four of them to start. The disembodied command was immediately followed by the emergence of three figures from a half-burned shack. The newcomers were human by all appearances. Two of them—a Knight and a much older man in a dark cloak—carried crossbows, which they leveled at the company. The third person, a dark-haired woman, carried only a short sword.

"If any one of you so much as takes a deep breath, you'll be dead before you let it out," the Knight promised.

The woman gasped loudly, causing her companions to glance away from their targets. That's when Mitto recognized the woman beneath the smudged and weary expression.

Else Fontane.

Keeping her sword at the ready, she took a step toward Mitto and said, "Tell me something only you would know about me!"

Mitto's mouth moved fruitlessly for a couple seconds before he blurted out the first things that came to mind, "You can drink more Dragon's Hoard than most men, you always beat me at dice, and I love you."

Else dropped her weapon and wrapped him in a great hug. Although she was crushing his ribs and causing the most exquisite pain to rip through his side, he returned her embrace with every ounce of strength he possessed.

It made no sense that the proprietress of Someplace Else was alive, armed, and in the company of two warriors. But reason no longer mattered to Mitto O'erlander.

Surrounded by death and ruin, he had found the one thing in the world he valued above all else.

Part 3

Passage I

Else walked as though in a daze, her thoughts leaping from tangent to tangent.

Ever since the attack on Rydah six nights ago, she had been overcome by a relentless numbness. The tragedy had been too sudden, so widespread, and she had been perfectly fine with avoiding the torrent of emotion swelling beneath the surface.

If she started crying, she might never stop.

But reuniting with Mitto had undone the façade, and now she struggled to close the floodgates of her heart. Ever since Rydah had been sacked and burned to the ground—she thought she could measure the time in years rather than days—she had held out a private hope that her dearest friend was alive and somewhere safe from the army of monsters that had appeared out of nowhere.

She almost didn't want to look at the man, lest he vanish like some wayward ghost. But she couldn't resist. Life on the road wasn't always conducive to a tidy appearance, but Else had never seen Mitto looking so filthy. Black stubble shadowed his cheeks, and there was no sign of the silly three-cornered hat he always wore. His clothes were spattered with mud and blood.

How had Mitto, a middle-aged merchant, managed to survive the monsters' invasion? Who were his friends, and what were they were doing at the massive graveyard that was Rydah?

And what, exactly, had Mitto meant when he said he loved her?

But this was no place for an inquisition, so Else contented herself with walking hand-in-hand with Mitto as they left the ruins of Rydah. When they finally reached the hideout—a stone cottage five miles or so outside of the capital—Else hardly knew where to begin.

Out of habit, she welcomed the newcomers to the dwelling.

She might have offered them a drink too, but the monsters had carried off whatever ale might have been on hand. As for the cottage's former owners, Else herself had happened upon the corpses of the elderly couple, mutilated and tossed onto a pile of broken furniture.

Because there was no guarantee the monsters had already been here, there was no guarantee they wouldn't return, no less than four sentries kept watch from the forest at all times. By all appearances, the other scouting parties were not back yet, and so, Else offered her guests a place on the floor. There would be hardly enough room for everyone to stand when the others returned.

Now she had no choice but to face Mitto. She watched him and his friends ease themselves onto the hard, wooden planks of the floor. The tall fellow with the fierce green eyes remained standing, however, as did Sir Dylan.

The Knight crossed his arms expectantly but said nothing. It's your show, he seemed to say. Get on with it! Else nearly smiled then. It was Dylan's impatience that had earned him a place among the scouting parties.

Mitto's eyes went wide when her other companion pulled back his hood.

"Loony Gomez?" he exclaimed. "In the name of all the gods, Else, what's going on here?"

She took a deep breath. It was not an easy tale to tell. The Knights had interrogated her the day after the attack, but she had still been in shock at the time. Now her defenses were down, and the thought of reliving her flight from the burning capital caused a wave of nausea to wash over her.

"You first, Mitto. I know you are who you say you are, but we also know some of the monsters have the ability to take on the appearance of humans. How well do you know your companions?"

"They aren't goblins. This man saved my life, and they"—he indicated the women with a wave of his hand—"are covered in goblin blood, a testament to their hatred for the bastards."

Else smiled sheepishly at the strangers. "Forgive my suspicion, but we can't be too careful. And please pardon my directness, but who are you?"

"My name is Opal," the red-haired woman said.

"And I'm Lilac," said the blonde with the sword. "He is

Othello. The two of us are former Renegades who were taken captive at Fort Faith. She's a friend of the fort's commander, and it seems that you already know Mitto. The four of us, along with two others, were sent to deliver word of the goblins' invasion to the capital. We had no idea…"

Lilac trailed off, and Else's stomach fluttered again. She didn't want to think about what had happened to Rydah and her people. She found it difficult to believe that the Knights of Fort Faith would send rebels in lieu of Knights, but Else had learned firsthand that war made for strange bedfellows.

The fact that she, Gomez, and Dylan were working together was evidence of that.

"Else," Mitto said in a soft voice she nearly didn't recognize, "what happened to our home?"

When Else started talking, she spoke quickly, hoping that her words would outpace her feelings. She barely took time to breathe, and when she felt her eyes begin to burn, the harbinger of tears to come, she ignored it.

As she related her flight from the doomed city, she focused all of her attention on Mitto's filthy, wonderful face.

Had she known that it was the last time she would ever see Bryant Walden, she would have said something meaningful to him. She might have thanked the high commander for treating her so kindly or kissed him on the cheek for good luck. She had no idea whether the Knight was married or not; she couldn't even guess what his reaction to such an impulsive move would have been.

In the days to come, Else would have plenty of time to ponder the heroic Sir Walden.

At the time, she hadn't even said goodbye. The high commander abruptly departed to ready his men for the battle against the Renegades, leaving her in the company of Lord Minus. Else would always remember Magnes Minus as a kind-faced man. Even when the Celestial Palace began to shudder beneath the blows that resounded like thunder—even after they looked out the window and found that a fleet of strange, tower-like ships sailing into the harbor—the Lord of Capricon kept his wits about him.

Lord Minus issued instructions to guardsmen and attendants

in a quick but calm voice. Even when he ordered one man to personally see to his wife's safety, Lord Minus's face remained unperturbed.

It occurred to Else the residents of the Celestial Palace had not been caught completely unprepared by the Renegades' assault. A small assembly of men-at-arms led her and the Lord of Capricon down a steep, winding staircase that had been hidden behind a tapestry.

Inside the cramped passageway, the booming clamor that shook the palace and sent showers of dust raining down on them. She worried the magnificent towers would topple, crushing her beneath tons of rock.

Nevertheless, she followed the Lord Minus and his retinue down in the bowels of the palace.

Finally, the stairs came to an end. The candlelight that had illuminated their decent was insufficient for her to see what was going on up ahead. She heard stone scraping against stone, and the next thing she knew, she was being helped down into a hole.

Else gripped the cold, metal rungs tightly with her hands and gingerly worked her feet against the wall in search for the next one. When she reached the bottom, she found herself in a large, bare-walled chamber that was lit by several candelabra.

Lord Minus and his wife, the Lady Corrine, shared a brief embrace. The lord then issued more instructions to his attendants, who retreated back up the rungs. A half a dozen Knights remained behind, and after the last aide was clear of the hole, the stone slab was slid back into place.

One of the Knights stood beneath the trapdoor and made frequent glances up at the stone. While Else knew that they were taking such measures in order to keep the Renegades and their allies out, the innkeeper couldn't help but note that they were simultaneously shutting themselves in.

After the echoes of retreating footsteps faded away, the room grew as quiet as a tomb.

"So you waited out the attack in the palace's keep?" Mitto asked. "And to think, if it hadn't been for Toemis Blisnes, Sir Walden wouldn't have had any reason to introduce himself to you at Someplace Else. That's a stroke of fortune. But I'm still not sure how Loony Gomez fits into it all."

"Who ya callin' loony?" Gomez demanded.

Else paid the old man no attention for she had a question of her own. "Sir Walden had said Baxter and another Knight followed you in order to keep an eye on Toemis. Did your paths cross?"

She knew the truth from his face before Mitto said a word. "Baxter and another Knight did catch up with us. While we were fighting off highwaymen, more Knights burst out of the woods. They were being chased by goblins. It was the first time I saw the monsters. We wouldn't have escaped if it weren't for Baxter …"

A lump formed in her throat, and again her eyes tingled with promise of tears. Stubbornly, she willed them away. "Did he…die quickly?"

Mitto shrugged helplessly. "I honestly don't know."

In the quiet that followed, Else remembered the many nights she and Mitto had shared with Baxter Lawler. She had always thought of him as a friend of a friend. But now she realized that beneath their playful bickering, a true friendship had formed.

The world was a far drearier place without Baxter in it.

Lilac cleared her throat and said, "Excuse me, Else, but what happened after you were sealed in the palace's keep? Were you able to wait out the attack?"

Else took another deep breath before replying, "We would have, except the Celestial Palace fell on top of us."

The rumbling was getting worse. When a particularly violent crash sent them all to the floor, Lord Minus ordered the hatch to be reopened so that they might survey the damage.

On the advice of one of the soldiers, they waited for several minutes longer until everything was still. In Else's opinion, the silence was even more frightening than the crashes had been. Finally, one of the Knights climbed the rungs, but no matter how hard he—or any of the other men—pushed against the stone slab, it wouldn't budge.

"Whatever does it mean?" Lady Corrine asked her husband.

"Something must have fallen on the opening," Magnes Minus reasoned. Even while making that ominous declaration, the lord sounded calm. "But do not fret. This room was designed with both protection and escape in mind."

Lord Minus walked over to a sconce that held an unlit torch and gave it an expert twist. Like in the stories Else had heard since she was small enough to sit on her father's lap, a section of the adjacent wall slid aside to reveal another dark passage. Else's anxiety only mounted. In the tales, secret passageways seldom led anywhere good.

Lord Minus brought the torch to life with the aid of a candle. After three of the Knights dutifully took their place in the lead, the lord took his lady by the hand and escorted her through the threshold of the passage. As the remaining three Knights were clearly waiting her to go next, Else swallowed her apprehension and started toward the tunnel.

But a shrill scream kept her rooted in place.

Corrine reemerged, covering her face with her hands. Lord Minus was right behind her. He wore a grim expression as he comforted his wife. To Else's bewilderment, the three Knights returned too, and the last man was dragging something large and limp behind him.

Her knees weaken when she realized that the something was a dead body.

"Who is it?" she asked in spite of herself.

No one answered at first. Lord Minus and the Knights formed a circle around the corpse and began talking in hushed tones. Feeling suddenly alone, Else made her way over to where Corrine sat on a three-legged stool. The lady appeared to have regained some of her composure, but her complexion remained as white as fresh milk.

Else took her hand. It was the first time she really looked at Corrine Minus. Although the Lady of Capricon had seen more than fifty winters, the deep wrinkles around her mouth and at the corners of her eyes did not mar her elegance, but rather instilled her with dignity and poise.

Corrine's dress was finely tailored, but it lacked the frills and flashy accoutrements Else would have expected of a noble-woman. But even in her everyday garb, Corrine would never have been mistaken for a commoner.

How did I end up here? Else wondered.

All at once, the crowd of Knights dissipated, and Lord Minus came forward to stand before his wife. "I cannot understand it. I recognize this man as one of the cooking staff, but how he found his way to the keep..."

"How did they die?" Corrine asked.

"*They*?" Else echoed incredulously.

Lord Minus produced a black-feathered arrow. "They were all laid low by arrows like these, but I cannot imagine who—"

His words were cut off by an eerie, high-pitched wail that resonated from the open passageway. The Knights formed a protective barrier between their lord and lady and the opening. The sound of scuffling footsteps drew nearer and nearer.

When the creatures poured into the room, Else could scarcely believe her eyes and feared whoever had dug the palace's escape route had inadvertently breached Thanatos' Crypt.

The monsters came at the Knights like slavering jackals, overwhelming the meager defenders in seconds. They crawled over the soldiers—scrambled over each other—in their eagerness to kill.

Paralyzed with fear, Else heard Magnes Minus's voice but couldn't understand what he was saying. Time seemed to slow impossibly, giving her plenty of time to contemplate the certainty of her death. Then something solid connected with the side of her head, and she lost consciousness.

Reliving that terrible day brought back all of the fear she had felt. Else paused for a moment before concluding, "I awoke to find myself in the woods...near enough Rydah to hear the screams of the dying. It was there that Corrine, Gomez, some of his friends, and I waited out the attack."

Else was aware of the shift in her audience's attention. Even Sir Dylan glanced away from window he had been staring out and looked at Gomez. Else surreptitiously dabbed at her eyes with the backs of her hands. She wished that she could shut out his voice, what she knew he would say.

"The first thing ya oughtta know is that the dead people in the passageway were all Renegades," Gomez said. "I know this 'cause me and m'boys followed 'em. They was plannin' to murder the lord an' lady, but the devils...or goblins, as you're been callin' 'em...wanted to do it themselves. An' they might've killed every last person in the keep if I hadn't done the single most foolish thing in m'life and stuck around."

When Gomez took a breath, Opal quickly interjected, "I don't mean to be rude, but who are you exactly?"

Sir Dylan crossed his arms and said, "He is the mysterious and ever-elusive Guildmaster."

Gomez let out a hardy chuckle that reminded Else of better times, but the guffaw died when he saw the blank expression on Opal's face.

"Don't tell me ya never heard of the Thief Guild!"

Opal shrugged. "Sorry."

Gomez's eyebrows nearly touched his hairline, which had been steadily receding for years. "What about you?" he demanded of the others.

Lilac shook her head and said, "Sorry...but you must forgive us. The three of us are relatively new to the island."

But Mitto was still gaping at Gomez. "You can't be serious!"

The merchant's reaction seemed to placate Gomez. "The perfect disguise, no? Anyway, after the Renegades shut down the Guild, I had nothing but time on my hands, so I did what I could to keep abreast of their plans. Through a fair amount of eavesdropping and bribery, I learned that the rebels were going to invade Rydah with the help of a secret army. Of course, I never would've guessed they had made a pact with monsters!"

"The Renegades likely didn't know they were dealing with goblins," Sir Dylan added. "They can take human form, after all. And even if Rydah's Renegade Leader wasn't bewitched by a spell, he didn't live long enough to regret the alliance."

Gomez cleared his throat dramatically. "The truth is, we don't know how the goblins got the Renegades to open the gates for them, but each and every rebel received the same reward...a swift and brutal death.

"But getting back to the story, my boys and I followed the Renegades through a maze of underground passages...some of the very tunnels the Guild was wont to use...but when we saw the goblins kill the rebels, we held back. I *should've* run. If I had, I'd likely be in Kraken now, nursing a mug of mulled wine."

"So why didn't you?" Opal asked.

The old man seemed taken aback by her query. He blinked, as though trying to find his bearings, and then resumed his account—and his favorite accent, Else noted.

"I dunno. Curiosity, maybe? Or maybe I'm just a suicidal ol' fool. M'boys an' I followed the goblins all the way to the keep, where they stormed Lord Minus and his men. I lost many friends in the fray, but we managed to save Else and Lady Corrine. But the Lord of Capricon wasn't so lucky."

Else closed her eyes, unable to stem the tide of tears any longer. She was grateful to have been unconscious when the kindly lord met his fate. She had learned of Magnes Minus's death from his widowed wife.

Thinking of how Corrine must have felt upon leaving the body of her beloved husband behind made Else's heart break. Lord Minus was dead, and there was no sign of Bryant Walden. According to Mitto, Baxter was lost too. The senseless tribulation was just too terrible to contemplate.

She must have started crying for she was suddenly aware of someone's arms around her. Whenever these fits had overtaken her in the past, Loony Gomez and Dylan Torc had given her a respectful berth. But right then, the proximity of another body alleviated some of her pain.

Burying her face in Mitto's chest, she whispered, "What now? What now?" again and again.

Mitto swept his fingers through her hair. "I don't know, Else, but we'll figure it out together."

Passage II

Seated in the middle of the floor of his room, his legs crossed and hands resting on his knees, Stannel willed all of the tension out of his body.

Keeping his eyes closed and his breathing steady, he focused first on one area and then another. Several minutes later, his entire body was relaxed. He felt lighter than air, as though his spirit might easily drift free of its corporeal shell.

In this state, the fine line between inner reflection and prayer became irrevocably blurred. He began by thanking the Great Protector for seeing him through the many trials of the day, including one particularly exhausting conversation with Lieutenant Petton. After reviewing his actions of that day and evaluating them objectively, he allowed his thoughts to drift toward the same preoccupations that had haunted him for the past few days.

Stannel remembered those who had perished at the old Fort Valor, friends and comrades he would not see again in this life. He asked Pintor to assuage the invisible wounds that marred him and sought comfort in the knowledge that the Gods of Good would guide their souls to Paradise.

He would see them again when his own time came to die.

Next, he asked his heavenly patron for guidance and wisdom. He let go of any reservations he still harbored about accepting the command at new Fort Valor. Stannel had learned long ago that doubts were snares in the road to reason. One cannot change the past, he thought. One can only control his present and adjust his course to the future.

Stannel started at the sound of someone rapping on his door. He just stared at the door for a few seconds. When the knocking came again, he stretched out his legs, stood, and went to it. He was loath to abandon his meditation, but he was well acquainted with the unfortunate fact that his responsibilities as commander took precedent over his personal wellbeing.

He opened the door to find Sister Aric holding a tray of food.

"Am I interrupting?" she asked in a pleasant voice.

"Nothing that can't wait," he replied. "Please, come in."

Ever since she had decided to stay on at the original Fort Valor, Aric had been Stannel's confidant, one of his dearest friends. She might have guessed that she was intruding upon his meditating because she knew all about Stannel's spiritual exercises.

Moreover, Aric was just about the only other person who knew the full extent of his extraordinary relationship with the Great Protector.

"I brought you some supper," she said, setting the tray on a bedside table.

Stannel saw that the meal was made up of a small portion of beef, a few raw vegetables, and a hunk of bread. The brass goblet that rested beside the plate was filled with water.

"Thank you, my friend, but you need not have bothered."

She raised an eyebrow.

"I am fasting."

Aric nodded slowly, but her smile dimmed. The two of them had long debated the positive and negative effects of fasting. Aric, who believed proper nutrition was paramount to maintaining good health, could not understand why a man would willingly starve himself for days on end.

As a priestess of the healing goddess, Aric was concerned with caring for the body. Stannel's training, on the other hand, had taught him that one could deny the flesh in order to empower the soul.

Today, Aric did not voice her protests about how he was making himself more susceptible to sickness—or what a fine warrior he would make if he lacked the strength to swing his claymore.

Instead she said, "Don't you think it might be a good idea to dine with the men...for their sakes, if not for yours?"

Stannel said nothing at first. He had, in fact, considered this aspect of his fasting. As the new commander of this fortress, he ought to spend time among his men, socializing with them and showing them what kind of leader—what kind of man—he was.

And to some degree, he had been doing so ever since Colt and his party departed.

Dinner, however, was a special case. Meals were a time for camaraderie, an event where a commander could relate to his men on a more intimate level. It was also an opportunity to make friends.

But the truth was Stannel wasn't interested in making new friends—not yet.

"They will always see you as an outsider if you hole yourself up in your room," Aric said. There was no reproach in her words. She spoke only out of concern for him.

"I concede your point," he began, "but I will not be a good leader to them if my thoughts are clouded. That is why I fast and meditate. I may not be their commander for long…for when Colt returns, I intend to abdicate…but in the meantime, I intend to do the best that I can.

"If that means I must immolate conviviality for pragmatism, then so be it."

Aric's expression softened. She took a seat in an old wooden chair that rested against the wall. Other than the bed and small table, it was the only other piece of furniture in the small room.

"Thank you for thinking of me, Aric," he said as he took a seat on the edge of his bed. "But I must do as I see fit."

"You always do," Aric replied with a little laugh. "But you can't blame me for being concerned. How are you really holding up?"

Stannel offered a slight smile. "I might ask the same of you. We have lost many friends."

The healer glanced down at her folded hands, and when she looked up again, her eyes held a faraway look. "When new initiates are accepted into Mystel's ministry, the first thing they learn is that death is a part of life. Man is mortal, and no matter how good of a healer you become, you will never become the master of death."

Stannel nodded.

"In many ways, we healers are not so different from the Knights, only our wars take place *after* yours. Our battlefield is the body itself. Every healer has lost patients. It's inevitable. In my profession, you become well-acquainted with death. He's the unwelcome visitor in every infirmary, always leering over your shoulder."

Stannel remained quiet. Although Aric had come to see to his welfare, she had come for her own as well.

"Many patients have died under my care. Each death is a loss, but a healer must never feel defeated by them. Although we wield the goddess's power, we are only mortals. When it is time for a person to die, nothing can thwart that destiny. I have lost many patients, and I have lost more than a few friends.

"But never before have I lost so many friends at once."

Her voice trailed off as she finished, and Stannel saw her eyes were glossy with tears.

"There was nothing you could do," he stated. "Nothing either of us could have done."

Aric produced an unconvincing smile. "I know that, and I hope you truly believe that too, Stannel. You were their commander, but even if you had been there, the result would have been the same."

Stannel nodded again. While meditating, he tried to cleanse himself of guilt. It was important to learn from the past, but one must never let it hamper the present or the future. The fact was, his men were dead, and he was alive. The gods—Pintor himself—must have had a reason for sparing him.

He could only pray he would prove worthy of that gift.

"How are your patients here?" Stannel asked, broaching this new topic as much to leave the past behind as to amass information pertinent to his new command.

"All of them are on their way to recovery." She signed. "All of them except for Toemis Blisnes, that is. The longer he sleeps, the more likely it is that he never will wake from the coma."

"What about Ruben?"

Aric smiled, and perhaps it was the first genuine smile of hers Stannel had seen since learning of Fort Valor's demise.

"Thank the Goddess, he will be fine," she said. "The goblin arrow didn't puncture any vital organs. Mystel willing, Ruben will be back on his feet any day now."

"What about the men who were injured before we arrived?" Stannel asked.

"Plake…he's one of the Renegades…well, he is faking his injuries. He says he suffers from headaches, but they aren't distressing enough to stop him from complaining from sunrise to sunset. In truth, he suffers from naught but a broken nose, which is healing nicely."

"And the Renegade Leader?"

"Aside from Toemis, Klye is perhaps my most perplexing patient. He had a burn on his hand, and his body is covered with more cuts and bruises than I can count, but none of them are enough to keep him bound to a sickbed," Aric explained.

"Klye is faking too?"

"No," she replied. "If it were up to him, he would have left the infirmary long ago. He's terribly weak, however. It must be an effect of the shaman's magic. He's recovering slowly, but there's little I can do to hasten the process, seemingly."

Stannel listened as Aric described the condition of Matthew Fisk, a Knight who had nearly lost his life to Lilac's enchanted blade, and was pleased to learn that Sir Fisk looked as though he was going to pull through after all.

A little while later, Aric stood and said, "I really ought to be getting back to the infirmary. I want to be there in case there is any change in Toemis's condition."

Stannel walked the healer to his door. "Don't forget to take care of yourself."

"I would say the same to you," she shot back with a smile. "Please call on me if you need someone to talk to…even though we somehow always end up talking about me!"

"You are more helpful than you know, my friend."

They said goodnight, and Stannel shut the door behind her. He paused for a moment, looking out the window at nothing in particular, before resuming the cross-legged position in the center of the floor. Shutting out the savory smells wafting from the tray of food and ignoring its effect on his empty stomach, Stannel closed his eyes and reached out for the warm embrace of the Great Protector.

Lilac was dirty and bone-weary, she and had a headache to boot. Despite all of that, she listened patiently to the horrible events that had happened in Rydah.

She had seen the results with her own eyes—the capital in ruins, its citizens slaughtered—but even after hearing Else and Gomez's account of the goblin attack, she had plenty of questions. Although she wanted only to curl up and sleep on the dusty floor, Lilac knew she must learn as much as she could before returning to the fort.

Since Else was sobbing in Mitto's arms, Lilac looked to Sir Dylan for the answers.

While many of the other Renegades, including Klye, had few good things to say about the Knights of Superius, Lilac had always held a great respect for the defenders of the realm. At times, she had envied her younger brother, Gabriel, who had made their father proud by joining the Knighthood. She had learned a lot about the Knights from Gabriel, including tips and techniques to improve her swordplay.

She couldn't help but be reminded of Gabriel when she was around Knights. Perhaps it was their general attire, or maybe it had to do with the way they carried themselves. Gabriel had certainly held himself with more dignity after being knighted. Whatever it was, Lilac had seen her brother's face while sparring with Dominic Horcalus. And Colt, who was roughly the same age as Gabriel had been, unwittingly imitated her brother from time to time.

Maybe it was her great longing to see Gabriel again that so frequently summoned his ghost. Certainly, Horcalus was more rigid and proper than Gabriel had ever been, and Colt, with his dark eyes and brown hair, didn't resemble her brother physically.

Nonetheless, Lilac couldn't help but see Gabriel Zephyr while looking at Sir Dylan.

Judging by his age, Dylan hadn't been a Knight for very long. There was an obvious listlessness in his bearing. When Dylan's gaze met hers, she realized that she had been staring at him.

Hoping her cheeks weren't turning red, she asked, "What has become of Corrine Minus? And what of the other survivors? Surely the goblins didn't kill everyone."

The Knight fixed her with a scrutinizing stare before replying. "Lady Corrine should be safely to Kraken by now. As for the others, well, a few were fortunate enough to escape the slaughter. A small contingent of Knights managed to hold the monsters off long enough for some of the civilians to flee. Those survivors are now residing in Hylan, where they depend on the farm folk for food and shelter."

"How many Knights accompanied them there?" she asked. "What is left of Rydah's garrison?"

"You certainly ask a lot of questions," Dylan returned flatly.

"We are here on behalf of Fort Valor in order to learn every-thing we can about the goblins' movements," Lilac explained. "Commander Stannel will want to know how many allies remain in the region."

Dylan's eyes narrowed. "I thought you said you were from Fort Faith."

Opal abruptly rose to her feet. "Fort Faith recently underwent a few changes after the goblins destroyed the original Fort Valor. Now Fort Faith is called Fort Valor, and Stannel Bismarc commands there instead of Saerylton Crystalus. I'd be happy to share the whole story if you have a day or two, but if you think we're goblin spies, nothing we say will change your mind."

Sir Dylan blanched at Opal's candor and didn't say anything for a few seconds. Lilac tried her best to hide a smile. It was nice to have Opal's sharp tongue on her side for once, not that she expected it would happen often.

"I...I didn't mean to offend," Dylan stammered. "It's diffi-cult *not* to be suspicious when the enemy can disguise himself so convincingly."

"We understand," Lilac said, "but we're going to have to trust one another if we are to have any chance at ejecting this foreign army."

When Dylan hesitated, the old man in the black cloak—Else had called him Gomez—said, "Gods above and below, Dylan, just tell the lady what they she wants to know. If they were goblin spell-casters, they'd have killed us long before now. In case you've forgotten, the monsters don't take prisoners."

Dylan seemed to struggle with the decision a moment longer before answering. "Three Knights escorted Lady Corinne to Kraken. The rest of the warriors...there are less than fifty...remain in Hylan, prepared to give their lives to stop the goblins' advance. But we have no way of knowing whether the enemy will pursue them south or if they will go west."

Or both, Lilac thought.

Surely there had been hundreds, maybe even thousands of warriors stationed in Rydah. Add their deaths to the Knights who perished at the original Fort Valor, and, by Lilac's calcula-tions, the goblins were well on their way to conquering the eastern half of the island.

"Who is in charge of the remaining forces?" Lilac asked.

"A sergeant by the name of Dale Mullahstyn leads the

Knights," Dylan said, "though Captain Ruford, an officer from Rydah's coastal guard has a say in what goes on. He's more experienced than Sir Mullahstyn.

"For the moment, they are preparing what defenses they can in case the goblins hit Hylan next. Volunteers like Else, Gomez, and myself, use this cottage as our base. We have been making daily trips to Rydah, looking for survivors and trying to learn what we can about where the goblins went. You were the first living people we've found."

Lilac nodded, committing the information to memory. She glanced over at Gomez and found him staring at her.

Perhaps the old man sensed her curiosity for he said, "You might be wondering why me and my boys are working with the Knights. Well, we're only too happy to do our part! Rydah was our home as much as it was theirs. And anyway, the goblins are the enemy of all humans. Even if we headed for Kraken or Steppt, the monsters would likely be right on our heels."

Lilac smiled grimly. The Renegades—Klye's Renegades, anyway—had come to that same realization.

"We should be leaving," Opal announced.

"At least stay the night," Gomez offered. "You'll not make it far if you're dead on your feet."

"Two of our companions are missing. We must find them and get back to the fort as quickly as possible," Opal replied.

Lilac cast a sidelong glance at the other woman. What was this talk of looking for Colt and Cholk? Hadn't they already decided that completing the mission was the most important thing? She wanted to confront the headstrong woman right then and there but thought it best not to argue in front of Dylan and the others.

Not that she had the energy for another disagreement with Opal.

"We understand," Dylan said. "But if I were you, I wouldn't go near Rydah. The goblins' camp is somewhere to the west of the ruins."

"Thanks for the warning," Lilac said. The idea of staying at the cottage to sleep for a while was tempting, but she knew they couldn't afford to waste time. "And thank you for your hospitality."

Dylan grunted. "What hospitality? We accuse you of being goblins and can't even offer you a meal...or a chair to sit in."

Opal rose to her feet. "Let's hope next time we meet, it'll be under better circumstances."

"Indeed," Dylan said.

Then the rest of them stood except for Mitto and Else. The merchant continued to hold the woman. Clearly, he had no intention of leaving Else's side anytime soon. Mitto had wanted only to reach Rydah. He had never planned on accompanying the troupe back to the fort.

Although she didn't know Mitto very well at all, Lilac was sorry to leave him behind. If nothing else, he was a brave man who had risked his life to get back to his home—and to Else, apparently. Lilac prayed the two the two of them would find peace together.

Her eyes met Mitto's in a silent farewell as Dylan walked her, Opal, and Othello to the door. The Knight muttered brief goodbye, and then the three of them were swallowed up once more by the cool night air.

Passage III

Othello took the lead without being asked. Lilac followed, aware of Opal's presence only by the sound of her footsteps behind her. A sliver of moon provided more shadows than light.

Her hand resting on the pommel of the vorpal sword, Lilac kept an eye out for signs of the enemy. As tired as she was, she wondered if she could muster the strength for another battle should the goblins attack again. Othello's quiver was nearly empty, and neither he nor Opal were adept at hand-to-hand combat.

Opal made no mention of tracking down Colt and Cholk after they left the cottage, and neither did Lilac.

Ever since she had joined Klye's band of Renegades, determined to protect Ragellan and Horcalus from assassins, she had felt a sense of purpose and of true accomplishment. In the end, she had failed Chester Ragellan, but Horcalus was still alive because of her efforts. Never before had she been a part of something larger than herself, and the combination of self-satisfaction and constant danger was more than a little intoxicating.

She had been glad to join Colt's company, not only for the chance of avenging Ragellan and her brother, but also because she yearned for the chance—any chance—to make a positive difference in the war.

By no small miracle, they had made it to Rydah. If the three of them were killed now, the Knights and Renegades back at Fort Valor might never learn what had become of the island's capital. She could only trust that the gods would get them back home safely.

And it would probably take divine intervention to dissuade

Opal from her fool's errand.

As they walked, Lilac stole what glimpses she could at the night's sky to confirm the direction they were traveling. But even though autumn's winds had swept the leaves from some of the treetops, many held fast to their foliage, like old misers hoarding what they must surely lose in the end.

She never once questioned Othello's choice in paths. If what the others said about Othello were true, the archer had spent most all of his life in a wilderness like this. Anyway, he seemed confident in his path.

At dawn they rested for a few hours, but none of them wanted to linger, so they resumed their hike with aching feet and grumbling stomachs. The forest looked entirely different during the day. At night, there were odious silhouettes lurking everywhere. In the daytime, however, the setting was more awesome than it was awful.

The colorful leaves on the trees and the sweet smell of those that had already fallen reminded Lilac of better days, back when she and Gabriel carefully constructed piles of leaves, only to scatter them a moment later while jumping into them.

They saw no sign of any goblins that day or the following night. When they stopped to make camp that next morning, Lilac was beginning to feel they might make it back to the fort alive after all.

As soon as they stopped, Lilac leaned against a tall, slender birch and slid down to a sitting position. Opal, on the other hand, announced she was going hunting.

"At this rate, we'll starve before we make it home," she said. "There has to be something besides goblins in this forest."

Without another word, Opal began walking away, but then Othello caught her by the shoulder. She immediately pulled out of his grasp and flashed him a dangerous look.

"I'll go," he said, nocking an arrow in his longbow.

Lilac thought Opal would surely argue. But slowly, Opal's countenance eased into a civil expression. Othello then strode past the woman, moving quickly but quietly through the trees.

As Opal watched him go, Lilac remembered another time Othello had managed to reason with the fiery-tempered woman. It had been during the Renegades' raid on Fort Faith. She, Othello, Klye, and Plake had stumbled upon Opal while searching for Prince Eliot.

Opal had leveled her crossbow at Klye, but then Othello had placed himself between the Renegade Leader and the woman. Opal had wanted nothing more than to put a bolt through Klye's heart, but Othello had talked her out of it.

Lilac marveled at the effect he seemed to have on the woman. Surely, Opal wasn't smitten with the taciturn forester— or was she? Suddenly, as though sensing Lilac's eyes upon her, Opal spun around. Her expression soured when their eyes met, but Lilac noted a faint blush painted across her cheeks.

Opal found a spot a couple of yards away, sat down, and stared out into the forest, avoiding the direction Othello had chosen. Lilac was happy to leave Opal alone. She was far too stubborn—not to mention hostile—for her liking. But even though the two of them sat in silence, Lilac didn't hear someone approach a few minutes later.

She jumped to her feet, her hand on the hilt of the vorpal sword, before she realized Othello had returned from a different direction. Pointedly ignoring Opal, who was walking over to join them, Lilac tried to pass off her alarm as eagerness.

"Well, that was fast," she said to Othello. "I'm so hungry, I could…"

Then she noticed that the man was empty-handed.

"There is something you must see," he said, looking at each woman in turn.

Without further explanation, Othello headed back into the trees, leaving Lilac and Opal to exchange uncertain glances before hurrying after him. Lilac felt her heartbeat quicken with every step. She couldn't imagine what Othello had found, but she doubted it was anything good.

Lilac began to notice peculiar things about the environment. Branches and vines littered the forest floor, cleanly severed from where they had previously hung. Also, the leaves on the ground had been trampled flat. A large group had come this way.

She looked over at Opal to see if the other woman saw what she was seeing, but Opal kept her gaze fixed straight ahead.

We're following a party of goblins, Lilac thought, and she was tempted to stop Othello right there and demand an explanation. By her calculations, they were heading due north. If the goblins—it had to be goblins—had come this way, then they should be heading in any direction but this one.

Then Othello stopped, and the scene that met her eyes was as unexpected as it was gruesome.

A dozen or more corpses lay scattered in what must have been at one time a green meadow. The clearing had been reduced to mud beneath the feet of many combatants. Whatever growth had survived the battle was stained black with goblin blood.

The forest was unnaturally still, as though even the carrion eaters were appalled by the dead monsters. Or perhaps it was the smell. Lilac brought her hand up to cover her nose, but that did little to deflect the nauseating stench surrounding the carnage.

"Who could have done this?" Opal asked.

Lilac could have wagered a guess.

Othello started forward once more, stepping over the bodies in his path. He stopped again a few yards away and crouched down by something shiny on the ground. When Lilac joined him and saw what that sparkling object was, her suspicion was confirmed.

There at her feet was *Chrysaal-rûn*.

"No."

The single word sounded impossibly far away, even though Opal was standing right beside her.

The mocking caw of a crow disrupted the mournful silence, sending a jolt of apprehension through Lilac. When she realized that it was only a bird—and not the allies of the fallen goblins— she expelled her breath in relief. Her eyes lingered on the solitary blackbird, however, for the sheer size of the thing was remarkable. Its oily black feathers seemed to defy the sunlight, and there was something about its eyes that didn't seem quite right.

The crow let out another shrill caw before taking flight and leaving the three humans to ponder the mystery of their missing companions.

Fingers dug painfully into the flesh of his upper arms. His feet dragged limply across the ground. It was certainly a strange way to travel, but even though he knew he should be moving his legs, he couldn't find the will to do so.

Colt's mind struggled trying to comprehend what was going on. It felt as though his entire body were made of steel, though he wasn't wearing any armor.

One of his eyes was swollen shut, but he was able to open the other. Brightness accosted the sensitive organ, and he couldn't see anything at first. After a few more steps—theirs, not his—his eye adjusted to the light. He even managed to lift his head a bit.

The scene that stretched out before him was hardly a rewarding one. It might have been a logging camp at one time. Hundreds of trees had been cleared from the area, their stumps scattered around the legion of tents that blanketed the clearing as densely as the trees once had.

A putrid odor hung heavy in the air—the smell of poorly ventilated forges, rotting food, and too many bodies sharing close proximity. Since he found it impossible to breathe out of his nose at the moment—possibly, it was broken—Colt was forced to taste the tainted atmosphere with every breath. A perpetual din of activity further polluted the forest air, though he couldn't understand a single word of what was being said.

The sight of so many goblins in one place was beyond disheartening.

It was only when his captors brought him to a halt near the edge of the camp that he perceived the pain in his feet. A glance down at the limbs revealed that they were bereft of boots and socks. The tops of his feet were raw and bleeding from scraping against the ground. He also became aware of various other hurts all over his body. If not for the grudging support of his captors, he would have surely collapsed.

He could not guess how long they waited outside the far-most ring of tents. The nearest shelter was remarkable only in that it stood two feet taller than the other tents. He wondered if they were waiting for permission to enter—not that he and the goblins around him could have all fit inside at once.

Then the goblins on either side of him straightened up and tightened their clamp-like hold on his arms. Squinting with his one good eye, he saw their improved posture was due to the arrival of three new goblins. The trio wore an assortment of armor. He figured the one in the middle was the highest-ranking, judging by the quality and condition of its gear.

Ironically, that goblin wore a breastplate emblazoned with the sun-and-sword standard of Superius.

As the lead goblin spoke to his comrades, using that harsh-sounding, unintelligible language he had been hearing for the past few days, he studied the creature in Knights' armor. Like all of the other goblins he had battled—with the exception of T'slect, he supposed—this officer wore a costume as mixed and motley as any harlequin. Aside from the Superian breastplate and standard-issue boots, Colt didn't recognize the design of the other accoutrements. Possibly, they had been smuggled from battlefields in other countries.

But what held his attention was what that goblin was carrying—a scepter as long as a quarterstaff, bedecked with inky black feathers and topped with a leering skull.

Without warning, he was thrust into the largest tent. Despite his wobbly legs, he managed to catch himself before he fell. Dazed, he took in his new surroundings. While the canopy was tall enough for him to stand upright, the tent itself was far from spacious. Two cots lying side-by-side nearly filled the entire floor of the tent.

One of the cots was occupied, but he caught no more than a glance before he was again shoved from behind.

He landed face-first on the vacant cot, causing new waves of pain to wash over his nose. Fighting the impulse to pass out, he forced his head to turn so that he was looking at the other bed. There, stretched out on the cot and lying in a most unnaturally stiff pose, was a man.

His body was gaunt; his skin, a deathly white. The man's eyes, which were fixed, unblinking on some distant place, added to the impression that he was, in fact, deceased.

Colt tried to watch the man's chest to gauge whether he breathed or not, but then he was being moved once more. He neither helped nor hindered the creature that flipped him onto his back. Then he was looking up at the goblin with the scepter.

By all appearances, the others goblins had left, and the two of them were alone. Colt thought he saw something red glint inside the sockets of the skull, but his interest in the staff was instantly forgotten when the monster began to speak.

"You have made a grievous error in stepping outside your fortress, Commander."

At first, he thought that the goblin was speaking his language, as T'slect had, but then realized he didn't *hear* the words so much as *know* them—like another voice inside his head.

Completely bewildered, Colt couldn't decide which was more astonishing—what the goblin was saying or the fact that he could comprehend the words in the first place.

"Yes, I know who you are, Commander. This one was unable to provide me with any satisfactory information regarding you or your fort." The goblin nodded its bald head at the emaciated man. "He knew your name and the number of Knights stationed at Fort Faith, but of the other inhabitants, he was altogether ignorant. He knew nothing of the midge or Klye Tristan's Renegades."

The goblin's toothy smile widened in response to Colt's horrified reaction. They had theorized that the goblins had learned a lot about Capricon's defenses thanks to T'slect's usurpation of the prince's identity. But hearing confirmation from the monster's mouth was all too dreadful.

Then another terrifying thought occurred to him. One goblin above all others would have known about the occupants of Fort Faith. T'slect, the shaman who had paraded as Prince Eliot Borrom, had seen both Klye and Noel firsthand.

"T'slect," Colt said, though it came out as a wheeze.

A smile splayed its dark lips. "You think I am the prince? I suppose you never saw him in his natural form, did you? No, Commander, I am not T'slect, and you won't see him again. It was thanks to that shortsighted fool that we were forced to begin the invasion before reinforcements arrived."

"Who—?" Colt started to ask, but his voice gave out. A series of painful coughs wracked his body.

The goblin merely watched him with a bemused expression on its face.

"You want to know who I am? I suppose I could satiate your curiosity. My name is Drekk't. Before T'slect's...discharge, I served as the general of the Capricon Campaign's Eastern Army. Now, I lead both the Eastern and the Western Armies."

Two armies, Colt thought with an involuntary shudder. Gods help us...

"The prince did me a favor by betraying our presence here, I suppose." Drekk't continued. "The men were growing restless. We are a race of warriors, you see, trained for battle from birth. It's not easy to restrain an army of goblins when the enemy is so near.

"I suppose I owe you and your magical sword a debt of thanks as well. When you bested T'slect...that self-righteous blunderer...you sealed his doom and made my promotion possible."

Colt was trying to make sense of what the goblin general was saying. Although he could somehow comprehend what the creature was saying, he was finding it increasingly difficult to find the meaning in it all.

I have to concentrate, he thought. *I must learn everything I can.*

"You are ignorant of our culture," Drekk't said. "Most of our enemies are. But I'll let you in on a secret. I just slandered one of the Chosen of the Chosen and one of the Emperor's own sons, at that!

"To speak ill of any shaman is punishable by death. Even though most all of my soldiers would agree that T'slect was a self-serving bastard, they would never utter it aloud. You are the only one in this camp whom I could ever dare speak my true thoughts to. It's ironic, wouldn't you say?"

Colt didn't answer. While he was pleased to hear that T'slect was out of the picture, he couldn't find much comfort in it, since Drekk't was obviously a shaman himself. What else, aside from *vuudu*, could explain how they were able to communicate?

He tried to dissect Drekk't's comments. What did Chosen of the Chosen mean? Was that just another way of saying shaman? How many of the goblins could use *vuudu*?

Those questions and more swam around and around in Colt's head. He couldn't seem to hold onto any one of them for long, however. His hold on consciousness had grown tenuous at best.

"There are many things that I will ask you," the goblin told him, "but I can see that you are in no condition to talk now. But believe me when I say you'll fare far worse before this is over. You'll come to wish your death had been as quick as the dwarf's."

Drekk't raised the skull-topped scepter, and this time he was certain he saw the eye sockets glow a deep red. Something strong but unseen seemed to coat his body like a second skin.

He couldn't move. The knowledge might have caused him to panic, but at the moment, he could barely comprehend the implications. One thought and one thought alone monopolized his mind—the very last thing Drekk't had said.

No matter how he tried to reason it out, he couldn't understand how he had forgotten that his dear friend, Cholk, was dead.

Passage IV

"Shut up, Plake."

Klye gave the order without thinking. It had become an automatic response to the rancher's ceaseless complaining.

He was convinced sharing a sickroom with Plake was punishment for all of the bad things he had done in his life. The threat of eternity in Abaddon had nothing on a week stuck with Plake Nelway?

"I would've thought the Knights were smarter than this," Plake said, undaunted. "I mean, what kind of a chance do six people have against an entire army of goblins? We were a band of ten, and now there're only nine of us. We barely made it to Fort Faith with our lives. And I don't care if Colt does have a magical sword. All it'll take is a handful of those poisoned arrows, and they're all dead."

"He certainly is an optimistic one, isn't he?" Aric said from her place at Matthew Fisk's bedside.

Klye scoffed. "He's just mad because Lilac is one of the six."

"Is he sweet on her?" Aric asked, not looking up from her work.

"You might say that," Klye replied.

Plake was on his feet and glaring down at him before the first word made it past his lips. "You shut *your* mouth, Klye. You don't know half as much as you think you do!"

Klye didn't flinch. "If I am mistaken, why have you been condemning me for letting Lilac go with Colt but haven't said a word about Othello?"

He watched Plake's face turn bright red. "I'll tell you why…I…I forgot Othello went with them. You have to admit he's an easy guy to forget. He has a way of disappearing when you're not looking right at him…and it's not like he says a whole lot."

Good cover, Klye thought wryly. "Sorry, I must have been mistaken."

Plake glared. Throwing himself back down on his bed, the rancher crossed his arms and brooded. Klye could hardly contain a smile. So that's how you get Plake to shut up, he thought.

Klye might have teased him more, but he wasn't a cruel man. He had the distinct impression Lilac didn't return Plake's affection.

Plake's sulky silence was short-lived. "Anyway, they might both be dead by now…Lilac and Othello, I mean. Only that merchant guy is actually from this miserable island, and he's the least likely to survive. They're probably all six of them dead already."

Sister Aric whirled around suddenly that Plake jumped.

"Haven't you ever heard the expression, 'If you don't have anything nice to say, don't say anything at all'?" she demanded.

Plake stared up at the woman, his mouth agape.

"If Plake adhered to that adage, he'd be as mute as Othello," Klye said, earning him another dark look from the rancher.

"I don't have to take this!" Plake shouted, leaping out of his sickbed again. "Even listening Scout prattle on about ancient history is better than getting insulted all day long."

Before slamming the door behind him, he added, "And if my health fails because you chased me out of bed too soon, it'll be on your head, Klye Tristan!"

Now Klye could contain his mirth no longer, and for the next few minutes, he leaned back against his pillow and laughed wholeheartedly. It felt good. When there was so much wrong in the world and so many bad things just waiting to happen, one has to laugh every now and then, he thought.

In truth, Klye was just as worried about the absent Renegades as Plake was. While Othello remained, for the most part, an enigma, he wholly respected the archer, and Lilac had become a friend and confidant.

Klye feared for the other members of the troupe too. He knew next to nothing about Mitto, and while neither Cholk nor Opal had ever had a kind word for him, he nevertheless hoped all three of them were all right.

He thought often about Colt, wondering what kind of leader the young Knight would prove to be. Although he and Colt had been nemeses up until recently, Klye had come to like the man. He truly hoped he would see him again.

"I think you hit a nerve," Aric said, taking a seat on the edge of Plake's bed to face Klye. "However did the two of you end up together? You're like water and oil."

"When Horcalus, Ragellan, Othello, and I were fleeing from Superius, we skirted the Paramese border. We stole some horses from a ranch owned by Plake's uncle. I still don't know whether the man sent his nephew after us, or if Plake decided to follow us on his own. All I know is that a day or two later, Plake charged into our camp, wielding a tree branch and demanding we return his uncle's animals."

"That's actually quite brave," Aric said, "albeit impetuous."

"He was drunk," Klye replied flatly, "infused with liquid courage."

Aric smiled. "Why doesn't that surprise me?"

"Don't even get me started talking about Plake and liquor. When we were in Port Town…"

As Klye told the healer about their misadventures in Port Town, starting with how Plake burned an inn to the ground, he found he couldn't stop smiling. At the time, he had been furious with Plake, whose insubordinate actions had resulted in Chester Ragellan's incarceration. But now, recalling the first time he had met Scout—not to mention how they had gotten tangled up with the pirates—Klye couldn't help but feel a bit nostalgic.

It had been less than a month ago, but it seemed so much farther back than that. And even though they had been in almost constant danger, Klye felt as though those were somehow happier times—back when he had fought alongside the charming and daring Leslie Beryl, when Ragellan was still alive, and before any of them knew about the goblins' sinister plans for the island.

It was quite the contrast to his bleak days in the infirmary.

Aware that he had trailed off, Klye cleared his throat and asked, "How long do you think it will be before I'm fully recovered?"

Aric let out an exasperated sigh. "How many times do you plan on asking me that?"

"Until I hear the answer I want. I'm beginning to feel like that old man, only *he* has the blessing of sleeping through his recovery time."

"Well," Aric said, "if you continue getting plenty of rest, eat three meals a day, and continue with your walks every day, I think you'll be as good as new soon enough."

"In other words, you have no idea," Klye concluded.

Aric rolled her eyes. "You're as pessimistic as Plake. But the truth is your injury is unlike any I have ever treated before."

"I guess that makes me special, huh?"

"So sarcastic," Aric lamented. "If only I had the power to heal your attitude."

"That, indeed, would be a miracle."

"Um…excuse me…Sister Aric…"

Klye recognized the voice as Ruben's. He craned his neck to get a look at the wizard, but Aric was blocking his view.

The healer rose and turned to face the far end of the room. "What is it, Ruben?"

"I think you'd better take a look at Toemis." The suggestion was punctuated by a groan from the old man.

Aric hurried over to Toemis's bedside, her long, white gown flowing in her wake. Klye sat up straighter and tried to peer over the prone form of Sir Matthew Fisk to get a look at the comatose old man—only, Toemis Blisnes did not sound so comatose anymore. He was coughing, and Klye thought he heard him ask for water.

"All right, all right," Aric said. "I will get you water, but you mustn't try to sit up. You need to take it slowly."

"Zusha," the old man croaked. "Where is my granddaughter? Zusha? Zusha!"

For the next few minutes, Aric endeavored to soothe the man, telling him his granddaughter was fine and that he shouldn't get so excited. But Toemis would not be placated until he saw the girl in the flesh. Aric looked around helplessly, first at the door where the Knights had formerly stood guard—Stannel had ordered them away days ago—and then over at Klye, who shrugged.

"You've seen how fast I can move," he reminded her. "It'll be midnight by the time I find the girl and bring her back."

Then Ruben spoke again. "I can find her."

"Are you sure you can manage?" Aric asked. "I would go myself, but I don't want to leave Toemis."

Klye saw the wizard slowly climb out of bed. "Don't worry," he said. "I'll be back before you know it…only…um…where *is* the girl?"

"Noel took her to get something to eat," Aric replied.

"Which means that they could be anywhere," Klye said.

His comment provoked a new stream of questions, demands, and curses from Toemis. Aric barely had time to cast Klye a reproachful look before returning to the arduous task of mollifying the old man. Meanwhile, Ruben made his way, stiffly but determinedly, to the infirmary door.

Colt's soul felt as numb as his body.

He couldn't fathom how he had forgotten Cholk was dead, but he knew it was true. In spite of the exhaustion that crippled his mind as assuredly as Drekk't's *vuudu* had paralyzed his body, sleep would not come.

Instead, he found himself reliving the terrible ordeals of the past few days...

When he awoke the morning after fighting that hopeless battle with Cholk, he was confused but happy to be alive. However, it didn't take long before his gratitude fizzled away, only to be replaced by a mounting despair. Surely, the goblins wanted him alive for some nefarious reason.

Colt knew very little about his enemies, but he suspected torture was part and parcel of their wartime protocol. As a Knight of Superius, it was his duty to seek death before betraying his country. He considered attempting an escape in the hopes that the goblins would slay him, but he could not abandon hope altogether.

Perhaps a chance for escape would yet come.

His mood was bolstered by the fact that Cholk had survived the fray too. The goblins were wise enough to keep the two of them separated, but knowing his friend was alive lent Colt strength. He and the dwarf had already been through so much during the short time they had known each other. They would find a way out of this predicament.

Throughout the laborious hike, Colt tried to keep his wits about him, studying the enemy in hopes of using any new knowledge against them in the future. The first thing he realized about his captors was that they were not at all hampered by the darkness. After the sun set, they made no sign of stopping or even slowing.

The forced march continued well into nightfall, teaching Colt something else about the goblins—they had incredible stamina.

When they finally stopped to rest, Colt collapsed to the ground, thankful for the respite. The break from walking was brief, however, and soon enough, he was none-too-gently prodded back to his feet by the tip of a spear.

For a split second, Colt considered wrestling the weapon away from the goblin. But he couldn't hope to escape with so many vigilant soldiers nearby. He could only bite his lip and suppress a cry when the spear pierced the bare flesh of his back.

The goblins had removed his armor from the start, and he had caught sight of one of the fiends wearing his leather cuirass and another, his coat. But there was no sign of the crystal sword. The thought of *Chrysaal-rûn* in a goblin's filthy hands was maddening, but Colt swore he'd get it back. He just had to be patient.

The Order had rules about how a Knight must treat his prisoner, but the goblins had no such laws, apparently. An occasional stone or clod of earth struck him in the back. His body was already covered with superficial wounds from when the goblins took turns prodding him with their odd assortment of weapons.

Colt did his best not to give the cruel creatures any satisfaction, ignoring their bullying with as much grace as he could muster. Throughout it all, his captives shouted jeers and taunts—at least Colt assumed that's what they were.

If the goblins' treatment of him was harsh, they were downright brutal to Cholk. He could estimate the dwarf's location by the guffaws and roars of the goblin soldiers that entrenched him. He could only guess what barbaric attention his friend was receiving. According to Cholk, dwarves and goblins shared a deep, undying hatred for each other. Now it sounded like Cholk was reaping the worst of that centuries-long feud.

The goblins' bloodlust seemed insatiable, but Colt noted that their captors were careful not to do too much damage to their prisoners.

He had no idea how far they had traveled, but they hiked for more than half the night before stopping. Colt got the impression that this break was to be longer for some of the goblins began working on a campfire.

To Colt's surprise, he was reunited with Cholk at this time.

The goblins tied them back to back, wrapping their wrists and ankles together with a long cord. When the goblins were satisfied with their work, they appointed two guards to watch over them. The rest of the monsters busied themselves with setting up camp.

Cholk started to say something to Colt but was rewarded with the haft of a poleax to the side of his head. The dwarf groaned but did not otherwise protest. After that, the two prisoners stayed silent.

Tired as he was, Colt resisted the urge to sleep. He didn't want to be caught dozing if the chance to escape presented itself. Cholk's proximity lent him a measure of comfort, even if they weren't allowed to speak.

Colt took the opportunity to count the goblins. There were around fifty of them, which was far fewer than the party they had encountered the previous morning. Apparently, these fifty had been charged with delivering the prisoners, while the other soldiers remained strategically positioned throughout the forest.

Colt had to admit the foreign army was coordinated. The realization did nothing to lift his spirits. The gods only knew how many of the Crypt-spawns had already made Capricon their home.

At some point, he must have nodded off because he was awakened by a sound slap across the face. Blinking back tears of pain, he glared up at the goblin crouched before him. The monster said something Colt couldn't understand and started to untie his bonds. All the while, several others kept arrows trained on him.

At first, he assumed it was time to resume the grueling hike. But then he noticed the campfires were still blazing. Confused, he glanced back at Cholk, who was also being relieved of his constraints.

"I'm guessing they want to have a bit of fun with us," he whispered.

Cholk earned a punch to the gut for talking, but the dwarf took the blow with hardly a flinch. Just then, Colt admired the brave dwarf more than anyone he had ever known, including his father, whose heroics were highly praised within the Knighthood.

There was no fear at all in Cholk's expression as the goblins forcefully led them through the congregation of their companions and into a small clearing.

When the circle of monsters closed in around them, Colt feared the end had finally come. But the goblins came no closer, remaining a few yards away. He looked around in absolute bewilderment. Meanwhile, all fifty-some soldiers were shouting raucously and waving their weapons in the air. Ghastly shadows from fires only added to the goblins' demonic appearance.

"They want us to fight each other."

Colt regarded Cholk with absolute amazement. "What? But how…?"

"Though I hate to admit it, their language isn't so different from my own," Cholk explained.

One of the goblins came forward into the circle and used its wickedly-curved poleax to push the two prisoners apart. Colt backpedaled, careful to avoid the weapon's razor-sharp edge. Cholk retreated to the far end of the circle. Before returning to his comrades, the goblin shouted something in its native tongue.

From across the circle, Cholk translated. "He said that if we don't fight to the death, they'll kill both of us."

"It's a bluff," Colt insisted. "They need us alive. Otherwise, they would've slain us long before now."

An arrow whizzed through the air and caught Colt in the shoulder. He fell to one knee with a cry. Breathing heavily, he barely had time to yank the shaft out of his arm before Cholk came barreling toward him. Too stunned to move, Colt caught the full brunt of the dwarf's charge, which landed him flat on his back.

When Cholk pounced knees-first onto his chest, all of the air rushed out of him. For a moment, he could only sputter and gasp for breath. All around them, the goblins cheered wildly.

"Never underestimate a goblin's love of bloodshed," Cholk muttered.

Colt blinked, unable to understand what was happening.

The blow that Cholk landed across his jaw nearly sent him into oblivion. Colt's head jerked to one side from the impact, and he spat out blood and a tooth.

Now there was no mistaking the situation. Cholk intended to kill him so that the goblins wouldn't kill them both. The realization hurt Colt more than any physical assault ever could. For the next second or so, he could only look up at his friend, his assailant.

"They know we're important," Cholk said, "but I get the feeling that there aren't any higher-ups in this bunch. Maybe they'll still get a reward for delivering our carcasses."

The dwarf punctuated his statement with another punch to his face. The strike connected with Colt's left eye, and he had to struggle once more to maintain consciousness. A part of him wanted to give up and die, to surrender to the pain coursing through his throbbing head. But another part of him wanted to look Cholk in the eye as the traitor landed the deathblow.

One thing was certain, Colt would sooner die than fight back. If Cholk wanted to take the life he had saved months ago, then so be it. But Colt, for one, refused to play the goblins' games.

The spectators' howls and shouts reached a pitched fervor. The cacophony only grew when Cholk placed his heavy hands around Colt's neck.

"I am prepared for the Last Great Deed," he heard the dwarf say, "but I think you have a greater part to play before this war is over."

Somewhere in Colt's befuddled mind, he was aware that Cholk wasn't squeezing very hard.

"Suicide is a great crime among my people, but to give your life so that another might live…well…I'd say that's honorable enough."

Then the dwarf's hands were no longer wrapped around his throat. With a speed that defied his form, Cholk lunged for the something beside Colt. When the dwarf righted himself once more, Colt saw he held the bloody arrow Colt had discarded.

Then everything became terribly clear.

"No," Colt whispered.

"Sorry I had to make it look so real," the dwarf said.

"Cholk…"

"May the gods help you, my friend."

Before Colt could act, Cholk reversed his hold on the arrow, plunged it into his neck, and pulled it across his throat. A fountainhead of blood spurted from the wound, cascading down Cholk's chest and onto Colt. Although the dwarf grimaced in anguish, Colt thought he saw satisfaction in his friend's eyes.

The crowd that had been so boisterous seconds before went absolutely silent. Only when Cholk toppled, lifeless, to the ground, did the goblins seem to comprehend what had happened. Screaming furiously, the throng closed in on the dwarf, and Colt could do nothing but watch as the goblins started hacking away at the one who had robbed them of their perverse sport.

Colt shut his eyes, eagerly embracing the dizziness that plunged him into unconsciousness.

Passage V

The Thief Guild and the rebels of Rydah had coexisted without conflict for more than a year, until the local Renegade Leader coerced more than half of the Guild's members into forsaking one illegal code of conduct in favor of another. The Renegades had accomplished in a day what governors, guardsmen, and Knights of Superius had failed to do in two centuries.

The Guild collapse was as sudden as it was unexpected. Every thief who had not wanted to get caught up in violent politics had been forced to hide or flee the capital altogether.

Ruben had been one of those refugees, though he hadn't strayed too far from Rydah.

He quickly learned highway robbery wasn't his forte. He had joined Falchion's crew out of necessity. And while he hadn't worked with any of them before, he almost immediately wished he had never signed on with the thugs.

They hadn't bothered to mask their contempt for him either, making it quite clear they saw him as the most worthless member of the band. Ruben couldn't help but blame the Renegades for landing him with Falchion and his crew, so he was far from thrilled when he awoke to find he was sharing an infirmary with several of them.

He didn't miss Falchion, Critter, and the rest, but at least he had known what to expect with the highwaymen. Renegades were a different story entirely, and when he learned that one of them was a Renegade Leader, he wanted nothing more than to retreat back to unconsciousness.

Ruben had spent the majority of his first day at Fort Faith in slumber. As the second day dragged on, his apprehension of Klye Tristan and his Renegades was dulled by the sheer tedium of the uneventful hours. By the time the second night rolled around, he considered escaping the sickroom, if only for a change of scenery.

There were, however, a few key factors that prevented him from doing so.

First of all, he had absolutely no skill for burglary. He wasn't the least bit sneaky or stealthy. His role had always been performing diversionary tactics. While he, in the guise of a beggar, distracted the mark with a woeful tale or stirred up trouble as part of a larger cast of rabble-rousers, another thief—a far more talented thief—would traipse onto the scene and relieve the victim of his valuables.

Also, he wouldn't have known where to go even if he could have somehow foiled the fort's sentries. As far as he knew, Fort Faith was in the middle of nowhere. The Port of Gust lay some-where to the north, but his odds of stumbling upon the right path in the middle of the night were somewhere between slim and nil. And, of course, there were the goblins.

But one reason above all prevented Ruben from escaping, something that transcended even his cowardice. Though he knew Sister Aric would never return his affection, he simply could not leave her.

If he had loved her before arriving at Fort Faith, he adored her now. Aric spent most of her time in the infirmary, tending to her patients. Ruben, who could not stomach the sight of blood, marveled at how calm the healer remained while treating gruesome injuries.

But it wasn't his aversion to gore that kept him from peeking at his own wound when she routinely changed his bandages. No, he took advantage of the close proximity to lose himself in the pure, unblemished whiteness of her skin; her small, perfectly shaped mouth; and, above all, her eyes, which, like a pair of gems, sparkled a different color depending on how they caught the light.

Perhaps what he liked best about her was that she never judged him. Aric knew he was a highwayman—he couldn't have denied that if he wanted to—but that didn't keep her from talk-ing to him. He longed to tell her the truth about himself—the full truth—even though Aric was far too polite to press him about his past. On the contrary, she was content to engage him in conversations about less weighty things, like joking about how bravely he had stopped the goblin's arrow with his abdomen.

But he didn't think that she would laugh if he told her he was no more a wizard than Toemis or the Renegade Leader was.

What difference does it make whether she believes I'm a spell-caster or knows the truth of my failed ambitions? he wondered woefully. She'll never feel for me what I feel for her.

Imprisoned as much by his injuries as his past crimes, Ruben had a lot of time to think—too much time. His emotions had more ups and downs than a gnomish kite. Passion and depression waged a war for dominance within his soul. And lurking beneath his affection for Aric—and disdain for himself—was the constant worry about what the Knights would do with him when he was well enough to leave the infirmary.

He had heard that Fort Faith had a dungeon...

After spending a week in bed, Ruben had jumped at the chance to find Toemis's granddaughter, though he knew next to nothing about the old man. He had volunteered for this noble quest to impress his ladylove. What *wouldn't* he have done for Aric's sake?

But now that every slow step was causing slivers of pain to shoot through his stomach—and he hadn't even traversed the first corridor!—he prayed he would find someone else to take over the mission.

To his astonishment—and private consternation—there seemed to be no Knights positioned anywhere near the infirmary. When he came upon an intersection and saw the retreating form of someone in the distance, a surge of elation shot through him.

"Hey, you!" Even though his voice was weak, the words resounded down the hollow, stony corridor.

The man at the far end of the hall turned around but made no reply. Neither did he move in one direction or the other.

"Please," Ruben persisted. "I need your help."

The person just stared back at him. Ruben squinted, trying to identify the man, but he was too far away to determine much of anything about the stranger. Unlike most of the fort's residents, the man didn't seem to be wearing armor of any kind. In truth, he looked a bit short for a Knight.

"What, are you deaf?" With a silent curse, Ruben continued inching down the hallway.

Then, from the other end of the hall, he heard someone say, "What's taking you so long, Arthur? If we don't hurry, the

Knights will scarf down all the good food before we get there."

Ruben watched as a second man appeared from around a corner. The newcomer—who looked to be wearing a black hood—saw Ruben at the same time Ruben saw him.

"Hey!" Ruben shouted.

"What?" asked the man in the hood.

"I need…I need your help."

The hooded man ran toward him, but the first man remained rooted in place.

"Wow," hooded man said, "you don't look so good. Hey, aren't you that wizard fellow that arrived with Mitto, Stannel, and that woman?"

"Aric," Ruben corrected crossly. "*Sister* Aric."

The man frowned. "I thought you caught an arrow in the gut. Do you really think you ought to be walking around by yourself? You're not trying to escape, are you? Because if you are, you're wasting your time. I've been exploring this fort for the past couple weeks, and the Knights seem to have thought of everything."

"I'm not trying to escape!" Ruben exploded. "I'm looking for the little girl and the midge."

That statement seemed to take the man by surprise. His brow crinkling in confusion, he asked, "You're looking for Noel? Are you two going to trade spells or something?"

"No," Ruben replied, forcing himself to take deep breaths. "The midge is keeping an eye on the girl. Her grandfather just woke up, and he's asking for her. I was sent to find her, but…"

"But you're in no condition to do much of anything. All right. Let's think. It's suppertime, so they're both probably in the dining hall. The Knights aren't crazy about sharing a table with a midge, but none of them have the stones to tell him to leave."

"Can you go fetch the girl and bring her to the infirmary?" Ruben asked, all but begging.

The man in the hood straightened up. "Of course I can. What else do I have to do? Hey, Arthur! Come here!"

The man at the end of the hallway didn't budge.

"He's not going to bite you!" The hooded man turned to Ruben and said, "Tell him you're not going to hurt him. He had a bad experience with a wizard recently…"

The thought that someone could be so intimidated by him

might have been hilarious in other circumstances. He was on the verge of calling out to the other man when the man in question started walking toward them on his own.

In a sidelong whisper, the hooded man added, "Arthur hasn't been himself lately, so don't be offended if he acts rude."

As Arthur drew nearer, Ruben saw he was only just barely a man, though there was a hardness in the youth's eyes that hinted at a different kind of maturity.

Arthur didn't look intimidated; he looked annoyed.

"I've got to go find Noel. He and that little girl are needed in the infirmary," the hooded man told Arthur. "Would you help...um...what's your name?"

"Ruben."

"Would you help Ruben back to his bed?" The man didn't wait for a reply before sprinting away. Over his shoulder he called, "Don't worry, Ruben. I'll find them!"

Arthur stared after his companion, his mouth opened in silent protest. He managed to say, "Scout!" but by then the hooded man was out of sight.

For a long moment, the boy looked off in the direction in which the man—Scout?—had fled. Ruben was beginning to think the boy was a bit slow in the head, but when Arthur turned to regard him, he saw no signs of dullness—only irritation.

"Um, hello," Ruben said.

At first Arthur only stared at him some more. It was a most unnerving experience for Ruben, who went to great lengths to avoid others' notice—except when performing a part for his fellow thieves. He wished he did know magic so that he might take a peek at the boy's thoughts.

Ruben was about to start back to the infirmary on his own, when Arthur finally spoke.

"Which way is it?"

Ruben gave a brief description of the way back to the sick-room. Arthur listened, eyeing him warily all the while. When he finished giving the directions, the boy grabbed his arm—causing Ruben flinch involuntarily—and draped it over his shoulder. Flushing profusely, Ruben averted his eyes and allowed Arthur to half-guide, half-carry him back to the infirmary.

They made the trip in uncomfortable silence. When they finally reached the infirmary door, Ruben extricated himself from the boy, muttering his thanks. Arthur didn't reply. He simply turned around and headed back down the hall.

Before reentering the infirmary, Ruben cast a final look back at Arthur. He knew acting when he saw it and couldn't help but feel Arthur had been putting on show for him—and perhaps for everyone else. People wear different faces and adopt new guises to hide their true selves…and their pain, he thought.

He wondered what demons Arthur was wrestling with.

Lilac watched the large blackbird until it was lost from sight. When she turned her attention back to the discarded crystal sword, Opal was reaching down to pick it up.

She reacted instantly, yanking Opal away from it. Caught by surprise, Opal didn't resist at first, but when she realized what was going on—and who was holding her back—she fought back. A well-placed elbow to the ribs sent Lilac staggering back a step.

"What in the hells do you think you're doing?" Opal demanded, leveling her crossbow at her.

"I'm saving you from a nasty burn," Lilac said, "though maybe I shouldn't have bothered."

"What are you talking about?"

Lilac saw Othello out of the corner of her eye, but the archer didn't seem to be in any hurry to help her. "During the battle in Fort Faith's western wing, before the goblin shaman was revealed, Klye disarmed Colt, but when he reached for the crystal sword, it burned his hand. The wound still hasn't healed completely."

Opal's expression didn't soften in the least as she considered Lilac's words.

"The crystal sword is a magical weapon," Lilac added. "We don't know all that it's capable of, and you'll be doing no one any good, save the goblins, if you scorch your fingers like Klye did."

Staring at the razor-sharp tip of the quarrel, Lilac wondered if Opal was capable of killing her in cold blood. She couldn't quite withhold a sigh when the crossbow finally returned to its place at Opal's side.

"Colt told me about his fight with Klye in the war room," Opal said. "In case you forgot, I wasn't there for that part. A certain Renegade Leader had granted me an unexpected introduction to his fist."

Lilac remembered—and clearly Opal would never forget it.

Opal turned her back to Lilac and crouched once more beside Colt's sword, though she didn't touch it. Lilac was no stranger to magical weapons. Like *Chrysaal-rûn*, her vorpal sword possessed an impossibly fine edge.

But aside from its antiquated design, the vorpal sword looked no different from an ordinary sword. *Chrysaal-rûn*'s appearance, however, hinted at a great magic. Lilac had seen firsthand the damage it could inflict. And the slew of goblin corpses around them was a testament to the weapon's raw power.

Who could say what else the crystal sword could do?

"Something terrible happened here," Opal stated. "Colt would never have willingly left *Chrysaal-rûn* behind. Either he was taken captive…"

"Or he's dead," Lilac finished.

Opal's glare might have made her regret her blunt words, but Lilac didn't want Opal to have any illusions about what had probably occurred in the clearing.

Opal stood upright once more. "I don't see a body here, do you?"

"I see plenty of bodies," Lilac replied, throwing her hands wide to indicate all of the fallen goblins around them. "Someone had to have killed them. We know by the presence of the crystal sword that Colt was here, but if he was victorious, why did he abandon his sword?"

"I don't know!" Opal snapped. "Maybe more goblins were on the way, and he dropped it and couldn't retrieve it."

"You yourself said that he'd never willingly leave it behind," Lilac pointed out.

Opal's glare intensified. "Fine. Then the goblins must have captured him, and I, for one, am going to rescue him."

Opal stood with her hands planted firmly on her hips, as though daring Lilac to argue further.

But Lilac wasn't about to back down. "This is madness! There's no proof Colt is still alive."

"There's no proof he's dead either!" Opal countered.

"Maybe he's somewhere under that pile of goblins there."

"You shut your mouth, Renegade!"

An invigorating warmth spread through Lilac's body, and she found her hand clutching the vorpal sword's hilt. She had always thought of herself as an even-tempered woman, but there was something about Opal that drained her patience faster than a drunkard with his ale.

"Colt didn't do this alone."

Othello's calm words diffused the tension immediately, and the women regarded the forester expectantly. Othello pointed down at the deep laceration that stretched across one goblin's chest, a wound that was visible even from a distance.

"The crystal sword did this, but..." Two great strides took Othello over to the next corpse. "...it did not do this."

The two women approached the goblin in question. The first thing Lilac noticed was that the creature's head was nearly severed from its body. She conceded Othello's point. Like the vorpal sword, *Chrysaal-rûn* cut cleanly. The goblin that lay before them looked as though someone had used a conventional weapon coupled with an incredible amount of strength.

It didn't take long for Lilac to realize who that someone must have been.

"Cholk," Opal murmured, echoing her thoughts.

"They were both here," Lilac agreed. "Might they have escaped?"

She looked to Othello for an answer, but he was already walking away again.

"I'm going to find out," Opal said.

"You can't be serious."

Opal was quick to cut her off, but rather than shout her words—as Lilac would have expected—Opal spoke them quietly, which she found even more unnerving. "I've never been more serious in my life."

"What about the mission?"

Opal shrugged. "I'm not going back to the fort without Colt and Cholk."

"Then you're a damn fool!" Lilac shouted.

"Call me what you will." Opal started back over to the crystal sword. "But I couldn't live with myself if I didn't learn what happened to my friends. One way or another, I'm going to find out. Complete the mission if you want. Maybe Stannel will even give you a full pardon for your efforts."

The words were like a slap in the face. "I'm not doing this for a *pardon*. I'm doing this because all of Capricon is depending on the Knights to protect them from the goblins, and right now the Knights are depending on us. You're being unreasonable, Opal."

Opal shrugged again. "Maybe. But I don't care. I'd rather be an unreasonable fool than a heartless bitch. If *you* could leave *your* friends to the goblins, you're no better than the monsters."

Lilac bit back a retort. No good would come of name calling. Seething inside, Lilac glared at Opal's back, cursing her for the insufferable fool she was. It would serve you right if I just let you tromp off after the goblins.

But Lilac's anger could not hold out long against Opal's accusation. What if Klye and Horcalus were missing instead of Colt and Cholk? Would she be so heart-set on returning to the fort if her dearest friends were in danger?

After the slightest moment of hesitation, Opal bent to pick up *Chrysaal-rûn*. Lilac expected the woman to cry out and drop it, but no harm came to her. Flashing a smug smile, Opal walked past Lilac and said, "Colt will want this once I find him."

Opal then made her way to Othello, who was still examining the forest floor, and said, "I have some experience in tracking, but I know you're better. Would you help me look for my friends?"

The earnest question took Lilac by surprise, and her astonishment only grew when Othello replied, "Yes."

Anger well up inside her again. Othello hadn't even glanced her way before throwing in with Opal! It wasn't jealousy; it was about loyalty. And too many times had she seen the charms of a beautiful woman compromise even the most intelligent of men. Maybe there was something more to the two of them than she had realized...

It would serve them right if I let them wander off together, Lilac thought. How long do they think two archers will last in hand-to-hand combat?

She considered completing the mission on her own. As long as she kept heading west, she would find the Rocky Crags eventually, and then all she would have to do is follow the mountains back to the fort. She thought she could manage it too. After all, she found Klye's Renegades all on her own.

Lilac contemplated this course for a second or two. Then she trudged after her companions, cursing herself for getting pulled into Opal's foolhardy plan. From somewhere far off, she thought she heard the mocking call of a crow.

Passage VI

Even before she had gotten caught up in the Renegade War, Lilac had spent most of her time traveling.

Between the errands she had run for her father, Baron Paris Zephyr, and trips she had taken for pleasure, she had explored one end of Superius to the other and visited a few of the other kingdoms of Continae.

Back then, she had basked in the thrill of seeing so much of the world, never staying idle for long. But having walked all day without rest or nourishment, Lilac now fantasized about finding a comfortable inn and sleeping for two days straight.

By the time they stopped to make camp, Lilac had lost all track of time. They had wandered into a section of forest populated by great evergreens, which blocked all but a few streams of sunlight. She could tell by the darkening patches of sky that night was not far off, but that was all she could ascertain. They chose a spot about thirty yards from where they had left the goblins' trail in case the monsters doubled back.

When Opal and Othello went out to hunt for supper, Lilac was left alone at the campsite to stew. She hadn't said a word to either of her companions since joining them on the hopeless quest to find Colt and Cholk. She didn't trust her tongue.

She couldn't decide with whom she was angrier. Opal possessed the ability to infuriate her like no one else could. Othello, on the other hand, was her friend. His siding with Opal had been a slap in the face.

Beneath her irritation, however, was the nagging feeling they were getting in way over their heads. Throughout their daylong hike, she noticed the path was taking them north and east—back near Rydah and where Sir Dylan had guessed the goblin army to be.

We should have returned to the fort and let Stannel decide what to do about Colt and Cholk. I shouldn't have let Opal pressure me into this suicidal course.

A little while later, the two archers returned with some hares and a squirrel between them. No stranger to roughing it, Lilac had learned long ago to be content with whatever food could be scrounged up. Anyway, she was so hungry that she might have happily eaten earthworms and crickets for supper.

Othello built a small fire that produced only a little smoke, and they ate in heavy silence. All the while, Lilac found herself watching her companions for signs of a deepening alliance.

They slept in shifts. During her turn for watch, Lilac tried to put her thoughts in order. She knew, whatever the wisest move might have been, it was too late to go back now. There was no use pondering "should have" or "could have." The three of them had to be united in purpose, or they were already defeated.

For better or for worse, they would learn what had happened to their missing companions.

She also tried to put Othello and Opal's nebulous relationship from her mind. She had far more important things to worry about than a budding romance.

They set off again when the morning light colored the sky a dull gray, retracing their steps back to where they had left the goblins' trail. While they still traveled in silence, Lilac felt a great improvement in her mood. Putting things into perspective —not to mention sleep and food—had mollified her temper.

The morning was blessedly uneventful, but what they discovered in the early afternoon sunk Lilac's mood back to the point of despair.

She knew that something was wrong when Othello jerked to a sudden stop and then slowly continued forward a moment later. A feeling of absolute dread washed over her as she followed. When Othello stopped again, Lilac forced herself to step beside him.

What she saw made her knees buckle unsteadily and bile rise in her throat. Lying there in the middle of the path was a pile of gore consisting of bloody flesh, broken bones, and dismembered appendages. The ground was stained a deep red.

"Oh gods," Opal gasped.

Tears clouded Lilac's vision. There was no need to ask who the mutilated corpse had been. Despite the fact that the remains had been torn nearly inside out, there was no mistaking the coal-black skin clinging to the various body parts.

It was by far the vilest thing Lilac had ever seen, and she would have given anything to be spared the gruesome sight. A sudden dizziness assailed her head, and she had to lean up against a nearby tree for support.

Opal fell to knees, her head buried in her hands. Lilac didn't know much about Opal's relationship with Cholk—how long they had known each other and whether they were as close friends with each other as they were with Colt. Lilac herself had said no more than a few words to Cholk. She had engaged him in combat more often than in conversation.

Fate had made them enemies first and allies second. But never had she wished such a deplorable fate for him…or for anyone.

Fixing her gaze on her feet, Lilac concentrated on steadying her breathing. When she was convinced her sparse breakfast was going to remain in her stomach, she made the mistake of looking up. There, hanging by rope from a low-hanging branch, was Cholk's head.

Eyes wide in horror, Lilac could only stare into the dwarf's dark, unseeing eyes, before falling down to her hands and knees and vomiting.

She heaved until her stomach was empty. After a time, she felt a hand on her shoulder, and looked up to see the tear-blurred shape of Othello standing over her. The forester helped her to her feet. She wiped her eyes in time to see Opal draw a small knife from her belt and reach up to cut the rope suspending the dwarf's head.

"Don't," Othello said, clutching the woman's arm suddenly.

Opal looked too weary to argue, though the confused look she gave Othello was enough to ask what she couldn't express vocally.

"We cannot leave signs of our passing," he explained, gently removing the knife from her grasp and returning it to the sheath at her hip.

"So we can't even bury him?" Opal asked. Lilac had never heard the woman sound so weak, so defeated.

"No."

Opal let out an unsteady sign. "I guess it's just as well. I don't know how we would have managed it…"

Without another word, Opal walked away from the grisly

remains of her friend. Othello strode after her. Lilac inhaled until her lungs were full and then let out the air slowly. The prospect of death had not frightened her overmuch before, but now she knew death would come only after a time of torment if she were captured.

Lilac could only pray Cholk had died before the goblins began dissecting him.

Brushing away the fresh tears that streamed down her cheeks, she hurried to catch up with Othello and Opal. Cholk was lost, but there was no sign of Colt. Apparently, the goblins had wanted the commander alive—for at least a little while longer. Lilac vowed she would save Colt from a similar fate or die trying.

She said a silent prayer for the dwarf's soul. In spite of herself, she cast a final look back at Cholk and saw a great blackbird descend onto the pile of remains. The crow seemed to stare at her for a moment before letting out a jarring caw. Then, without ceremony, the bird began to peck at the dead dwarf.

With a shudder, Lilac turned around and followed her companions deeper into the dense forest.

Colt's thoughts dwelled on Cholk for innumerable hours. He tried to remember every conversation he had ever had with the dwarf.

He lamented how little he knew about Cholk. He didn't know where in Thanatan he had come from or why he had left his homeland in the first place. He hadn't even learned Cholk's surname! Cholk had been evasive with all questions pertaining to his past, though now that the dwarf was gone forever, Colt wished he had pressed a little harder.

I don't deserve the honor of your sacrifice, Colt told the dwarf's ghost. I made a terrible commander, and I'm not even much of a Knight. I've failed the company, and I've failed the mission. To make matters worse, I got captured, and the gods only know what the goblins plan to do with me now.

You should have killed me, Cholk. You were the stronger of us…

His eyes stung as tears welled up in his eyes. Since he couldn't move no matter how hard he tried, he was unable to wipe away his salty sorrow. Eventually, the tears overflowed their small pools and streamed down the side of his face, leaving a tickling sensation in their wake. It felt as though his entire body were crafted out of granite, and he could only lie there like a toppled statue.

Colt tried not to feel sorry for himself. After all, he had gotten himself into this mess—had gone so far as to find a loophole in the Knighthood's law so that he could abandon his post and personally join the company bound for Rydah. He had no one but himself to blame for ending up in the goblin war camp.

When he wasn't mourning the loss of Cholk, he was worrying about the remaining members of his company. Had they escaped the goblins? Were they all dead? Captured? He had no way of knowing, but he secretly hoped that if they hadn't escaped the ambush, they had found a quick death.

Death was far preferable to this.

He felt his heart tremble at the thought of Opal lying dead in the wilderness, her soft skin ripped open by a blade, her shapely body riddled with black-feathered arrows. The thought of losing both Cholk and Opal was more than he could bear.

Colt had no way of keeping track of time except for the gradual changes in illumination inside the tent. He could make out the beginning and the end of a day, but the hours themselves drifted by tediously and unremarkably. He supposed he should be grateful his captors weren't torturing him. Then again, leaving him alone to ponder all of the terrible things that might have happened to Opal and the others was torture enough.

He drifted in and out of consciousness, though his sleep was never deep or restful. He still couldn't see out of his left eye. He was also aware of other scrapes and bruises on his body. Most of all, he tried not to think about the emaciated body on the other cot.

At one point, he awoke to find Drekk't standing over him. Once again, the goblin general carried the skull-tipped scepter. It was difficult to judge the goblin's intentions. To Colt, all goblins seemed to wear the same expression at all times. Their slightly slanted, catlike eyes and black-lipped smirks always held the promise of horrors to come.

"I hope you have rested. I have many things I would like to ask you." As before, Colt's mind translated Drekk't's foreign words into comprehendible sentences.

Colt had a rejoinder on the tip of his tongue, but since he had no control over his extremities, he couldn't speak the sarcastic reply. He laughed inwardly, wondering how the goblin intended to interrogate a mute.

You'll have to remove your hex, he thought, and the moment I can move again, I'm going for your throat.

For an instant, Colt feared Drekk't had heard his thoughts as clearly as he had heard the meaning behind the goblin's strange words. But the general appeared none too concerned with the momentary stalemate. Colt watched, then, as the skull portion of the staff came closer and closer until he was staring into the dark caverns that had once contained eyes.

An involuntary shudder coursed through his body.

Drekk't started talking again, but this time Colt couldn't understand the words. In spite of his ignorance, he sensed something powerful in the phrases. He's casting another spell on me, Colt realized, but no matter how hard he struggled against his invisible bonds, he could do nothing but sit and stare at the old, yellowed skull.

As Drekk't completed the incantation, the skull's eyes glowed red.

Pintor, protect me! Colt prayed.

The Knights of Superius had a long history of mistrusting magic, and Colt was no exception. He had been privy to a plethora of magical feats since coming to Capricon—thanks to Noel and *Chrysaal-rûn*—but there was something different, something terrible about the goblins' spells. Gooseflesh crawled over his arms and legs, and his stomach twisted in knots.

The goblins' *vuudu*—as Noel had called it—emanated evil and evoked terror.

Colt would have tensed if he could. As suddenly as the rite began, it ended. Drekk't withdrew the fearsome scepter. In the next few seconds, nothing seemed to change at all. Colt found the uncertainty of the spell's effect as terrifying as the spell itself.

"How do you feel, Commander?" Drekk't asked. The goblin's tone was lighthearted, almost conversational.

Colt had another snide retort in mind, but then to his surprise, he heard himself reply, "I'm scared out of my wits."

A wide grin spread across the general's face. "You should be. Are you frightened because you have heard tales of goblin...hospitality?"

"No," Colt answered. Panic filled him anew, drenching his skin in a cold sweat. He couldn't stop his mouth from speaking. It was as though he were listening to someone else talk. "I know nothing about goblins other than what I have witnessed firsthand."

Drekk't nodded sagely. "So what you have *seen* has instilled you with fear?"

"Not exactly."

"What do you mean by that?" Drekk't pressed.

"I fear your magic more than I fear death."

Drekk't stared at him thoughtfully for a moment before glancing down at the staff in his hands. "Truth be told, Commander, I don't care for it myself. I am not a shaman, you see. As a priest of Upsinous, T'slect could channel our god's power without the use of a talisman. I, however, must use this."

The general raised the skull scepter.

"This was a gift from the Emperor. With T'slect and his abilities out of the equation, we needed a new way for our troops to maintain communication."

There were many things he would have liked to ask Drekk't. If nothing else, he might have tried to keep the general talking to give him time to think of a plan of escape. But he remained paralyzed and could speak only when something was asked of him.

"In my opinion," the general continued, "shamans depend too much on *vuudu*. That was one of T'slect's many flaws. I use this staff only out of necessity. I am a warrior. My skills are best demonstrated with a blade."

How comforting, Colt thought dryly.

He found it odd that his captor was sharing so much information about himself. Maybe, like Colt, Drekk't felt his authority created distance between a commander and his soldiers. Maybe he didn't have anyone else to confide in.

Or maybe Drekk't was just toying with him.

"But I won't lie to you, Commander," Drekk't said. "Were it not for this staff, I would be forced to resort to more barbaric methods to get you to talk. *Vuudu* makes my job easier, and it spares you much pain. And unlike torture, this spell ensures I learn the truth...the *whole* truth. Do you understand?"

"Yes."

"I have told you a little about myself. Now I want you to

know about you," the goblin said. "What is your name?"

"Saerylton Crystalus."

Drekk't looked momentarily confused. "But your comrades call you Colt?"

"Yes."

"And you are the Commander of Fort Faith?"

"No."

"What?" Drekk't's easy manner deteriorated immediately. He glanced suspiciously at the skull staff and then back at Colt. "You cannot lie to me, Commander. The Emperor showed me what you look like, and when you were captured, you were wielding the same magical sword that destroyed T'slect's illusion. Now...*what is your name!*"

An unpleasant prickling sensation swelled inside Colt's head, as though the spell was reacting to the intensity of Drekk't emotions.

"I am Sir Saerylton Crystalus, former Commander of Fort Faith."

Drekk't's hairless brow wrinkled in surprise. "You were demoted? Interesting. Who commands Fort Faith in your absence?"

"There is no Fort Faith anymore."

Drekk't was scowling once more. The buzz in Colt's head grew into a throbbing ache. In other circumstances, he might have laughed at the goblin's confusion. Maybe you should stick to swinging a sword, he silently taunted.

Drekk't was quiet for a moment before asking, "What has become of your fort?"

"Fort Faith has become Fort Valor."

"Fort Valor has been destroyed," Drekk't stated.

Colt said nothing.

Drekk't paused for another moment, and to Colt it seemed as though the general was considering recasting his spell in order to be sure that his prisoner was, in fact, telling the truth. Finally, he rephrased his question. "Who is in charge of the castle you came from?"

"Commander Stannel Bismarc." The confession left a bitter taste in Colt's mouth.

Drekk't followed up with a few more questions about Stannel. Specifically, he wanted to know how the Knight had escaped the devastation of his own fortress and come to command at Colt's fort. The forced interview was an awkward exchange, but in the end, Colt told him everything, hating himself more and more with every word.

Abruptly, Drekk't changed the subject. "What about the midge?"

"His name is Noel," Colt provided.

"As if that matters," the goblin spat. "Why did the midge come to stay at your fort?"

Colt probably would have laughed aloud if he been capable of it. "I don't know."

The general's wild eyes narrowed dangerously. "You don't know?"

"No."

"Are there any other wizards at your fort?"

"Maybe."

Drekk't looked as though he was going to resort to violence after all. Gritting his sharp teeth, the goblin said, "What do you mean by 'maybe'?"

"Stannel arrived with an injured man who was dressed like a wizard, but he might be dead by now."

The general cursed. "What about the other forts on the island? Are there wizards residing at any of the others?"

"There's only one that I know of," Colt said. "A spell-caster was stationed at Fort Miloásterôn to work with the Knighthood."

Drekk't said nothing for a while. Colt imagined that the general was organizing all of the new information in his mind. In the momentary silence, Colt could do nothing but fume. I should have followed Cholk's lead and killed myself, he thought. I've put everyone in danger.

He had never felt so pathetic, so despicable. What Drekk't said next made Colt scream inwardly.

"I want you tell me everything you know about everyone who is currently residing at your fort, starting with Klye Tristan."

Passage VII

Rain had been pouring on them an hour before they were finally forced to stop. Drenched and shivering, Lilac held her knees to her chest and watched the column of goblin soldiers march past. She hardly breathed, peering through the branches of a pine and mouthing a silent prayer that none of the monsters would give her evergreen a second glance.

Othello and Opal had ducked beneath an adjacent spruce. Despite their nearness, Lilac felt utterly alone.

There were perhaps twenty of the creatures walking single-file along the game path the three of them had been following. They had no way of knowing whether these particular goblins were the ones who had killed Cholk and taken Colt, but Lilac half expected to see a bolt from Opal's crossbow fly from the branches of the other tree.

And then we're all dead, she thought.

The arrow never appeared, though, leaving Lilac to deduce that either the hot-tempered archer had finally found some personal restraint or Othello was physically pinning her arms to her side. Whichever the case, Lilac thanked the gods for small miracles. Their only chance of survival was to lay low and hope none of the goblins looked too closely at the trees.

From what little she could see of the passing fiends, they didn't appear to be too watchful. The troupe hastened by with a single-minded determination. The goblins were extremely confident, it seemed. Then again, judging by what Sir Dylan had said, a large-scale counter-attack against the goblins wasn't likely to occur anytime soon.

She waited a full three minutes after the final goblin was lost from sight before disengaging herself from the tree. Once she was free of the scratchy branches and the sharp needles, she saw

Opal and Othello emerging from their hiding place.

"Where do you think they were going?" Opal asked, looking back the way they had come—the direction that the goblins were headed.

Lilac wiped her brow, brushing the dripping rain out her eyes. "Who knows? Maybe they're going back to look for us."

But if those were the same goblins we've been tracking, the ones from the ambush, then what have they done with Colt? she wondered. Lilac had seen no sign of their missing companion among the goblins. Apparently, Opal hadn't either because if she had, not even the full pantheon could have held her back!

No one voiced their concerns about Colt, however. If he wasn't with those goblins, then he was still somewhere farther up ahead. They resumed their hike without further hesitation. Taking a final glance over her shoulder to make sure the goblins hadn't doubled back yet again, Lilac wrapped her arms around herself and, shivering, fell into place behind Opal.

They walked maybe an hour more before they were forced to hide again. Were it not for Othello's uncanny awareness, they might have walked directly into the approaching soldiers. This time, there were closer to fifty than twenty of the monsters. Like the prior group, these goblins were all armed to the teeth.

Lilac kept an eye out for Colt but saw no sign of him—living or dead. She was beginning to wonder if the Knight had escaped capture after all.

When the danger had passed, the three of them returned to the path once more.

"We're getting close," Othello announced, staring farther up the trail.

"Close? Close to what?" Lilac demanded.

Othello didn't answer. And how could he, when he didn't know their destination? While the forester was possessed of remarkably acute senses, he wasn't clairvoyant. She regretted snapping at the man but didn't apologize. The tension was getting to her. They had had too many close calls for one day.

And yet Lilac suspected she knew the answer to her own question. For the past couple of days, they had followed the goblins' trail north and east. The appearance of so many goblins could only mean they were heading directly into the goblins' war camp.

An hour later, the forest suddenly came to life.

Arrows rained down from the treetops, which had appeared empty a moment ago. There were enemies on the ground too, though Lilac nearly caught a shaft to the head before spotting her assailant. The goblin—along with the rest of its allies—was bedecked in a camouflaged shroud of some sort.

As the enemy archer reached for another arrow, Lilac's eyes caught the movement. She was on the verge of charging at him when she heard the snap of Opal's crossbow. The wretched creature let out a strangled cry and pitched backwards.

Lilac blinked and in doing so lost sight of the wounded foe. She had little time to consider the goblins' method of concealment, however, for another arrow planted itself in the ground less than a foot away from her.

She frantically searched for the new threat, but aside from the arrows pockmarking the forest floor, everything was silent and still again. Meanwhile, Opal was quickly reloading her crossbow while Othello methodically nocked an arrow. The only evidence that he had already fired once was the dead goblin dangling from a nearby tree.

Without warning, Othello pulled back on the bowstring and let go. Lilac hadn't a clue what he was aiming at. She heard rather than saw the missile hit its mark. The shrill wail might have indicated a fatal hit, except the wounded goblin scrambled out of its hiding place. The monster's cloak, which, Lilac noted, was the same color as the landscape and coated with dying leaves, fluttered out behind it like a sail.

"Not so fast," Lilac mumbled, racing after the creature.

Vorpal sword in hand, she easily outpacing the injured goblin. When she was nearly upon her quarry, the monster stopped and spun around. Lilac saw a glint of light and dove to the side. The knife ripped through her shirtsleeve and at least a few layers of skin. Pushing the pain from her mind, Lilac swung her blade in quick strokes.

After throwing the knife, the goblin drew a short sword, but the meager weapon was cleaved cleanly in half when the creature attempted to parry the vorpal sword. The goblin had only enough time to pull a bug-eyed face before she plunged her blade into the miserable creature's chest.

Black blood sprayed her in the face. She spat and with the back of her free hand smeared the foul ichor away from her mouth. Now the cold rain seemed more like a blessing than a curse.

Lilac hurried back to where she had left her companions. Opal was swinging *Chrysaal-rûn* at three goblins. All of them were wearing camouflage cloaks, though Lilac had no trouble seeing the fiends now that they were moving.

With a cry, Lilac surged forward and caught one of the monsters in the back. It fell, snarling, to the ground and didn't get back up. The remaining goblins turned back to back, renewing their offensive against their respective opponents.

Lilac dodged the sickle-shaped head of her adversary's halberd, but she wasn't quick enough to avoid the other end of the long weapon, which struck her kidney. Blinking away the pinpricks of pain that blossomed in her vision, Lilac accepted the blow with a grunt and made a wild swing with the vorpal sword to drive the goblin back.

The monster sneered in victory as it batted the sword aside. It was already coming at her with the sharp end of its glaive before it realized its weapon had split into two parts.

At the unexpected loss of balance, the goblin tried to adjust its swing, but by then Lilac was waging an offensive of her own. Careful to evade the clumsy swing of the sickle, Lilac aimed for the creature's other hand. An instant later, both the glaive's haft and the goblin's hand fell to the ground. The monster screamed, but Lilac silenced it with a stroke that separated head from body.

Opal ran her goblin through at the same time. Lilac saw the tip of the crystal sword burst through the doomed creature's back. The goblin slid free of *Chrysaal-rûn* and slumped down next to its companions.

But Opal hadn't escaped the melee unscathed. Blood—red, human blood—stained the front of her jerkin. Before she could ask Opal whether she all right, she spotted a brown-clad goblin in a tree overhead. Instead of a bow, the creature held what looked like a horn.

It was bringing the instrument up to its lips.

She knew if the monster were allowed to blow the horn, the forest would be quickly overrun by goblin reinforcements. And yet she had no way of stopping that from happening. The goblin seemed to move impossibly slow. She could even see its chest rise as it took a deep breath.

Time resumed its normal speed as a green-feathered arrow streaked through the air and pierced the goblin's windpipe. A clipped, sputtering sound blurted from the horn before it and the goblin plummeted to the earth.

Then the forest was eerily quiet.

"We have to keep moving," Othello said. He strode over to his latest kill and pulled the arrow free.

"He's right," Opal said. "These were sentries of some sort. It's only a matter of time before they're missed."

"Opal, are you…" Lilac started to say, but the woman had already turned away.

Still clutching the crystal sword, Opal walked deeper into the unknown. Her quiver was completely empty, but if her wound was causing her any distress, she didn't show it.

Lilac gave Othello a desperate look, but the forester wasn't paying either of them the least bit of attention. Othello had removed the cloaks from two fallen goblins and was already heading for a third.

Now why didn't I think of that? Lilac wondered.

When Othello tossed her one of the coats, Lilac snagged it in midair and draped it over herself. It stank of the sweat and blood of its previous owner, but at least it added another layer of protection against the rain. Lilac watched as Othello caught up with Opal and handed her one of the cloaks.

After a short time following the trail, Othello, who had once more taken the lead, motioned for them to stop. Lilac's heart pounded in her chest, and when the forester lowered himself to his stomach, she too went low.

Now what? she wondered. Just how man gods-damned goblins are there in these woods?

Lilac slowly crawled forward next to Othello. As she did so, she realized the forest seemed to come to a sudden end ahead. But any excitement she might have felt in leaving the forest behind was instantly lost when she saw what was out there.

The large clearing was ringed on all sides by trees that seemed to go on forever. Hundreds—perhaps thousands—of tents covered most of the field, leaving a ring of twenty yards between the tree line and the camp.

Dark smoke wafted up from different parts of the settlement, and Lilac could make out groups of goblins walking the perimeter of the camp.

She couldn't even guess how many soldiers there were in all. And none of the tents looked any different from the others. If

Colt is in there, Lilac thought, we could search for a week and still not find him—and that's assuming the goblins don't find us first.

She looked over at Othello and then Opal, wondering what they made of the bleak situation. To Lilac's surprise, Opal was back on her feet.

"I know where Colt is," she said and then stepped into the open.

The Renegade Leader's words echoed in his head: "At this rate, Sister, it'll be just you and me."

During his time in the infirmary, Ruben had had plenty of time to study Klye Tristan. There had been times when he was jealous of how easily the rebel spoke with Aric, and even though he was pretty sure Klye hadn't meant to imply anything romantic, Ruben wasn't thrilled with the prospect of leaving the two of them together.

He didn't want to leave the infirmary at all.

But Ruben couldn't refuse Stannel's invitation to relocate to one of the fort's spare rooms. The commander's decision wasn't an offer, but an order. And he counted himself lucky Stannel hadn't sent him to the dungeon.

Stannel had decided Ruben, admitted highwayman, was to be treated like one of the Renegades. He was free to roam the fortress, but at the first sign of insubordination, he would be confined to a cell beneath the castle.

Matters could certainly be worse, Ruben reminded himself, lying in his new bed. He had been tossing and turning for the past hour or more, trying to convince himself Klye had no impure interests in his ladylove. If he had to compete with the Renegade Leader—who was both reasonably handsome and undeniably charming—for Aric's affections, he would most certainly lose. He could only pray Klye had another woman in his life.

Ruben's only consolation was Aric's promise to check on him. He didn't know when these visits would occur, but the prospect alone buoyed his spirits. Other than his love for Sister Aric, Ruben was lost. His life's path had taken a most unforeseen twist thanks to the Renegade War, and he hadn't the foggiest idea where to go from here.

He had spent so much of his life pretending to be other people that he was starting to wonder if he knew who Ruben Zeetan was anymore.

Convinced sleep would never come, Ruben pushed back the blankets. Slowly, he eased his legs over the side of the bed. Ever since he had pushed himself to fetch Zusha two days earlier, he had grown noticeably stronger. Perhaps Aric's generous reward for accomplishing his task—a beautiful smile—had something to do with it.

Whatever the case, Ruben was now determined to take an active role in his recovery. The quicker he rebuilt his strength, the sooner he could return to the infirmary. Maybe Aric would take him on as an assistant.

He shivered as his bare feet made contact with the stone floor. He hurried over to his shoes and slipped them on. Wrapping his gray wizard's cloak around him—it was all he had—Ruben made for the small room's only exit. But he paused when his hand touched the knob.

What if one of the Knights came upon him and thought he was trying to escape? Was a late-night stroll worth the risk of ending up in the dungeon with those pirates?

Ruben stared at the door for a few seconds longer before yanking it open. None of the Knights—Stannel in particular—had ever seemed threatened by him in the least. He glanced down at his costume, a further mockery to his impotence. If I really were a wizard, Ruben thought, I could use a spell to free myself from this place. I wouldn't need to hobble out of here like a cripple!

He pulled the frayed robe around him tightly in an effort to ward off the draft in the corridor. Slowly, he made his way down the hall, trying his best not to use the wall for support. Considering he had had a goblin arrow in his stomach a week ago, he thought he was doing remarkably well.

Ruben hadn't wandered far before he heard signs of someone up ahead, an incessant buzz of speech that rent the silence of the night. Curiosity urged him onward, though he figured it was only some sentries walking their rounds. If there were Knights prowling about, it would be wise to show himself before they assumed he was skulking about with a sinister purpose.

He rounded a corner and realized he was quite mistaken. Farther down the hall were two people, but even in the dimness of the corridor, Ruben saw they weren't Knights. It was the old man, Toemis Blisnes. The bundled-up figure beside him was surely his granddaughter.

Like Ruben, Toemis had been taken to a private room earlier that day. Aric had been reluctant to let the old man out of the infirmary, but Toemis had insisted vehemently. Aric had eventually consented on the condition that Toemis remain in bed for the next few days.

Ruben was half tempted to grab the old man by the shoulder, spin him around, and scold him for breaking his promise. Something held him back, however. Toemis was moving with a singular purpose through the winding halls of the fort. The little girl struggled to keep up with him.

He remembered hearing that Toemis had served as Fort Faith's cook long ago, and while that would explain how he knew his way around so well, it didn't explain why he was up and about in the middle of the night.

Ruben glanced around, looking for some help—divine or otherwise. When nothing presented itself, he hiked his robe up to his knees and quickened his pace so as not to lose sight of the peculiar old man.

Although Ruben had spent the past few years of his life as a thief, he lacked the know-how of a true cat burglar. The only thing he could think to do was to walk on his tiptoes. Gradually, he closed the gap between himself and his quarry. As he got closer, he was able to make out some of what the old man was saying.

"...to end this once and for all. Fort Faith is doomed. It's only a matter of time before the enemy comes. There's nothing I can do about that. They're all destined to die..."

The more Ruben overheard, the more convinced he was that Toemis had lost his mind. At the very least, the old man was disoriented. No one knew why Toemis had returned to Fort Faith after so many years, though those within the infirmary had speculated. Plake had even gone as far as to predict that the old man knew of a hidden treasure, valuables that the Knights had hidden before the ogres attacked the fortress during the Thanatan Conflict.

But who was the enemy Toemis now spoke of? Was he referring to today's goblins or the ogres of yesteryear? Was the old man reliving the past, or was he adhering to a course he had concocted long ago?

Ruben wasn't ready to make his presence known to Toemis yet. He followed at a distance, catching bits and pieces of the old man's one-sided conversation. The fragments only confused him more. Suddenly very tired, he was considering turning back when Toemis stopped suddenly.

Toemis stared at an old tapestry clinging to the wall. Holding his breath, Ruben watched the old man run a bony hand over its woven surface, as though he were inspecting the quality of the material. Then Toemis slipped his hand behind the decrepit decoration.

"This had better still work," Toemis muttered, and the cryptic sentence was followed by a loud clicking sound, like a latch falling into place.

A second later, Ruben doubted his eyes. He watched, awestruck, as the tapestry—and the stone behind it—sunk into the wall. The old man gave the indented masonry a hard push, and it swung inward, revealing a dark recess beyond.

A secret passageway! Ruben marveled. Had Plake been right about a treasure after all?

Either Ruben had made a noise to betray himself or the old man's cautious nature prompted him to look behind him then. Toemis's beady eyes glared daggers at him, and suddenly Ruben found it very difficult to speak.

"Oh...hi...I...I just happened to be...and you...with the wall...and..."

"I will not be stopped!" Toemis shouted and pulled a knife from somewhere.

The old man was on him quicker than Ruben would have thought possible. It was all he could do to avoid the blade that stabbed out at him repeatedly. Ruben could only backpedal frantically. When his back bumped up against another wall, he nearly swooned out of sheer panic.

"Please!" Ruben cried. "I don't want your treasure!"

"This isn't about treasure," Toemis spat. "It's about redemption!"

The knife lashed out once more. Ruben tried to duck, but he couldn't move fast enough. Pain exploded at his right temple, and he was vaguely aware of falling. Surprised that the knife hadn't killed him instantly, he just lay there, trying to clear his thoughts, but already he could feel the darkness closing in around him.

The last thing he saw was Toemis disappear into the passageway, granddaughter in tow.

Passage VIII

Lilac could only gape as Opal walked boldly toward the goblin camp. The darkening sky and her camouflage cloak provided some cover, but in a matter of seconds, the vigilant eyes of goblin sentries would surely spot her.

"She's lost her mind." Lilac stood up. Maybe if she were lucky, she could drag Opal back into the forest without the goblins seeing them…

A strong hand wrapped around her arm. "Don't."

She spun around to confront Othello. "Why not? She's going to get herself killed!"

"She made her choice," the forester replied. "And sometimes one can accomplish what two cannot."

Looking up into Othello's eyes, she again found herself wondering about his motivation. What he said made sense, and anyway, Opal wasn't likely to back down without a fight. But how could the man be so coldly logical when Opal's life was at stake? Had she read too much into his behavior earlier?

Lilac knew one thing for certain—she wasn't going to unravel the knot that was Othello Balsa anytime soon. Tearing her gaze away from the forester, she looked back at the clearing, where Opal had already covered a little more than half of the distance to the outer ring of tents.

"Where does she think she's going?" Lilac asked.

She watched in helpless silence as Opal continued forward in a straight line. She found the woman's destination a second later. There *was* a tent unlike the others. Not only was it larger than those around it, but also it was positioned a bit farther away from the rest. It seemed a likely place to begin the search for Colt, and yet there was no guarantee that was where he was being held.

"How can she be so sure?" Lilac asked.

While she didn't expect a reply from Othello, she glanced back at him to see if maybe she could read his intentions.

To her complete astonishment, the forester was gone.

Ruben awoke with a start. He was aware of a dark shape hovering over him and a stinging sensation that caused his cheek to pulsate in time with his racing heartbeat. It took him a couple of seconds to put two and two together and realize that person crouched beside him must have slapped him in the face.

He also remembered Toemis and the knife.

Caught somewhere between a lying and sitting position, Ruben tried to drag himself away from danger, only to find his back up against a wall. At his sudden movement, the other person scrambled to his feet and hastily stepped back.

The two of them just stared at each other then. As his eyes adjusted to darkness, Ruben recognized the other man. It wasn't Toemis—as he had initially feared—but Arthur, the young Renegade who had helped him back to the infirmary days ago.

He couldn't guess why the boy was out of bed at such an hour. But Ruben wasn't one to question good fortune on the rare occasions he found it.

His sigh of relief changed into a groan when he tried to stand. Without his fear to distract him, he was suddenly aware of the throbbing ache that originated from some point on his forehead. He gingerly explored the area until his fingers came upon a bulbous lump.

Conceding that matters certainly could have ended up worse—for instance, Toemis could have struck him with his the sharp end of his knife—Ruben thanked whatever god or goddess had guarded his life. Perhaps that same deity had sent Arthur to him.

"Could you help me up, friend?" he asked.

Arthur didn't budge. At first, Ruben was confused by the boy's apparent reluctance, but then he remembered his accursed disguise. Apparently, Arthur had exhausted all of his courage in the act of waking a sleeping wizard. Now the young Renegade looked as though he were on the verge of running away.

"Don't go!" Ruben blurted.

The sudden command caused the boy to flinch.

"I mean, please don't go," Ruben said, keeping his tone as amiable as he could manage. "I'm not going to hurt you."

The boy's expression revealed a plethora of skepticism.

Feeling more and more ridiculous by the moment, Ruben sighed and then uttered the confession he had been wrestling with for the past week and a half. "The truth is I couldn't harm you even if I wanted to...which I don't. I can't hurt anyone, at least not with magic. What I'm trying to say is that I'm not a wizard."

Arthur regarded him suspiciously. "What are you talking about?"

"I don't know any magic," Ruben explained. "It's just a ruse. A farce. A disguise."

Ruben tried to look as unthreatening as possible as the boy looked him up and down. Now hardly seemed like the time to go into *why* he had found it necessary to don the persona of a spellcaster. If Arthur didn't know he was chatting with a former highwayman, now was not the time for enlightenment.

"I don't believe you," Arthur said.

Ruben looked up at the ceiling and laughed in exasperation. "Do you think I would have allowed a man who's old enough to be my grandfather to get the better of me if I knew even a single spell?"

"Huh?"

"You don't think I did this myself, do you?" Ruben demanded, pointing at the lump on his forehead. "It was Toemis! I happened upon him and his granddaughter while I was strolling along...I couldn't sleep, you see...and, well, to make a long story short, I saw him open a secret passageway in the wall. And when *he* saw that *I* saw him, he came at me with a knife."

As Arthur considered his story, Ruben took the opportunity to rise to his feet. His head still hurt, but at least the dizziness had receded. Arthur watched him but made no move to help.

Ruben had to admit his tale sounded unlikely at best. He was ready to surrender to the fact that the Renegade wasn't going to believe anything he said, when he thought of another way.

"I can *show* you I'm telling the truth," Ruben announced.

Groping at the wall behind the dilapidated tapestry, he searched for the trigger Toemis had used to open up the wall. After a few seconds, his fingers met an indentation. Within that grove was a metal handle of sorts. Ruben tugged at the lever, trying to move it in several different directions before yanking the thing upward.

The mechanism fell into place with a loud click, and the wall gave way. With moderate effort, he was able to push the stone portal wide open. He regarded his companion with a victorious smile.

But Arthur wasn't even looking at him. Instead, he was staring at the revealed passageway, mouth agape. For a moment, neither of them said anything.

It occurred to Ruben he had no way of knowing how long he had been unconscious. How much of a lead might Toemis have? What was the old man up to anyway? Were he and his grand-daughter in danger?

There was no way of knowing the answers to those questions, but he knew someone had to find out. And he was the only person who could catch Toemis now. There simply wasn't though time to alert the Knights and provide them with a satisfying explanation.

As though to emphasize the need for haste, the wall began to slowly inch shut behind him.

Whatever the old man was planning, he had to be stopped.

"You're a Renegade, right?" he asked.

The question must have taken Arthur by surprise because he paused before replying, "Well…yes…I guess so…"

That was good enough for Ruben. While Arthur was young, he was far more experienced than Ruben when it came to adventuring if even half of the stories he had heard about Klye's band were true.

"I need your help, Arthur. I don't know what Toemis is up to, but I'm damn sure it's not good. Come on, we might be able to catch him."

Ruben took the first step into the narrowing doorway. A glance back revealed Arthur standing exactly where he had been.

"Look," Ruben said, "if you're worried about the Knights… Toemis is a shifty character at best. The Knights will probably reward you if you help me bring him back. You might even get a pardon."

Arthur didn't move.

The wall was already halfway closed, and it showed no sign of stopping. "Think of the little girl!" Ruben shouted. "Gods only know what she's been caught up in!"

Ruben took another step into the darkness so as not to avoid the slowly sliding wall. He could no longer see Arthur's expression, but could tell the Renegade hadn't budged.

His frustration getting the better of him, Ruben said, "Why am I wasting my breath? You're a Renegade, a villain yourself. Honor among thieves and all that."

Wrapping his anger around himself like a cloak—and pointedly ignoring the fact that *he* was a thief—Ruben turned his back to Arthur and started walking. He maintained a hurried pace despite the fact the passageway was pitch-black, hoping his indignation would outpace his fear.

Silently, he cursed Toemis and Arthur and, after a while, himself.

A moment later, a resounding thud echoed down the secret corridor, indicating that the wall had settled back into place. The unsettling sound made Ruben pause. The way back was now sealed shut. Standing alone in the darkness, he considered abandoning the foolish undertaking.

If he shouted loud enough, maybe Arthur would reopen the passageway. It would be a cowardly thing to do, but then again, Ruben was as much a hero as he was a wizard.

So what *are* you then? he demanded of himself.

And then Ruben knew this was something he absolutely had to do. He couldn't take back all of the rotten things he had done in the past. He couldn't undo the past few years living as a thief. But if he ever wanted to put the past behind him, he had to start behaving like the honorable man he wanted to be.

Feeling considerably less afraid, Ruben pressed onward. No matter where the tunnel might take him, at least he knew that, for once, he was doing the right thing.

Her heart thundering in her breast, Opal fixed her gaze straight ahead.

Not trusting herself to look away from her destination, she maintained a quick but controlled pace. She could almost feel the sharp, predatory eyes of the goblins boring into her. The temptation to break into an open run was nearly overwhelming.

With each step, she expected to hear the cry of alarm. She imagined the entire goblin army spilling out from between the pitched tents, surging forward to engulf her like a hungry, black tidal wave. For that matter, even a small delegation of goblins would make short work of her.

She didn't have to look back to know her companions weren't following her. She was alone, and her quiver was empty. While she did have *Chrysaal-rûn*, Opal knew next to nothing about how to wield a sword. By some miracle—or maybe dumb luck—she had managed to fend off the goblin sentries with the enchanted blade.

She had surprised herself at how natural and instinctive her movements had felt. It was like she had been swinging a sword all of her life.

Of course, her skills hadn't surfaced in time to deflect the spearhead that grazed her belly. She was aware of the wound, though she might have expected it to hurt more than it did, considering the size of the red stain that had blossomed on the front of her shirt.

She wanted to brand Lilac a coward for hanging back, but as much as she disliked the Renegade, Opal knew that simply wasn't true. Ever since the ambush that had separated them from Colt, Lilac and Othello both had faced the goblins with courage—even though they could have abandoned her at any time.

Opal couldn't blame the Renegades for not following her plan. She didn't quite understand it herself.

The only things she was certain about just then was where to find Colt and that she must rescue him. She didn't know *how* she knew he was in that tent. She might have chalked it up to intuition, but she had never bought into that.

Yet it was more than hope, and something greater than faith propelled her forward with a power beyond what her injured body possessed alone. Tightly clutching the crystal sword's hilt, Opal set aside logic and succumbed to the mysterious force.

She made it all the way to Colt's tent without being spotted. She would have paid a goodly sum to see the look on Lilac's face, but as it was, she didn't even allow herself a private smile. It was far too premature to celebrate.

Even though she *knew* that Colt was inside the tent, she still had to eliminate whatever was keeping him there. And then there was the matter of getting away without getting killed in the process.

She glanced longingly at her crossbow, which hung from her

belt. What she would have given for one bolt more! Biting her lip, Opal gripped *Chrysaal-rûn* with both hands and eased open the tent's flaps with the tip of the transparent blade. Here goes nothing, she thought, stepping into the flimsy shelter.

She spotted Colt immediately. Despite the single, inadequate candle, which cast more shadows than light, she could clearly see he was in rough shape. His near-nakedness and the fact he was lying prone provided her with an unobstructed view of his many injuries, including a festering wound on one shoulder, dark cuts crisscrossing his legs and abdomen, and a black eye. He looked thinner, too.

But Colt wasn't alone.

A goblin spun around and regarded her with a look of shock. The creature was one of the larger specimens she had seen. In its clawed hands, it carried a morbidly decorated staff.

For a moment, the two of them just stared at each other. *Move!* her mind screamed, and her body answered the call, letting out a yell and lunging for the monster. She thrust *Chrysaal-rûn* at the creature's black heart and watched in awe as the tip of the blade homed in on the precise location she had been aiming for.

Gods above, she thought, I should have been a Knight!

She wasn't at all concerned when the goblin brought his staff up to block. She had seen the crystal sword cleave through solid steel. What chance did a wooden stick have?

The two weapons met with a loud smack, but the skull-tipped staff did not break. Opal looked confusedly from the crystal sword to her opponent's face, which was twisted in a savage smile. She pushed with all of her might, hoping pure desperation would fuel the sword's magic—for surely it had failed to kick in—but the staff held strong.

Slowly, the goblin began driving *Chrysaal-rûn* back toward her.

Opal pulled back and swung again. Her second stroke was as graceful and polished as the first, seeking the goblin's unguarded flank with supreme accuracy. But the monster deftly parried the stroke with its own weapon, sending her sword out wide. *Chrysaal-rûn* sliced cleanly through the top of the tent, but no harm had come to the skull-staff.

Before she was even aware of what she was doing, she came in low, aiming for her enemy's knees. The goblin was ready for her. This time, after knocking the blade aside, the goblin came through with a kick to her bloodstained midsection.

She staggering back, grimacing against the pain boiling up from her earlier injury. It was enough to send her down to one knee, but she didn't dare close her eyes, lest the dizzying pain rob her of her senses. Pushing the agony down to somewhere deep inside of her, Opal pulled herself back up to a standing position and squared off in a defensive stance she must have unwittingly learned from Colt.

But the goblin didn't advance. The fiend remained standing where it had been, though now it leveled the skull-end of its staff at her. When she saw the monster's lips moving, she realized the true danger.

As she swung the crystal sword in a wide arc, hoping to knock the staff out of the creature's hand, Opal saw the skull's eye sockets glow a deep red. There was no flash of light or explosion, but she didn't need either of those things to know the goblin's spell was finished.

Chrysaal-rûn hit an invisible wall. She reacted by pulling back. Or at least that is what she tried to do. The crystal sword was stuck fast, as though the air had solidified around the blade, trapping *Chrysaal-rûn* like a fish in a frozen pond. She decided to release the bewitched weapon and attack the goblin with her bare hands.

That was when she realized she couldn't move at all—that it was her body, not the crystal sword, that was stuck.

Staring up at the hellish scenes, which his imagination continuously displayed on the tent's canvas roof, Baxter was only vaguely aware of the goblin general's comings and goings.

Lately, when the general spoke, he spoke to someone else, and the words were nothing but gibberish. He hardly noticed when the current conversation abruptly ended. His mind had already drifted far away from the here and now.

But the familiar noises that followed—the scuffling of feet, ricocheting weaponry, heavy breathing mixed with fervent grunts—reached a part of him that the madness had yet to consume. He recognized the sound of battle for what it was and, and along with that realization, came to understand that someone had finally come to challenge his captor.

He tried not to get his hopes up. If his expectations were dashed, he might lose his mind for good. Instead, he focused all of his senses on the battle, listening for clues as to which of the combatants was gaining the upper hand and using what limited view he had of the fight to guess his rescuer's identity. Despite his efforts to remain detached, he couldn't suppress his hope and joy when he caught sight of a magnificent blade tearing through the tent-top.

The skirmish was brief—woefully brief.

When he heard the general mutter the familiar words to a spell, he knew all was lost. The would-be hero was doomed to be paralyzed, just as he and the other prisoner had been. Baxter's only chance of escaping the goblin camp had come and gone in the blink of an eye.

Despair blanketed his mind like a black cloud, and Baxter decided not fight back against the madness. He felt something change inside of him then. So sudden and so strange was the feeling that he feared—and hoped—it was death coming to claim him at last, but as nothing around him seemed to change, he was left to conclude it was just another hallucination.

In frustration, he let out a deep sigh...

...a sigh that held the answer to the mystery, the renewal of hope, and the key to his freedom.

Passage IX

Ruben had taken no more than a few steps before stopping again. This time, his hesitation was not due to fear, but rather the response to the single, disembodied word that resonated through the passageway from somewhere behind him.

"Hello?"

He recognized the voice as Arthur's. The young Renegade had changed his mind and squeezed through the narrowing threshold at the last minute. Ruben didn't know why he had decided to join him after all, but he didn't dwell on it. He was thrilled to have the company.

"I'm over here, Arthur!"

It didn't take the boy long to catch up, and when Ruben could make out his silhouette in the darkness, he added, "Glad you could make it."

The only reasonable thing to do was follow the hidden hallway until a different way presented itself. It was difficult to determine how long they walked the dismal corridor. Because of the darkness, they were forced to take it slow. Spider webs clung to Ruben's hands and face, and the passageway seemed to grow colder with every step.

Invisible obstacles caused them to trip and stumble, and only Arthur's quick reflexes saved Ruben from taking a nasty tumble down an unexpected stairway.

After a time, their eyes adjusted somewhat, not that there was much to see. The tunnel was narrow and completely comprised of stone. There were no forks or divergences whatsoever. Aside from the single flight of stairs, which spiraled down for a considerable expanse, the passageway followed a strictly straight route.

Finally, they reached what appeared to be a dead end. Ruben

squinted at the barrier, searching for the mechanism that would reveal a new path. There had to be one. Toemis couldn't have vanished into thin air.

"Come on," he mumbled. "Where in the…wait a minute…I think…"

His fingers found a lever identical to the one he had felt behind the tapestry, and Ruben pulled it upward. He couldn't stifle a triumphant laugh as the wall caved in a fraction of an inch. Looks like I'm getting the hang of this adventuring thing after all, he thought.

A wintry breeze wafted into tunnel, giving him a vicious case of gooseflesh. Ruben paid it no mind. Placing his open palms squarely on the stone door, he gave it an expert push and started forward once more.

He nearly walked right into the solid stone before realizing that the thing was stuck. A second attempt widened the threshold by a mere two inches. With a frown, Ruben put his shoulder to the barrier and shoved with all of his strength. The wall gave way, groaning in protest until it could go no further.

Not trusting the old contraption to hold, Ruben hurriedly squeezed through the opening. Once on the other side of the threshold, he took a few steps forward in order to give Arthur enough room to follow, but then he stopped in spite of himself.

While he had had no way of knowing where the passageway would lead, he certainly hadn't expected to end up outside. Thanks to Plake's hypothesis, he had been expected to arrive at a small room filled with piles of gold and silver. He and Arthur might have been able to overpower greedy, old Toemis in that scenario.

After wandering for so long in the cramped, stale corridor, Ruben thought that the air smelled downright refreshing. The night was cold, however, with but a sliver of a moon shining down from the heavens. A chorus of chirping crickets ebbed and flowed according to the whimsy of the breeze.

Under other circumstances, it might have been a beautiful scene.

He glanced back at Arthur, wondering what his fellow adventurer made of the situation. The boy had his back to him and was apparently studying the wall they had just passed through.

Ruben looked past Arthur, expecting to find the outer wall of the fortress, but to his amazement, he saw only hard, rocky earth. The fort was nowhere to be seen. The passage they had just stepped out of might have resembled a cave where it not for the unnatural, square shape of it.

When the wall closed again, Ruben could scarcely discern where the opening had been in the first place. Deciding he needed a better look at their surroundings, he climbed up the side of the ledge. He kept low to the ground once he reached the top of the rise, not wanting to be spotted by Toemis or the sentries back at the fort.

The fort was more than a mile away.

Arthur joined him at the top of the ledge, and the two of them stared in silence at the unexpected discovery. Not only had the passageway provided them with a way out of the fortress, but it had also taken them far from it—far enough away to escape unnoticed. Although he couldn't quite make out the sentries walking the battlements, Ruben felt exposed. He cast a cursory glance at the expanse of moonlit countryside around them, before sliding back down into the gully once more.

He tried not to think about the fact that they were now trapped outside the fort—there was no lever on *this* side of the passageway—and focused his thoughts on where Toemis might have gone. He was still determined to find the old man, even if doing so had become significantly more difficult.

Where they stood now must have been a riverbed at one time, though judging by how the ledge had collapsed in several places—not to mention the existence of the tunnel—it had dried up a long time ago. If Toemis had wanted to avoid being seen by the Knights, which he clearly did, he would have probably followed the ditch until he was a bit farther from the fort.

But which direction had the old man taken?

Ruben looked left, then right, and then left again, but neither direction provided any clues. From everything he'd heard, Fort Faith was in the middle of nowhere. There had to be a logical explanation to the old man's behavior. Ruben just had to reason it out.

Meanwhile, every second he stood there thinking took Toemis and his granddaughter farther and farther away. Desperate for help, he looked to Arthur, who was staring up at the stars.

"Do you know where we are, Arthur?"

His brow crinkled in uncertainty, the Renegade said, "We're

west of the fort. You can just make out the Rocky Crags over that way." He pointed in the direction opposite of the fortress. "The Divine Divider River should be somewhere nearby, too...maybe a little farther to the south and west."

Ruben's surprise must have registered on his face for Arthur quickly added, "We came to Fort Faith from the west, so I know a little about the area."

Hope swelled in Ruben's breast. "Do you think you could track Toemis?"

"No," Arthur was quick to reply. "I don't know anything about tracking. Othello or Scout might have been able to help you there, but I..."

The boy trailed off, and Ruben looked away. The sad fact was neither Othello nor Scout was here, so it was up to the two of them to figure out how to find the old man.

We've got to think like Toemis, Ruben decided. It sounded like a reasonable approach, only they couldn't *think* like Toemis until they figured out what he was after, and they couldn't do that until they knew where he was going and why.

"What I can't figure out is why he paid good coin to come to Fort Faith in the first place if he was going to up and leave right away," Ruben snapped.

"Well, he is an old man, and he's traveling with a little girl," Arthur said. "Maybe he just needed a place to stay for a while."

Ruben cast Arthur a sidelong glance. "So, you're saying what he's really after has been something near the fort all along?"

Arthur shrugged. "Maybe."

"He chose Fort Faith because it's the closest shelter to wherever he really wants to go. But then he got injured. And even after he recovered, the Knights wouldn't let him leave, not with so many goblins about. So he sneaked away at the first chance he had."

Arthur looked at him thoughtfully but said nothing.

"They didn't have any bags with them when I...met them," Ruben said. "Toemis isn't planning on stopping until he gets to his secret destination. What does that tell us?"

He was talking more to himself than Arthur. He willed his brain to work harder, to use the facts to put the final pieces of the puzzle together.

"An old man and a little girl can't walk forever," Ruben continued, hoping that his ranting would lead to something.

"They don't have any supplies, so they're not likely to make any long stops. If there's an ounce of truth to his tale, Toemis probably knows the area well. He probably knows a dozen places nearby to hide out…"

"Hideout," Arthur echoed.

"What?"

"Hideout!" Arthur wore a big smile. "I think I know where Toemis is going…or where he *might* be going…if he needs shelter, a place to hide out."

"Where?"

"Port Stone. It's southwest of here."

"There's a town nearby?" Ruben asked.

"No. I mean, yes. Yes and no," Arthur stammered. "There used to be a town near the mountains, but it's been deserted since the Ogre War. The Renegades…*we* used Port Stone's inn as a hideout. Some of the buildings are still standing. If Toemis wants a comfortable place to wait out the night, he might be headed there."

Ruben nodded, his thoughts racing a mile a minute. While there was no way to know with certainty, it was the only reasonable course they had. If Toemis hadn't stashed his treasure inside the fort, maybe he had buried it in the neighboring town.

"Arthur, do you remember the way to Port Stone?"

The boy gave their surroundings another glance before saying, "Maybe."

"That's good enough for me," Ruben said. "Lead the way!"

Rather than use the skull-topped staff to bludgeon her, the goblin regarded her with a smug smile. When the monster began chanting again, she struggled but no matter how hard she fought against the spell, she just stood there like a fool.

I *am* a fool to have tried this alone, Opal thought. She wondered what Lilac and Othello were doing. Were they waiting for a sign from her, confirming she had found Colt? Or had they abandoned her and all hopes of rescuing Colt altogether?

Even as Opal prayed for a rescue, a part of her hoped they were heading in the opposite direction. She had squandered the element of surprise, and even if this goblin hadn't alerted its allies yet—even if they followed her to this tent unseen—neither Renegade was a match for the skull-staff.

The goblin's second spell did no more damage than the first. She had no idea what the hex had accomplished until the monster spoke.

"You humans are full of surprises. I underestimated your desperation...and your stupidity."

As the goblin came toward her, Opal saw it wasn't looking at her, but at *Chrysaal-rûn.*

"So this is the blade that thwarted T'slect," the goblin said. "Rumors of the talisman have already spread through the camp. I have been told that it can cut through metal as easily as cloth. Truly, this weapon could be a great asset to our cause."

Opal watched—could do nothing *but* watch—as the goblin took another step forward, bringing its face mere inches from the crystal sword's keen edge. Again, she tried to break the spell and drive the glassy blade into the creature's ugly, bald head. Her rebellious arm refused all commands.

"My soldiers tried to take this sword upon capturing the commander and the dwarf, but its magic prevented it. And when they tried to wrap it in a hide, it burned a hole through the leather. They were forced to leave it behind, much to my chagrin."

The goblin contented itself with studying the crystal sword, its sickle-shaped pupils scouring every inch. Out of the corner of her eye, Opal saw movement. Colt lay perfectly still, probably trapped under the same spell that she was, but the man on the other cot—a man Opal hadn't even noticed until now—was stirring. Since she couldn't even move her eyes, Opal saw him as little more than a blurry shape.

"I am very pleased you brought this blade to me," the goblin said. "Even if I cannot make use of it, at least my enemies will not either."

The mysterious man rose stealthily, if shakily, from his cot and moved toward the monster. As he drew nearer, Opal was able to make out more details. He might have been handsome once, though now his features were raw-boned. His body was gaunt and weak; his movements, awkward and uncertain.

The goblin stepped directly in front of her, obscuring her view of all else. The fiend was so near she could smell its fetid breath and could make out the individual black veins within its eyes. A wave of revulsion flowed over her when the monster touched her.

"Human females are intriguing animals. You resemble goblin

females to a degree, but you are much fatter." The goblin painfully squeezed one of her breasts. "Personally, I find you repulsive, but some of my soldiers might be interested in exploring the ins and outs of your...pliable anatomy."

Opal's fury gave way to terror. This wasn't the first time she had had to endure the unwanted advances of a man—and she supposed this goblin was technically male—but now she had no way to defend herself against busy hands...or worse...

The goblin fell forward then, nearly knocking her over. At first, she thought it intended to molest her after all, but then it let out a great cry and spun around. The emaciated man was down on one knee and holding the goblin's knife, coated in thick, black blood.

The man didn't get a chance to attack again for the goblin drew its sword and plunging the blade deep into the haggard man's chest. He slumped to the ground with a groan but made not a sound after that.

The goblin limped over to the where the man had fallen, and Opal saw a long gash stretching from its lower back down to one of its thighs. She understood every wicked word that dripped from the fiend's maw as it picked the wretched man up by his neck. The monster made dread promises and cursed the man's ancestors a thousand years back.

In a sudden and savage outburst, the goblin tore out the man's throat with its talon-like fingers.

A strange feeling washed over her. She might not have realized what the sensation portended, except at the same time, her fingers relaxed, and the crystal sword fell to the ground and landed beside the skull-staff. Even as she realized that she was free from the spell, she heard a commotion from somewhere outside the tent, which was immediately followed by a thunderous boom that shook the ground.

The sound of angry voices and stomping footsteps snapped her out of her daze. Scooping up *Chrysaal-rûn*, she threw herself at the goblin. Upon seeing she was free, the goblin threw itself backward. Unable to check her momentum, Opal could only do her best to avoid falling on her own blade as she tumbled into the wall of the tent. Her collision nearly toppled the thing.

Even as she struggled to regain her feet, she knew that she would be too late. She expected to feel cold steel rip into her back at any moment. Miraculously, the attack never came, and when she managed to right herself, she saw why.

Colt was grappling with the goblin.

The two combatants were laying half on and half off of Colt's cot. The goblin must have fallen on top of the Knight because Colt was on the bottom, trying to get a firm hold on the creature's neck while simultaneously avoiding the flailing sword. Jabbing its armor-clad elbow into Colt's ribs, the monster finally managed to extricate itself from Colt's grip.

When the goblin saw her and, more importantly, the crystal sword, it hesitated, glancing over at where the skull staff lay. Go ahead, Opal silently taunted. I'll cut you in half before you're halfway there! Apparently the goblin had come to the same conclusion, for it hesitated, glaring at her with unadulterated hatred.

Colt kicked out at the monster and connected with its wounded leg. The goblin crumpled, but as it fell, it grabbed onto the wall. The entire tent came down with it. Unable to see anything, Opal tried to push the heavy tarp off of her, but it was a useless endeavor. A couple of swings with *Chrysaal-rûn* freed her from the stifling environment.

The first thing she saw was the injured goblin limping away from the fallen tent. Next, she noticed the upright bulge in the canvas that was making exaggerated movements and calling her name. Finally, she took in the throng of goblin soldiers that were arriving on the scene.

Ignoring the monsters for the moment, Opal cut a hole for Colt. She didn't know what she expected the Knight to say, but she was surprised when he grabbed her by the shoulder and said, "Where is it?"

Opal held *Chrysaal-rûn* out to him.

"No, not that! The *vuudu* staff! Where is it?"

Seemingly oblivious to the enemies surrounding them, Colt dropped to his knees and patted the ground around him. Opal was too stunned to do anything but go along with it. "I think it fell somewhere over here," she said.

When her hands found a round object that was connected to a longer, thinner shape, she didn't hesitate. She used *Chrysaal-rûn* to rip the canvas and pulled back the material. She reached for the skull-tipped staff, but Colt yanked it out of her grasp, rising to his feet in the same motion.

Opal stood too and saw some of the goblins stealing up on

them. Their advance ceased as soon as they saw *Chrysaal-rûn*—and the skull-staff.

If any of them had brought a bow, we'd be dead already, Opal thought.

At that moment, another explosion shook the camp. A blaze of fire streak up to the sky from somewhere in the distance. The goblins surrounding them appeared to be gripped by indecision, alternating their stare from the black, billowing smoke to the two humans. Of the wounded goblin there was no sign.

Opal grabbed Colt by the arm and said, "Follow me."

She ran headlong at the goblins standing between them and the forest. Weary though she was, she expertly cleaved through the line. Beside her, Colt used the skull-staff like a club, beating down any foe that came too near. There were a dozen or more goblins right behind them, but Opal knew if they stopped to drive even one of them off, the rest would pounce like ravenous wolves.

Having cut a path through the pack, the she and Colt sprinted for the forest. The trees all looked the same, so she could only guess at the general direction from which she had come. And even if I do find the way back, there's no guarantee we'll find any help there, she thought. Nevertheless, they kept moving. Losing their pursuers in the trees was the only choice they had.

When Opal saw Lilac step out of the forest, flapping her arms like a crazy bird, she laughed out loud and altered her course.

Passage X

When Opal didn't reemerge from the tent after several long minutes, Lilac considered her options. She had no way of knowing what had happened to the woman, but to find out would mean sharing in Opal's fate.

If she had seen which direction Othello had gone, she might have followed. She doubted she could convince the forester to abandon Opal. Then again, there was a chance he had already left them both. Lilac shook her head and prayed he would return.

Meanwhile, there was nothing to be done but watch and wait…and worry.

Someone was behind her. She didn't know how she knew, but the certainty struck her with staggering force. An icy fist clenching her heart, she tightened her grip on the vorpal sword and spun around, expecting to find goblins sneaking up on her.

"Greetings," said a fair-haired man atop a chestnut charger. "I had not expected to see you again so soon."

"Dylan!" Lilac gasped, nearly swooning in relief. Behind the Knight, riding horses of their own, were Gomez and two other men she didn't know.

Gomez made a mock bow from up in his saddle. "Well met, m'lady."

"May I ask just how you ended up here?" Dylan said. "I thought you and your companions had departed for your fortress."

Lilac didn't know whether the Knight asked out of curiosity or suspicion, but she was too cheered by his presence to be insulted by any insinuations. "We were headed for the fort when we found the…um…remains of one of our lost companions. We followed the goblins' trail in hopes of saving the other."

Dylan silently digested the information.

"And what brings *you* so far from Rydah?" she asked.

Now the Knight's expression eased a bit, and Lilac thought she saw a slight smile tug at the corner of his mouth. "We needed to find the precise location of the goblins' war camp. I volunteered for the job, as did Gomez and two of his boys, Tryst and Lucky."

Lilac studied the "boys" in question. While she didn't know which man was Tryst and which was Lucky, she assumed that Lucky was the one whose face *wasn't* fixed in an unrelenting grimace. If Dylan had seemed at all skeptical of her story, the man she figured for Tryst was openly dubious.

Both were old enough to have children of their own. Still, if Gomez had been the leader of a guild of thieves, she supposed the older man might have referred to all of his male employees as "boys."

"Are you sure this woman is who she seems to be?" asked the scowler. "Might be she's a goblin wrapped in a spell."

Lilac caught a glimpse of something shiny near the pommel of the saddle. The man had a dagger in each hand. He gripped them by their blades, as though he were getting ready to throw them. She looked back to Dylan, whom, she assumed, was in charge of the mission.

The Knight turned in his saddle to regard the suspicious thief, but it was Gomez who spoke.

"Shut yer yap, Tryst." Lilac thought he sounded more like a scolding father than a master criminal. "If she was a goblin, she'd not likely be standin' here all by her lonesome. And if I'm guessin' right, it was her handiwork we saw back there."

"If you're referring to the dead goblins, you're correct." Lilac said. "But I didn't do it alone."

"Where *are* your friends?" Dylan asked.

Lilac opened her mouth to answer, but she was interrupted by a deafening boom from somewhere behind her. She turned in the direction of the racket and saw black smoke billowing up from the goblin camp. She was near enough to the fire to smell the noxious fumes but far enough away that she couldn't make out the source of the blaze.

Her first thought was Opal had slipped out of the tent while her back was turned and was fighting for her life deeper within the camp. But she immediately dismissed the idea when she spotted the larger tent, which was shaking. Unusual shapes pushed the canvas walls to their limits throughout the scuffle inside.

Come on, Opal. Get out of there! Lilac silently pleaded.

The rest of the camp was a flurry of activity. Some goblins pushed their way towards the fire and others ran in the opposite direction. Very few of the monsters were paying any attention to the tent. The fire was providing an excellent distraction. And at that moment, Lilac understood what—or, rather, who—had caused the explosion.

"Othello," she whispered.

"What's happening?" Sir Dylan had dismounted and stood beside her.

"A diversion, I think," she replied. "Opal entered that tent over there to rescue our friend, Colt."

Even as Lilac drew Dylan's attention to the tent, the thing collapsed. Three shapes could be seen struggling beneath the tarp. Lilac breathed a sigh of relief when one of them proved to be Opal. The woman looked to be in one piece.

Someone else—a goblin—crawled out from under the far edge of the tent. Rather than stay and fight, the monster limped away.

They watched as Opal rushed over to the third form and cut through the material with the crystal sword. When Colt pulled himself out of the entangling cloth, Lilac thanked the Benevolent Seven.

Her breath caught in her throat, however, when a ring of goblins formed around the pair.

"They'll not make it," Dylan predicted gravely.

Lilac prayed that Knight was wrong. For the moment, the goblins hung back. She supposed it was *Chrysaal-rûn* that kept them at bay. Still, she knew from experience that as the goblins' numbers grew, so too would their courage.

Even with the crystal sword, there were too many for Opal and Colt to fight off alone.

The two humans did the only reasonable thing they could do. They ran. Lilac held her breath as Opal slashed through one goblin while simultaneously pushing past another. She wondered why the woman hadn't returned the crystal sword to its rightful owner, but then she saw that Colt carried a weapon of his own.

"Come on," Lilac muttered. "You can make it…"

But Opal was heading in the wrong direction. Without

hesitating, Lilac stepped into the clearing and waved her arms. Opal must have spotted her then for she immediately corrected her course.

"What in the name of the Pit, the Crypt, and Abaddon does she think she's doing?" Tryst demanded. "She'll lead 'em right to us!"

"Turn those horses around and get ready to ride," Dylan barked.

Lilac didn't bother to see if the others obeyed. She couldn't take her eyes off of Opal and Colt. The goblins were fast, but the two humans kept ahead of the mob, which seemed to grow larger by the moment.

Even if they do make it to the forest, Lilac though, we're in for the run of our lives.

She glanced back at the others and found Dylan atop his horse once more. As for the others, they had already brought their mounts about. Her eyes met the Knight's, and she couldn't find the words to make her request.

But Dylan answered her unspoken question in a mild voice. "You'd best climb up. Though we've only just arrived, it's time we all were leaving."

His heart filled with hope, Ruben set out for Port Stone at a quick pace.

It wasn't long, however, before the rigors of the hike began to slow him down. Aside the brief rest they had taken after exiting the hidden passageway, they had been walking for the past two hours. Such physical exertion was beyond his custom, and he had only just gotten over an injury.

Moreover, neither of them were dressed for the weather. The cold wind penetrated his threadbare wizard's robe and the clothes beneath, robbing Ruben of whatever enthusiasm he might have had left.

They were forced to stop several times to rest. Ruben felt guilty for holding them up, though Arthur never protested when he asked to take a break. They hadn't spoken much since deciding to head for the deserted port, and yet Ruben felt as though the distance between him and the young Renegade had diminished somewhat. Arthur seemed to have snapped out of whatever spell had held him earlier.

Unfortunately, Arthur had exchanged his mask of apathy for an expression of unease. Ruben supposed he wore a similar look. The farther they traveled, the more time he had to consider the many dangers around them.

First, there were the goblins. If their path crossed, he and Arthur would surely die. And then there was Toemis, who possessed a knife and the will to wield it. They were unarmed, and even if they had weapons, Ruben was no warrior. He could only hope that Arthur would pick up the slack or, better yet, that they might avoid violence altogether.

Eventually, they heard the sound of water and soon after came upon a wide river. Arthur verified it was, in fact, the Divine Divider River and that Port Stone lay somewhere on the other side.

For a moment, Ruben simply stared at the glossy black surface of the water. The river was much wider than he had expected. A quick survey of the area revealed no bridge or ferry. On the best of days, Ruben might have been able to swim across, but now he felt exhausted just thinking about it. Gods above and below, the water was probably cold enough to freeze the blood in their veins!

"How are we going to get across?" he wondered aloud.

"There's a pier in Port Stone that serves as a bridge. We could cross there," Arthur said.

Without another word, the two of them started walking again, following the river south. They had gone less than a mile when Ruben caught sight of something on the other side of the water. He blinked twice, hoping his weary eyes weren't playing tricks on him.

But the image remained—outlines of buildings and a long stretch of planks extending across the river.

We found it! Ruben marveled. At that moment, it didn't matter that Toemis might not be there. He reveled in their achievement. He was beginning to think there wasn't anything he and his unlikely companion couldn't handle. We may not have brawn, but we've got our wits, he thought triumphantly.

His zeal began to fade, however, as they made their way across the rickety pier. From a distance, Port Stone had been a welcoming sight, but as they got closer, the place had a far less friendly feeling to it. War and time had taken a toll on the town, robbing it of all vibrancy and color. The port was unnaturally still, with only the wind and the occasional creak from a dilapidated building to break the ghostly silence.

All that Ruben knew about the Ogre War was what he had heard in song and story. Those bards of magnificent talent, whom he had admired since youth, painted tragic panoramas of fire and slaughter. Ruben himself had never seen an ogre, but as he took in the desolate scene all around them, he imagined the minstrels had not needed to exaggerate in recounting the brutes' ferocity.

The son of a gravedigger, Ruben had long ago become acquainted with death and what it did to the human body. He had buried too many corpses and had spent too much time in the cemetery to put any stock in tales of stubborn spirits who refused to pass over to the other side. There were too many things in *this* world to worry about—things that were solid and real—without inventing phantasmal concerns.

But while the graveyard where his father had worked had held a sense of peace, Ruben found Port Stone far less tranquil. It wasn't so much a place of eternal rest as it was a permanent monument to destruction and the aggressive end to life. The only things that moved were the shadows.

He blamed his exhausted mind for his discomfort. It's because I've been on guard all night against goblins, he told himself. Gods above, there are no such thing as ghosts!

"Where should we start looking?" Ruben asked, speaking more to banish the eerie silence than anything else. Although few of Port Stone's structures remained standing, there were enough hiding places to keep them searching all night.

"When I was here with the Renegades, we stayed there." The boy pointed to a largish building straight ahead of them. "It's an inn…or at least it was."

As they crossed what must have once been the town square, Ruben realized a new day would be dawning soon. Already the first rays of morning were smothering out the stars with dull, gray light. He let out a great yawn in spite of himself.

They approached the inn cautiously. Ruben watched the windows, searching for signs of someone within. When he reached the door, he inched it open slowly, causing a wail-like screech to fill the derelict inn. Gritting his teeth against the sound, Ruben thrust the door open the rest of the way. He was both relieved and disappointed to find the place unoccupied.

"The rooms are this way," Arthur whispered.

The boy pushed past him and stepped lightly across what might have been a common room. Their search of the inn yielded nothing but empty beds. Ruben found himself yearning for the old, worn-out mattresses. His eyelids felt twice as heavy as they should.

When they reached the last room—which was also Toemis-less—Ruben said, "Maybe we ought to take a rest. An hour or so of sleep will do us both some good."

"What about Toemis and his granddaughter?" Arthur asked.

"Well," Ruben began, straining to find a justifiable reason for the indulgence, "aside from the fact we're nearly dead on our feet, I think we'll have an easier time of finding Toemis once the sun rises. Besides, if he wanted to wait out the night here in Port Stone, we'll have no trouble spotting him when he tries to leave. It'll be faster than searching every house."

Arthur rubbed the back of his hand across as his eyes as he thought it over. "I guess that makes sense."

"It's settled then," Ruben announced. "We'll sleep just until the sun comes up and then wait for Toemis to make his move."

The room contained two beds, so they each took one. Ruben was so tired he might have contentedly curled up on the floor. As it was, the stiff, smelly mattress felt like a small piece of Paradise. He closed his eyes and almost immediately fell asleep.

His last conscious thought was of how he wouldn't be Ruben the Highwayman, but Ruben the Hero when he returned to the fort with Toemis in tow.

Opal's and Colt's eyes widened when they reached the trees and saw Dylan and the others.

"There's no time to explain," Lilac said from her place behind Dylan. "Mount up, so we can ride away from here!"

Although he had never before seen Gomez before, Colt extended a hand to the former Guildmaster, who helped him up onto his horse. The commander carried what looked like a staff of some sort. Black feathers and a leering skull decorated the grayish rod. Lilac had no idea why the Knight would want to keep such a horrible-looking thing, but now was hardly the time to debate differing tastes in weaponry.

Opal hesitated. "Where is Othello?"

Lilac blinked in surprise. She had forgotten the forester entirely! "He wandered off. I suspect he's the one who started the fires."

"We have to wait for him," Opal said.

"If we wait, we die!" Tryst argued.

"He's right," Dylan said. "We must flee. If you are coming, get on a horse. If not…"

Opal just glared for a moment, and Lilac realized with a start that *she*—not Dylan or Tryst—was the recipient of that angry look. Lilac felt ashamed for considering leaving Othello behind. But they simply could not wait.

A few of the goblins came crashing through the trees. They abruptly halted upon noticing the mounted humans, but Lilac knew that their surprise would quickly wear off.

Cursing loudly, Opal joined Lucky on his horse. With a forceful cry, Dylan urged his charger into motion. The forest began whipping past Lilac at a remarkable speed. One misstep, she thought, and we'll be thrown from the animal. At their current pace, they'd be lucky not to break their necks.

Lilac held onto Dylan tightly. She was tempted to bury her face into the Knight's back, close her eyes, and try to shut out reality. Instead, she turned partway around. Gomez's horse was blocking her view of the others, and all she could see of Colt was the skull from his staff peeking over the thief's shoulder like an emblem of death.

Passage XI

Stannel searched the two men for signs of conspiracy, but both Dominic Horcalus and Klye Tristan looked genuinely surprised by the news.

It was a reaction he had seen all too often that morning—from the sentries on duty last night to Lieutenant Petton, who stood at his side now. Why, Stannel himself must have worn a similar expression when Aric had told him of her missing patients less than an hour ago.

When a scouring of the fortress revealed that Arthur was gone too, Stannel had made for the infirmary with all haste. The Renegades' bewildered faces didn't inspire confidence in a quick resolution, however.

"This makes no sense," Horcalus said. "Why would Arthur have left the fort in the company of virtual strangers? How could he even have managed it? This must be a mistake."

Since taking command of the fort, Stannel had spoken with Horcalus on two separate occasions. The first time had been during the interview process—he had spoken one-on-one with all of the Renegades—and the second time, they had chatted for a while when, by happenstance, Stannel had wandered into a room where Horcalus was sparring with an invisible opponent.

He knew most of his men kept their distance from the Knight-turned-Renegade, but Stannel liked Horcalus, who if nothing else, was a polite and companionable fellow.

"We are not mistaken," Petton replied. "And you two would be wise to divulge everything you know about the boy's escape."

Klye glared at the lieutenant but said nothing.

"Arthur had been acting strange lately," Horcalus said, "but I assumed it was because of the tremendous strain of recent events. Could I have mistaken scheming for suffering? No, it isn't possible. Arthur is incapable of such machinations. If he has left the fort, then he has done so under duress."

Petton scoffed. "It is far more likely that the young rebel and the highwayman took Toemis and his granddaughter as hostages."

"To what end?" Klye demanded.

"We can speculate and argue about scenarios all we like, but we will likely not know the truth until we track them down." Stannel turned to the Renegades. "Neither of you believe Arthur willingly fled the fort, but do you have any idea of where the boy might have gone if he had a say in the matter?"

Klye let out a deep breath, looking up at the ceiling as he thought. "I don't know an awful lot about Arthur. We met him in Port Town, where he was working as a dockhand. I figured the only reason he stayed with us was because he hated his job. Or maybe he was afraid to go back."

"I suppose rebels don't need to be very selective in their recruiting," Petton said wryly. "Why bother asking about past crimes when you're hiring a man to do more?"

"No one *forced* Arthur to join my band," Klye shot back. "But if you want to talk about allying with shady characters, let me remind you who had been following the orders of a goblin prince up until a few weeks ago."

Petton tensed, and Stannel held up a hand. "That is enough, gentlemen. We haven't the time for bickering."

"Arthur is from Hylan," Horcalus said softly. "From what I gathered, he had never been away from home until he went to Port Town. He knew the island no better than we Superians did. I'm not even sure he would be able to find his way back to Hylan from here.

"But as you both know, our band stayed at the Port of Stone for a short time before...well...coming here. Arthur might have returned there...*if* he had a choice."

"Port Stone," Petton muttered. "It is the nearest refuge. Some of the buildings still stand. It would be the obvious place to begin our search."

"Very good," Stannel said to Petton. "I shall lead a small party on horseback to Port Stone. You will continue investigating here. I am eager to learn how four of our guests managed to leave the fortress without being seen by our vigilant sentries."

Petton hesitated for moment before saying, "With all due respect, Commander, this matter does not necessitate your personal involvement. Let us not forget there is a goblin army out there. If something should happen to you…"

The lieutenant trailed off, leaving Stannel to consider the implications. Whatever Petton's motivation for trying to talk him out of going, he could not refute the lieutenant's logic. He had not forgotten—*could not* forget—that the attack on the original Fort Valor had occurred while he was away.

What if the goblins mounted an offensive while he was gone?

Stannel took a deep breath to clear his mind and banish all doubt. If this mystery with Arthur and the others was to be resolved without worsening relations between the Knights and Renegades, it needed to be handled delicately. And there was nothing remotely diplomatic about how the lieutenant interacted with the Renegades.

While he wanted to believe that Petton's professionalism and honor held more sway than his personal prejudices did, Stannel could not risk sending Petton—or anyone else—to fetch the truant rebel.

"I will take two with me," Stannel announced. "Sir Horcalus, would you please accompany me?"

Horcalus looked shocked, but no more so than Gaelor Petton. The lieutenant looked as though he were in a great struggle to govern his tongue.

"The honor would be mine," Horcalus answered.

Stannel turned to Klye. "Were you in better shape, I would ask you to join us as well. I am a perfect stranger to the boy, and I should think Arthur would welcome a familiar face or two, whatever the circumstances. That being said, do you think the fellow in the black hood would be willing to come along?"

"You cannot be serious!" Petton shouted, but then, as though remembering himself, he added a hurried, "Commander."

Stannel regarded him patiently.

"What makes you think they won't stab you in the back and join their companion the moment the fort is out of sight?" Petton demanded.

"Faith."

Gaelor Petton crossed his arms but didn't argue further.

"I would like to come too."

Stannel glanced behind him to find Sister Aric standing in the doorway.

"Two of the missing people are my patients," she said. "I pray you won't need my services, but we should be prepared for the worst."

He might have tried to dissuade her. As the only healer at new Fort Valor, Aric was in some ways even more valuable than he. Taking in her determined expression, Stannel knew she would not soon forgive him if he ordered her to stay behind. But that wasn't the reason he granted her his permission…

As he left the infirmary, with Aric and Horcalus following close behind, he gave Petton a curt nod. He knew his lieutenant was unhappy with his decisions, but Stannel would not allow others' opinions to distract him.

For good or for ill, he would abide by his own wisdom, trusting that the Great Protector would take care of the rest.

She has many questions she wants to ask, but she won't bother Toemis.

He is angry about something. Why else would have hit that man with his knife? She thinks maybe Toemis is still angry at the thief for trying to rob them before. Toemis used to be a quiet and gentle man, but he isn't anymore.

She and Toemis left home in a great hurry, and now they are leaving in a hurry again.

She is surprised when the castle wall opens up like a door. When they come out of the castle, it is dark outside, but she isn't afraid of the dark. Larissa used to worry she would be afraid of the dark because Julian told her scary stories about ghosts and goblins.

In a way, Larissa had been right. She *had* seen monsters at night, but they were never scary or mean. Sometimes they even talked to her.

She and Toemis walk for a long, long time. She can't remember stopping, but they must have because Toemis is waking her up. They are in a town, but it is not really a town. Many of the houses are falling apart. She thinks maybe she sleepwalked to the town.

When she sleepwalks, she never remembers how she got where she is.

Without eating any breakfast, Toemis takes her hand, and they start walking again. Now they are going uphill. The ground is very hard. Toemis is walking so fast she falls. He drags her back to her feet and keeps going.

She tries to listen to what Toemis is saying, but he is mumbling. She hears the name Julia a lot, but she doesn't know a Julia. She thinks he must mean Julian, but Julian is dead. He was killed by wolves.

When Toemis stops, they have already climbed a good way up the mountain. Even though the sun is up, the air is colder up there, and it's harder to breathe. She wants to sit on the ground to give her legs a rest, but since Toemis does not sit, she won't. He looks down at her, and for the first time since leaving the empty town, he speaks to her.

"I am sorry about this, Zusha," he says, "but it has to be this way."

She thinks he is apologizing for making her walk so far in the cold. She doesn't say anything back to him. She is used to keeping quiet. She has never liked to talk much. Larissa called her a "quiet child." But Larissa is dead too. She was killed by people.

"I had wanted to reach the top of the mountain," Toemis says. "That's where the curse began…"

She watches the steam flow from Toemis's mouth as he talks. It reminds her of when Toemis smoked his pipe back home. But when Toemis used to smoke, he never talked. Larissa told her that she and Toemis were two of a kind because they were both so quiet most of the time.

"I should have died that day. We *both* should have. But today, I will finish it. Today, it will all end…gods forgive me!"

The way Toemis is talking makes her feel uncomfortable. When she sees Toemis is holding his knife again, she starts to worry even more. She thinks maybe Toemis is going to kill himself. Maybe he is apologizing because he's sorry to leave her all alone in the world.

"No," she whispers. She wants to run at him and grab the knife away from him, but then Toemis takes a step toward her.

"You were never meant to be born because your father should never have been born. You are both of my blood. You both carry the curse."

Toemis is inching nearer as he talks. She can't take her eyes off of the knife.

"In order to end the curse, you and I must die. I have to take you with me!"

Toemis lunges at her. She tries to jump out of the way, but Toemis's free hand grabs her by the shoulder. His fingers are even colder than the air. His grip is so tight it hurts. She pulls away, but even though Toemis is an old man, he is still very strong.

Her eyes are blurry with tears. Toemis's eyes are clear and dark as ink.

"Please don't struggle, granddaughter. You'll only make it worse."

But she doesn't obey him. She pulls and pulls with all of her might. She can't get away from him, though. She is looking at the knife again, which is slowly coming closer.

A glint of sunlight reflects off the tip of the knife, and then all she can see is white. Her body starts to tremble, and her skin tingles as though hundreds of tiny ants are crawling all over her. She shakes so much that the ground beneath her starts to shake too.

She hears a little girl shouting. The voice sounds familiar, but she can't understand the meaning of the words. Then, as suddenly as it left, her sight returns. She sees an old man standing before her, holding a knife. He draws back with a terrified expression. She realizes she is free from his clutches, but at the same time, she can't figure out who the old man is or why he was holding her to begin with.

She turns away from the old man and forgets about him as soon as he is out of sight. Aimlessly, she places one foot before the other, walking for the sake of walking. Without giving a thought to where she is going, she ascends the mountain.

Ruben burst out of the inn, nearly tripping over the hem of his robe in the process. The sun was well above the eastern horizon, shedding its light on the ruined town. How could he have overslept? Gods above, what time was it anyway?

Wiping the sleep from his eyes, Ruben glanced down one end of the road and then the other. There was no sign of Toemis or his granddaughter.

"It's hopeless!" Ruben lamented, kicking at the dusty ground. "They could be a hundred miles from here!"

Arthur joined him outside, but Ruben couldn't look the boy in the eyes. Not only had he failed the quest, but he had failed Arthur as well. The boy had stepped blindly through a secret passageway and wandered the countryside in the middle of the night on the presupposition that he, Ruben, would lead them to their quarry.

What are we to do now? he wondered. If we go back to the fort empty-handed, they'll throw us in the dungeon for sure!

Fixing his gaze heavenward, Ruben found himself looking up at the wide mountain looming over Port Stone. He shivered then, though he couldn't say why. It felt as though someone was looking at him, as though the mountain itself were staring him down.

"You don't suppose the old man just wanted to give mountain climbing a try, do you?"

Arthur's reaction to the facetious question frightened Ruben more than anything they had encountered since leaving the fort. The boy's face drained of all color, and his eyelids opened so wide Ruben feared his eyeballs would pop out of their sockets. Taking a series of small steps away from the mountain, Arthur struggled to get any words out of his gaping mouth.

"We can't go up there, Ruben. That's Wizard's Mountain...and I've met the wizard. His name is Albert Simplington, and he told us that if anyone ever trespassed on his mountain, he'd kill them and then hunt *me* down and do terrible things before killing me!"

Ruben might have thought Arthur was pulling his leg, except no player could have so perfectly affected that look of sheer terror. "Slow down, Arthur. What exactly are you saying?"

"That wizard was why we left Port Stone to find a new hideout," Arthur said. "He could've killed us all if he wanted to, but he didn't. I don't know why. Maybe he thought we would keep people away from his mountain. Scout said there's a treasure or something hidden up there—"

"A *treasure*?" Ruben interrupted. "That has to be what Toemis is after!"

Arthur was already shaking his head. "No no no..."

"Come on, Arthur!" Ruben pleaded. "It's the only chance we have. If Toemis did spend the night here, he has a big head start on us. Somehow I know he went up there. I can *feel* it."

"No no no..."

Ruben scanned the tree-strewn slopes of Wizard's Mountain,

and for a split second, he imagined he actually saw Toemis.

"Look, Arthur, I'm not going to give up. If there really is a wicked wizard up there, then Zusha needs our help more than ever. And if Toemis is climbing the mountain, we had better get him down before said wizard realizes he's there."

That comment made Arthur flinch. "We don't *know* they are up there."

"Well, I'm going to find out," Ruben announced. "You can either come with me and help me get Toemis before Albert does, or you can wait here."

Ruben brushed past Arthur and started toward the mountain. He felt guilty for pressuring the boy, but while he felt that pursuing Toemis was the right thing to do, he didn't want to go alone—wizard or no wizard. As he strode purposefully through the deserted port, Ruben resisted the urge to glance back at his companion.

A short while later, after stumbling upon a small trail that meandered up the mountainside, Ruben heard the sounds of someone following him. Arthur eventually caught up with him, though Ruben refused to reduce the grueling pace he had set. Even after an hour of walking, he dared not slow down.

Once again, he had made a hasty decision, gambling everything on the small chance that he was right. Goblins, the old man and his knife, and now a xenophobic wizard—it seemed increasingly unlikely he and Arthur would survive this adventure.

You're not some hero from a bard's tale, Ruben scolded himself. You're going to get yourself killed and take poor Arthur with you. You would have been better off if you had forgotten you had seen Toemis Blisnes in the corridor and just gone back to bed.

But Ruben kept right on walking, pushing himself higher and higher up the mountain's rocky slopes. It was far too late to turn back now. Besides, disappointing Sister Aric was a fate worse than death.

They were startled to a halt when the sky filled with hundreds of birds.

The birds—mostly sparrows and wrens, though Ruben spotted a falcon or two—moved like a single organism, spiraling and undulating in a most unnatural fashion. The motley flock whirred overhead before eventually disappearing back the way he and Arthur had come.

Once birds were gone, the scene was eerily quiet. The trail that they had been following came to a steep rise up ahead, prohibiting their view of what lay ahead.

"Come on," Ruben said, feigning confidence. Clutching his flapping robes, he slowly advanced and, keeping himself as low to the ground as possible, peeked over the embankment.

On the other side of the hill were Toemis and his granddaughter.

Ruben was so stunned by the sight of them he could only exchange a wordless look with Arthur crouched beside him. Toemis held the girl by the shoulder. The old man was holding his knife.

"Wait…he's not going to…" Ruben gasped.

Before Ruben could finish, Arthur vaulted over the ledge and ran at Toemis. Ruben followed, hoping they would reach the old man before he completed the horrendous act.

He heard Arthur shout, but his cry was immediately lost beneath the voice of the little girl. The sound was far too loud to have come from Zusha. It seemed to emanate from all around, buffeting them like a sudden gust of wind.

Then the ground began to shake. Ruben lost his footing and hit the rocky trail hard. At first he feared the deafening yell had caused an avalanche, but he didn't have long to ponder the earthquake for suddenly a burst of white light flared from up ahead.

Surely they had run afoul of the dreaded Albert Simplington!

But when the blinding radiance disappeared, he saw only Zusha standing where the light had been. Toemis had fallen to one knee. Now freed, the little girl started walking away.

Ruben expected Toemis to give chase, but the old man didn't move. Toemis appeared to be staring off into the distance, looking past the spot his granddaughter had occupied only seconds ago. As Ruben got to his feet, he glanced off to his right, wondering what was preoccupying the would-be murderer.

What he saw was nearly enough to send him back to the ground.

Not far from the mountain trail, the earth continued to churn. Ruben watched, transfixed, as what appeared to be arms and then legs separated themselves from the rocky soil. When the thing stood upright, Ruben realized he was looking at a creature made entirely of solid stone.

The behemoth resembled a man in that it had a head, a body, arms, and legs, though it was more than twice the size of any person Ruben had seen. Even from a distance, he could see the giant's eyes glowed bright orange.

The stone colossus took a step forward, followed by another. It moved slowly, each step sending dust and pebbles cascading down its massive form. When the loose dirt had all fallen away, Ruben saw the creature's flesh was a light, dull gray. Its skin—if the stony shell could be called skin—was not at all smooth, but bore many sharp angles and fissures.

The creature moved slowly and unerringly toward Toemis Blisnes.

Passage XII

The all-night ride seemed like a dream to Colt. He feared that if he closed his eyes, Opal and the others would melt away and be replaced by the same patch of tent-top he had been staring at for days.

They stopped sporadically to let the horses rest, but such reprieves were short-lived. Inevitably, the dreadful silence was interrupted by the distant shouts that would prompt them to renew their arduous pace.

Eventually, Colt dozed off, unabashedly resting his head against the other man's back. He didn't know the rider, didn't know anything about the rescuers who were taking him away from the goblins. At the moment, he didn't care. All that mattered was Opal was alive and she had saved him.

Upon waking from that first of many naps, he was startled to find the skull-staff in his hands. He was overcome by the impulse to cast the vile thing to the ground, but he remembered all too clearly why he had taken it in the first place.

Colt would never forget the terrible things that the staff was capable of...

He tried not to look at the skull. He didn't know what he would do if those vacant eyeholes flared to life. The rod itself felt incredibly cold in his hand. Colt suspected it was the result of his imagination. And yet he would have gladly endured far worse than numb fingers to keep the skull-staff away from the goblins.

Between the uneasy interludes of sleep, Colt reflected on the hellish events of the past few days. His thoughts went back to Cholk, who had given his life for him, and the emaciated man with whom he had shared the tent. Colt had mistaken him for dead. Who was he? Colt wondered. Why did I survive, but not either of them?

Cholk had believed that he, Colt, still had a part to play in the war. Colt didn't know what to think, but he swore he would his best to deserve the dwarf's sacrifice.

Later, when he awoke again, the rays of dawn lanced at his bleary eyes. Gods, he thought in wonder, when was the last time I saw the sun? He was aware of a gnawing hunger that made his stomach complain loudly and realized it had been days since he had eaten anything.

He groaned as he tried to stretch his limbs. He feared spending even one more hour on horseback would cramp his legs forever. Colt listened for the signs of their pursuers but heard nothing other than the chirping of morning birds. Maybe the bastards have finally given up, he thought.

Even if they hadn't, Colt was beginning to think that fighting off the hoard would be preferable to more riding.

He was on the verge of asking the old man in front of him where they were headed, when the man who shared a mount with Lilac ordered the company to halt.

"Commander Crystalus," he said with a sharp salute. "It is an honor to meet you. I am Sir Dylan Torc."

This was the first good look Colt had gotten of the man. Now that they were but a yard apart, Colt could see the man wore a breastplate emblazoned with the sun-and-sword standard of the Knights of Superius. He wore no helm and carried no shield, but Colt saw a quiver and crossbow hanging from the saddle. His sword likely hung at his left hip, as with most right-handed warriors.

Dylan looked to be in his twenties, a couple of years older than Colt at best. The Knight's brownish-blond hair was disheveled, but he looked none the worse for their nightlong race.

"Well met," Colt replied, saluting Dylan in return. "A thousand thanks for your assistance."

"It was my pleasure, Commander," Dylan replied, "but I confess that it was pure chance we came upon you when we did…or a gods-sent miracle."

Colt listened as Dylan related the circumstances that had brought him and his companions to the goblin camp. When the Knight mentioned the sacking of Rydah and what came after, Colt could only listen in stunned silence. He didn't want to believe any of it, but he saw in Lilac's face that she had seen the truth of it with her own eyes.

He might have been surprised to learn that Dylan's companions—Gomez, Tryst, and Lucky—were all thieves, but it hardly seemed important in light of the tragedy that had befallen Capricon's capital.

"Where are we headed now?" Colt asked, swallowing the lump in his throat.

"We're almost home," Gomez said, "if my estimates ain't too far off."

Since he was seated behind the older man, Colt couldn't see Gomez's face. He looked to Dylan for an explanation.

"We're less than an hour from the Rydah-Hylan Highway. Our hideout is not far beyond the road," Dylan said.

Colt conjured up a map of the island in his mind to get a sense of direction. "We're headed *east*?"

Dylan nodded. "East and south."

Colt let out a long breath. "It's the wrong direction."

"Huh?" said Gomez over his shoulder.

"What do you mean, Commander?" Dylan asked.

"I must return to Fort F—Valor as quickly as possible," Colt said. "My mission was to get word of the goblins to Rydah. Obviously, that's a moot point now, so I must get back to my fort and help prepare its defense."

Dylan frowned. "I can appreciate your anxiousness, Commander, but I think you would be better off waiting a little while before departing. You need to recover your strength, and besides, the goblins are no doubt scouring the forest for you. We had all better lie low for a time."

Colt considered the Knight's advice. It all made sense. Even with the benefit of a horse, Colt was in no condition to travel. He might be able to push the pain from his wounds far from his mind, but will alone could not hope to make up for the weakness of his body.

The detour would also afford him the chance to meet the individuals in charge of Rydah's remaining defenders. Perhaps he could even coordinate an offensive between them and the Knights at new Fort Valor.

And yet Colt worried about the cost of a delay. He had had the chance to slip through the goblins' fingers before but had lingered to fight beside Cholk. That choice had resulted in his getting captured, and Cholk had died anyway.

Now—thanks to the magic of the skull-staff—Drekk't knew most everything about his fortress's defenses. If he didn't reach Fort Valor before the goblins did, the gods only knew how many more friends he would lose.

"What's going on?" Opal asked. The woman had dismounted and stood between Dylan's and Gomez's horses.

"I'm trying to convince the commander to stay with us and rest for a while before returning to his fort," Dylan said.

Colt looked down at Opal, wondering what she would say. He valued her opinion; Opal was as intelligent as she was beautiful.

"You're an ugly mess, Colt. I think some food, sleep, and medical attention would do you a lot of good. We can start out for Fort Valor as early as tomorrow if you're up for it, but I think all of us need a rest before we head back."

Colt turned to Lilac. "What say you?"

Lilac looked taken aback at the question. "I agree with Dylan and Opal. We've been lucky so far, but luck always runs out. Besides, if Othello is still...if he's still in the area, he might come looking for us at the cottage."

Othello? Colt stole a quick glance back at the last horse and found only the remaining thief seated there. Dear gods, he thought, I had forgotten all about the forester! And what had happened to Mitto? Maybe I ought to have a brief respite, he thought. At least it would give me a chance to sort out what had happened in my absence.

"We cannot linger here," Dylan said. "You must make your choice, Commander."

Colt tried not to think about how much was riding on his decision. He had thought he left the burden of command back at the fort with Stannel, but even as the leader of a small company, he could not escape the double-edged blade that was being in charge.

Letting out a long sigh, Colt made his choice.

Ruben couldn't see Toemis's face, couldn't guess what the old man was thinking.

Toemis wasn't moving. He appeared to be staring at the approaching giant and then, as though surrendering to his fate, let the knife fall from his fingers.

"We have to help him," Ruben said.

Arthur shot him a look of absolute bafflement. "Why?"

"We need Toemis to tell the Knights that it's his fault we all ended up here," Ruben explained. In spite of the mounting fear that sat in his belly like a ball of lead, he forced himself to walk forward. "We need him to corroborate our story. And besides, it's the right thing to do."

Arthur only sighed. Ruben knew exactly what the boy was thinking. How could the two of them hope to stop the giant rock-thing? Ruben didn't know the answer. All he knew was he couldn't just watch as Toemis was squashed like a bug.

Despite its lumbering pace, the creature was already almost upon its prey.

Come on, Ruben. Think! Think! Think!

Arthur launched himself forward and shouted at the top of his lungs. Ruben couldn't tell if the cry was an attempt to bolster his courage or to distract the monster. He could only watch as the boy charged headlong at the rock creature, helplessly waiting to see whether Arthur would get there in time.

As it was, Arthur reached Toemis at about the same time as the stone giant did. The beast moved far more quickly than it had been, swinging one of its massive arms at the old man. Arthur tried to knock Toemis aside, but all he managed to do was put himself in the way. Ruben thought he heard a sickening snap as the rock-hard fist slammed into both Toemis and Arthur.

The two men went sailing through the air and landed a few yards from the giant.

Hardly aware of what he was doing, Ruben ran to the giant. He must have scooped up Toemis's knife on the way for now he was holding the meager weapon out before the monster. For a moment, he just looked into the smoldering orange eyes that stared back at him without any apparent emotion.

When the giant began moving both of its hands in his direction, Ruben took a swipe at the oncoming appendages. He might as well have been trying to stab the mountain itself. The knife bounced jarringly off the rocky flesh, leaving nothing but a white scratch behind.

Ruben tried to dart out of the way, but the colossus was quicker than he would have thought possible. The creature's large, stubby fingers caught hold of his gray robe, and when the monster jerked its boulder-like arms up, Ruben was lifted six feet off of the ground.

Desperately, he tried to free himself from the garment, but then the giant's other hand took hold of his midsection. The cold, unyielding fingers squeezed him, forcing the air from his lungs and causing his ribs to ache.

"Let him go!"

Ruben identified the speaker as Arthur by the voice alone. He couldn't see anything besides the rock creature's massive chest, and already that image was beginning to fade as darkness clouded the edge of his vision.

Oddly, the realization he was dying wasn't accompanied by fear. Instead he found his mind assailed by a multitude of questions he would never know the answer to. Why had Toemis come to Wizard's Mountain? Where had the rock giant come from? Would he ever see Aric again?

As his hold on consciousness weakened, he saw Sister Aric clearly in his mind. He heard her speak his name. What was I so afraid of? he wondered. Bearing my soul to her should have been the most natural thing in the world. I squandered so much of my life living in fear...

Then he could resist no longer, and the darkness washed over him.

Stannel set a grueling pace for Port Stone. Though his gaze swept across the open plain—seeking the missing humans and prowling goblins alike—his mind was sifting through what he knew about Toemis, Arthur, and Ruben, recalling Mitto's misgivings about the old man, everything he had learned from his interview with the youngest Renegade, and how he had never seen Ruben cast a single spell.

No matter which way he looked at the situation, he could not get his mind around it.

When they reached Port Stone, Scout quickly located four sets of tracks. The riders followed the trail back out of town and up the side of a mountain. Scout led the way, keeping his eyes on the ground even as he spoke with Horcalus, who rode directly beside him.

After a few minutes, Horcalus slowed his horse to bring his mount side-by-side with Stannel's.

"Do you know the name of this place, Commander?" he

asked.

Stannel paused before replying, "No, I don't believe I do."

"It's called Wizard's Mountain," Horcalus said, "and unlike the port below, it is inhabited."

Before Stannel could seek clarification, a woman's voice echoed all around them. He thought he could make out individual words, but they didn't make any sense. When the strange chanting ceased, the ground began to shake.

The tremors were weak, but Stannel saw the quake's effects were more severe higher up the mountain. Trees quivered as though terrorized by a violent tempest, and in several places, rocks tumbled down the mountainside, creating a veil of dust in their wake.

Stannel urged his horse into a gallop, trusting Aric and the Renegades would follow. The way was steep for a time, and he could only pray his mount wouldn't lose its footing. When he saw the trail made an even sharper incline ahead, Stannel was forced to bring the horse to a full stop.

He had already dismounted and taken hold of his horse's bridle when the rest of his companions caught up with him. A shout rose up from the other side of the hill. With Horcalus's ominous declaration still ringing in his ears, Stannel released the bridle, unsheathed his sword, and ran up the ledge.

When he reached the top of the hill, he immediately spotted three of the four missing people. Arthur and Toemis lay near each other not far off the trail. Ruben, on the other hand, was being held by a giant creature that appeared to be constructed from solid rock.

Stannel might have suspected Ruben was responsible for conjuring the amazing creature but for two things. First, he was almost certain Ruben Zeetan wasn't a true spell-caster, and second, the would-be wizard looked to be seconds away from getting the life squeezed out of him by the enormous creature.

"Ruben!" Aric shouted.

Stannel ran toward the creature. Over his shoulder, he yelled, "Get Arthur and Toemis and flee!"

"What about you?" Horcalus asked.

"Do as I say!"

Stannel didn't know if he would reach the stone giant before it killed Ruben, but he had to try. As he drew near, the creature's fiery eyes trained in on him. The monster released its hold on

Ruben and turned to face him. Ruben plopped to the ground, where he lay as still as a corpse.

Stannel slowed his advance somewhat. "Stand down!"

The stone giant took a great step forward, then another.

So much for ending this civilly, Stannel thought.

In his peripheral vision, he saw Horcalus, Scout, and Aric moving toward where Arthur and Toemis lay. The creature of stone took another step toward him.

Stannel steadied his breathing and mentally prepared himself for the confrontation. Some men said fear was as dangerous as an enemy's blade. Others claimed fear produced strength in the face of combat. As for Stannel, he believed the gods would decide whether he lived or died, and no amount of worrying would change anything.

The stone giant looming over him, Stannel made a silent appeal to the Great Protector for the strength and wisdom to see him through the battle. He then sheathed his sword and loosed the mace from his belt. The feel of the weapon's smooth handle seemed to drain some of the tension from his body.

He stared up into his opponent's furnace-like eyes, waiting for it to make the first move. When the creature finally attacked, it moved far more quickly than expected. Stannel narrowly avoided the first enormous fist that came barreling down at him with the force of an avalanche and could do nothing but brace himself as the second crumpled his pauldron and shoulder.

The giant lifted one petrified tree trunk of a leg and tried to step on him. Stannel darted to the left, barely evading the attack. The impact of giant's foot against the ground shook the earth, but Stannel kept his footing. As the creature's right hand came at him again, he gripped his mace with both hands and swung with all of his might.

He felt the familiar tingling sensation spread through his arms into his hands and through the mace. The bronze glow washed over him like a rare glimpse of sunshine on a cloudy day. It was in moments like these, the times when Pintor granted him a small portion of his power, Stannel felt simultaneously immense and tiny—exalted and humbled all at once.

His mace met the creature's arm with a clamorous boom. The rocky limb exploded, pelting Stannel with shards of stone and something else that he couldn't immediately identify. A small cloud lingered in the air, and Stannel was forced to take a few steps back, coughing in order to expel the dust from his lungs.

When the air had cleared somewhat, Stannel saw the giant's arm had completely broken apart between the elbow and shoulder. Red-orange liquid spewed from the wound, smoking and hissing as it dripped from the shattered appendage.

Stannel realized he too was smoking for the molten substance had splattered all over him. He quickly pulled off his helmet and breastplate, throwing the scorching-hot armor to the ground. The liquid was already eating holes through the steel.

His mace, however, appeared not at all damaged by the corrosive solution.

Stannel studied his adversary, waiting for the giant to act. But the creature didn't move. It made no sound either. Stannel was beginning to suspect that the deep, mouth-like crevasse underscoring the burning eyes was more for show than utility. If the monster could feel pain—and Stannel sincerely hoped that it could not—it had no way of expressing it vocally.

The two adversaries stood perfectly still, staring at each another for what seemed a long time to Stannel. He wondered what the creature was thinking and if it were even capable of thinking. Is this a natural beast or a magical creation? he wondered.

Suddenly, the stone giant lurched to the side. Stannel tensed, but the creature was not advancing. It slowly turned itself around before ambling off in the opposite direction. Stannel briefly considered finishing what he had started, but he couldn't bring himself to slay a foe unprovoked and from behind, no less.

As he knelt down beside Ruben to check for signs of life, Stannel glanced repeatedly at the magnificent creature, praying it would keep walking.

Passage XIII

Stannel gave Arthur his undivided attention as he provided a brief account of the past twelve hours.

Aside from some bruises and a twisted ankle, the young Renegade had weathered his latest adventure well. Ruben, on the other hand, had yet to regain consciousness. Aric had had to reassure Arthur that Ruben would fully recover before he answered Stannel's questions.

As for Toemis, the old man didn't look like he would live long enough to confirm or deny Arthur's allegations against him. Aric crouched beside Toemis, muttering prayers to Mystel. The old man's breathing was slow and shallow. A thin, red stream trickled down the corner of his mouth. The healer had not wanted to move him for fear he was bleeding internally.

Neither Stannel nor the two rebels beside him said nothing when Arthur came to the end of his story. He studied the boy's face, searching for signs of treachery. It wasn't his nature to be suspicious, but he was far too shrewd a man to take everything he heard at face value.

Arthur did not return his stare. He was looking over at Ruben again.

Stannel wanted to believe Arthur. Everything he had said was possible, even if much of it was improbable. Stannel walked away from the Renegades without saying a word and came to kneel beside Aric. He didn't even have to ask the question.

"I don't think I can save him," she said quietly. "His heartbeat is weak, and his breathing is irregular. He has several broken bones. And he has only just recovered from his past injuries…"

And he is old, thought Stannel.

Just then, Toemis's eyes popped open. Aric inhaled sharply

in surprise. When the old man's dark eyes met his, Stannel found himself again wondering if Toemis Blisnes were truly capable of doing the wicked things Arthur told.

He expected Toemis to ask a question like "Where am I?" or "What happened?" Instead, he said, "I'm dying."

"Don't say such things," Aric said, brushing his sweat-soaked bangs from his forehead. "You can fight this, and Mystel willing, you will be as good as new before long."

The old man let out a laugh, which instantly changed into a loud, hacking cough. When he tried to speak again, Aric insisted that he conserve his strength.

"No," Toemis croaked. "I'm going to die on this mountain, and that's how it should be. But before I do, I want to tell you *why*."

Aric started to protest, but Stannel silenced her with a gentle touch. If Toemis had last words—a final confession, as it were—then the old man had a right to speak.

When Toemis continued, his voice was soft and scratchy. "I haven't been honest with any of you. I did work at Fort Faith at one time, but I wasn't a cook. I was a Knight. I was also young and foolish and fell in love with a miner's daughter from Port Stone. I spent every free moment with Julia, and I knew I would marry her one day.

"But then the ogres came. I was called to defend the fortress while Julia and her family remained in the town. From reconnaissance reports, we knew the ogres outnumbered us Knights more than ten to one. Many wanted to abandon the fort and fall back to Steppt, but our commander refused to give Fort Faith and Port Stone to the brutes.

"It was hopeless, and we all knew it. Our deaths were guaranteed. Young as I was, I might have happily given my life for the cause, but I knew once the ogres finished with Fort Faith, they'd move on to Port Stone. The thought of an ogre ravaging my fair Julia was too much. I had to go to her, no matter the consequences."

Toemis's squinty eyes stared up at the sky. Stannel suspected the man was peering back through time to the dark days of the Ogre War. Stannel had met a few of the older Knights who had lived through the Thanatan Conflict—as the Ogre War was currently being called—but none of them had been eager to discuss their harrowing clashes with the ogres.

"I fled to Port Stone, using the same secret tunnel as last night. I had learned of the passageway's existence by sheer luck, having overheard my commander speak of it to his lieutenant. It was to be the Knights' last hope of survival if the keep fell.

"But I wasn't going to wait for that eventuality. I stole away from the fort and hurried to Port Stone, where I convinced Julia to run away with me. Abandoning her family…just as I had left my only family, the Knighthood, behind…Julia and I fled under the cover of night, hoping to outpace the ogre armies and leave Capricon altogether.

"The ogres arrived the early the next day. From atop this very mountain, Julia and I watched the brutes overrun Fort Faith and then the Port of Stone. From up here, I watched my comrades get slaughtered for a hopeless cause. A part of me died that day too, but I was happy to trade my honor for my life…and for love.

"It was during the voyage across the Strait that I learned I was to be a father. Julia and I married as soon as we reached West Cape. We stayed in a small town, and I worked odd jobs until the baby, our son, was born. It was a difficult birth, and Julia was still very young. She died the day after our son was born, and I named him Julian in her honor."

Toemis paused again, and Stannel saw tears welling up at the corner of the old man's eyes. Horcalus, Scout, and Arthur had wandered over to listen to the old man's life story. The mountainside was silent as everyone waited for him to continue.

"Were it not for the babe, I would have killed myself. Eventually, we settled down in Gresshel, a small town in Param. I worked as a militiaman for the next thirty-some years. It was a far cry from being a Knight of Superius, but being a warrior was all I knew.

"As Julian grew up, I realized that while he resembled his mother in appearance, he wasn't much like her in spirit. He was a troublesome child, though I blame myself for that now. I let him get away with anything, for he was all I had left of Julia. It only got worse when he reached adolescence. We argued every day about one thing or another. One day, he left Gresshel without saying goodbye."

A coughing fit seized Toemis, and for a moment, Stannel feared the old man's tale must end prematurely. After a few seconds, however, he waved away Aric with a grimace.

"I didn't hear from Julian for eighteen years," he said at last. "Perhaps it was coincidence that he returned to Gresshel on the first day of my retirement. He brought with him a bride almost half his age. Julian had changed much in the years he was gone...none of it for the better. And he now had Larissa to take out his frustrations on.

"Julian spent most of his time scheming down at the tavern. He would disappear for a while, but he always came back. Once he was gone for two years. I did what I could to comfort Larissa. I lied to her, telling her Julian would return once he had 'found his fortune,' as he was wont to say.

"Meanwhile, we lived off of my savings and Larissa's sewing. She became like a daughter to me, like the child I should have had in Julian's place.

"When Julian did return, he was none the richer for his absence. He begged Larissa for forgiveness, swearing he would never leave her again. How I wished she would refuse him...to rebuke Julian like I never could. But Larissa loved him despite his many flaws.

"Nine months later, Zusha was born. We knew she was different from the very first day. She didn't cry at all, even when the midwife slapped her bottom. When Zusha opened her eyes, we saw one was blue, like Larissa's, and the other was brown, like her father's. She was a sleepwalker. We would find her out in the garden some mornings...and then her episodes started happening during the day as well."

After Toemis's next coughing fit, Aric trickled some water into his mouth.

"He needs to rest, Stannel. Now is not the time—"

"No!" Toemis shouted, his voice suddenly loud and strong. "The truth must be told!"

To calm him, Aric assured him they would let him speak, though she didn't look happy about the compromise.

"One afternoon, Zusha disappeared. We searched all day for her, only to find her lying on the ground in the nearby wood. When we approached her, all manner of reptile and creeping thing scattered—snakes, lizards, turtles. Zusha's eyes were open, but she didn't respond to our questions. It was as if she were in a trance. We took her home, where she slept all through the following day. When she awoke, she couldn't remember anything about her time in the woods.

"Because of her peculiarities, Zusha had few friends. She spent most of her time at home. But while Larissa loved her daughter more than anything in the world, Julian kept his distance. In the end, we would've all been better off if he'd never come back."

Toemis stopped again, though this time he seemed to be organizing his thoughts.

"One day, Julian got it in his head to rob the town's treasury. You see, they had given him a job as a militiaman after I gave my word he was as trustworthy and hardworking as I had been.

"Julian planned to steal every coin in the treasury and flee before anyone was the wiser. And he might have succeeded too. He got the money without a problem, but then Julian made a mistake…an error that was the first of its kind in the man's life.

"Julian came back for his family.

"While I was out, he came for Larissa and Zusha and convinced them to run away with him. By the time he gathered supplies for the road, the theft was discovered, and the crime was traced to Julian. The militia came after him in full force. With a wife and daughter in tow, he couldn't hope to outpace his pursuers.

"When they tracked him through the wood and demanded his surrender, Julian's stubbornness rose to new heights. In desperation, he grabbed Zusha, only six at the time, and held a dagger to her throat. He threatened to kill her if anyone came closer.

"I wasn't there, but there were enough eyewitnesses to confirm the unnatural events that happened next. Not wanting the little girl's bloodshed on their hands, the militiamen backed off. Larissa was too frightened to do anything, but she didn't need to because suddenly, the forest was filled with howling wolves.

"When the wolves attacked, each and every one of them went for Julian. The wolves tore him apart. Zusha remained untouched, however. After killing my son, the beasts dispersed. The town treasury was retrieved, and Larissa and Zusha were allowed to return to Gresshel.

"Some described it as a miracle, claiming Cressela herself protected Zusha, but others whispered she was a changeling or a demon-child who had the ability to command nature. We kept to ourselves after that and were content in our own simple way.

"We might still be living in Gresshel were it not for a certain boy who had made it his life's mission to torment Zusha. Whenever she played outside, the boy would be there, teasing her. Usually, my presence at the window was enough to frighten him away, but as he got older, he got braver."

Toemis coughed, clenching his eyelids shut as a spasm wracked his chest. Throughout the telling of his story, his voice had grown more and more hoarse. When Toemis started again, his voice was even quieter than before.

"A few months back, the bully and his gang mustered up the courage to approach Zusha where she was playing in the garden. I don't rightly know what happened next. Larissa and I were in the house, and we heard an awful screaming. By the time we got outside, all but a few of the boys had run away. Only their leader was still in our yard.

"The screaming was coming from the bully. He was covered in birds of all sorts and sizes. They were pecking him like he was made out of grain. Larissa and I managed to scare them away before they did any permanent damage, but by then a crowd had formed around our house.

"His mother and father were out for blood. They riled up the rest more of the townsfolk, accusing Zusha of being a witch. They said it was only a matter of time before she killed someone. They wanted to burn Zusha alive, but I still had some friends in the militia. They scattered the mob, and I thought that was that.

"The mob came for her in the early morning. Wielding kitchen knives and pitchforks, they broke down our door. When the bully's mother tried to push past Larissa to get into Zusha's room, Larissa shoved her back. A scuffle ensued, and before I could do a thing to stop it, someone's blade found its way into Larissa's breast. She died almost instantly. The mob panicked, and everyone fled.

"It was at that moment…with my daughter through marriage dead in my arms…that I knew what I had to do. It was only a matter of time before trouble turned up again, so I collected my granddaughter and all the gold Larissa and I had been saving for Zusha's future. We left Gresshel and didn't stop until we reached a port in West Cape and set sail for Capricon."

You then landed in Rydah, where you hired Mitto O'erlander to take you back to Fort Faith, Stannel silently concluded.

Now, Toemis's eyes were closed, and Stannel worried the

elderly man—who had to be at least eighty years old—would die before he provided the final piece of the puzzle. After a few seconds of silence, however, Toemis went on.

"There was but one thing to do," he echoed. "I brought a curse upon my family the day I betrayed the Order. I put my personal desires above my duty. I should have died an honorable death at Fort Faith alongside my comrades. It was on this mountain that my soul was tainted, and this is where I will die, paying my debt to the gods."

"But what about Zusha?" Aric asked. "Why did you bring *her* here?"

Toemis's gray lips tightened into what could have been a grin or a grimace. "Just as I was responsible for Julian's sins, I am also responsible for Zusha's. Julian was a bad seed. Zusha is something far worse. In her, the curse has manifested itself through unnatural proclivities. She's an abomination."

"That's ridiculous!" Aric interjected. "You don't actually believe—"

"Don't you?" Toemis demanded. "You saw that creature she called to protect her. I didn't think she would use her magic against me, but the evil grows stronger in her day by day."

"She's not evil," Aric argued. "She's just a girl!"

Toemis didn't seem to hear her. "Gods forgive me for leaving her behind. Gods forgive me…"

Then the old man said no more.

Stannel continued to stare down at Toemis even as Aric tried to breathe life back into him. He knew that the healer was wasting her time, but he also knew that Aric would never forsake her duty. She would try to revive him until there was no hope whatsoever.

Eventually, Aric ceased in her efforts and rose to her feet. "There was nothing I could do. He would not fight for his life."

Stannel nodded. There were tears in Aric's eyes, though he didn't know whether they were a result of Toemis's story or his death. He decided it was probably both. Aric held the highest regard for life, no matter what sins her patient had committed.

She wouldn't want to leave Wizard's Mountain without Zusha…

Stannel said a prayer to the Great Protector to watch over the former Knight's soul before turning away from the body. He now faced Horcalus, Scout, and Arthur. All three men wore solemn expressions.

Stannel stepped past the Renegades and looked up the mountain trail, wondering where the mysterious, not-so-little girl was headed.

Passage XIV

Night covered the land by the time they returned to new Fort Valor.

Although he had slept most of the way back from Wizard's Mountain, Ruben still felt tired. It was as though the magnitude of the recent events was only hitting him now, leaving both his body and mind heavy with fatigue.

Miraculously, aside from this lethargy, a few sore ribs, and a plethora of bruises, Ruben felt all right Yet he didn't argue when Sister Aric told him he would be spending the night in the infirmary for observation.

Once they reached the stables, Stannel quickly departed. Arthur and his Renegade friends did not dawdle either, and Ruben supposed the three of them were off to report what had happened to Klye Tristan. His eyes lingered on Arthur as the boy limped away. The two of them had shared quite an experience together, and he wished he could think of something profound to say to his erstwhile partner.

As he and Aric made their way to the infirmary, Ruben's thoughts turned inward. He had never been closer to death than when the stone giant had seized him with its massive hands. He was lucky to be alive, though he couldn't help but feel a bit useless. This was, after all, the second time Aric had had to save his life. While Stannel had wounded the giant, Aric was the one who tended to his wounds, the one who would, again, nurse him back to health.

Ruben wished that he could repay the favor and be her hero just once.

He wondered if Aric would have mourned him? What was he to her? Just another patient? A criminal? Had he ever given her a reason to think otherwise?

When he stopped suddenly, Aric paused a few steps later and gave him a confused look.

"Are you all right, Ruben?"

Looking into Aric's sapphire eyes, he realized imminent death was far easier to bear than the promise of rejection. But he also knew that he could not turn back now. He would not live another day trapped in a lie.

"I have a confession to make," he said finally. "I am not a wizard. I don't know any spells. The only reason I ever donned this gray robe was in order to trick people into believing I was a wizard so I could intimidate people into handing over their money. I've spent the past few years working in the Thief Guild in Rydah, and when it disbanded, I became a highwayman."

Aric said nothing at first. "Why are you telling me this?"

"Because...because I'm tired of pretending to be something I'm not. I'm just an ordinary man, and it's not right for you to go on believing I'm special. I should have told you right away, but I thought you'd at least respect me if you thought I could wield magic. I...I didn't want you to think less of me."

Aric's face eased into a smile. "Ruben, the first time I saw you, you were filthy, gagged, and hog-tied on the floor. How could I possibly think less of you?"

Ruben blinked in surprise. Then he laughed in spite of himself. "Just so you know, I'm never going to steal again. I never liked doing it anyway."

"How did you get involved with the Guild to begin with, if you don't mind my asking?"

Ruben certainly did not mind. This was the longest conversation he had had with Sister Aric, and he never wanted it to end.

"Ever since I was young, I wanted to be a stage-performer. Only, I wasn't very good at singing or acting. I couldn't earn a living doing what I liked best, and the only other thing I knew how to do was dig graves...my father's job. One day, a cousin of mine told me about a friend of his who worked for the Guild. Capricon was a long way from Superius, but I was desperate for work.

"In the Guild, I was able to apply my modest talents to stealing. I didn't like taking other people's money, but that wasn't my job...not really. My role was to distract the mark while one of my cohorts lifted the valuables. I never got comfortable with being a criminal, but I have to admit it felt good to earn a living through my acting. But I'm done with that now."

After a moment of silence, Aric said, "You're wrong."

Ruben's heart lurched. "What?"

"Before…you said you were just an ordinary man, but you're wrong," Aric said. "I knew you were more than a thief the first time I saw you. And you proved me right when you risked your life to save Zusha from her grandfather. Not just anyone would do that."

"But I wasn't able to help her. I almost got Arthur and myself killed in the process," Ruben pointed out.

"But you *tried*. Only the gods are perfect, Ruben. We mortals can only try to be the best people we can. And as for your magic, I was pretty sure it was all a ruse from the start. Stannel had his doubts too."

Ruben had started to smile, but at the mention of Stannel, he frowned. "You've known the commander for a long time, huh?"

"Yes," Aric said. "Stannel is a good friend, but he sacrifices so much for his duty. I hope to make some new friends during my stay at this fort."

"I'll be your friend," Ruben offered, quickly averting her eyes from hers. He wanted to say more, to declare his undying love, to pledge his life for her happiness, but he didn't want to scare her off.

Small steps, he thought.

Aric smiled warmly, and Ruben felt truly blessed for being the one responsible for it.

"I'd like that, Ruben. I really do think you are a good man." She reached for his hand, and Ruben was happy to let her take it. "Come now, let's get you to the infirmary."

Ruben grinned all the way to his sickbed. He didn't need an examination to know he was in fine shape. In truth, he had never felt better in all of his life. And even if he were to drop dead just then, he knew he would have at least one friend to remember him.

Stannel sat alone in the small room that served as his office. He had only just dismissed Lieutenant Petton, who continued to plead his case against Arthur—and the rest of the Renegades— even after learning the true motive behind why Ruben and Arthur had fled the fort.

He continued staring at the door long after Petton practically slammed it behind him. As long as the Renegades remained at the fort, there would be strife between the Knights and the rebels.

So be it, he thought wearily.

Arthur and Ruben had revealed the hidden passageway's location, and he had already assigned two guards to watch the portal to prevent future breakouts. He planned on inspecting the passageway himself—who knew when such a thing might come in handy?—but first, there was something else he wanted to investigate.

From a creaky drawer in his desk, Stannel removed a single tome. All throughout Petton's tirade, his thoughts had been on the book, which he had taken into his personal care after assuming command. As he paged through it now, his thoughts returned to Toemis's tale and, more specifically, to Zusha.

Stannel felt awful for having abandoned the girl on Wizard's Mountain. He had wanted nothing more than to scour the entire mountaintop to locate her, but after learning about the Renegades' encounter with Albert Simplington, the mountain's unneighborly wizard resident, Stannel had been forced to consider the matter realistically.

Searching for Zusha would have put everyone's life at risk, and Stannel could not in good conscience extend his absence from the fort. During the ride back, he had debated whether or not to send some of his Knights to pick up the trail, but between the goblins and Albert Simplington, he couldn't justify endangering the lives of his men.

As a result, Stannel felt as though he had sentenced the girl to death.

What chance did she have on her own? he wondered. Granted, Zusha wasn't as young as any of them had thought, but with so many dangers out there, how could a sheltered lass like Zusha hope to survive?

Then, if Zusha truly were the one responsible for summoning the rock creature, then perhaps he was underestimating her.

Stannel considered that Zusha might be better off alone. After learning of her fantastic abilities—her curse, as Toemis had called it—how would the Knights of Fort Valor have treated her? People tend to fear what they don't understand, he thought, and the Knights of Superius have a long history of distrusting magic.

As his eyes scanned the pages, Stannel said a silent prayer for the girl. He knew what it was like to be the target of suspicion and derision. He wielded the power of the Great Protector in a way that very few—if any—other Superian Knights could. He had never looked at his abilities as a curse, though he was wary about exhibiting his extraordinary abilities in public.

Now that the trumpets of war had sounded, how long could he hope to keep his own skills a secret from his men? What would their reaction be when they inevitably found out what *he* was capable of?

Stannel stopped flipping the pages when he spotted the name "Toemis Blisnes" in a flowing script, followed by the date of his arrival at Fort Faith, his rank at that time, and a brief list of his responsibilities. The page was yellowed with age and smelled of mold.

The tome, which was a long-dead commander's logbook, had been fortunate to survive the Ogre War, though it was common knowledge that ogres had little use for books—aside from kindling.

Stannel had not doubted Toemis's dying confession. Nevertheless, it was strange to see the old man's name in the book. The physical proof of Toemis's residency at the fort forced Stannel to consider the events that had transformed a Knight into a cold-blooded killer. Stannel supposed a man might go through many changes after branding himself a coward.

Toemis had said the ogres had outnumbered the Knights of Fort Faith ten to one. Might there be as many goblins out there now? he wondered. Or more?

Stannel had been preparing for war throughout most of his adult life. He did not fear any mortal enemy for he did not fear his own death. But as Commander of Fort Valor, he had to wonder if the motley residents of the fort could physically and mentally weather a siege.

How might the Knights and Renegades react in the face of certain death?

How many Knights would flee, like Toemis did?

Would the Renegades fight alongside their former enemies or run?

Looking down at the faded page, Stannel clapped the

logbook shut. Though the sun had long since set, he had much to do before seeking the comfort of meditation. For one thing, he had promised Aric he would come by the infirmary so she could take a look at his shoulder.

He would probably have to repair the considerable damage done to his helm and breastplate himself...

Gingerly, he rose to his feet and made to leave the room. Before closing the door behind him, he glanced back at the small, old desk and recalled his first meeting with Colt. He didn't blame the young commander for embracing a mission that took him far away from his responsibilities, but Stannel prayed Colt and his companions would return with all haste.

Not only did Stannel desperately need word of what was happening in the East, but also he was beginning to think that in Fort Valor's case, two commanders were better than one.

Bring them home, Pintor, he prayed as he traced the outline of the pendant always tucked beneath his tunic.

"Quit squirming! Do you want this to take all day?"

Mitto was too busy gritting his teeth against the sting of cold water on his tender flesh to reply. Else insisted on washing his wound every morning to prevent infection. Some of the cottage's residents claimed the goblins coated their blades with a poison, though Mitto had his doubts.

In a matter as serious as this, however, he thought it better to be safe than...well...dead. And though Else's ministrations caused him some physical discomfort, he didn't at all mind watching the woman dote on him.

The ruination of Rydah, the destruction of Someplace Else, the death of Baxter Lawler—all of these things weighed heavily on his mind. Both he and Else had lost so much, but they were truly fortunate to have found each other. That the innkeeper had thrown in with a bunch of Knights and professional thieves was still something he couldn't quite get his mind around...

Most of Rydah's survivors had sought refuge in Hylan, but rather than hide along with the other townsfolk, Else was doing her part to fight back, despite the fact that she had no skill as a warrior. Mitto suspected that were it not for his unexpected arrival, she would have gone with Dylan and Loony Gomez to look for the goblin camp.

"Ah!" he gasped. "I swear, Else, it didn't hurt this much when the wound was dealt."

"Quit complaining," Else snapped. "I'll be done in a minute."

Mitto eyed the woman as she gently wrapped a new bandage—crafted from an old tablecloth—around his waist. His injury still pained him every now and then, particularly when Else changed the dressing, but the discomfort was lost in the warmth he felt as she wrapped her arms around him to secure the bandage.

He wondered why he had never noticed her loveliness before. No, he corrected, that isn't right. I always knew she was a wonderful woman. I just never realized how precious she was to me until I almost lost her.

As he watched her take the bloodied rags over to a water pail, he thought he was seeing her for the first time. And if he were not mistaken, he had seen something new in her eyes when their gaze happened to meet. How strange, he thought, that I should find love in the midst of war. In the days of peace, when I had had nothing but time to court her properly, I did nothing. Now, when the two of us could die at any moment, I find I want nothing more than to grow old with her.

He hadn't said anything more about his love for her since his surprise confession at Rydah's ruins, but she couldn't have forgotten what he said. *He* certainly couldn't forget. In fact, he could hardly think of anything else. But he would not broach the topic for there were more important things to worry about. More importantly, Mitto didn't think they *needed* to address the subject.

He felt his love being returned in ways that mere words could not express.

Else's turn for guard duty would come soon. The cottage-turned-outpost was perpetually guarded by half-a-dozen watchmen at all times. Mitto had asked to help, but Else forbade him to step foot outside the cottage until he was fully recovered. Until then, Mitto was left to sit and wait, counting the minutes until Else's safe return.

He was in the process of watching Else tie her hair back in a thong when the sound of voices outside the cottage caught their attention. He sat up straight, ignoring the pain that lanced from his wound, and tried to identify the speakers. Humans or goblins? The sound was too muffled to be sure. Slowly, he reached for his quarterstaff. Meanwhile, Else had her hand on the short sword hanging from her belt.

When the door swung open, Mitto tensed but then immediately relaxed again. He was filled with relief at the sight of a human and was overjoyed that that human happened to be Sir Dylan Torc. Most everyone—Mitto included—had feared they had seen the last of the bold Knight when he and his companions had set off for the goblin camp.

To see the man alive and well brought a big smile to Mitto's face.

Gomez and Tryst entered the cottage after Dylan. Mitto had to look twice at the fourth member of the party, not believing his eyes. He expected to find Lucky bringing up the rear but found Colt there instead. The young commander looked far worse for their time apart, though Mitto was happy to see the man was alive at all. Despite Opal's faith she would find their lost companions, Mitto had given Colt up for dead.

How unfortunate that the commander had missed his friends by a span of days...

But then Mitto watched, dumbfounded, as Opal and Lilac too crossed the threshold. He waited, expecting the tall archer and the dark-skinned dwarf to come next, but his hopes were dashed when Lucky appeared in their place, closing the door behind him. Mitto's mind was flooded with questions, but he kept silent, knowing all would be explained in time.

Unfortunately, he would have to wait a full day to hear their story. After the newcomers wolfed down a modest meal, they found a place on the floor to sleep. Within an hour of their unexpected return, Loony Gomez was snoring rhythmically off in one corner, and even Sir Dylan—whose abundance of energy often led to insomnia—had nodded off, his head resting in his arms.

As Else was currently on watch—and since her replacements themselves were sleeping—Mitto might have been left with only his curiosity to keep him company. But there was one man who had resisted the lure of sleep in spite of his obvious need for it.

Across the room, Colt sat with his back against a wall, his eyes staring out at nothing. Mitto wondered about the grotesque staff that lay across his lap, but Mitto's eyes didn't linger long on the skull-topped rod. Instead, he studied Colt, marveling that this could be the same man he had met at Fort Faith.

Colt appeared to have aged ten years in that short time. The flesh on his face was waxen, and he looked as though he had lost a lot of weight. There was a haunted look in his eyes, as though he had witnessed some truly harrowing events. Using his quarterstaff for support, Mitto crossed the room, carefully stepping over the prone forms of those who sleeping.

As much as he wanted to ask Colt what had happened, Mitto started by saying, "It's good to see you again, Commander."

Colt nodded, and Mitto couldn't decide if Colt was looking at him or through him. Mitto didn't know what else to say. He could only assume by the dwarf's absence that he was dead. He supposed the same was true for Othello, though he didn't want to believe that. Othello had saved his life, after all.

"Don't worry," Mitto said, uttering the first words that came to his mind. "We'll find a way to push those monsters back into the pit they crawled out of."

Colt didn't reply, and Mitto was in the process of extricating himself from the Knight's presence, when the Knight smiled faintly. Now Mitto could see Colt was looking directly at him, his eyes blazing with an alertness that made Mitto tense up in spite of himself. The look on the commander's face, combined with his simple, yet confident, reply, sent a shiver down Mitto's spine.

"We'll find a way," Colt agreed, "or die trying."

Martyrs
and
Monsters

An excerpt from
Volume 3 of
The Renegade Chronicles

Prologue

The stiffness creeping into his long limbs made each stride more difficult than the last. Rivulets of sweat tickled his cheeks, but the cold night air was no match for the heat that consumed his skin and burned his lungs—a fire that rivaled the inferno he had left far behind.

He knew they were back there. Every now and then, a cry rent the stillness of the forest, a sound that resembled nothing so much as the baying of hounds. Even when they were silent, he sensed their nearness.

Othello was no stranger to the hunt, though usually the roles were reversed.

His empty quiver pounded against his back with every exhausting stride. He refused to cast aside his longbow, which he clutched awkwardly against his breast. The bow was one of his few possessions, and tossing it aside would only give his pursuers proof of his passing.

The predators—foreigners to the island until recently—stuck to his trail with a persistence he begrudgingly admired. He had done his best to conceal his path in the beginning, but they had found him anyway.

Now his flight was chaotic, desperate.

The shouts were growing louder by the moment. He wondered if they could smell him. The creatures certainly resembled animals in their ferocity, and some said they could see in the dark. But they weren't mere beasts. They spoke a language he didn't understand, and they knew magic. Perhaps they were using spells to track him now.

He ran so far he might have outpaced dawn itself. When he glanced over his shoulder, he saw not the welcoming rays of morning light, but rather his first unobstructed view of the hunters. Some called them monsters. He couldn't disagree.

Looking ahead once more, he focused a dense copse of aspens a few yards away. The forest had thinned out without his noticing. If he could only make it to the trees, he might be able to alter his course and lose them.

Othello cried out in pain as the arrow tore through tendon and muscle. His wounded leg buckled. His momentum sending him tumbling to the ground. He came down hard, skinning his elbows and biting his tongue. His longbow clattered against the trunk of a tree.

He rolled unto his back to assess the damage. The shaft was crude in design but effective. Blood glued his buckskin pants to his leg.

There wasn't even time to remove the arrow. The creatures were already closing in on him. The six of them were breathing hard as they loped toward him. Spearheads and sword tips preceded their advance. A seventh goblin hung back, fitting a second arrow into its bow. If there had been more than one archer, he would already be dead.

Then again, he would likely die anyway.

Swallowing the metallic tang in his mouth, Othello tucked his legs beneath him and sprang forward. The pain that coursed through his injured leg nearly sent him back down to the ground, but he pushed through it. He grabbed the shaft of the nearest spear with his left hand and drew his one remaining weapon with the right.

The goblin would have been wise to let go of the spear. As it was, the creature ended up the victim of its own slow reaction and Othello's momentum. The goblin could do little more than pull a surprised face as Othello's hunting knife slid into the hollow beneath its sternum.

He shoved the dying monster into one of its compatriots while avoiding the descending blades of the others. He then launched himself knife-first at the closest goblin. A dark, horizontal line appeared across the creature's neck. An instant later, black blood oozed down the goblin's chest.

Othello didn't even see the second corpse hit the ground. He was already turning to face the remaining foes.

The four held their grounds, alternating their glances between him and their fallen comrades. They had underestimated him, and he wondered if their taste for self-preservation would slake the thirst for vengeance.

Although outmatched, Othello knew he could take at least one more of the monsters with him to the grave. So...who will it be? he silently prodded.

The goblins seemed to be considering that very thing. They eyed his blade, slick with dark blood. Adrenaline or exhaustion caused the creatures to undulate before him. The shadows dancing in the distance were making him dizzy.

It was only when a second shaft planted itself just below his clavicle that he remembered goblins were wont to poison their arrows.

The impact sent him staggering backward, but he somehow managed to stay on his feet. The goblins kept their distance. With their toxins in his blood, he was as good as dead. They wouldn't risk getting gutted by his knife.

He thought he heard a goblin laugh as he pushed himself, unsteadily, toward where the archer stood, reaching for another arrow. He dove at the creature's chest with all of his might, planting his knife hilt-deep into the goblin's body.

But his aim had been off, and the wound wasn't fatal.

The goblin rained down a series of blows about Othello's head and shoulders, splintering its bow for its trouble. The creature's gangly arms possessed great strength. The howling, flailing monster raked its claw-like nails across his face before he could pull away.

Othello kicked out with his uninjured leg, connecting with the handle of the knife still lodged in the archer's chest. The creature let out a pathetic yowl and pitched forward. Slumped but still standing, he turned to the remaining goblins.

None of them had made a move to help their companion. They were, at that moment, exchanging words in their strange tongue while glaring mercilessly at him. Then, as one, the four stepped apart and waited for him to come forward so that they could surround and slay him—or for the poison to finish the job for them.

Othello wiped the sweat and blood from his eyes with a filthy sleeve. The toxin burned in his veins, and he shivered in spite of himself. The ground beneath him pitched back and forth like the deck of a ship in a squall.

The goblins smiled in cruel delight. Confident he was no longer a threat, the four of them came forward, giving him a wide berth as they spaced themselves evenly on all sides.

Weaponless, nauseated, Othello fingered the wooden object he had unconsciously removed from a small pouch at his belt. With one finger, he traced the symbols that were carved into the reddish surface of the coin-like token. He didn't know what the glyphs meant, but his father had insisted that it was elfish writing.

He hadn't asked his father why he had given him the token when he had left home. And he didn't question his sudden need to caress the heirloom's smooth surface. If it was a good luck charm, as he had long suspected, he needed its magic now more than ever.

Something sharp tore into the back of his shoulder. With a wild cry, he lunged at his adversary, groping for the goblin's sword arm. It was all he could do to hold the blade down and away from him. As they struggled, he used his opponent for support.

Somewhere in the back of his mind, he wondered if he would have been able to defeat the hunters if they hadn't drugged him. That thought evaporated when the other three goblins made their presence known, their jagged blades biting into his flesh.

Othello roared, but the sound came from someone—or something—else. He forgot all about his missing friends and the burning war camp as he grappled with the predators. There was only pain and the need to survive.

The primal game of kill-or-be-killed lasted mere seconds.

ACKNOWLEDGMENTS

To properly recognize every person who supported The Renegade Chronicles since I first put fingertips to keyboard in 1997 would fill another entire book. To spare the lives of a few trees, I'll attempt to keep my kudos concise and thank everyone who encouraged my creativity throughout the years, including:

Family members who nurtured my imagination by making sure I always had paper and pencils to map out new worlds and by exploring those places with me.

Dear friends who called me "weird but in a good way," indulged me when I spoke of made-up people and strange plots, and provided feedback along the way.

Educators who taught me the craft as well as bolstered my confidence—even though I was only interested in writing stories with swords and magic.

Comrades-in-arms whose critiques made me the writer I am today, especially the Allied Authors of Wisconsin.

To recognize a few of those individuals by name:

Robyn Williams, who motivated her little brother to try his hand at the written word and who inadvertently helped invent two main characters in this series.

Stephanie Williams, my incredible wife, whose interest in Altaerra and its populace in 1994 prompted me to record those stories in copious notebooks and who has supported me in so many ways over the past two decades.

Judith Barisonzi, who taught me the fundamentals of story-telling, how to write on deadline, and the truth that great writing transcends genre.

Alan Hathaway, who inspired me to pursue my dream and also made accommodations so I could make it a reality.

Jake Weiss, a good friend and brilliant designer who exceeded all expectations for the cover art.

Fern Ramirez, who always sees the best in a story even while seeking out its flaws.

And last but not least, Tom Ramirez, who has played a variety of parts since we met at that auspicious rummage sale in 2005—from surrogate grandfather and role model to tireless cheerleader and invaluable friend.

It's been a long, strange journey, and I consider myself very blessed indeed.

DAVID MICHAEL WILLIAMS was exposed to sword-and-sorcery fantasy at the tender age of 12. He dove headlong into fiction writing when he competed in a short story contest in sixth grade. While the tale—a glorified battle scene, really—garnered no accolades, two of its characters survived for many years thereafter and appear in The Renegade Chronicles.

David lives in Wisconsin with an amazing wife (who somehow puts up with his storytelling addiction) and two larger-than-life children.

Visit his website at david-michael-williams.com.

Made in the USA
Charleston, SC
15 December 2016